REDEEMING LUKE

Wings of Hope

A NOVEL BY
DARLENE WELLS

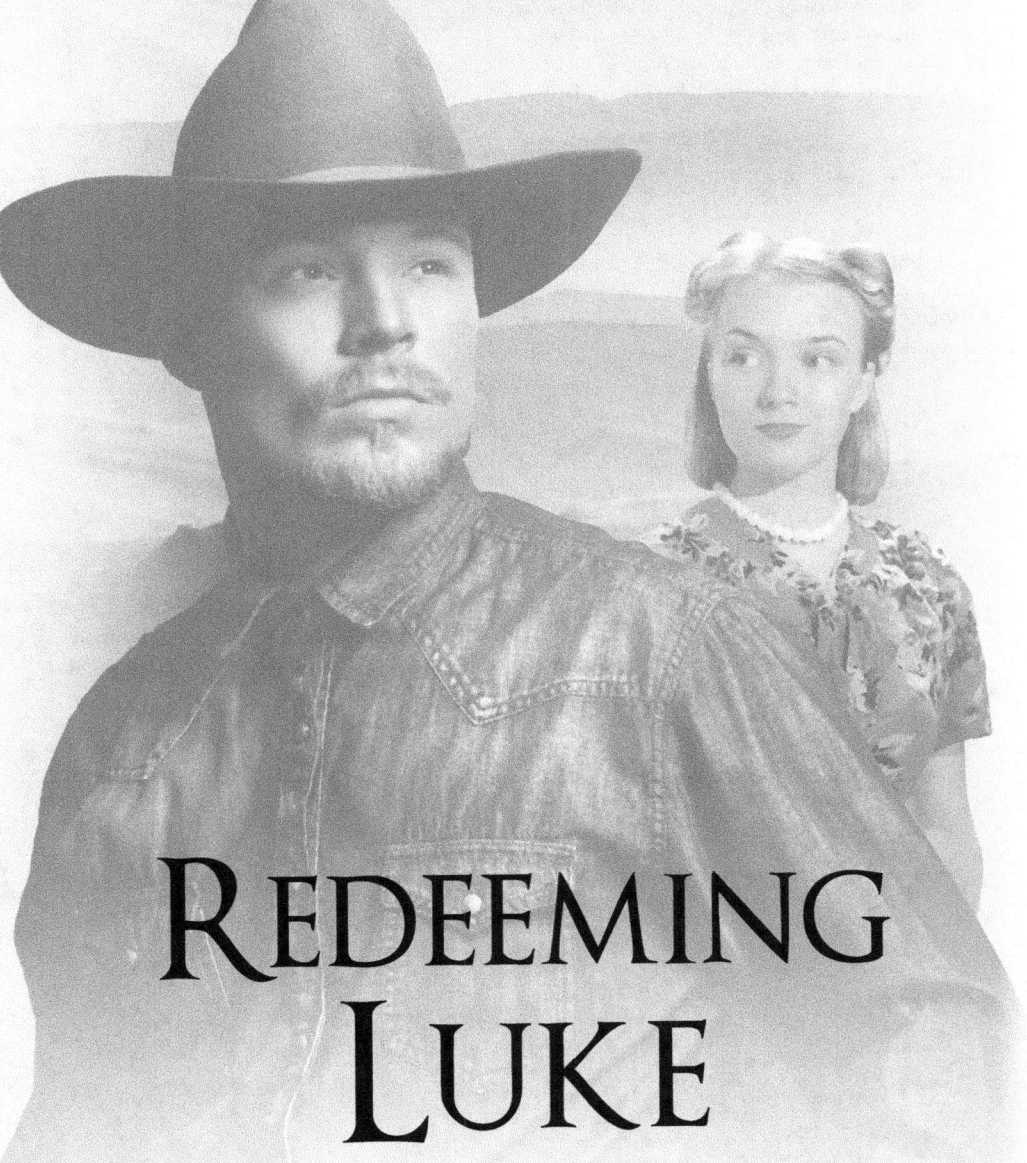

REDEEMING LUKE

THE DAYS OF GRACE TRILOGY
VOLUME I

Published by Wings of Hope Publishing Group
Established 2013
www.wingsofhopepublishing.com
Find us on Facebook: Search "Wings of Hope"

Printed in the United States of America

Wells, Darlene
     Redeeming Luke / Darlene Wells
     Wings of Hope Publishing Group
     ISBN-13: 978-0692329344
     ISBN-10: 069232934X

This is a work of fiction. Names, characters, incidents, and dialogues are products of the author's imagination and are not to be construed as real. Any resemblance to actual events or people, living or dead, is entirely coincidental.

Cover design and interior layout by Vogel Design in Hillsboro, Kansas.

Dedicated to my husband,
Rick,
for loving me unconditionally
and always encouraging my dreams.

A NOTE TO READERS

Petaluma is a real town located just 10 minutes down the freeway from my home in California. However, some creative licenses were taken when my research did not yield enough information and certain scenes in this novel occur in fictional locations. I ask any Petaluma historians to bear with me.

Praise be to the Lord,
who this day has not left you without a kinsman-redeemer.
Ruth 4:14 NIV

ONE

Petaluma, California, 1936

By the time the lazy morning sun peeked over the Mayacama Mountains, casting its gilded warmth across the smaller hills and pastures of the North Bay, Luke Morgan had already snagged six steel-head trout from Petaluma Creek. Fat, cumbersome bumblebees bounced and buzzed among a vivid rainbow of wildflowers. A frog plopped into the flowing water not too far downstream, and something rustled in the tall grass behind him. Probably a rabbit foraging for breakfast. The sounds of nature coming to life and the hum of a tractor in the distance notified Luke the rest of the world was now awake with him. Mornings like these made all the work it took to get this land worth it.

Luke took a moment to breathe in the scent of wet earth and clean water. This was a far cry from three years ago when he was working on the Golden Gate Bridge, living in a boarding house in San Francisco, putting every spare penny toward payment for this ranch. His plan had been to stay to the end of construction. The bridge was set to open one year from now. What could he have done with all that money? Bought a couple more horses? Maybe start a herd of beef cattle? But that's not how life had unfolded for him.

Enough useless speculation. Luke scrubbed his hand over

his face and closed the tackle box on the flat rock beside him. He pulled a string of trout from the water. With one more glance at the chuckling water splashing over and around rocks in its path, he wondered how the bridge's completion would affect the flow of the creek. It was more river than creek, and Petaluma and the rest of Sonoma County depended heavily on the waterway to get eggs and other dairy products into San Francisco and the rest of the country beyond.

Luke stood, wincing at the ache in his left knee, lingering effect of a minor injury from his time working on the bridge, and allowed his gaze to roam the quiet pasture. Normally a layer of cool, unruffled, white fog hovered above the ground at this time of day. Thanks to the Pacific Ocean a few miles west, temperatures tended to stay well within pleasant bounds in Sonoma County. But already the month of May warned of worse things to come when summer arrived next month. As if the blasted Depression wasn't enough. He only hoped things didn't get as bad out here as they were in the Plains.

His stomach grumbled on cue with the blossoming sunrise. He squinted through the increased daylight and spotted Gabby about twenty feet away. Her russet velveteen coat glistened. Her full mane lifted with the morning breeze. She swatted at a fly with her tail, head held high, as if she were royalty and not a simple, albeit beautiful, ranch horse. Luke slapped his hat against his right leg and blew a high-pitched whistle through his teeth.

The horse leisurely turned to look in his direction. Another sharp, impatient whistle, and Gabby sauntered over, her reluctance demonstrated in short, slow strides. He never could figure out if he owned that horse or if she owned him. Luke gripped the fish and tackle box and swung into the saddle. He tugged his hat over his eyes, gave Gabby a gentle nudge of his heels, clucked his tongue, and directed the mare back to the house.

A peaceful five-minute ride later the white with black trim ranch house came into view. The horses in the corrals chewed their breakfast, bits of straw sticking out of their mouths as they watched Luke and Gabby trot by. With a trained eye, Luke observed them, noting that Duke seemed to favor his right leg. He made a mental note to check the horse later. Lucy looked nice and healthy. Her foal would be here soon. Grayson stood at attention as if to say, *Don't worry, Captain. I'm keeping them all in line.* As they approached the house, Ruckus, his German Shepherd, met them, darting back and forth dangerously close to Gabby's hoofs.

"Lay off, Ruckus," Luke grumbled. The larger animal shook her head and whinnied in annoyance. At three years old Ruckus should know to stay out from under the horse's feet.

Luke stared down at the dog. "One of these days she's going to lose her patience with you."

Ruckus lifted his strong, brown chin in defiance and continued to prance in and out of Gabby's path.

Luke guided the horse into a corral with the three other horses, the only ones she would tolerate. He dismounted, removed the saddle and blanket from her back, and swung them onto his left shoulder. He glanced back at the horse as she pawed the ground.

"I know, I know. I'll be back later to brush you." He pointed a finger at the animal. "You know, you're getting a little too pampered for my taste, lady."

He pulled the gate shut behind him as he left the corral, then ducked into the barn where the sweet smell of hay, sawdust, aged wood, and worn leather surrounded him like old friends. Luke flipped the saddle on a bale of hay. The blanket he tossed over a rope, stretched taut and connected at each end of the barn. Ruckus danced and whimpered around his legs.

Luke groaned and knelt down, rubbing the dog's ears. "You're getting to be as demanding as Gabby." Ruckus licked Luke's face, throat, and ears for as long as Luke could stand it. "Ugh. Enough." He gave the dog a gentle shove.

A glow of light in the kitchen window drew his attention. Luke squinted beyond the open barn door. It was barely light enough to be 7:00 a.m. Ruth was never up this early. He usually had to light a fire under her to get her out of bed in time for school.

A twinge of concern wrinkled his brow. What was she up to in there?

Ruckus tilted his head and barked once. Luke patted the dog's furry cheek and stood, then headed to the house.

He rubbed the back of his neck. This was all still so foreign to him. What did he know about raising a child? And a female teenager at that. Not a day went by that he didn't wonder what on God's green earth his sister had been thinking.

Kate had sent Luke photos of his niece through the years and written letters about her often. But it didn't change the fact they were strangers to each another when he'd met Ruth at the train station in San Francisco four months ago.

Luke struggled to recall the last time he'd seen Kate. He left so many people behind when he ran at seventeen years old. His stomach knotted. Kate, especially, had been through so much. First her husband abandoned her when he found out she was going to have a baby, leaving her to raise her daughter alone. Then she got sick. And he wasn't there to help her through any of it. He left her to their parents to help.

Upon reaching the back porch steps, he stomped his boots on the top stair and opened the door that led into the kitchen. The smell of too-strong coffee, burnt eggs, and charred bacon chased away the unbidden memories he'd found himself tangled in. Ruth, wearing her pink robe dotted with white and purple flowers, stood over a waste basket. She mumbled as she angrily scraped food from an iron skillet with a metal spatula.

He bit the inside of his cheek so as not to laugh. "Uhh...morning?"

She stood up straight. Her brow formed a tight V over her eyes even as her lower lip quivered. Was she going to cry or throw the frying pan?

Ruth shook her head, sending loose waves of hair swirling around her cheeks. She slapped the pan on the stove top with a loud clank and waved her arm at the stove. "I can't get used to this ancient thing. It gets too hot too fast, and it burns everything!" She crossed her arms, scowling at the offending appliance.

Luke rubbed his fist against the sudden ache in his chest. Sometimes it took his breath away how much Ruth resembled his sister. She had her mother's auburn hair, beaming green eyes, fair complexion, and expressive face.

He picked up some old newspaper from the counter and began to wrap the fish he'd caught for storage in the icebox. How was a man supposed to know the right thing to do with an angry girl? Females. They should come with instruction books. Horses made more sense to him.

"I know how you feel. That thing has been burning my food for years." He held his breath and risked a glance at her. The left corner of her mouth twitched into a quarter of a smile. He'd take it as a win.

Luke set the fish aside and approached her. "Next time try less wood, and open the damper." He showed her where the lever controlling the damper was located and demonstrated how to use it. Ruth stared at the oven, her arms crossed. Luke stepped around her, used a towel to pick up the hot coffeepot, and poured himself a cup.

He took a swig. The acrid taste mounted a sneak attack on his taste buds and burned his tongue. It took all the willpower he possessed to force the mud down his throat instead of spitting it into the sink. Turning his back to her, he squeezed the bridge of his nose. He'd taught her more times than he could count, but she still couldn't make a decent pot of coffee any better than she could fry bacon. Lord help the man who married this girl someday.

"Why, uh..." Luke ran his scorched tongue against the roof of his mouth. "Why are you doing all this anyway?"

Behind him, Ruth spoke in a defeated tone, "I thought you might be hungry."

"You were right. I'm starving." Luke put the offensive cup of coffee on the counter. Then slid it farther away. How could he fix this? He faced her again and leaned over the stove. He pushed a couple of pieces of blackened food around the skillet with his finger. "Were any innocent eggs or bacon strips spared in this attack?"

Ruth cocked her head at him, eyes narrowed. "No."

"Hmm." Luke scratched his temple. "Well, we have to eat something. Go get dressed for school. We'll leave early and have breakfast at Nella's."

Ruth's emerald eyes brightened. She stood up on her tippy toes and kissed his cheek. "Okay. Give me five minutes." She started out of the kitchen, but stopped short in the doorway. She scanned the mess that spread from the table to the oven to the counters to the sink. Ruckus had already begun licking up burnt bits from the floor as if they were manna from heaven. "I feel like a real sap leaving this mess for you."

Luke crossed his arms over his chest and raised a brow.

She bit her lower lip and ducked her chin. "I mean...I'll clean it up when I get home?"

He agreed with a single dip of his head. "I'll meet you in the truck."

The fifteen minute drive to Nella Jackson's diner passed mostly in silence, with intermittent mutterings about the heat. Luke cranked the window down and rested his elbow on the door. A cloud of dust swirled behind them in the rearview mirror. The chug-chug of the truck's engine and a persistent rattle made worse by the old dirt road rendered conversation difficult.

As they drove by Bailey Turner's chicken farm, Luke raised his voice over the racket. "I hope this heat doesn't do harm to the hatcheries."

Ruth coughed and waved her hand in front of her face.

Suppressing a sigh, Luke cranked the window back up.

Fields of Petaluma wildflowers danced in the breeze beyond the dirty windshield.

"You know," Luke tried again, "Petaluma is called The Egg Basket of the World." He pointed toward the creek flowing perpendicular with the road they traveled. "The eggs get shipped down the Petaluma Creek there into the San Francisco Bay. Then out to the rest of the country."

She offered a polite smile.

Luke adjusted his hat on his head. "You probably already know that, huh?"

A slow exhale seeped past her lips. "It's nearly all anyone talks about around here. Chickens and eggs, cows and milk and butter."

At her bored tone, Luke decided it best to leave the girl to stare out her window in peace. He certainly wasn't going to come up with anything more exciting to discuss than chickens and eggs, cows, milk, and butter.

At long last, downtown Petaluma came into view. Luke veered left onto Petaluma Boulevard. He found an open space in front of the Chicken Pharmacy next door to Nella's and parked.

Ruth met Luke at the front of the truck, her brow pinched. "What on earth is a Chicken Pharmacy, anyway?"

Luke stared up at the sign on the building. "I know it opened in '23. Farmers go there to get vaccines, medications to delouse their chickens and such."

Ruth scrunched her nose. "Yuck." She turned on her heel and strolled ahead of Luke to Nella's.

Just like her mom. Always confident. Always in charge. By the time he caught up to her, she was already engulfed in Nella's ample brown arms.

"Look how pretty you are this mornin'! What a lovely dress. It's exactly the color of the wisteria in my backyard." Upon spotting Luke, Nella straightened her skirt and fluffed her short gray hair. "And there's your good-lookin' uncle."

It didn't matter how bad things seemed around her, Nella oozed joy. Her dark eyes danced with mischief. Her round, cocoa-colored face beamed with a perpetual smile. "How are you this fine mornin', Luke?"

Luke touched the rim of his hat. "I'm doing all right. How about yourself?"

"Oh, I'm fine, just fine. Y'all have a seat and I'll get you some milk."

Luke considered the amount of money in his pocket and held up a hand. "We'll have water."

Nella scowled and snapped a finger at him. "You'll have milk. You've got a growin' young woman there and you need your strength to keep up with her." She winked at Ruth. "It'll be on the house. Now, scoot." She waved them away. "Go sit down."

Luke followed Ruth through the diner. Silverware clanked against porcelain plates, ice rattled in glasses, community chatter about the heat and various dairy farm issues competed with the smooth tone of Billie Holiday singing "Summertime" through scratchy speakers. Luke offered an obligatory smile to familiar faces seated around red-and-white checkered tables. Ruth found a table for the two of them, perfectly positioned beneath one of the antique polished oak ceiling fans. Nella's diner always seemed to fascinate Ruth.

Luke picked up the menu from the table.

Ruth twisted around in her booth and watched Nella walking toward the kitchen. "Has Nella ever been married?"

Luke perused the menu. Maybe he'd have the pancakes. Not that he'd be able to taste them. He ran his scorched tongue along the roof of his mouth again. "Nope. Not to my knowledge."

Ruth pivoted to face him again. "She told me she's from New Orleans. I just adore her accent! How long has she lived in Petaluma?"

"I'm not sure. A long time." He read the handwritten sign on the wall that displayed the day's special. Eggs, bacon, and pancakes—ten cents. Perfect.

"Have you ever been to her house?"

"Several times." Luke laid the menu aside.

Ruth leaned forward, eyes alight with curiosity. "What's it like? I mean, is it real fancy? She acts like it would be simple, but I get this feeling it's not."

Luke rubbed his chin and shrugged. "I don't know. It's nice."

Ruth slumped back in her booth. "That's not an answer."

What did she want from him? "It is too an answer. How is it not an answer?"

Ruth leaned in, biting her lower lip. Waves of auburn hair spilled over her shoulders. She whispered, "Does she have any relatives at all? Anyone to live with her, to keep her company?"

Luke leaned in until he was inches from her perfectly shaped nose. Ruth's eyes sparked with anticipation. He matched her whispered tone. "No. No, she doesn't."

Ruth's shoulders drooped. Her upper lip curled in dissatisfaction.

What was it with women and all their details? Why did he feel like he'd let her down somehow? And why did he feel the need to make it up to her? He scratched his temple, then raised a brow. "She's got three cats. Abraham, Isaac, and Goliath."

Ruth tilted her head. "Shouldn't that be Abraham, Isaac, and Jacob?"

"That's what I thought. I started to ask her once why she had two named after Bible heroes, father and son, and then the third one after a Bible bad guy." He cupped his hands together over the table. "I was here in the diner, eating a tuna fish sandwich. She was sitting across from me. And right when I started to ask her, this black and white striped cat—fattest cat I've ever seen—pounced from out of nowhere. He snatched my sandwich and took off."

Ruth's nose wrinkled as she giggled. Just like her mom. "You're making this up."

Luke leaned back and draped his arm over the back of the booth. "Cross my heart. He ran right out that front door. I've never seen a cat so big move so fast."

Nella approached with their glasses of milk and set them on the table. "Well now, what's so funny?"

Ruth accepted her glass from Nella. "Luke was telling me about your cats."

Nella's laugh jiggled her brown neck and cheeks. "I s'pose he told you 'bout Goliath. That cat's been on the wrong side of the Good Book since the day he was born. So, tell me, what's new with the two of you?"

Luke picked up his milk and took a drink. Folks didn't come to Nella's only to eat. They came to Nella's to be loved on and showered with attention. And perhaps, on occasion, for the diversion of local gossip. Luke wasn't normally one for idle chatter, but his reverence for the woman made her the exception. Nella knew more about him than anyone else in town, besides J.D. Hudgins. She never meant to harm anyone with her stories and would be crushed if she were to learn she had.

"Luke's thinking about taking on another horse," Ruth offered. "He'd have to build a new corral though."

"Oh, I'm sure it'd be a fine one, too, what with havin' such sturdy hands." Nella playfully batted her eyes at Luke, eliciting a chuckle from him. "You know, speakin' of corrals"—she squeezed herself into the booth next to Ruth and lowered her voice, forcing the other two to lean in—"I heard yesterday that cranky old Silas Holden was caught drivin' moonshine up to Santa Rosa two nights ago." She *tsked* once and added, "I'd say it's 'bout high time. Ever'one 'round these parts knows Silas has been bootleggin' since his sweet saint of a mama died in 1924." Nella slapped the table. "So, I guess he's gonna be corralled for a long while himself."

Ruth's mouth formed a shocked O. Nella's brow lowered again. "And, you know Eileen Broadmore, over on Washington Avenue? She was comin' outta Payne's Mercantile last week when a young man bumped into her. Well, he acted terrible sorry an' helped pick up her groceries an' all. It wasn't 'til Eileen got home she realized her wallet was gone! That boy bumped into her on purpose so he could take her money. Can you believe it? A grifter! Right here in Petaluma!"

Ruth's brows squished together. "What's a grifter?"

Nella waved her hand in no particular direction. "Oh, darlin, it's a person who swindles folks. They travel from town to town, trickin' folks and pullin' stunts like this one."

Eyes wide, Ruth gasped. "Did she call Sheriff Calvert?"

Luke hid a smile behind his hand.

Nodding, Nella leaned in closer to Ruth. "She went to the station and took Connie Smith with her 'cause, apparently, Connie saw the whole thing. So they went to the sheriff an' Eileen told him what happened. Then he asked Connie what she saw. And what do you guess she said to him?" Nella's dark eyes bore into Luke.

Luke rested his chin in the palm of his hand. "I haven't a clue."

"Connie told Sheriff Calvert the boy who took Eileen's wallet looked like Kim Samson's grandson, Ethan. He's been staying with Kim, what with his mama an' daddy not bein' able to afford to feed him out there in Kansas. Well, Kim was fit to be tied when she found out! So she showed up at the sheriff's office with Margie McKenna, who told the sheriff it couldn't have been Ethan because Ethan had been at her house all day, replacin' rotten boards in her front porch." Nella slapped the table top again.

Luke and Ruth exchanged a puzzled glance.

"Oh!" Nella maneuvered her ample self out of the booth and pulled a pad of paper and pen from her apron pocket. "Where is my mind? You have school to get to, young lady. You don't have time to be sittin' here listenin' to an old woman flap her gums! What would you like, chérie?"

"Wait." Ruth grasped Nella's hand. "Who was the grifter?"

"Oh, who knows." Nella shook her head. "He's prob'ly long gone by now. Most likely Santa Rosa's problem now." She bent down so as not to be heard by other patrons. "If I find out anything else though, I'll be sure to let y'all know." She straightened again. "Now, what would y'all like for breakfast?"

Ruth cast an amused grin at Luke, like a little kid who just experienced her first ride on a carousel. "I'd like two eggs— scrambled, bacon, and toast with strawberry preserves."

"Okay." Nella scribbled on the note pad. "And how about you, gorgeous?"

Luke pointed at the sign. "I'll have the special."

"Comin' right up." Nella patted Ruth's shoulder before leaving them.

Ruth took a sip of her milk. "I like her so much. She reminds me of our next door neighbor in Montana, Mrs. Fulbright."

"If she's anything like Nella, the name Fulbright suits her."

Ruth stared past Luke, seeming to watch a scene play out in front of her. "When Mom got sick, Mrs. Fulbright brought dinner over for me every night. Her son and his wife and their two boys lived with her. She said fixing one more plate of food was no trouble."

"I'm sure it wasn't." The familiar clench of guilt gripped Luke's heart. "She sounds like a great lady."

Ruth stared at her glass of milk, tracing the rim with her finger. Every once in a while she offered these glimpses into what life was like with his sister. Painful reminders to him of how much Kate needed him and he wasn't there.

They waited in silence until Nella returned with their plates. He never knew how to fill those awkward moments. Never knew what to talk to Ruth about. She didn't seem to have any more ideas than him.

He dug into his food. There wouldn't be time to stop and eat any time soon if he wanted to finish sinking the rest of the posts for the corral. Ruth ate a few bites, but mostly pushed the food around on her plate. It seemed the memory of her mother's illness stole her appetite. Luke tried not to think about the ten cents being wasted. But ten cents would go a long way in helping to pay for a new pair of work gloves.

Luke finished his breakfast and checked his watch. "We better get going."

He left twenty-five cents on the table to cover their meals and the milk. They waved to Nella on their way out.

"Bye now." Nella smiled. "Good luck on your new corral, Luke."

Luke touched the brim of his hat. "Thanks, Nella."

"And you." She pointed at Ruth and winked. "You enjoy your lunch under that romantic old oak tree with Grady. He's a good-lookin' young man, too."

Ruth's eyes widened. Her gaze darted to Luke. She ducked her head and rushed past him out the door.

Luke stepped closer to Nella, tipping his hat back on his head. "Who is Grady?"

Nella stared past him to the door. "Oh, dear. Oh, I am so clumsy." Her lips pressed together.

"Nella." Luke stepped in front of her, blocking her view of the door through which Ruth had escaped. "I don't know anyone named Grady."

Nella wrung her hands. "Well, his family, the Akins, moved here from Oklahoma a month ago after the bank where his daddy worked closed up shop. I guess the bank couldn't survive what with all the wheat an' corn fields gone under 'cause of the drought." Her dark brows lifted. "They're one of the lucky ones though. I understand they still have plenty of old money."

"So why come here? Why not stay in Oklahoma and do something different?"

"Mr. Akins is a cousin to Caleb Elder. They bought Caleb's cattle ranch. Caleb's mama lives in Arizona an' her health is failin'. He took what they offered an' moved to take care of her." Nella shrugged her round shoulders. "I guess Mr. Akins figured, any which way, life here in California would be better than what's happenin' out there."

Luke rubbed the stubble on his chin, musing at the thought of a banker trying to become a cattle rancher. "And they have a boy, this—what's his name again?"

"Grady. He's seventeen." She reached up and laid her hand on Luke's shoulder. Her chocolate eyes peered into his. "He seems like real good people. He's real polite. Kinda shy even."

Unconvinced, Luke's eyes narrowed. "What's all this about lunch under a *romantic* oak tree?"

Nella smiled sheepishly. "I've seen them there every day, eatin' lunch together for the past two weeks. It's sweet, really." Nella held her hand to her bosom. "Does my heart good to see two young people discoverin' love for the first time."

Luke tugged his hat down lower on his head. "Yeah, well, it does something very different to *my* heart."

Two

R uth waited in the truck for Luke, her eye on the diner's door. She pressed her nose to the vehicle's window and squinted, but the glare of the sun on Nella's perfectly polished glass obscured her view. She adored that sweet old lady, but right now she could strangle her.

Ruth covered her cheeks with her palms. What was Nella thinking, spilling the beans like that? She dropped her hands and peered at the diner again. Were they talking about Grady? Was Luke asking questions about him? Was he curious about the boy she was falling in love with? Was Nella telling all of Grady's good qualities? Would Luke listen to her if she did?

She had broken his rules. But they were such hooey. She was sixteen years old. No dating was a dumb rule. Completely unrealistic. She closed her eyes and leaned her head against the seat with a groan. She'd known Luke was bound to find out about Grady eventually, but she'd rather it had been in her own time and on her terms.

Ruth startled at the protesting creak of the worn-out truck door. She picked at a dry cuticle. The churning questions in her mind abruptly gave way to concern over Luke's unpredictable reaction to this news. In her peripheral vision she saw him ease his long legs into the truck. He shifted his position behind the steering wheel a couple of times. Ruth focused on a crack in the old windshield. They sat in silence for a punishingly long moment. Why wasn't he saying anything?

She scooted closer to her door.

"Why didn't you tell me about this boy?"

Indignation at his demanding tone replaced fear. Why should she have told him? It was none of his business. She lifted her chin. "You didn't ask."

The sound of his long inhale then exhale warned that she stood on a very dangerous precipice. She was keenly aware of his dark gaze on her. Her stomach rolled. He possessed such an eerie calm, it spooked her.

"I've asked you several times if you were making friends at school."

Ruth straightened her spine, determined not to turn back now. But she refused to look at him. "I told you I've made a few friends."

"The only friend you've told me about, or ever had over to the house, is Olivia Hawkins. And last time I checked, she was not a boy."

A swell of irreconcilable emotions pressed against Ruth's ribcage. She wanted to tell someone about the boy who had stolen her heart. She wanted to gush about how wonderful Grady was, how kind he treated her, how he listened to her as if everything she had to say was important. How he made her feel things she'd never felt before.

A woman holding a little girl's hand passed by on the sidewalk. Why did her mom have to leave her? Why did God think it was okay to leave her all alone with no one to talk to?

"Ruth." Luke's deep voice intruded. "Stop playing games with me. Why didn't you tell me about Grady Akins?"

How dare he think he had any say in who her friends were? He'd only known her for four months himself. And whose fault was that? His.

Ruth twisted in her seat. "You never cared to know anything about any of my friends! Why should Grady be any different? You have no right to be angry. You aren't my father, and you aren't my mother. You're just the poor sap who got stuck with me because my mother died." Why on God's green earth had her mother chosen to send her to him?

His stare held her in some kind of invisible grip. The muscles in his jaw flexed. He breathed slowly, as if he were counting each breath. Ruth held her own breath. He had never raised his voice to her. Had never lifted a hand. Maybe it was only a matter of time...

He faced forward, gripping the steering wheel so hard the blood left his knuckles, turning them white.

Ruth reached for the door handle. "I'm going to walk to school."

"No. You are not."

Her hand stilled on the handle. She slowly withdrew her hand and clasped it with the other on her lap.

Luke turned the key in the ignition three times until the engine sputtered to life.

The five-minute drive from Nella's to Petaluma High School may as well have been five hours. Ruth defied the hot tears stinging her eyes. She bit her inner lip, determined to make it to school without falling apart. She had grown used to Luke's quiet ways, but his silence right now was unbearable. If he'd only say something, even if he yelled at her, at least she'd know what he was thinking. She could fight back.

She gathered her books and her lunch in her lap before they reached the school, tapping her foot on the floorboard, anxious to be out of his presence. At last the two-story school presented itself, a refuge from the never ending clamor of thoughts in her head and feelings deep in her soul no one but Grady knew about.

As the truck jumped and jolted to a stop, she threw the door open and escaped Luke's crushing silence and disapproval. She slammed the door behind her. Finally free from Luke's presence, Ruth drew in a steadying breath.

The grove of eucalyptus trees that bordered one side of the school waved their branches, filling the air with their spicy scent. It mingled with the smell of hay, fresh cut grass, and blooms on a nearby magnolia tree. She crinkled her nose as a warm breeze ushered into the pleasant mix of aromas the obnoxious smell of manure from a nearby dairy farm.

Chirping birds played background vocals to the excitable chatter and laughter of students on the school steps and lawn. The vise around Ruth's heart loosened. She approached the steps. Clusters of girls stood in packs. They giggled and fussed with their skirts, making eyes at the boys, who returned the flirtatious attention in kind. Ruth scanned the grounds until she spotted Grady. Their eyes met. He patted his friend's shoulder and, with a quick word, left his friends and jogged over to where she stood.

The flush of heat that raced through her chest and sent her heart into a gallop inspired a delightful amnesia regarding the tense drive in the truck with Luke. A contented sigh accompanied the smile she offered. Oh, she would never, ever be stuck on another boy. He was all she'd ever dreamed of. She adored the way he slicked back his light brown hair. He had a strong brow and dreamy chestnut-colored eyes. And to think, of all the girls at Petaluma High School, she was the one he wanted.

"Mornin', Ruth."

She loved his Oklahoma accent and the dimple on his left cheek when he smiled. "Morning, Grady."

He reached for her books. "Can I carry those in for you?"

Ruth tittered. "It's only a few steps, silly."

Shrugging, he took the books, which she gladly gave up. Grady held her gaze long enough to bring the wild butterflies in her stomach to life. Grady's attention suddenly diverted. He motioned behind her. "Is that your uncle?"

Ruth turned to see Luke in his truck, watching them. He hadn't driven away? Luke got out of the truck and strode toward them. Ruth pressed her lips together and closed her eyes.

"He doesn't look happy," Grady whispered in her ear.

The thrill of his breath against her skin was short-lived. She opened her eyes, her cheeks burning. Luke stopped in front of them. Grady's attention bounced between Ruth and her uncle. She said nothing.

Grady held his hand out. "Um, hello, sir. I'm Grady. Grady Akins."

Luke accepted the gesture and pumped Grady's hand once. "Luke Morgan."

Ruth stepped between them, breaking their handshake. She tipped her head to meet Luke's scrutiny. "Did I forget something in the truck?"

Luke hooked his thumbs around his belt loops and innocently lifted his shoulders. "Nope. Just thought I'd come meet your *friend*."

The bell announcing the start of school rang out.

Ruth breathed a prayer of thanks for the respite. "We have to go now." She grabbed Grady's elbow, tugging him along with her.

Heavy footsteps followed close behind.

Ruth gritted her teeth and abruptly stopped and turned back. She stomped toward Luke, twisting Grady's arm and dragging him with her. "What are you going to do? Follow me to class?"

Luke stared at Ruth's arm, linked with Grady's. "I was thinking, I haven't actually met any of your teachers." He studied the school and surrounding area. "Seems like as good a time as any."

Students rushed past them in a blur, bumping them out of the way. "You cannot follow me to class," she hissed.

Luke bent down and whispered, "I'm pretty sure I can."

Ruth sucked in a furious breath. "Fine! Follow me! I don't care!"

She dropped Grady's arm and stormed ahead of them both. She could hear the echo of Luke's boots above all the squeaky sneakers, tapping pumps, and soft thumps of saddle shoes on the linoleum hallway floor. She reached her first class. Ruth stopped and threw her arm open wide in the direction of the classroom's open door. "This is our English class."

She snatched her books from Grady, whose wide-eyed confusion continued to dart between her and Luke. She hugged her books to her chest. "You can leave now."

Luke eyed Grady. He craned his neck to look through the classroom door. "I haven't met your teacher yet."

Ruth's right eye twitched. "She doesn't have time to meet you. She's has a class to teach. That's what she does. She's at work, Luke."

As if summoned, Ruth's teacher stepped out into the hallway.

"Good morning, Ruth." Miss Darby smiled at Ruth, then gaped at Luke. Ruth was used to women gawking at her handsome uncle.

He always seemed as oblivious as could be. Miss Darby quickly recovered and held out her hand. "Hello, I'm Emma Darby. Ruth's English teacher."

Luke shook her hand. He regarded Ruth. "I thought Mrs. Landry taught English here."

Now it was Miss Darby's turn to study Ruth. "Mrs. Landry moved to San Francisco to live with her daughter and son-in-law."

Ruth swallowed hard. "We should go in now." She caught Grady by the elbow again. "Come on."

Grady followed Ruth into class. "Why didn't you tell him about our new teacher?"

Ruth didn't answer. She left Grady at his desk in the front row and hurried to her seat, avoiding all the curious stares from fellow students. Why hadn't she told Luke about the new teacher? Because Luke wouldn't have cared. Because she was only one of six teachers. He wouldn't have asked questions about her favorite teacher the way Mom would have, or baked cookies for Miss Darby, or invited her to dinner.

Olivia Hawkins, Ruth's best friend, rushed into the classroom, made her way between their classmates' desks, and slipped into the one next to Ruth. "What's happening?" Olivia whispered. "Where is Miss Darby?"

"She's with Luke." Ruth whispered back. "Right outside the door. Didn't you see him?"

Olivia's already large blue eyes grew even larger. Her blonde curls bounced as she shook her head. "I was digging in my purse for a pencil, just trying not to be late. Why is he here?"

Ruth kept her eye on the classroom door. "Nella told him that she saw me having lunch with Grady under the oak tree."

"Oh." Olivia's nose crimped. "What's wrong with that? He's not sore about it, is he?"

"Yes, he is. Or maybe not. I don't know. I don't know if he's sore about me having lunch with Grady or sore that I haven't told him about Grady."

"Do you think he found out about—"

"No!" Ruth quickly scanned the others sitting around them. Fortunately, everyone else was taking advantage of the teacher's absence, too engrossed in their own conversations to pay any attention.

"Are you crazy?" She pointed her finger at Olivia and whispered, "And he won't find out either. Right?"

"Of course not! What do you think I am? A snitch?"

Ruth peeked across the room at Grady. He was laughing with two other boys. He caught her mooning at him and winked. The way her heart twittered in her chest, she could almost forget Luke stood right outside.

Miss Darby returned to the room. "All right, class. Please stand for the 'Pledge of Allegiance' and for prayer. Come on now, hands over your hearts. Oliver, will you lead us please?"

Oliver walk to the front of the class. The same pair of overalls he wore everyday bore a new stain on the bib. Some of the kids made fun of Oliver's dirty clothes. But what choice did the boy have except to wear them? Since his mother's death from tuberculosis, he had no one except a drunken father to see to his needs. Rumor had it they were headed for the poor farm in Santa Rosa.

Oliver faced the flag. The rest of the class stood with their palms pressed to their hearts. They all recited, "'I pledge allegiance to the Flag of the United States of America and to the Republic for which it stands, one nation, indivisible, with liberty and justice for all.'"

After a brief pause, Oliver led the class in prayer. "Almighty God, we acknowledge our dependence upon Thee, and we beg Thy blessings upon us, our parents, our teachers, and our Country."

"Thank you, Oliver. You may all sit down now." Miss Darby pointed to the blackboard. "Everyone, the assignment is on the board. Please spend the next thirty minutes reading the text, and then we will have a discussion time about Mr. Dickens's writing style."

Olivia and Ruth both groaned as they opened their books. They would both much rather read romance books.

"Ruth?" Miss Darby held her hand out toward the door. "May I see you outside for a moment?"

Ruth winced at Olivia, then stood to join her teacher.

"Let's step away from the classroom door." Miss Darby guided Ruth several steps down the hallway. "It's much too hot to close it on the other students."

If Miss Darby didn't want the other kids to hear what she had to say, this was not going to be pleasant.

"I enjoyed meeting your uncle."

Miss Darby's warm smile always managed to reach the aching, lonely place deep inside Ruth. The same place in her heart that longed for her mother sometimes seemed a little less lonely when Miss Darby was around. Olivia and Ruth had decided, after seeing the movie *Swing Time*, their teacher looked like Ginger Rogers. Without all the Hollywood makeup and fancy clothes, of course.

"I'm wondering why you didn't give him the letter I sent home to all the parents, introducing myself?"

Ruth fidgeted with a button on her dress. "I don't know. I guess I thought it didn't really matter." She added quietly, "I didn't think he would care."

The teacher inclined her head. "He seems to care a great deal, Ruth. But even if he didn't, I trusted you to give the letter to him. If you're going to hide things from your uncle, things I ask you to share with him, you and I are going to have a very difficult time trusting each another. I really don't want that to happen."

Ruth's throat tightened at the realization she'd disappointed Miss Darby. "I'm sorry, ma'am. It won't happen again."

"I appreciate that." The teacher placed her hands on Ruth's shoulders. "And...I'm sorry to have to tell you this...but your uncle has requested that we not allow you to spend time alone with Grady Akins while you're on school grounds."

Ruth stared at Miss Darby, her mind blank. She waited for the rest of the story. Surely her teacher had talked Luke out of such a ridiculous idea. But Miss Darby didn't seem to have anything to add.

Ruth folded her arms across her chest. "He has no right to do that."

Miss Darby lowered her hands from Ruth's shoulders. "Yes, he does. He is your guardian."

Ruth's pulse raced as panic and anger flashed like lightning bolts through her chest. Not allowed to have lunch with Grady? "No, he can't do this! We aren't doing anything wrong!"

Startled by the sound of her own voice echoing off the yellow metal lockers that lined the walls, Ruth stepped away from her teacher. She held her arms tightly to her chest. Had everyone in class heard her?

"I'm sorry, Ruth. I know you and Grady like each other very much." Miss Darby's gentle tone assured Ruth she meant what she said. Maybe even that she agreed Luke's demand was ridiculous. "But I have to honor his request."

Tears pressed at the back of Ruth's eyes and stung her nose. "But it's not fair."

"Your uncle is only trying to protect you the best he knows how."

"He's treating me like a child." Ruth stamped her foot on the ground. "I'm not a child. I'm sixteen years old. Lots of girls get married at my age. All I've done is eat lunch with a boy."

The teacher pinched Ruth's chin between her thumb and forefinger. "You're right. You are not a child. So don't behave like one." Miss Darby's ocean blue eyes nearly swelled with understanding. "Show your uncle that you are a mature young woman by honoring his rules. Earn his trust."

Ruth rubbed away the stinging tears. How would she tell Grady?

"I know you've suffered a great loss, Ruth." Miss Darby took Ruth's hand. "I can only imagine how much you must miss your mother. And I want you to know, anytime you feel you need someone to talk with, you can talk with me. Anytime. About anything. All right?"

Ruth nodded, but she absolutely could not talk about her mom right now.

Miss Darby gave Ruth's hand a gentle squeeze. "I have to get back to the class. You take a few moments to gather yourself, and then join us when you're ready."

Ruth dipped her head so Miss Darby wouldn't see the tear falling down her cheek. "Yes, ma'am."

Miss Darby went back to class. Ruth crossed to the other side of the hallway and leaned against the lockers. How was she going to tell Grady that Luke wouldn't even let her eat lunch with him? They already had to sneak around to see each other outside of school because of Luke's stupid "no dating" rule.

Now they couldn't even be together while at school? What if Grady decided being with her wasn't worth the hassle of having to put up with Luke? What if that snooty Gretchen Manor got her way and stole Grady?

Ruth muffled a frustrated cry and kicked a locker door. She would not lose Grady. Not ever. No matter what Luke said or did.

THREE

Luke gently pried loose the stone wedged between Duke's hoof and shoe. The stone bruise explained why the animal had been limping earlier. He untied the leads he'd used to cross tie the animal so as not to get kicked. Fortunately, Duke's owner wouldn't arrive for another two weeks to ride. The minor injury would be healed by then.

The last thing Luke needed was the owner of a horse he boarded to get browned off and take his horse elsewhere. Luke was lucky to have a business that catered mostly to the wealthy. Folks who had enough money to weather the financial devastation of the Depression that had put so many others in bread lines. He couldn't afford to lose even one of his high-priced boarders.

Duke nudged Luke with his nose.

"Feel better, ol' boy?" Luke patted the horse's neck. "You can thank me later."

Duke blew hot air out his nostrils and shook his head.

Luke led the horse back to his corral and then left the barn in search of fresh air. The heady, sweet scent from the jasmine vine climbing a fence near the barn door hung heavy in the afternoon heat, but not even the slightest breeze dispersed it among the hills and valleys of Petaluma. He removed his hat, ran his hand through sweat soaked hair, then replaced the hat and wiped his hand on his pant leg. A ride to the creek for a long, cool soak sounded inviting. If only he had the time.

He checked his watch. Two-thirty. Ruth would get out of school in fifteen minutes. Pressure built in his chest, pushing against his ribcage. Maybe he should pick her up. He'd been on edge ever since finding out about that Grady kid last week. He peered over at his truck.

What should I do, Kate? Go get her? Watch her every move? How do I keep her safe?

He squinted up at the scorching, unrelenting sun. He pulled his hat lower, over his eyes. He'd stay right here. There was still work to be done. Ruth knew the rules. No boys. If she chose to break the rules, then— Well, he wasn't exactly sure what he was supposed to do if she broke the rules. For now, he'd have to hope she chose to obey.

Luke went back into the barn, snatched a brush off a hook on the wall, and approached Maude. He clicked his tongue a few times and ran his hand down the mare's long black nose. "Ready for your brush down, old girl? Come on out here."

He unlatched the gate that held Maude in her stall and led her out into the open barn. This was where he felt most at home. The rustle of straw under his boots, the familiar sights and smells. No one chattering away at him. A man could think in a barn. If he did have an urge to talk, horses were good listeners. And even better at keeping secrets.

Luke had about finished brushing Maude when a knock drew his attention. Who knocked on a barn door? He swept the brush toward Maude's hind quarters and caught Grady Akins's form in the doorway.

What had he been just thinking about no one chattering at him? He kept brushing the horse.

"Mr. Morgan?" Grady called from the open barn door. "I was wondering if I could talk to you for a minute."

Maude's coat nearly glistened. Her brushing was done, but Luke figured the animal wouldn't complain about a little more attention.

Behind him, Grady cleared his throat. "It's...uh...it's about Ruth and me."

Luke's attention darted to the boy.

Grady raised his hands in a defensive pose. "I mean, it's about Ruth. I mean me. I mean, I want to talk to you about me. And her." His Adam's apple bobbed up and down.

Luke resumed grooming Maude. "Spit it out, kid. We'll be here all day at this rate."

"Right. Okay. I wanted to ask your permission, sir, to take Ruth to the church social next Saturday night."

"Don't call me 'sir.'"

"Okay. Mr. Morgan."

"Don't call me that, either."

Grady heaved a sigh. "What should I call you then?"

Luke couldn't help but grin, knowing the irritation he was causing. "My name is Luke."

"All right. Luke. So, may I have your permission to take Ruth to the church social?"

Luke led Maude back to her stall and latched the gate. He hung the brush on the wall where it belonged, then crossed his arms over his chest and studied Grady. The kid had a tall, sturdy build and intensity in his eyes, disturbing in its familiarity. Only his slightly rounded cheeks gave away the fact he was only seventeen years old. He wore clean, store-bought clothes, and he'd slicked back his hair. Luke remembered Nella saying Grady's family had money. Had the boy ever worked a day in his life?

"We don't go to church."

"I know that." Grady took a tentative step inside the barn. "Ruth used to go, though. Back in Montana. Before her mother died. She misses it."

Luke searched his memory. Had Ruth mentioned to him wanting to go to church since she got here? He slapped some loose horse hair from his pant leg. "She told you that?"

"Yes, sir—I mean, Luke."

Luke adjusted his hat on his head and stared out the barn door.

Ruckus lay in a shaded spot under an old redwood tree. Ruth had never said anything to him about wanting to go to church in all the time she'd been here. Why not? Did she think he wouldn't let her go? *Would* he allow her to attend services? Or would he stand in her way because of his own experiences?

He squinted at Grady. "What kind of church do you go to?"

"Petaluma Valley Christian Church."

"Your parents go there, too?" Luke stalked across the barn and picked up a pitchfork. Grady's eyes widened. What, did the kid think Luke was going to attack him? Might not be a bad idea to put a little fear into the boy. Luke stabbed the fork into a pile of straw, inches from the boy's leg.

Grady jumped back.

"Have you gone deaf?" Luke found satisfaction in the beads of sweat that appeared on the kid's forehead.

Grady's eyelids twitched. "What?"

Luke pulled the fork out of the pile, bringing with it a bundle of loose straw. He tossed it into the stall next to Maude's, then returned to plow the fork back into the pile.

Grady continued to eye the pitchfork, alarm etched into his face.

"I asked if your parents go to this church, too."

"Oh. Yeah. Both of them. My dad is a deacon and my mom plays the piano..."

Luke recognized himself in the young man standing before him. The courage mixed with anxiety at confronting the father of the girl he wanted to date. A dad who was a deacon and a mama who played the piano. A boy who went to church every Sunday. Always did and said the right thing, having no clue what kind of heartache life could throw at him. No idea that one wrong choice could change his life forever.

And cost the lives of others.

Luke tossed another heap of straw into the stall. "Has Ruth told you my rule about dating?"

Grady's shoulders sagged. "Yes, she has."

"Then why are you here? You were spending a lot of time with my niece already without my permission, weren't you?"

"We ate lunch together if that's what you're talking about. I didn't think you would see that as dating. We were in view of everyone, including teachers."

Truth be told, the lunches in the school yard weren't what bothered Luke. What kept him awake at night was worrying about what could happen when they weren't surrounded by a school full of kids and teachers.

The boy shoved his hands in his pockets and returned Luke's stare.

Weighing the danger level of a church social would take some time. "I'll think about it."

Grady's brow wrinkled. "All right. Uh, when will you let me know your decision?"

Luke struck the straw pile with the pitchfork again. "When I've made it."

"Oh. Right. Okay. Well—thank you." His thank-you sounded more like a question. "I'll just wait to hear from you then." The kid stood there as if Luke might decide to give him an answer immediately after all.

Luke had nothing else to add. It seemed to take a minute, but finally the kid got the hint and left him in peace. Luke rubbed Maude's nose and peered into her large eyes. "I'll be lucky to get out of this without an ulcer, won't I?"

When the sun sank low enough to cast long shadows on the ground, Luke stood and straightened his back. He had replaced three fence posts, and found a large, errant portion of barbed wire in the field where he exercised the horses. Thank goodness a horse hadn't found it first. He walked across the field toward the corrals. He tended to the horses with food, water, and a final quick inspection, then trudged to the house to wash up.

He opened the door to the kitchen and nearly stumbled at the aroma of food cooking. His mouth started watering. Ruth stood at the counter, shredding lettuce into a bowl. Was he in the right house?

Olivia Hawkins greeted him with a smile bright enough to light a moonless night. "Hi, Luke!"

"Hi." Luke took in the scene before him. "Is that real food I smell?"

Olivia's blonde curls bounced around her shoulders. "And how! I taught Ruth how to fry chicken."

Luke pointed from Olivia to Ruth. "*You* taught *her* how to cook?"

Ruth spun around to face him. "What do you think I am? A dumbbell?"

A smile tugged at the corner of Luke's mouth. "Sorry, kid. But you have to admit, your cooking was not going to win any blue ribbons up to now."

Ruth playfully stuck her tongue out and kicked up a heel before returning to shredding lettuce.

Fortunately, her mood from this morning had not carried over to this evening.

Olivia giggled. "We've got potatoes, lettuce, tomatoes, and peas from the garden, too."

"It sure smells good."

Ruth glanced up at him, smiling. "Let's hope it tastes as good as it smells."

Luke wasn't about to question her good mood and break whatever spell she was under. He tossed a wink at Olivia. "You staying for dinner?"

"No." She stuck her bottom lip out in true Olivia style. "I have to go home and make dinner for my dad and brothers. Mom is still in Washington visiting my grandma."

Olivia's mother had been gone a while. Luke feared there might be more going on than what was being said. "Your dad find work yet?"

"No." Olivia sighed. "He said he might take the ferry to San Francisco and see if he can get work on the bridge. Mom didn't want him to. She said it was too dangerous."

Luke's aching knee reminded him how dangerous it could be.

He'd lost a good friend on the job, too.

"She's right. There are some dangerous jobs on the bridge. But there are also perfectly safe positions available. I'd be happy to put in a word for him if he'd like. I know all the men in charge."

"That's right!" Olivia's eyes widened and her smile returned. "You worked on the bridge. Oh, that would be swell. Can I tell him you'll recommend him?"

"Sure. No problem."

"Thank you." Olivia gathered her books from the table. "I gotta go. I'll see you at school tomorrow, Ruth."

"See ya, Liv."

"Olivia, wait." Luke went to the ice box and pulled out the fish he'd planned to fry for dinner. "Take these with you. I caught them this morning."

"Are you sure?" The girl stared at the newspaper-wrapped fish as if he'd handed her a fully cooked pot roast.

"I'm sure."

"Thank you, Luke. My dad and the boys will love it." Olivia tossed them one last smile before leaving.

Luke liked Olivia. She brought a burst of energy with her whenever she came over. He watched Ruth at the counter, now cutting up tomatoes and dropping them in the bowl with the lettuce. Did Ruth ever giggle like Olivia? Did her face ever light up and her eyes sparkle? He'd certainly never seen it.

Ruth glanced over her shoulder. "You were okay just now. You have your moments, you know that?"

Luke rubbed his neck. "Yeah, well... I'm gonna go clean up."

Ruth carried the bowl of salad to the table. "Okay. Hurry, though."

Luke returned from washing the barn dust from his hands and took a seat at the table. He paused a moment to appreciate the glossy skin on the chicken, bright green peas, red tomatoes on a bed of crisp lettuce, and steam curling up from the thick brown gravy. Food he hadn't had to cook.

Luke picked up the platter of chicken and served Ruth, then himself. They each dipped into the other dishes on the table and began to eat. He wracked his brain for something to say while the clanking of silverware echoed into the silence. May as well go with the lead story before she heard it at school tomorrow.

"Grady came to see me this afternoon."

Ruth's fork paused midair. "Yeah...he told me he was going to ask you about the church social."

Luke buttered a slice of bread, took a bite, and spoke around the mouthful. "He did."

Ruth put her fork down. She sipped her milk and patted her lips with a napkin. "Well, do I get to know what your answer was?"

"I told him I'd think about it."

"What kind of answer is that?" She fell back in her chair and huffed. "Why couldn't you just say 'yes'?"

Luke swallowed his food. He studied the table. The food. All the work she'd put into it. He was being plied. She probably had a cake hidden around here somewhere, too. Did older women teach girls this trick or did it come naturally? Well, it wouldn't work. He wasn't going to fall for it.

Luke shoveled a forkful of peas into his mouth. He chewed and swallowed. "I don't know him."

"Fine. What do you want to know?"

"I'm not talking about his middle name or his favorite color."

"Then come to the social. You can get to know him there."

Luke lifted a brow at her. "No thanks."

"So let me get this straight." She folded her arms. "I can't eat lunch with him in front of the entire town because you don't know him. I can't go to the church social with him because you don't know him. But you won't go out of your way to get to know him. How is that fair?" Her green eyes blazed, challenging him to think through his next move very carefully.

Luke closed his eyes and pinched the bridge of his nose. How did women do that? How did they formulate their arguments so fast? And how did they make a grown man shrink with one look, even at only sixteen years old?

Truth was, she had him cornered. He had no real reason for

keeping her away from Grady, who actually seemed like a perfectly good kid.

You were a good kid once, too.

Luke dodged the thought and its accompanying memories. "I have my reasons."

FOUR

Emma Darby balanced an armful of essays and her pocketbook in one arm and opened the front door with her free hand.

She unloaded the papers and purse onto the desk Nella had given her and shook her arms to get the blood flowing again. She wedged the door open with a broken broom handle as a breeze outside manifested. Hopefully it would cool off her little home, such as it was. And it wasn't much. At all.

She blew out a heavy breath and scanned the one-room cabin. Jasper Loomis had known exactly where he was sending her when he offered to rent his "charming cottage" to her. Sighing, she picked up a fragment of peeled wallpaper from the floor. She should have expected as much. Payback—or control. It had always been one or the other with him.

It had the necessities, at least. Walls. A ceiling. Functioning kitchen and bathroom. She mopped her forehead with the back of her hand and went to the icebox for the pitcher of cold water. After pouring herself a glass, she moved a kitchen chair to the doorway and sat down to take advantage of the breeze. Dust rose in little puffs from the nearly bare yard and settled into the patches of crab grass. Maybe she should have moved her chair beneath the willow tree several yards away. Now that she was off her feet, though, she didn't have the energy.

Emma drank the last of the water and stared at a broken board on the porch. Jasper had said she was making a mistake. That she wouldn't make it on her own and would be back. There had certainly been days when she questioned if he was right. She smiled with satisfaction. Today was not one of them.

She had been getting closer to Ruth Morgan ever since the incident with the girl's uncle a couple of weeks ago. Her first heart-to-heart with Ruth wasn't exactly the way she'd hoped to start, but she'd seen something in the young girl's eyes hinting at a desire to connect. They had found a sort of kinship in each other since that day.

And Luke Morgan—he was certainly a surprise. Not an altogether unpleasant one. The epitome of tall, dark, and handsome. She'd had some difficulty concentrating on his words and not on the depth of his round, dark eyes.

But handsome though he may be, everything about him evoked caution. Could he be another Jasper Loomis? Her instincts rejected the idea. Luke didn't seem like the type to control or manipulate. He was...a tortured soul.

Emma shook her head. She'd been reading too much poetry. And she certainly had enough to keep her busy that she needn't waste time thinking about some mystery man.

Time to get to work grading papers and preparing the rest of the week's lessons. She moved her chair to the desk. Thumbing through stacks of essays and notes, she searched for her lesson plan and grading book. Where was it hiding? She searched her large flour sack bag and under the desk, then checked outside to see if she had dropped it.

Then she remembered. She had let Ruth borrow it earlier in the day. She searched the sky and noted that the sun had begun its slow descent into the horizon, but there would be at least an hour of daylight still. She regarded the dirt driveway that led to Old Adobe Road. Ruth lived about a half mile away. Not a terribly long walk, especially with the heat starting to dissipate.

Was there any way she could avoid it? The stack of completed student assignments glared at her. If she didn't grade and record them tonight, it would only mean twice as much work tomorrow. And there was still the lesson plan for the next day. She hadn't been at this job long enough to come into class unprepared. What if it got back to the principal?

"May as well go for a stroll." She retrieved a light sweater, stepped outside, and locked the door behind her.

The relative cool of the early evening provided a lovely walk. She breathed in the scent of eucalyptus trees and wild jasmine. As disenchanted as she was with her little shack, Emma did enjoy living in the small California town. Petaluma offered beautiful rolling hills, farms, dairies, and open fields, as well as the conveniences of downtown.

She passed by two farm homes before reaching the address she had for Ruth. It was a nice looking place. Well cared for. Single story, painted white with black shutters, and fronted by a large covered porch. A stately oak tree shaded the yard and several other varieties of trees and bushes dotted the property. Not far beyond the house she spotted a barn with red peeling paint and, farther back, another older-looking barn and large corral holding a few horses. Even they seemed to enjoy the drop in temperature as they trotted in circles. Only one russet-colored animal stood off by itself, whisking flies away with its tail.

Something about the animal made it special, and the horse knew it. In her mind's eye, she could picture Luke sitting atop one of the beautiful animals. Tall and in control. Brooding and mysterious.

Suddenly the thought of meeting Luke Morgan at his home, unannounced, struck her as terribly foolish. He didn't seem the type to enjoy unexpected company. What had she been thinking? But she couldn't have called ahead. She didn't have a telephone. She should leave. But she had to have the lesson plan book tonight. And what if Luke or Ruth had already seen her through a window? There was no turning back.

Emma smoothed her skirt and continued forward. The porch steps squeaked but the porch itself was inviting, with a few potted plants and flowers and a fresh coat of paint. She couldn't help but imagine sitting out here on a porch swing reading a book. The aroma of rosemary carried on a light breeze, and she sought out the full bush covered with its tiny purple flowers at the end of the porch. She closed her eyes, took in a deep breath and slowly released it before reaching out to knock on the door.

She whispered under her breath. "Dear Lord, please let Ruth be the one to answer."

Muffled voices echoed from inside. It sounded like an argument.

Emma hadn't seen any cars other than one truck when she'd approached the house. Recalling the incident at school, she feared Luke and Ruth had still not found a way to communicate. She really should leave. Right now.

Before she could turn to go, the door swung open. Emma found herself looking at Luke Morgan. He towered over her, broad chest and shoulders filling the doorway, eyes questioning. Goodness, he was more handsome than she recalled.

Emma swallowed around a lump in her throat. "I—I'm sorry to come by unannounced. But I don't have a telephone."

Luke inclined his head toward her, brow furrowed.

She absently lifted her hand to her throat. "You see, I...I can't find my lesson plan book. I think Ruth has it."

Ruth peeked out from behind him. "Miss Darby?"

Her voice must have startled him because he blinked and stepped aside, rubbing the back of his neck. "Uh—sorry. Come in."

She scooted by the giant of a man, unable to ignore the very masculine scents of a man who worked outdoors. Straw, dirt, leather. He closed the door behind her. She focused on breathing through the unexpected flips her stomach continued to make in his presence. "Hello, Ruth. How are you?"

"I'm all right." Ruth glared at her uncle, but then smiled at her. "Have you had dinner? We just finished, but we have leftovers."

"Oh, no, that's quite all right. Thank you."

"How about a cup of coffee? And we have some chocolate cake Nella made. You know Nella, right?"

"Yes, I do. She's a wonderful lady." The girl's eyes sparked with anticipation. Didn't she have many visitors? Of course, as she considered the idea, Emma couldn't imagine many people dropped by Luke Morgan's home simply to chat. "I don't want to take up too much of your time. I needed to come by to get my lesson plan book."

"Oh!" Ruth snapped her fingers once. "I forgot to give it back to you. I'm such a ninny. I'll get it right now."

Emma held out her hand, intending to stop the girl and suggest they retrieve the book together, but Ruth rushed out of the room. Emma stared after her like a child stared after a lost balloon. She slowly faced Luke again. She couldn't help but notice his denim pants bore evidence of the day's labor, dusty patches of dirt on the knees. Dried sweat marks around his collar testified to a man not afraid of hard work.

He hooked his thumbs in his belt loops. Emma tore her focus away from the man whose presence seemed to fill the room. Yellow and white gingham curtains hung on the windows. Four blue colored glass canisters filled with beans and rice added color to the worn counter top. Cheerful white daisies, surrounded by the remains of a chicken dinner on the oak table dressed up a simple milk glass vase.

"You have a lovely home."

"Thanks." He rubbed his neck. "Ruth brought a lot from her mother's house."

"I'm sure it's comforting for her to be surrounded by her mother's things."

Luke nodded and rubbed his neck again. Emma suppressed a grin at the nervous habit.

Ruth reappeared with the book. "Here it is."

Emma pressed her palm to her heart. "I thought I had misplaced it. I spent quite some time searching before I remembered you took it. I tell you, sometimes I think if they were to put my brain in a bird, the poor thing would fly backward."

Ruth laughed.

At Luke's confused look, Emma explained, "I loaned the book to Ruth so she could copy her extra-credit assignments."

"Extra credit?" He scowled at Ruth. "Are your grades in trouble?"

Ruth began to fidget. "I... Um..."

Luke's gaze bore into Emma. "How bad is it?"

"Well, she's in danger of failing my class." Emma quickly added, "But with these extra-credit assignments, she'll be back up to a passing grade."

"Why haven't I heard about this before now? Don't you send a note home or something?"

Emma risked a glance at Ruth.

Luke followed her gaze. "Ruth." His voice lowered. "I am in no mood to run around in circles with you."

Ruth eyes darted between the two of them. "Miss Darby gave me the choice of asking you to come to school to meet with her or tell you myself."

"When?"

The young girl seemed to shrink before Emma's eyes. "A couple of weeks ago."

The muscles in Luke's jaw flexed. "About the same time you were supposed to tell me you had a new teacher?"

Ruth bowed her head. "Yes."

Tension seemed to palpitate in the small room like a heartbeat. Emma was terribly out of place here. She headed for the door. "I should go so the two of you can talk about this."

"No, don't."

Luke blocked her way with an outstretched arm. She jerked to a stop, barely avoiding a collision with his muscled bicep.

"I need to know if there's anything else I should be informed about." His focus landed on his niece again. "How am I supposed to know what's going on if you don't tell me? How am I supposed to make sure you graduate from high school if I don't know you're practically failing subjects? How do I do *anything* for you if you decide for yourself what's important to tell me and what isn't?"

"There's nothing else." Ruth shook her head. "Honest."

Luke gave a snort of derision.

Ruth's emerald eyes pleaded with Emma. Emma swallowed hard

and stepped forward. "May I say something?"

Luke raised a brow at her. "Don't you think it's about time you did?"

Was he actually blaming her for any of this? She resisted the urge to kick him in the shin. The last thing she wanted was to lose her temper in front of a student.

She lifted her chin and squared her shoulders. "Ruth and I have talked about the importance of trust. We agreed to start a clean slate with each other. But I think you should know, Ruth has also shared with me—" Should she tell him what Ruth had said to her in private? If only she could glean some kind of reaction from Ruth. But the girl's attention remained glued to the floor.

"What? What did she tell you?"

The battle of whether to speak or to leave gave her pause. Her heart went out to Ruth. Clearly these two did not have ideal communication. Ruth needed someone to help her say what she couldn't say for herself. "Ruth feels you have no interest in her schoolwork."

Luke stared at Emma for a moment as if stunned by what he'd just heard. His strong forehead twitched and his shoulders sagged. "Ruth, is that true? Why would you think that?"

"You never talk to me. Mom would always ask how my day was." Ruth's words seemed to tumbled out of her like blocks from a child's toy box. "Mom always asked what we studied in class, and always asked if I needed help with my homework, and—" She pressed her lips together in a firm line.

Luke stood before his niece, mute.

Emma's heart wrenched in her chest. These two desperately needed to talk to each other, yet neither of them seemed to know how.

"You see?" Ruth raised her arms and then let them fall to her sides. "He has nothing to say about my schoolwork. Or anything else about me. All I am is an obligation he got thrown in his lap."

"That's not true," Luke snapped.

Ruth gave a start. Her eyes darted to him.

"I—" He rubbed at the back of his neck. "I don't—" His chest emptied of air.

Emma approached Ruth, though her better sense screamed this was none of her concern and she'd best not overstep her boundaries as a teacher.

"You have to understand Luke's position, Ruth. Your mother knew what to do because she was your mother. She raised you, she knew you. From what you've told me, the two of you had a very special bond and a close relationship, the kind I wish all my students had with their mothers. But your uncle"—Emma witnessed a shadow of defeat settle in his dark eyes—"is new to this. He's never had a teenage girl. You want him to come to you. You want him to know what to do and what to say, to know what you need and when you need it. It's really unfair to him."

Ruth opened her mouth as if to argue.

Emma held up a finger. "It is. It is unfair. If you want Luke to talk with you about school, you are going to have to help him. Waiting for him to do it, and then getting angry when he doesn't, is not right." Emma stepped back, waiting, praying for one of them to speak, to confirm she'd done the right thing.

Ruth finally sighed and rolled her eyes. "I'm sorry, Luke. I promise not to keep anything about my schoolwork from you again."

The emphasis she placed on the word *schoolwork* was not lost on Emma. She watched for Luke's reaction. He met Ruth's apology with a silent stare.

He pointed his finger at Ruth. "I will not put up with any more deceit from you." His baritone voice carried a warning, bordering on anger, while pleading hid behind the intensity of his words.

"Yes, sir."

Emma wanted to take the girl in her arms. Assure her everything would be all right. She could not imagine the uncertainty and fear Ruth must have faced, losing her mother and riding alone on a train from Montana to San Francisco to live with an uncle she'd never met, and to find such an imposing figure as Luke Morgan.

She recalled her own first encounter with Luke. Standing easily over six feet tall, the black hat he wore added to his height and intimidating stature. Dark facial stubble and espresso-colored eyes peering from beneath the hat's rim had momentarily unnerved her when they first met. The gravel in his voice had done little to put her at ease. Here in his home now, though, she had a different view of him. For one thing he wasn't wearing the hat. Subtle waves of hair nearly as black as his hat curled at the nape of his neck, softening his rough edges and invoking the image of a young boy's unruly mop.

Who was this man? A dark and brooding enforcer of rules? A loving and concerned uncle? He seemed to be, in fact, a six-foot-three walking contradiction.

"Miss Darby?"

Emma nearly jumped at the sound of Ruth's voice.

Luke's squinting eyes lit with a flicker of mischief above the faintest of smiles.

A swell of heat rolled up the back of her neck and into her cheeks. She forced a smile at Ruth. "I'm sorry... What?"

"I asked if you would like a piece of cake." The young girl's voice pleaded with her to stay. "We always have dessert while we listen to the radio, and it's almost time for Burns and Allen."

They listened to the radio together? Well, that was a positive sign. "I don't want to intrude."

Crinkles formed around Luke's eyes, taking the edge off his thousand-yard stare, as if he'd made some discovery while delving into her soul without her permission. He offered a half nod. "You're welcome to stay."

Emma opened her mouth to accept the invitation, but she couldn't find her voice. No. She should definitely leave. The pace at which moods and emotions changed in this house made her dizzy. She would do well to put as much distance between herself and Luke Morgan as possible.

Ruth bit her lip and pressed her palms together.

Emma's stomach sank. How could she disappoint her? Maybe it would be best if she stayed after all. Just to observe her student's home life. A good teacher strives to understand her students as much as possible, right? "I suppose I could join you. For a bit. Thank you."

Luke motioned behind him with this thumb. "I'll get the radio going."

Emma enjoyed lighthearted small talk with Ruth as she helped clear the dinner dishes and cut the cake. Once they filled three plates with wedges of chocolate cake, Emma followed Ruth into the living room. Luke bent on one knee in front of the old Zenith radio and turned the dial back and forth until the crackle and hiss of interference gave way to a man's voice. Ruth gave Luke a piece of cake, and he lowered himself into an overstuffed chair, his long legs stretched out in front of him on a wooden footstool.

Emma diverted her eyes before he could catch her staring again. Ruth's touches were noticeable in this room, too. A pillow adorned with a cross-stitched rose decorated the sofa. Sky blue fabric draped across the tops and down the sides of the windows. An amber pressed-glass lamp on the sofa table bathed the room in a pleasant yellow glow.

She joined Ruth on the couch and took a bite of cake as a news brief began. The hasty cadence of the reporter spoke of tensions rising in Europe as Adolf Hitler continued to rally his army. Emma's heart sank at the possibility of another war. How many more lives would it cost this time? Especially if somehow America were drawn in. Next, the reporter gave an account of the scandalous activities of King Edward in London. It seemed he was involved with a divorced woman, causing quite the uproar in England.

"Olivia and I saw a picture of Edward in *Life* magazine today at Meyer's," Ruth gushed. "He's dreamy."

Emma smiled at the spark of innocence and youthful ideas of romance in her student's eyes. "He may be dreamy, but his activities could cost him the throne."

"How?" Ruth set her now empty cake plate on a round redwood coffee table. "He's the king. He can do whatever he wants." She licked frosting from her finger.

"Yes, he can. But it causes people to question how seriously he takes his role as king. Many people think he's bringing shame to his family and to the throne."

"So, he has to walk away from the woman he loves? Just because other people don't approve?" Ruth cast an accusing look at her uncle.

Luke didn't seem to notice. "He'll abdicate."

Surprised at his contribution to the exchange, Emma attempted to draw him in more. "Give up the throne? You think he will?"

"It's the right thing to do." His sure stare and the conviction in his voice pinned Emma to her seat.

"Is that what abdicate means?" Ruth asked.

"Yes." Emma peeled her attention from Luke. Again. "If he were to abdicate, his younger brother would become king."

"How romantic." Ruth leaned back and sighed. "To have a man give up the throne of England for you?" She stared off into the distance, lost in the dreams of love and courtship of a young girl.

Luke took his last bite of cake and put the plate on a side table. "You'd be far better off focusing on your grades."

"There's more to life than grades," Ruth retorted. "Like church socials."

Emma watched the muscles in Luke's jaw twitch.

Ruth crossed one leg over the other. "Miss Darby, do you think a church social is wrong?"

"I never said going to a church social was wrong," Luke interjected.

Ruth rolled her eyes. "Fine. I'll clarify then. Miss Darby, do you think it's wrong for a seventeen-year old-boy to ask a sixteen-year-old girl to a church social?"

Emma's mouth went dry at the challenge in his eyes.

"I— I don't think— I mean—" Emma set her own plate on the coffee table. "Clearly, whatever is going on here is between you and your uncle."

"But you can still answer the question. Is there anything wrong with two teenagers going to a church social together? You see, Petaluma Valley Christian Church is having a social on Saturday."

"Oh, that's the church I go to. Yes, I know about the social."

"You go there, too? So you see Grady there?"

"Yes. I see him and his family there every week."

Ruth leaned in. "Well, he asked Luke if he could ask me to go with him." Ruth shot Luke an angry glare. "And Luke said he'd 'think about it.'"

"And it's what I'm going to do." Luke stood. "I'll be in the barn."

Emma watched, slack jawed, as he simply walked out of the room without another word.

Ruth slumped back on the sofa. "That's where he always runs off to."

Emma stared at the empty chair Luke had vacated. "Just like that?"

"When he's in this kind of mood, yes. Sometimes I wake up in the middle of the night and go to the kitchen for a glass of water, and I see the light bulb on out there."

Emma worried her brow. "He seems upset. Maybe I should leave."

"Oh, you don't have to." Ruth grasped Emma's hand. "Really. Please. He'd rather be out in that old barn than in here, anyway. Stay and listen to 'The Burns and Allen Show' with me. Please?"

Once again Emma couldn't bring herself to let Ruth down. She seemed so lonely, and Emma didn't want to leave her listening to her favorite radio program alone.

"All right. I'll stay for the program. But then I really must go home."

"Okay." Ruth curled her legs beneath her and hugged a decorative pillow to herself.

They listened and laughed at George Burns' and Gracie Allen's witty banter about George's singing voice. When the show was over, Emma stood and gathered the cake plates.

Ruth took the plates from her. "They are so funny."

Emma followed Ruth to the kitchen. "Yes, they are. It's been a long time since I heard that show."

Ruth took a metal tub from under the kitchen counter and positioned it in the sink. She turned the faucet on and waited for the water to get hot, then sprinkled soap flakes into the tub as it filled with water.

"I enjoyed this evening." Emma handed Ruth a plate to wash.

"I've missed listening to the radio."

"Don't you have a radio?"

"No. I had to sell mine, with a few other things, to make the move here to California."

Ruth washed another plate, rinsed it, and handed it to Emma to dry. "That's awful. I'd just die without a radio."

Emma laughed. "I promise, you would not."

"I'd be bored to tears, that's for sure. What do you do without a radio?"

"I read." Emma shrugged. "And grade schoolwork."

Ruth giggled. "How absolutely dreadful." She handed Emma the last glass and rinsed the wash cloth. "This was really nice. Maybe you could come back another night and have dinner with us?"

"Maybe." Emma dried the glass, set the towel down, and gave Ruth a hug. She gathered her pocket book and assignment book. "But for now, I really do need to go."

"All right." Ruth peered out the window. "Did you drive here?"

"No. I walked. I don't have a car."

"Well, it's dark out. You can't walk home alone." Ruth took Emma's hand and led her out the kitchen door.

"Where are you taking me?"

"To Luke. He'll drive you home."

FIVE

A number of hay bales balanced one on top of another at various angles and faced differing directions. A saddle straddled the bale in the center. The metal cage, as he called it—he'd have to find a better name for it soon—closed around the saddle. Luke circled the bales and the cage, eyeing the angles. He knelt on his good knee and examined the soldered points. The two light bulbs hanging from the ceiling swayed to and fro. He squinted through the dancing shadows and reached for two joined pieces of metal, testing them for strength. They came apart.

Luke grumbled under his breath. He thought he'd gotten that joint strong enough.

"Luke?"

He jumped to his feet. Ruth and Emma stared back at him from the open barn door. He reached for the canvas and covered his project. "What are you doing out here?"

Ruth stepped forward. "Miss Darby needs to go home."

They needed to come out here to tell him this? "Okay. Well. Goodbye."

Ruth huffed, planted her hands on her hips, and cocked her head at him.

Luke stared back. Females! Why couldn't they ever just come right out and say what they wanted? He held his arms out. "Sweetheart, I think this is one of those times Miss Darby was talking about earlier. You're gonna have to help me out."

Over Ruth's shoulder Emma covered a grin with her fingertips. What was so funny?

Ruth wasn't as entertained. "It's shocking that I even have to help you out." Ruth spread her arms. "Luke, Miss Darby has to go home. And it's *dark* out." She motioned toward the door, open to the night.

Luke stared out at the night for a moment until her convoluted message took hold. He scratched his chin. "Oh. Yeah. So it is."

Emma's eyes still held a spark of amusement.

Luke rubbed at his neck. "I'm sorry. I was distracted here with my—"

Her attention moved to the canvas. Luke reached for the chain connected to the light closest to the canvas and gave it a tug. The canvas disappeared into blackness. Almost. He strode to the other chain and tugged. The barn went black.

"Now we can't see even to walk back to the house." Ruth's voice rang with indignant disapproval.

He answered by flicking on the flashlight he'd hooked in the side pocket of his dungarees. He aimed the beam for the house and fell in step with the women.

"I really can walk home," Emma said. "It's not too far. And it's still a pleasant evening."

"No, no. Ruth was right to come and get me. I don't mind." In fact, it disturbed him how much he didn't mind.

"Luke never lets me walk the roads at night," Ruth said. "Even if it's only to go over to Olivia's."

They reached the house, and Ruth offered to get the keys to the truck. Luke led Emma to the vehicle, opened the door, and waited for her to tuck her feet inside before he closed it.

Ruth brought the keys to him.

He pointed to the cab. "Hop in."

"I think I'll stay home. I've got a lot of extra credit work to do, remember?"

Ruckus pawed at Luke's heels, tail wagging, anticipating a ride.

Ruth grabbed the dog and held him back. The smile on her face spoke of a teenager's overactive ideas of romance. He muttered to himself, walking around to the driver's side. He got in and turned the key a couple of times before the truck rumbled to life.

"Which direction?" he asked above the commotion of the engine.

Emma pointed east. "Right past Finnegan's Hatchery."

He tugged on the pull switch to bring the headlights to life, and then drove toward the hatchery. He should say something to her, right? Be polite. Nothing came to him. Had he completely lost all ability to interact with a pretty woman? He cast a brief look at her. She stared ahead, her delicate profile silhouetted against the dark night. She seemed at ease with the silence. Was that possible? A woman at ease with silence? He'd only known one in his life. The sweetest thing that ever happened to him. Until he destroyed her.

Emma pointed to her right. "The next driveway."

Luke steered the truck onto a short driveway leading to what appeared to be a small cottage. The headlights on the truck revealed a place in need of a fresh coat of paint, a couple of shingles repaired. The porch looked none too sturdy. Why did she live in a place like this?

"I'll get your door." He got out of the truck and met her on the passenger side, proud he'd remembered at least that much chivalry. He opened her door and held out his hand, which she accepted. Something foreign shifted in his chest at her touch. A spontaneous protective instinct struck him at the way her grip on his hand tightened as she gingerly stepped out onto the running board, trusting him to steady her.

"Thank you." She smiled.

A flash of warmth chased up his neck. Thankful for the cover of darkness, Luke held his hand out for her to lead the way to the front door.

Emma paused at the first porch step. "You'll want to walk on the right side."

Luke tested the step. The spongy texture beneath his feet confirmed his suspicions. The boards were rotted. "Who owns this place?"

Emma unlocked the door. "A man named Jasper Loomis. He lives in Arizona."

"You'd think he'd have put a little work into the place before letting you move in."

She continued ahead without answering.

A high pitched squeal suddenly assaulted his ears. Emma nearly fell through the rotted boards before Luke realized the screech came from her. He snatched her elbow and pulled her to safety. The blur of an animal catapulted out the door, across their feet, onto the yard, and disappeared into the bushes beyond.

Emma held her hand to her heart, breathless. "Oh, my word!" She peered around Luke. "What was that?"

Again the cover of night saved him as he swallowed his laughter. "I think it was a raccoon." Luke lowered his hand from her elbow. He stared into the dark house. "I wonder how it got inside?"

"I have no idea." Emma cautiously stepped in the house and lit an oil lamp. She warily eyed the floor around her, rubbed at her arms and rejoined Luke on the porch. "Well, it's gone now, thank goodness. I'm sorry I screamed like that. I'm so embarrassed."

"Don't be. That was quite a welcome home."

She pushed a loose curl behind her ear. "That's for sure. Thank you for the ride, Luke. I really am sorry to have interrupted you tonight."

"It's no problem." He studied the bushes behind him. "Say, do you mind if I come in?"

Emma's eyes widened. Her jaw dropped.

"I—I don't mean like that." Luke sputtered. Was it possible to make a bigger fool of himself? "I was thinking maybe I can figure how that animal got in your house."

"Oh!" Emma's shoulders relaxed. "Of course. I'd like to know, too. I'm not sure I'll sleep very well otherwise."

In the corner of the one-room cottage, a mattress covered with a feminine quilt of blue and pink flowers lay on the floor. Not on a bed frame. Only a mattress on the floor. A small desk stood against the opposite wall with neatly stacked papers and a few books on it. Next to the desk, a wardrobe dwarfed the already small space. To his right was a kitchen. Of sorts. A stove, a sink, and an icebox filled one wall and an old beat-up pine table with two mismatched chairs sat across from them.

Between the "bedroom" and the "kitchen" was a loveseat that had seen better days. A crocheted blanket of blue and white yarn spread across the back. Two side tables each held an oil burning lamp. Luke hoped a bathroom was behind a door the size of a closet. He hated the idea of her having to use an outhouse. Irritation nagged at him. Why did such a beautiful, educated, well-spoken woman live like this? She didn't even have electricity.

"I don't know where it could have come from." Emma's voice broke into his thoughts.

Luke rubbed his neck and inspected the worn baseboards. "Animals will find a small opening, maybe a little hole started by a mouse, and they'll work at it until they can fit through."

"Oh."

Her worried tone drew his attention. "We'll find where it came in and make sure it can't come back." *Or bring any friends with it.* "May I?" He pointed to the closed door.

"Yes, of course. It's the bathroom."

Luke opened the door to what amounted to little more than a closet with a sink, toilet, and bathtub crammed so tightly she must have to leave the door open to actually utilize the room. He scanned the area and closed the door again.

"I don't see anything in there. Do you mind if I move the desk?"

"Not at all. I'll help you."

They worked together to scoot the desk away from the wall. Sure enough, after they'd moved the piece away from the wall, they saw a hole large enough for a small animal—or a fat raccoon bent on squeezing itself—to get through.

Emma leaned down to get a better look at it. "You were right."

Luke scratched his temple. "At least it didn't mark its territory." At her scrunched brow he held up a hand. "Trust me, you don't want to know." He chuckled as understanding dawned on her face.

Her cheeks blossomed pink. "I suppose we could move the wardrobe over here to block it."

"Good idea."

They moved the wardrobe out enough for Luke to scoot the desk into its place. Then they pushed the wardrobe into the desk's original spot.

Luke said, "I'll come by tomorrow and patch up the hole."

"Oh, no, you don't have to do that."

He held up a hand. "It's all right. You can't have wild animals roaming in and out of here. That Loomis guy is going to pay me to fix it." Luke scanned the room. "Along with some other things around here." He stepped out onto the porch and tested several patches of squishy wood planks. "You know, the guy has got a lot of nerve charging you rent before this place was repaired."

She hugged her arms to herself. "Well, I—I relocated in such a short amount of time, there wasn't time to search for a place before I came. I really should be thankful to have a home at all."

Why had she had to move so quickly that she didn't have time to find a proper place to live? And why did she act as if it was her fault the place was in such rotten shape? "Just the same, if you'll let me contact him, I'll take care of it."

"I certainly won't argue with anyone who wants to help. I would appreciate it." She added quietly, "I have a feeling you'd get further with him than I would."

What exactly was the relationship between her and this Loomis guy? "All right then. You can give his number to Ruth at school tomorrow."

"I'll do that. Thank you. For everything."

"You're welcome." He lifted his hand to touch the rim of his hat, then remembered he wasn't wearing it. He rubbed his neck. "Good night."

He waited for her to close the door and then listened for the latch to engage. Why did he go and do a thing like offering to fix her house? As if he didn't have enough work to keep up with at his own place. Work that now waited.

He drove home and parked outside the barn. Not ready to go to the house, he pulled the old barn door open, its creaks and groans joining a chorus of frogs and crickets. He stepped inside, took two steps to his right and reached up to tug on the chain that brought a single light bulb to life. Ruckus followed him, as he did every night, the faithful dog sauntering to an old blanket in the corner. He'd lumbered in a circle three times and plopped down facing the open door, ears twitching, at the ready for the slightest intrusion of a raccoon or possum. Luke ambled to the center of the barn and pulled on another chain, illuminating the back portion of the barn.

He drew in a long breath and blew it out slowly. The scent of pine trees swirled around him. Crickets chirped incessantly. He closed his eyes and listened for the sound of water gurgling in the creek. This was his favorite time of day. When the heat and demands of the day melted away into the soothing smells and sounds of evening. Sometimes he liked to sit on the bank of the creek before the sun went down and watch the boats make their way toward the San Francisco bay with their loads of eggs and milk. Those boats would be all but gone once the bridge opened.

This wasn't the prettiest barn in town by any stretch of the imagination. The walls moaned in a strong wind. Some spots in the roof needed repair before the rain started up again in winter, but it was his sanctuary. A respite when he needed to get away. And tonight, he needed to get away.

Emma Darby's face formed in his mind as if carried on the night breeze. She was a pretty little thing with delicate features. A halo of blonde curls and a pink heart shaped mouth that tipped into an easy smile. But fire hid behind those innocent blue eyes.

What would it take to light that fire?

He smiled at the memory of the blush on her cheeks when he caught her staring at him. How long had it been since a woman looked at him like that? Give her time. Soon enough reality would replace whatever she thought she saw in him. He didn't want her attention anyway. He'd only hurt her. It's what he did.

Then there was Ruth. Luke pinched the bridge of his nose. He couldn't seem to do anything right with her. He couldn't believe it when Emma told him Ruth thought he didn't care. He'd taken her in, hadn't he? He even quit his well-paying job on the bridge a year early to provide a steady home life for her. She had food and clothing and stability.

And what was that business about not hiding anything else about her *schoolwork*? The question in Emma's eyes told him she'd caught it too. A handful of possibilities flew through his mind. None of them good.

"Shake it off, Morgan. You're too young to worry yourself to death over a teenager and too old to be mooning over a pretty woman." Ruckus tilted his head at his master's voice.

Luke reached for a dusty, yellowed canvas and pulled it back to reveal a metal contraption that would make no sense to anyone but him. And that was fine. It didn't need to make sense to anyone else. Not yet.

Six

"Ruth! Gimme a push!"

Ruth laughed at Olivia's youngest brother, four-year-old Samuel. He wore denim overalls—a size too big—with no shirt and had wedged himself into the old tire swing hanging from the oak tree in the Hawkins' front yard. His blond hair needed washing and sweat smudged the dust on his cheeks. His skinny little legs swung with all their might trying to get the heavy tire to move.

Ruth gave him a healthy push. "You need to grow longer legs, shorty."

"I know." He held his legs out in front of him as he flew through the air, the soles of his feet caked in blackish-brown dirt. "Push me higher!"

"Okay. Hang on."

"Look at me! I'm flyin' like a thuper fatht airplane!"

Ruth laughed at his adorable lisp. She hadn't pushed him nearly that hard, but to a four-year-old, it must feel it. "Be sure you have a safe landing. Your mama will be none too happy with me if she comes home to find you've flown away." She gave him a salute. "Safe travels, Captain Hawkins."

"Yeth, ma'am!"

She climbed the steps to the Hawkins' front door and knocked.

Olivia called from the direction of the kitchen. "Come on in."

Ruth let herself in and crossed the living room of the small clapboard house to join Olivia. "Samuel needs a bath."

"Like I don't have enough to do. I'll throw him in the creek later. He'll love it." She tossed a kitchen towel at Ruth. "You're right on time to dry dishes for me."

Ruth caught the towel. "Gee, thanks." She picked up a dripping glass and ran the towel over it, absorbing the beads of water. "When is your mom coming back, anyway?"

Olivia dunked a dirty plate in the dish water. "I don't know."

What could be taking Mrs. Hawkins so long to return to her family? People in town were beginning to gossip, but Ruth chose not to question Olivia. She had other reasons for being here anyway. "So...listen, Liv—"

"No." Soap bubbled dripped from Olivia's pointed finger. "Don't say it."

"Come on." Ruth pressed her hands together beneath her chin and interlocked her fingers. "Just this once."

"Just this once?" Olivia let out a sarcastic laugh and crossed the kitchen, reaching into the laundry piled on the kitchen table. She retrieved a worn T-shirt and folded it.

"You are going to get caught. Luke is already watching you like a fox watching a hen house since he found out about Grady. Besides, I thought you said Grady asked Luke about taking you to the social."

"He did."

"Why would you want to go and mess everything up then?"

"You think Luke is actually going to say yes? Besides, it's been three weeks! The social is only a couple of days away now. He's not going to let me go. I just know it."

Olivia folded pair of her father's denim work pants. "You never know. But one thing's for sure. He'll say no if he finds out you're sneaking around. He'll lock you in the house and not let you out till you're old and fat and gray with hairy moles growing off the end of your nose and no one to care about you but a house full of black cats."

Any other time, Ruth would have laughed at her friend's

melodramatic prediction. Olivia's bright eyes and bouncing blonde curls added a sense of whimsy to nearly everything she did and said. Ruth stuck her lower lip out. "No, he won't."

Olivia lifted a brow at her. "Come on, I'll finish folding this load and then we'll go to the five-and-dime to look at the new magazines. I hear Greta Garbo is on the cover of *Photoplay*."

Ruth laid the kitchen towel in a blank space on the table. "I already promised him."

"Promithed who?" Samuel's voice sent Ruth's heart galloping. "And what'd ya promithe?"

Ruth's eyes darted to Olivia.

Samuel tugged on Olivia's skirt. " Livvy, can I have an apple?"

Olivia tossed a pair of socks on the table and crossed to the counter. She retrieved an apple from a bowl and handed it to Samuel. "Now, scoot. And don't come back in."

"Why?" Samuel bit into the apple. He spoke through the mouthful, juice dripping down his chin. "It'th too hot out-thide."

"Well, it's no different in here. Now, go. You can pick more apples from the Reinman's orchard."

Samuel didn't budge. Olivia knelt in front of him. "Listen, if you go outside and don't come back in until I say, I'll take you down to the creek for a swim."

Samuel's dirty face lit. He scampered out of the kitchen.

Ruth leaned against the counter, filled her cheeks with air, and dramatically released it.

Olivia shot her a disapproving look. One Ruth's mother would have given had she still been here.

Ruth opened her mouth to plead her case again, but the rumble of an engine drew her attention to the dirty kitchen window. Mr. Hawkins' old Ford kicked up a cloud of dust as it grumbled its way to the house. She had to get an answer from Olivia before he came inside. If Mr. Hawkins caught wind of this, he'd go straight to Luke.

"Oh, look. My dad's home." Olivia made a stack of folded kitchen towels.

"I have to go, Liv. Please?"

Olivia set her hands on her hips and exhaled. She stared out the window. Mr. Hawkins' heavy boots sounded on the steps outside.

"Liv," Ruth hissed.

"Fine!" Olivia waved her hand toward the back door. "Go. And don't get caught."

"I won't, I promise. Thank you. You're the best friend ever. Remember, I was here for two hours. See you at school tomorrow." Ruth slipped out the backdoor of the Hawkins home and ran in the direction of the old abandoned barn a quarter mile away, her heart nearly bursting with anticipation.

Just as her legs began to give out from fatigue, she spotted the faded barn with peeling red in the middle of the field of orange California Poppies. Grady leaned against the wall, chewing on a piece of straw.

She hollered his name.

He held his arms wide open and Ruth ran to him. He wrapped his arms around her, picked her up off the ground, and hugged her tight. Ruth could barely breathe after such a long run, but breathless giggles erupted anyway. Was there any more exhilarating feeling in the world than this? She couldn't imagine it.

Grady lowered her feet to the ground and touched her cheek. "I was startin' to wonder if you were comin'."

Goosebumps sped down her neck and into her arms. "I know. I'm sorry." She brushed his hair away from his forehead. She loved how that one curl always seemed to fall. "Liv gets all worked up sometimes. She's scared we're going to get caught."

Grady nudged a rock on the ground with his shoe. "It would be a lot easier if we didn't have to sneak. You think maybe Luke will change his mind about you datin' and let us go to the social together?"

"I don't know." She took Grady's hand and led him into the barn. They couldn't be too careful. "His rules are so dumb." She plopped down on a hay bale, stewing over Luke's stubbornness and unfair rules.

Grady took her hand in his. "He's only tryin' to protect you. He don't want you to get hurt."

What a silly worry. "You would never hurt me."

"No, I wouldn't. But Luke don't know that."

Ruth jerked her hand away from his. She stalked to the middle of the barn. The hair on the nape of her neck prickled. "Why do you do that?"

Grady blinked. "Do what?"

"Take his side. All you ever do is make excuses for him."

"I'm not makin' excuses. I'm only sayin' I understand why he has the rules. I mean, look at us. We're creepin' around behind his back. We're doin' exactly what he's so afraid we'll do."

Ruth's throat tightened. Of course she felt guilty. Even ashamed in moments of brutal honesty. But why was it so wrong for her and Grady to want to spend time together? Why couldn't Luke try to understand? "We wouldn't have to sneak if he would loosen up, even just a little bit."

Grady scuffed to her. Ruth loved the way the sun streaking through the cracks in the roof highlighted his brown hair with strands of caramel. Her frustration melted away as he took her in his arms again.

He pressed his forehead against hers. "Are we really gonna spend our time arguin' 'bout your uncle? 'Cause I'd much rather kiss you."

Ruth slipped her arms around his neck. She stood on her tiptoes to reach him and lost herself in his kiss. Her fingers ached to touch his face, his hair. Shivers of pleasure flooded her. All thoughts of Luke, of Olivia, and of school evaporated as her heart entangled itself around his.

Emma added a pinch more sugar to the lemonade and tasted it. Perfect. If he liked his lemonade sweet. She held a finger to her lips. Should she make another batch? One sweet, one tart? She eyed the small crock that contained her sugar. If only she had more. At twenty cents a pound, she couldn't afford to use it up too quickly.

Why was she so concerned about how he liked his lemonade

anyway? If he didn't like it, he didn't have to drink it.

She put the sugar crock away and placed the pitcher on a tray next to two glasses filled with chunks of ice, then carried it outside. Luke had made good on his promise to contact Jasper about making repairs to the cottage. Not that she ever doubted he would. From the moment they met, he'd struck her as a man who didn't made promises he did not plan to honor. And he didn't seem to expect anything in return. What a breath of fresh air that was.

His first item of business had been to patch the hole the raccoon had used to slink into the cottage. A shudder rattled her shoulders. The thought of the creature roaming around in her home, touching things with its icky little fingers, made her want to wash everything in sight.

She followed the spicy fresh scent of sawdust and the *zip-zap, zip-zap* of a handsaw clawing its way through wood. Rounding the corner of the house, she found him, his back to her, black hat on its perch atop his head, perspiration soaked through the back of his white shirt. Chiseled muscles strained against the shirt. Emma stopped short at the sight while he continued to saw through the wood plank. Emma mentally shook herself, embarrassed by her observations. She cleared her throat.

Luke turned and straightened.

"I…" Her voice crackled like an old woman's. She swallowed and tried again. "I made lemonade." *There ya go, Emma. Dazzle him with your brilliance.*

His charming grin only intensified the flush in her cheeks. As hot as it was out today, maybe he wouldn't notice.

Her arms began to ache. She'd misjudged the weight of the full pitcher and ice-filled glasses. She had to put the tray down somewhere. Quickly. She turned a half circle and scanned the area for a good spot.

"So, can I have some?"

She spun toward his voice. The tray flew out of her grip. Lemonade seemed to spread through the air at a snail's pace. Emma thought she could count each individual droplet. The sweet refreshment splashed over the pitcher and glasses, which shattered on the hard, dry ground. Dirt floated on top of the liquid for a brief moment before absorbing it. Ice chunks formed little mud puddles, and the sun's rays bounced off broken shards of glass.

Emma slowly lifted her eyes to meet Luke's.

He didn't even try to hide his amusement as he slapped sawdust from his hands and tilted his head at her. "I guess not."

What was it about the man that transformed her into a bumbling idiot? She attempted a good-natured laugh, but it sounded shrill even in her own ears as humiliation sank her stomach.

Luke bent down on one knee, picked up the larger pieces of glass, and set them on the aluminum tray. She couldn't even force her body to move, to assist him. She stood there like a store mannequin, watching him pick up after her.

Finally he unfolded his long legs and stood. His height shielded her eyes from the sun. He held the tray to her with a wink. "Water will be fine."

Emma accepted the tray with a mute nod and retreated to the shelter of her house, praying she wouldn't trip over her own feet to complete the day's entertainment. In the kitchen, she set the tray on the tiny counter beside the sink. She swiped the back of her hand across her forehead. Was it the heat of the day or simple mortification making her sweat? How was she going to afford to replace these items? Her left eye burned. She dabbed at it and blinked rapidly to try to alleviate the sensation.

At the sound of footsteps on the porch, she hastily reached into the cupboard for two more glasses. She'd better not drop these, too.

"Come on in, Luke. I'm in the kitchen." As if the kitchen were in the east wing of her grand home. She turned the cold water handle on the faucet and filled the first glass as his footsteps echoed on the wood floor behind her.

"Mind if I sit down?"

"Not at all." She offered a smile and carried the water to him. "Better take it before I spill it all over you."

His smile sent her already unsteady heart into a tailspin. "I hope those weren't heirlooms of some sort."

She lowered herself onto the chair across the table from him. "No. Just some old hand-me-downs I managed to gather before moving here." She sat with her palms flat against the table, as if balancing to keep herself from falling out of her seat.

He drank half his water. "Thanks."

"You're welcome." Her eye continued to sting.

"I have the board cut for the hole in the wall."

Had a drop of lemonade gotten into her eye? She delicately dabbed her eye with her finger. The sting intensified. What if it wasn't lemonade? What if a piece of glass had worked its way into her eye? She tried to blink away the discomfort.

"All I have to do is—" He shifted in his seat. "Did you get dust in your eye, or are you flirting with me?"

Mortified, she rushed to the sink. "I think some lemonade splashed in it." She retrieved a clean dish towel from a drawer and dabbed at her eyes, praying no glass was imbedded in her eye. He coughed twice, but she heard a chuckle hiding behind the fakery. Could this day get any worse?

"Do you need some help?"

His open amusement irritated her. "No, I do not." She dabbed at her eye again and splashed a bit of water on it. The sting dissipated. All she had to donow was regain some sense of control and self-respect.

Squaring her shoulders, she rejoined him at the table. "So tell me, are you going to let Grady take Ruth to the social?"

His brow quirked.

What in the world had possessed her? "I'm so sorry. It's none of my business. I don't know why I—" She clamped her lips together. She really should never speak around him.

"I don't know." He seemed to search her face for his answer.

His calm response surprised her. She'd already blundered her way this far into the subject, she may as well press on. "It's only three days away. Don't you think they deserve an answer so Ruth can prepare?"

His brows squished together. "Prepare for what?"

Emma resisted rolling her eyes. "She's a teenager, Luke. She'll want to decide what dress to wear. How to wear her hair. She may have some...special needs."

"What in the world kind of special needs would she have?"

Emma smiled at his naiveté. "Well, for example, does she own a pair of silk stockings?"

Luke shifted in his chair. He dragged his hand down his cheek. "I don't know. Why would I know that?" He raised his hands in the air as if being held up by a gunman. "I don't want to know that."

At last it was Emma's turn to enjoy his discomfort, though she took the high road and chose to hide her amusement. "Exactly. If she can't even approach you about silk stockings, she certainly can't approach you about anything more personal. She needs time, Luke. Don't wait until the last minute to tell her she can go."

"You're assuming I'm going to say yes."

"Why wouldn't you? It's an innocent church social." She leaned slightly toward him. "Luke, if you continue to forbid them from seeing each other for no rational reason, they are only going to start sneaking around behind your back. Trust me. I'm a teacher. I work with teenagers. I know what I'm talking about."

Dark eyes snapped at her. "Ruth wouldn't dare."

Emma shrugged one shoulder. "Maybe she wouldn't. On her own. But Grady, he's a seventeen-year-old boy. He's a good boy, but if you force his hand, he will do what seventeen-year-old boys do. The way Ruth feels about him, it's only natural she'd follow right along."

Luke tipped the brim of his hat back. He rested his arms on the small table, invading her personal space. "You're not exactly convincing me to let her go with him. Not if you think he'd lead her somewhere she shouldn't go."

"You're twisting my words. I do not think that about him. I'm only telling you what you must already know. You were a seventeen-year-old boy at one time. How would you have reacted if you had feelings for a girl and her father forbade you from seeing her for seemingly no rational reason?"

His eyes flashed with— With what? She wasn't sure. He pulled back, diverting his attention to the wall behind her. She'd hit a nerve. What was it?

He pushed his chair away from the table and stood. "I better get back to work."

She sat at the table alone, wondering where he had gone in his memory. What was that place, that time, that person? What had broken Luke Morgan?

Emma swept a broom across the floor of her classroom with more vigor than was really necessary. For the past two days, her thoughts had often wandered back to Luke. Had he given Ruth permission to go to the social tomorrow? She assumed not, since Ruth hadn't said anything to her about it.

She focused on the chatter of students outside the open windows before school began. If only she could sweep Luke Morgan out of her mind. She did not move here to be so affected by another man.

She turned to retrieve the dust pan from the coat closet and nearly plowed into a dark figure planted in front of her. Yelping like a startled puppy, she swatted at the man with her broom. He grabbed the broom in a grip of steel. She struggled to wrestle it back, fear clawing at her chest, until she saw his eyes.

Releasing the broom with a shove, she furiously swept her hair out of her face, straightened her best silk skirt, and glowered at him. "What on earth are you doing here, sneaking around like that?"

"I was hardly sneaking around." Luke handed the broom to her, his lips twitching. "Trade this thing in for a pair of gloves and you'll be the next Joe Lewis." He quickly scanned her from head to toe and gave her a rakish grin. "Then again, maybe not."

Stunned by his blatant flirting, Emma's mouth fell open. A proper lady would have slapped him. An elegant lady would have given him a tongue lashing. But there wasn't anything elegant or proper about the feelings those black velvet eyes evoked in her. It was a wonder her trembling legs held her upright.

He relaxed against a student's desk and stretched out his long legs. He shifted the black hat on his head. "I need a favor."

Emma steeled herself against the effect he had on her, frightened she might say yes to anything he suggested.

"You were right about Ruth. There's no— How did you put it?" He squinted at the ceiling and held a finger in the air. "No rational reason she shouldn't go to the social with Grady."

He came all the way down here to the school to tell her this?

He rubbed his neck.

The habit told her there was more to his visit.

"You, uh, were also right about the other thing."

She foraged her memory. "What other thing?"

"You know." He waved his hand in the air. "All that other...stuff."

Try as she may to recover the other *stuff*, Emma came up blank.

"Silk stockings," Luke blurted. "You were right about silk stockings."

Laughter erupted from the doorway. Emma gasped. Three young men, students of hers, had crossed the classroom's threshold. They chortled and slapped each other on the back.

Luke stalked toward the boys. Emma darted in front of him and held out a hand, nearly issuing a warning to Luke not to hurt her students, but he stepped around her and reached the door before she could. He unceremoniously shoved them into the hallway and slammed the door.

Emma stopped short and gaped at the closed door.

Fishing in his pockets, Luke walked back to her as if nothing had happened, while she wondered how she would ever earn the respect of her students again. He handed her three one-dollar bills. "Do you mind taking Ruth shopping today?"

Those eyes. Oh, those eyes... She fought past the paralyzing affect he had on her, the anger at her loss of control over her own classroom, and the impossibly frustrating inability to stand up for herself. What made him think she would jump to do whatever he wanted her to?

Ruth. She would do it for Ruth. And he knew that.

Emma snatched the money from his hand and took it to her desk, mostly to put distance between them. She dropped the money in a drawer. "You're making the right decision."

He adjusted his hat and stared out the window. "Take her for a chocolate soda, too. Make a day of it."

She planted her fists on her hips. "Is that an order or a request?"

He rubbed his neck, studied the chalkboard as if he'd find the answer there, and then walked out of the room.

Emma plopped down in her chair and held her fingertips to her temples. Another hairpin turn on the Luke Morgan roller coaster.

SEVEN

Ruth folded a piece of paper against her desk like an accordion to make a fan. Her mind wandered back to her sweet meeting with Grady two nights before. She brought her fingers to her lips, remembering his kiss. Her skin flushed at the thought. Being with him, talking and holding each other close, was wonderful. Only with Grady did she ever feel truly safe to share her heart. The more time she spent alone with him, the more she craved time alone with him.

Warmth crept into her cheeks. She hoped no one noticed. The old Whitman place had been abandoned for months and the barn offered privacy for clandestine meetings. It was all so exciting and romantic. Last night had become a little too private though. She ducked her head and glanced around. She would be so ashamed if anyone knew how quickly things had escalated.

At least he hadn't gotten angry when she pushed him away. Instead she found herself drowning in his gentle brown eyes.

"I would never do anything to pressure you, or hurt you, Ruth. I love you." He'd taken her hand, led her out of the barn, and led her home, her virtue intact.

"Good idea."

Ruth's attention jerked to her left. "What?"

Olivia pointed to the paper fan. "I said that's a good idea. I'm melting here. By the end of class all you'll see is an Olivia Hawkins puddle on this chair."

Ruth slumped against her seat, fanning herself. Between the heat and thoughts of Grady, she could not concentrate.

Within minutes the sound of thirty crinkled paper fans waving against stale air filled the classroom. Miss Darby looked up from her desk. She held her pencil to her lips and studied the class. She stood with a sigh and mopped her forehead with a handkerchief. "Class, I have a homework assignment for you."

A collective groan drowned out the paper fans.

"Since Mr. Green, the science teacher is gone for the week and I am filling in for him, I want you to study the Petaluma Creek. What kinds of plants and flowers grow on its shore? Which shores are rocky and which are sandy? I want you to bring specimens of plant life and even insects, if you so choose, to class tomorrow."

She leaned against the front of the desk. "The best way to study a subject is to dive right in. Get as close to the subject as you can. Therefore"—a playful smile spread across her pretty face—"I suggest you all go dive into the creek and start studying."

The class cheered and hollered. Desks and chairs screeched against the linoleum floor as students scurried to empty the room.

Olivia and Ruth paused on the school steps together. Olivia sighed. "I could simply die, it's so hot. Just like Greta Garbo in *Camille*." She held her hand to her forehead and quoted with dramatic flair, "'I'll be beautiful again—when I'll be well again—won't I?'"

Ruth laughed. "It wasn't the heat that killed Camille."

Olivia dropped her hand. "I know. But it sounds more romantic than consumption." She waved her paper fan back and forth in front of her face. "Let's go to the five-and-dime for a chocolate soda. My treat."

"Where did you get money to treat?"

"I babysat for the Millers last night. They paid me fifty cents."

"Well, if you're that rich, I will definitely let you treat."

Olivia's blue eyes sparkled. "And I'll still have enough money to buy a copy of *Photoplay*."

Ruth mopped her forehead on her sleeve. She scanned the well-kept lawn in front of the school. Everything was so still. Not a single tree branch or a blade of grass moved, as if the heat had sapped the energy out of every living thing. Across the lawn she caught Grady watching her. His wink sent chills trickling down her spine. She would much rather spend the day with him in their secret place. But he had taken a job working in the Kelsay's plum orchard today.

"Okay." Ruth sighed. "Chocolate sodas await."

The rumble of an engine drew Olivia's attention. "Hey, is that Luke?"

Ruth's gaze jerked in the direction Olivia pointed. Sure enough, it was Luke's truck.

Liv grasped Ruth's arm. "What is he doing here? Do you think he found out? Oh, this is bad, this is bad, this is bad!"

Ruth pulled her arm away. "Stop it. There's no way he found out. You said no one ever asked about me. As far as he's concerned, I was at your house." She swatted at Olivia. "Stop fidgeting. You're making me nervous."

They stood close together and watched Luke exit his truck. He met Grady across the schoolyard. Ruth sucked in a breath. Olivia muttered under hers. Luke spoke to Grady. Grady's mouth spread into a smile. Luke's expression never changed. Luke shoved his hands in his pockets. He spoke again.

Ruth's palms began to sweat. "What are they saying?"

Olivia bounced on her tiptoes. "If only I'd paid more attention to that spy movie. The one where the spy had to read people's lips. Maybe I could have learned something."

Grady held his hand out to Luke. Ruth held her breath again. Luke accepted it and gave it a single pump, then went to his truck and drove away.

Ruth and Olivia raced down the steps. They reached Grady, both of them out of breath. Ruth tugged on Grady's shirt. "What was that about? Why was he here?"

Olivia shook her hands in front of her as if shaking water from them. "Did he find out? Are you in trouble? I promise I never said a word!"

Grady laughed. "Calm down, girls. Everything is fine."

Ruth gave his shirt another tug. "Then please tell us what he said."

"I will if you'll give me half a chance." Grady took Ruth's hand. "Come on, sit down."

The three of them sat at a picnic table. Ruth slapped his shoulder. "Grady Akins, if you don't tell me what my uncle was doing here and what he said to you right now, I'm going to leave and never speak to you again."

He leaned in close to her. His eyes bore through to her very soul. "Really? You'd leave and never speak to me again?"

Gooseflesh popped up all over her arms. She glowered at him even as her stomach turned to jelly.

"He said I can take you to the church social."

Olivia shrieked and bounced up and down on the bench, rocking the whole table.

Ruth wasn't sure she'd heard correctly. "He—he what?"

Grady wrapped his arm around her shoulder. "I get to take you out. In front of everyone. We get to spend the whole day together."

She was going to go on a real date with Grady! With Luke's permission!

Grady leaned in and whispered in her ear. "I want to kiss you so badly right now, Ruthie. But I don't want to jinx it."

Ruth caught her breath. Oh, the way he made her feel...

He gave Ruth a quick peck on the cheek. "For now, I gotta get over to the Kelsay's orchard. I'll pick you up tomorrow at one o'clock, beautiful."

His smile and the spark in his eyes set her heart to pounding in her ears. She could only nod her agreement.

Olivia blew out a dramatic sigh and collapsed against the table top, her blonde curls splaying out. "I can't take all this excitement. It's simply terrifying."

Ruth laughed and squeezed her friend's shoulder. "Oh, Liv, everything in life is simply terrifying to you." She spotted Miss Darby standing on the steps of the school. "I wonder why Luke changed his mind."

Olivia raised her head and rested her chin in her palm. "Who cares? As long as he's starting to loosen up."

Ruth contemplated this sudden change in attitude with Luke. He'd been helping Miss Darby make repairs at her house and the last time he went there, he was quieter than usual when he came home. He hadn't even eaten at the table with her. He took his dinner out to the barn. She knew something had happened between the two but hadn't given it any further thought until now.

Ruth unfolded her legs from the picnic table. "I'll be right back."

"Where are you going? What about the five-and-dime?"

"I'll be back in a minute."

Ruth met Miss Darby on the school steps.

Miss Darby smiled. "I thought you'd be down at the creek."

"Maybe later. I wanted to ask you a question."

"Oh?"

"Did you say something to Luke about me going to the church social?"

Miss Darby offered a coy shrug. "I might have mentioned it."

Ruth couldn't suppress her smile. "Well, he said yes. He said we could go."

Miss Darby beamed. "I'm so happy for you. You and Grady will have a wonderful time."

"I know. I'm excited. Thank you so much for talking to him for me. Except..."

"Except what?"

Ruth lowered her chin. "I only have one real nice dress. I know it's silly, but Grady has seen me in it so many times." She sat on the top step, tucking her scuffed brown loafers under her blue plaid skirt. "It would be real neat to have a new dress for my first date." She toyed with a small stick.

Miss Darby lowered herself to the step next to her. "Well, then, I suppose it's a good thing your uncle gave me this." She reached into the pocket in her skirt and brought out three dollars.

Ruth stared in disbelief at the bills. "He gave you money? To buy me a dress?"

Miss Darby lifted her slim shoulders. "Or for whatever I deemed important for a young lady's first date."

"Oh, Miss Darby!" Ruth threw her arms around her teacher. "Thank you! Thank you so much!" An unexpected vision of her mother flashed in Ruth's mind. Her throat tightened. Was she betraying her mother? She backed away from the embrace.

Miss Darby touched Ruth's hand. "What's wrong?"

"I—I always thought my mom would be the one to take me shopping for this."

Miss Darby touched Ruth's back. Something a mother would do. "I know I'm not your mother, Ruth, and I could never replace her. But I would be honored if you would allow me to stand in for her this afternoon."

Ruth leaned into Miss Darby's arms again. She missed her mother terribly, but Miss Darby, who was so beautiful and refined—everything she wanted to be, wanted to help her. Ruth had been lonely for so long. But not today.

Today she had a mom.

EIGHT

Emma sipped her chocolate soda at Meyer's Five-and-Dime's laminate lunch counter. Although the red vinyl stools were less than comfortable on such a warm day and the ceiling fan did little to stop the trickle of sweat down her back, her heart remained full as she listened to Ruth and Olivia chatter about the dress Ruth would buy.

Emma thought back to earlier in the morning. Every encounter with Luke proved that the man was a tangled ball of contradictions. She found herself wanting to unravel those contradictions and get to know who he really was. But a niggling voice warned her she might not like what she found.

"What color will you get?" Olivia's animated voice coaxed Emma's attention back to the present. "I think you should get green to go with your eyes."

"I don't know. What do you think, Miss Darby?"

Setting aside thoughts of Luke, Emma joined in. "Green would be lovely." She caressed one of Ruth's auburn curls. "It would also look beautiful with your hair."

Ruth leaned in closer. "I can't thank you enough for convincing Luke to let me go. How did you do it, anyway?"

"Oh, I wouldn't lay too much of the credit at my feet. I think your uncle would have come around eventually."

"No, he wouldn't have." Ruth pushed her half-finished soda aside. "It had to have been what you said."

"Ruth. Honestly. It wasn't all me. Luke hasn't learned yet how to go about keeping you safe while giving you a little freedom at the same time."

Ruth didn't argue. She traced the rim of her glass with her finger.

Olivia sipped her strawberry soda through a red and white striped straw. "I think he's afraid of something bad happening to you. I think it's why he smothers you."

Ruth's shoulders slumped. "If that's true, why doesn't he just talk to me about it?"

Emma and Olivia both answered with a raised brow.

Ruth laughed. "You're right. He's not big on talking."

The bell above the store's entrance jangled, and a moment later Nella's voice rang with cheerful surprise. "Isn't this a happy sight." She met them at the soda counter and nearly encircled all of them at once in her full arms. "What are we girls gigglin' at today? As if three beautiful young women like yourselves need a reason to be happy."

Ruth returned Nella's hug. "We're trying to figure out why Luke is so afraid of me going out with Grady."

Nella's smile froze. Only for a split second, but there was definitely a reaction to Ruth's comment. Nella had information about Luke. The look Emma exchanged with the older woman compelled her to change the subject.

"Luke gave Ruth some money to buy a dress. She's going to the church social with Grady tomorrow."

Nella's clasped her hands together. "Oh, that is wonderful." She patted Ruth's cheek. "You know, I was afraid my big mouth had ruined your chances with that young man. Luke seemed none too happy."

"He wasn't. But Miss Darby managed to change his mind somehow."

"Oh, she did, did she?"

Emma's heart thudded at the knowing look in the woman's eyes. "Uh, I think we better get over to Burke's Department Store."

Nella winked. "You girls have fun."

Emma gave the soda jerk forty-five cents for the three sodas, and the trio set out together. She left feeling like a secret she didn't even know she held had been discovered.

The girls flitted from one sales rack to another in the store. It wasn't a large store, but it met the needs of a small town. Emma trailed behind, perusing dresses for herself. Not that she could afford to purchase clothes right now. Her last new dress had been a gift from Jasper Loomis. She never wore it anymore, but it still hung in her closet. She couldn't get rid of it. Not yet.

Squeals of delight alerted that the girls must have struck gold. She followed the high-pitched voices and found Ruth in front of a mirror, holding a dress.

Olivia cupped her hands to her cheeks. "Oh, it is divine. Just divine. Hurry and try it on."

Ruth giggled and grasped Olivia's hand, pulling her behind the curtain. "Help me change."

The giggles coming from behind the curtain heightened Emma's anticipation. "Come on out, girls, I'm dying to see it."

After much girlish commotion, Ruth reappeared. The green georgette dress reflected in Ruth's emerald eyes. It fit her waist and flared at the bottom. She looked more mature and even more beautiful. Ruth held her arms out to her side and twirled. The lovely dress curled around her legs.

Ruth bit her lower lip. "What do you think, Miss Darby?"

Emma studied Ruth. "I think you look stunning."

The uncertain eyes of a girl transformed into the hopeful eyes of a young woman. Ruth pivoted to study her reflection in the full-length mirror again, twisting and peering at the mirror over her shoulder.

Olivia fluffed Ruth's hair and smoothed the shoulders on the dress, gushing over every detail, like a lady in waiting. "I adore the pearls on the bodice. Aren't the pearls divine, Miss Darby?"

"Yes, they are." She recalled her first church social. The excitement, fear, and wonder that flooded her young heart as she stared at her own reflection in a new dress. That sweet, mysterious moment a girl realizes she has blossomed into a young woman. Ruth's eyes held the same awe in her eyes now. What a privilege it was to be here with her for such an important day.

Oh, Ruth. Your mother would be so proud.

"What about shoes?" Olivia asked.

"Oh. I didn't think of that." Ruth stretched to reach the price tag on the back of the dress. "How much is the dress?"

Olivia reached for the tag. "Here, let me. Oh!" She held the tag in one hand and clamped the other over her mouth.

Ruth twisted, grasping for the tag. "What? What's wrong?"

Olivia whispered, "It's three dollars and fifty cents."

Ruth's smile melted and Emma's heart sank. The dress was so beautiful on Ruth, and the way her face had lit up when she'd seen herself in the mirror, Emma hated to disappoint her. She scoured her mind for a solution. "Let me go and talk with the sales woman. Maybe it's on sale."

"It would be marked if it was." Ruth ducked her head. "It's okay. I'll find a different dress."

"It couldn't hurt to ask. I'll be right back." Emma rushed through the store, eyes darting from corner to corner, until she found the woman who'd greeted them when they first arrived, working on some sort of paperwork beside a sales counter. "Excuse me, ma'am. I have a question about the green georgette dress over in that corner."

The older woman patted her silver, neatly rolled bun. "Yes? What about it?"

"The tag says it's three dollars and fifty cents."

The woman tilted her head at Emma.

"Well, um, I was wondering." Emma could hear the girls chattering on the other side of the store. "Might there be a mistake? Perhaps it's on sale and the price hasn't been corrected on the tag?"

"Young woman, I assure you the tag is correct." She waved her hand at nothing in particular. "I am responsible for pricing all the merchandise myself."

"Oh, I didn't mean to offend you." Emma reached for the woman's arm. "But...if you could...double-check?"

The saleslady backed away and pursed her lips. She lifted her slanted eyeglass, hanging from a chain around her neck, and perched them on the tip of her nose. She reached for a book and flipped through several pages. She ran her finger down a line of items and prices.

Her stern expression lifted to Emma again. "That is the correct price." She lifted a sharply arched brow, accentuated by the angle of her glasses. Her lips remained in a firm red-stained line. "As I said before, if it was on sale, it would be reflected on the tag."

"I understand, but"—Emma gathered her courage—"the young lady I brought simply adores it, and she looks stunning in it."

"I'm glad she likes it." The woman frowned and closed the book. "What exactly do you want from me?"

Emma had never tried to haggle over the price of a dress or anything else for that matter. But someone had to take up Ruth's cause. "I was hoping perhaps the dress will be going on sale soon? And perhaps you could give us the sale price today."

The woman patted the bun again. "Young lady, do you know how many people come in here and try to get me to drop my prices simply because they can't afford what they want? If we were to do that, we would be out of business. May I suggest you make your daughter a dress rather than buy one?"

"She's not my— Oh, never mind. Here's the situation." Emma took the woman's elbow and guided her away from the counter.

"Excuse me!"

"I'm sorry but this is very important." Emma led her to the corner behind a rack of men's suits. "You see, Ruth—that's the girl I brought in—her mother passed away, and now she's living with her uncle. He gave me three dollars to purchase a dress and silk stockings for her so she can go to a church social—her first date—with the boy of her dreams."

The woman eyed Emma for a long moment. Emma held her breath, unable to read the woman's harsh expression. The tense lines in the woman's face softened. "Come with me."

Emma anxiously followed her, glancing back at the girls. The sales woman opened a receipt book and flipped through a few pages. "It would appear that it has been quite some time since the georgette dresses have been on sale after all."

Emma leaned in. "Yes?"

"I suppose it's time to run another sale. Maybe it will bring in more customers."

Emma exhaled with relief. "That would be wonderful. Thank you. So, what would the sale price be?"

"You say you have three dollars?"

"Yes. I mean, no. I spent forty-five cents of it already. We had sodas at the five-and-dime." Emma dug the remaining money from her coin purse and held it out to the woman in her open palm. "I have two dollars and fifty-five cents."

The woman pinched the bridge of her nose. "And you want silk stockings, too? I am sorry, but I cannot reduce the dress more than seventy-five cents. It simply is not possible."

Doing the math in her head, Emma realized she didn't have enough for even the dress, let alone the stockings which were another seventy-five cents. She rested her elbows on the counter and rubbed her temples. She had a dollar and twenty five cents of her own in her pocketbook she'd planned to use for groceries. If she didn't buy some of the things on her list, she could help pay for the dress and stockings.

She would not allow Ruth to leave this store without that dress and proper stockings. As for shoes, she had a pair at home hidden in her closet, unused, that Ruth could borrow. They went with the dress from Jasper.

"We'll take them."

The sales woman raised her eyebrows at Emma. "But I thought you only have two fifty-five. I cannot reduce the price any more than I already have."

"It's fine. I can cover it. We'll take the dress and the silk stockings. Except, please don't say anything to the girls about the price."

The woman waggled her head and waved Emma away. "Fine, fine. Tell the girl to bring the dress to me, and I'll get the stockings."

Emma hurried back to Ruth and Olivia. Ruth had changed into her blue cotton blouse and plaid skirt. She and Olivia were looking at a small rack of dresses marked for sale.

Breathless, Emma grasped Ruth's elbow. "Get the dress, Ruth. It's on sale."

"But it doesn't say that on the tag."

"I know. But I talked to the saleswoman, and she realized it's time to put the dress on sale."

Olivia squealed, ran to the green dress, and swiped it off its hanger.

Ruth hugged Emma. "I don't know how you keep making this stuff happen, but thank you. Thank you so much." Ruth's eyes nearly gleamed.

Emma's heart swelled, being able to play even a small part in Ruth's happiness. She had made the right choice, sacrificing a few groceries for this important moment in Ruth's life. "You're welcome. Now let's go get that dress wrapped."

Luke busied himself outside while Olivia and Ruth primped for the social. He even did Ruth's chores for her, milking Verna, feeding the chickens, and gathering eggs from the hen house. The sun blazed high in the noon sky. A combine droned in the distance, spreading the sweet scent of dry hay in the air. Luke stared at the house. Should he go back in yet? He'd left as soon as the giggling had begun two hours ago. He couldn't remember a time when he'd felt so out of place.

Ruckus stared up at his master, his head cocked as if trying to understand this sudden lack of confidence.

Luke patted the dog's head. "No time like the present, I guess." He crossed the dirt driveway to the house and let himself in through the kitchen. Ruckus barked and pushed his food bowl to the center of the room. Luke opened the icebox and retrieved a bowl of leftover beans and rice and put it on the floor. Ruckus gobbled the food, tail wagging.

Luke rubbed his knuckle behind Ruckus's ear and then left the kitchen. He entered the living room at the same time as Olivia and Ruth.

He stopped short. Ruth wore a green dress and white high-heeled shoes. Her hair spilled out from beneath the brim of a green felt hat with a pink band wrapped around it. Luke struggled to find his voice. "You—you look like...your mother."

She dipped her chin and a rosy flush crept into her cheeks. "Oh, nonsense. Mama was beautiful."

"Yes, she was."

Her lips parted into a smile. Olivia stood quietly beside Ruth. Luke reprimanded himself for not noticing her. "You look real pretty, too, Olivia."

"Thank you." She twirled once. "Ruth gave me one of her older dresses."

"I hope that's okay?" Ruth's brows raised, questioning.

He could only recall seeing Olivia in one or two dresses since the day he met her, and they hadn't been anything as nice as the one Ruth gave her. Another characteristic Ruth inherited from Kate. His sister couldn't stand for anyone to feel left out. "It's fine. It really suits you, Olivia."

So what now? Should he give some kind of fatherly speech? What did fathers say to their daughters who were heading out on their first date? He knew what he wanted to say, but he couldn't find the words.

The sound of an engine outside grew louder as it approached the house. Ruth rushed to the window. She fussed with her hat. "It's Grady. His father let him drive his Packard. Olivia is riding with us."

The girls gathered their pocketbooks and primped one another's hair and dresses until a knock sounded at the door. The giddy preening ceased. Ruth and Olivia stared at Luke.

Luke glared at the door. He could still stop this.

"Ahem." Ruth pursed her lips, motioning toward the door. She didn't just *look* like her mother. She fidgeted with the snap closure on her purse, anticipation in her eyes. Olivia giggled.

Luke swallowed the sour taste in his mouth and approached the front door. He paused with his hand on the doorknob for a moment, then opened it.

Grady squared his shoulders and extended his hand. "Hello, Mist—uh—Luke."

Luke reluctantly shook the boy's hand. He stepped aside and motioned for Grady to come in. He watched as Grady caught sight of Ruth. The kid's face went blank in stunned silence.

Luke recognized that look. He remembered the way his own heart galloped and his stomach tumbled at the sight of the girl he loved dressed up and looking more beautiful than anything he'd ever seen, and all for him. That was the moment he knew for sure he was in love.

Luke coughed, nearly choking on the thought. That was Sadie and him. This was Grady. And his niece. And this was not love. Ruth was a beautiful girl, and Grady had two healthy, perfectly working eyes in his head. That's all.

Please, God, let that be all.

Had he just prayed? "You better get going, I guess." He resisted the urge to shove Grady out of the house and close and lock the door behind him.

The three teenagers filed out the door.

Luke caught Grady before he stepped off the porch. "What time is this thing over?"

"Baptisms should be done before dark. About eight o'clock, I'd guess."

"Then you'll have her home by eight-fifteen."

Grady opened his mouth, but at Luke's arched brow he clamped it shut and nodded.

Luke patted him on the shoulder, maybe a little harder than necessary, maybe not. "Good answer."

NINE

After the kids left for the social, Luke retreated back to the barn. He picked up a saddle and threw it over a hay bale.

Did he do the right thing, letting Ruth go with Grady? It wasn't like they would be alone. But at what age was it appropriate for a girl to start dating? Did Kate have a rule about this? Emma didn't seem to think it was a problem. That offered some solace. He trusted she wouldn't have endorsed the idea if it wasn't the right time for Ruth.

This thinking in circles made him crazy. He needed to stay busy. Keep his mind off this mess until it was over. But it never would be over now, would it? This was only the beginning. He'd opened the door. And he knew well enough that two teenagers would keep pushing that door wider and wider. Like his memory kept doing. That door he'd managed to keep closed and locked tight for the last seventeen years had been rattling since the day Ruth came to live here. The ghosts he kept contained behind that barricade were no longer cooperating with their imprisonment.

Luke snatched a clean cloth from the wooden box where he kept them. Taking his frustration out on the scratches and dirt in all the nooks and crannies of a saddle felt like a much better use of time than all this *thinking*.

He ran his thumb over the name stamped into the leather. "Raffle.

Dumbest name for a horse I ever heard." He lifted his arm to swipe away the sweat on his forehead and cast a look at the stately, black, quarter horse standing nearby in his stall. "No offense, ol' boy."

A stiff breeze blew through the open barn door, scattering hay around his boots and stirring up dust and the scent of horse manure. Luke straightened his back and allowed the air to rush over him. He may as well set an electric fan in front of a wood stove. In this hundred and two-degree heat, the breeze fought a losing battle. The weather didn't care that he had work to do though, and if he didn't get this saddle perfect he'd be in for a tedious, condescending lecture from Raffle's owner, Mr. Bracken.

Luke held the cloth in one hand and reached for a bottle of oil on the workbench with the other. In his haste, he bumped the bottle with his knuckle, sending it airborne. He spit out a string of curse words and bolted for the bottle even as he watched the contents ooze out onto the ground. He plucked up the bottle and inspected it. How much had he spilled. Too much to finish the saddle and do the next one.

He clenched his teeth against the irritation crawling up his spine. With a very expensive mud pie forming on his barn floor and the saddle only half finished, he would have to drive to the store to buy more. He threw the cloth on the workbench and stalked out of the barn to the house. He grabbed his keys off the kitchen counter and headed for his truck, the screen door slapping against its frame in his wake.

As he drove to town, Luke fended off thoughts of Ruth and Grady. He'd actually considered driving down to the social to satisfy the nagging worry that worked at his brain. But he'd rather walk into a snake pit than into a crowd of church people.

And then there was Emma Darby. Another one he couldn't get out of his mind. Emma had a way of getting him to agree to things he wouldn't ordinarily approve. Like letting Ruth go to that blasted social with Grady. How did a woman he barely knew hold so much sway over him? It had to be more than a pair of pretty blue eyes. Luke shook his head. This road his mind kept trying to take him down was a dangerous one. One he had no interest in traveling.

After arriving in town, Luke parked the truck in front of Lyman's Feed and Supply and went inside. The bell above the door jangled, announcing his entry.

Jim Lyman lowered a clipboard down to the counter. "Afternoon, Luke."

"Jim." Luke approached him, the wood plank floor creaking beneath his feet.

"What can I help you with?"

"I need some Neatsfoot oil."

Jim's brow pinched. "You run out already?"

"No." Luke suppressed his irritation at having to converse when all he wanted was to get his oil and get back to work. "Spilled it."

"Ouch. That's an expensive accident."

"Yeah. It is." Luke stared at the man.

The store owner's smile faded. "I'll, uh, get a new bottle for you."

Luke answered with a nod and watched Jim walk away. He flipped through a seed catalog at the counter while he waited for Jim to return. Maybe he'd add on to the garden for next year. The bell above the door jangled again.

"Hello, Luke!"

Luke's irritation faded at the sound of the familiar voice. J.D. Hudgins approached with a wide smile. Luke accepted the pastor's outstretched hand. "What are you doing here? Shouldn't you be at the social?"

"I'm on my way there. I just got back from visiting Buster Kelsay at the hospital in Santa Rosa."

There were few people Luke actually considered among his friends. J.D., , with his shock of white hair and dancing blue eyes, was one. Nella another. And Buster. Just the mention of Buster's name could lighten a person's mood. "I heard he got pretty banged up in that automobile accident. How's he doing?"

"As stubborn and ornery as ever." J.D. chuckled. "Making the nurses blush and the doctors wonder why they didn't become lawyers."

Luke smiled at the adept description of one of Petaluma's favorite citizens.

Jim returned with Luke's bottle of oil and set it on the counter next to the register. "Here ya go, Luke. That'll be eighty-five cents. Hi, Pastor. How are you doing?"

"Fine, Jim, fine." J.D.'s smile always spread into his eyes. "I came by to see if you might have some extra—or used—burlap sacks. Seems Barbara forgot to get them for the sack races."

"Sure I do. I'll get them for you right after I ring up Luke's oil here." Jim finished the transaction with Luke and trotted off again.

Luke picked up the bottle of Neatsfoot. "Good to see you, J.D."

"You, too. Say, I hear Ruth is over at the social. Rumor has it she's going with Grady Akins."

Luke rubbed his chin and stared out the store window to the street where his truck waited. Once again he revisited the choice to allow Ruth to attend the social. Seemed that's all he did these days. Relive decisions over and over, never knowing if he'd made the right ones.

"Something bothering you, son?"

Luke shifted his focus back to J.D. "I don't know." He rubbed at his neck. "Just wondering if I should've let her go with him."

J.D. hooked his thumbs on his suspenders. "I see. Well, if it helps, I've gotten to know the Akins family since they moved here. Grady seems to be a fine young man."

It didn't help much, but Luke appreciated his friend's attempt at setting his mind at ease.

J.D. patted Luke's shoulder. "You know, I was thinking about you the other day. About you and your niece."

Luke recognized the familiar glint in the man's eye. J.D. Hudgins was the only preacher Luke had allowed to get close to him since he came to Petaluma. And he was the only preacher who could ever get away with saying some of the things he'd said to Luke over the years.

"I was reading in my Bible. In the book of Ruth."

Luke adjusted his hat. "Kate's favorite story. She always said if she had a daughter she'd name her Ruth."

"Really?" J.D.'s wide smile could disarm the most hardened of men. "Well, isn't that interesting."

Luke squinted at the spark of understanding in the man's eyes. He knew something Luke didn't know. It made Luke curious but cautious. He may not be on speaking terms with God, but he knew J.D. Hudgins was. Sometimes it made Luke squirm, knowing J.D. could talk to God about him behind his back and that God answered him. Luke didn't care one bit if people gossiped about him...unless the Almighty was on one end of the conversation.

J.D. leaned against the counter and crossed his arms over his broad chest. "When was the last time you read the story?"

"Not sure I ever did read it myself. Kate read it to me. She gushed all the way through it. Said it was the most romantic love story in the Bible next to Samuel and Rachel."

J.D. smiled his knowing smile again. His voice held an air of mystery. "Oh, it's a love story all right."

Luke slipped his thumbs in his belt loops. This must be how a mouse felt when being toyed with by a cat. "Okay. I'll bite. What do you mean?"

"Oh, only that it's like a lot of things in life. There's plenty more going on than what folks see on the surface."

Jim returned and plopped a stack of burlap on the counter. "Here ya go, Pastor. Will six be enough?"

"That'll be perfect, Jim. How much does the church owe you?"

"Nothing at all. I'm happy to contribute."

"Thank you. You are very generous. Why don't you come out and join us at the creek when you close up? We'll be having baptisms and some hymn singing."

"I might do that."

"All right then." J.D. gave Luke a wink. "You really oughta dust off your Bible and give that 'love story' a closer look."

Luke studied Pastor Hudgins for a moment. It wasn't like the man to push Luke to pray or read his Bible or even attend church. The fact he was doing it now sparked Luke's curiosity. "I'll think about that. See ya later, J.D."

Luke carried the bottle of oil to his truck and set it in the passenger seat. As he twisted the key to start the truck, J.D. exited the feed store and started down the sidewalk, carrying the burlap sacks and mopping his forehead with a handkerchief. Luke scanned the area for the pastor's Buick but didn't see it. He slowly drove forward until he met up with J.D.

He spoke to the pastor through the open passenger window. "You aren't walking all the way to the social in this heat, are you?"

J.D. stepped up to Luke's truck. "Oh, it's not too far. We're up on the south shore."

"Where's your old Buick? How'd you get all the way to Santa Rosa and back?"

"I caught a ride with Jack Marsdale."

Luke adjusted his hat and stared down the road. The last thing he wanted was to go anywhere near that social. But it was too hot out for seventy-one-year-old J.D. to walk that far. "Hop in."

"Are you sure? I wouldn't be taking you away from important work, would I?"

Luke shook his head. "Nothing I'm excited about getting back to anyway."

J.D. opened the door, moved the bottle of oil, and climbed in with a grunt. He flopped the stack of burlap sacks across his lap and closed the door, chuckling. "To tell you the truth, I was dreading that walk. This heat wave is worse than any we've had in some time, isn't it?"

"Sure is." Luke pulled the truck away from the curb and drove in the direction of the creek. As he stopped for the D street drawbridge and pulled aside for a steamer to pass by, he considered the opportunity this afforded him to check on Ruth.

"I understand you helped Emma Darby at her place."

Luke couldn't avoid the man's amused grin. "You know, for a preacher, you're sure caught up on all the gossip in town."

J.D. chuckled and smoothed his hand over his short white hair. "I can't help but hear when folks talk within earshot, now can I? She's a good woman, that Emma."

Luke returned his attention to the bridge ahead of him.

"A real good woman."

A smile tugged at the corner of Luke's lips. *Nope. Not today, J.D. I ain't biting.*

The steamer finally passed, and the bridge moved back into place. Luke drove on. They arrived at the spot on the creek J.D. identified. He gathered the sacks and got out of the truck. A small crowd of people milled about several yards away. Their easy banter and laughter carried to Luke's ears.

He watched a young boy chase a little girl in circles until she hid behind her mother. Sunlight bounced off rippling water in the background, and folks splashed at the water's edge. A long buried part of him wanted to join them. To be a part of something bigger than himself again. For all the rotten memories he had of church, there were good ones, too. How different would his life be right now, if he hadn't ruined everything all those years ago?

"Luke, hello!"

Barbara, J.D.'s wife, trotted toward his truck, waving her hand and wearing her easy smile that always made him feel like he'd come home from a long journey. She'd pulled her normally perfectly coifed blonde hair into a short, casual pony-tail. Her trousers were rolled up, revealing bare ankles and feet. A rare sight for a modest pastor's wife. But Barbara Hudgins never did put on airs. Luke always thought she and his mother would have been the best of friends.

"Hello, Barbara."

"I'm so glad you're here." Barbara wagged a finger at him. "You are exactly the person I need."

J.D. shifted the burlap sacks in his arms. "Luke isn't here for the social, Sweetheart. He just gave me a ride from the feed store."

"Oh?" Barbara raised a brow at her husband, then tossed a smile to Luke. "Thank you Luke. Goodness knows J.D. shouldn't have even attempted to walk all that way in such heat." She jabbed her finger at J.D.'s chest. "You are not a young man anymore."

J.D. kissed her cheek. Barbara playfully pushed him away and walked to Luke's window. The two of them reminded Luke so much of his own folks. He rubbed his hand against a familiar twinge in his chest.

"I know you aren't here for the social, Luke." Barbara's expression pleaded. "But we could sure use your help if you don't mind. It would only take a few minutes."

Apprehension crawled into Luke's chest and tied itself into a knot. He didn't want to have to talk to any of these people. Not that they were all bad folks. But that didn't mean he wanted to socialize with them here. In no time at all he'd be inundated with questions. *"Oh, are you coming back to church?" "Will we see you on Sunday?" "You know, you can stay and get baptized."*

Barbara pointed. "Emma is down the beach a bit farther, setting up chairs for the baptism service. It's an awful big job for one person."

Emma, huh? Maybe he could help out. For a few minutes.

J.D. dropped the burlap sacks on the ground at his feet. "Now, sweetheart, Luke has things he needs to do. Besides, there are plenty of blankets around. We don't need chairs. How about you go and get one of the young people to come get these burlap sacks for me?"

Luke opened the door of his truck and hopped out. "I can help."

J.D. white eyebrows shot upward.

Barbara smiled like the cat that swallowed the canary.

Luke ignored them both and pointed west. "You said she's down that way?"

"Yes. She'll be so pleased so see you." Barbara winked at him. "To help with the chairs, I mean."

TEN

Emma carried another wooden folding chair closer to the water's edge and placed it next to the first three. She took a moment to watch the gentle current flicker in the sunlight.

The letter she'd slipped in her trousers pocket felt like a lead weight. Jasper Loomis's handwritten words still rang in her mind with threats and accusations. Why had she even stopped at the post office on her way here?

As she made her way back to the pile of chairs, she noticed a man approaching. She squinted and held her hand up to shield her eyes from the sun. She hoped it wasn't Kevin Branson. She didn't know how many more times she could politely sidestep his invitations. But Kevin didn't wear a black cowboy hat. Her stomach flip-flopped.

Emma pressed her hand to the pocket concealing Jasper's letter. "Well, this is a surprise."

Luke adjusted his hat. "I'm not here for the social. Barbara asked me to help you with these chairs." He frowned at the chairs piled unceremoniously on the ground.

Emma sighed and patted her forehead. "That would be the work of Ben Carver. He brought them from the church in his truck."

Luke smirked. "I'm guessing his chubby fingers are now wrapped around a juicy piece of fried chicken."

Laughing, Emma picked up a chair. "Apparently you know him."

"Enough to never count on him for physical labor or get stuck behind him in a potluck line." Luke grabbed two chairs and followed her back down to the creek bank.

Emma unfolded her chair and planted it solidly on the ground. "Do you know Pastor Hudgins and his wife?"

"Yeah. They're good people."

"Yes, they are."

How much did the Hudgins know about Luke? Did they have the answers to all the questions that plagued her about him? She followed Luke's lead, back and forth from the chair pile to the organized rows, until the job was complete. Emma dusted her hands. The sparkling water flowing downstream reflected a clear blue sky, while birds flitted from one tree to the next. She closed her eyes and breathed in the fresh, clean air. "It's going to be a beautiful service."

"I suppose so."

He didn't seem in a hurry to leave. Maybe he'd stay if invited. "Would you like to sit for a few minutes?"

Luke's eyes narrowed as he peered toward the sound of laughing adults and squealing children. Emma hoped no one would come this way and intrude on this time with him. He rubbed his neck. "Sure."

They sat in the front row of chairs, one chair between them. He didn't speak. Apparently, she would have to initiate any sort of dialog between them. "Sonoma County is a really beautiful place. All the hills, and valleys, creeks, and lakes."

Luke leaned forward and rested his elbows on his knees. "Yeah. It is."

Emma tapped a finger against her leg. "I can't wait to see the ocean."

"You haven't been to the ocean yet?"

"Not yet, no. I plan to though."

He seemed to study something in the distance. "I could take you sometime."

His offer rendered her briefly mute. The rugged strength of his firm defined jawline, long straight nose, and strong brow in profile struck again. Tearing her attention away lest he catch her staring, she found her voice. "I'd like that."

She sensed his eyes on her and risked a glimpse. Pinned to her seat by his penetrating gaze, Emma did her best to hold her own. The quirk of his lips both thrilled and infuriated her. Why did he find such pleasure in her discomfort?

He bobbed his head once. "All right then."

Emma fingered the hem of her blouse. It seemed the water was the only safe place to look.

Luke scuffed a rock aside with his boot. "Can I ask you a question?"

She shifted in her seat and swallowed "Of course."

"How did a woman like you get tangled up with a guy like Jasper Loomis?"

Jasper. The mention of the man's name sent a tremor down her spine. She'd known it was only a matter of time before he intruded between Luke and her. The letter in her pocket dared her to tell him the truth. "I've wondered what he might have said to you when you called about making the repairs."

"Enough to let me know he never deserved you."

Emma crossed her ankles. Suddenly the gentle current of the creek roared in her ears.

"He still thinks you're going to come running back to him, you know."

Clearly Luke had known more about her all this time than she knew about him. She couldn't bring herself to make eye contact. "I know he does."

"That's why he sent you to that place."

"Yes."

"But he doesn't charge you."

The air left her lungs, yielding only a whispered, "No."

He shoved a large rock with his boot. "Why do you stay there?"

Unable to sit any longer, Emma stood and moved closer to the water's edge. Birds chirped around her. Children laughed in the distance. Water lapped against the shore of the creek. In spite of warm breezes stirring the white feathery pampas grass on the bank, a chill swept through her veins. Did she want to lay her secrets bare to Luke Morgan? She squeezed her eyes shut at the sound of his boots crunching on the ground, approaching.

He stood beside her, thumbs pushed into the edges of his pockets. He didn't press her. Truth was, she felt safe with him by her side. There was an aura about his stance, his silent patience, which made her want to unburden her heart.

She drew in a breath. "Jasper's family is very wealthy, very powerful in Pine Bluff, Arizona. Among other things, they control the school board. He invited me to dinner repeatedly, but I always turned him down. Until he threatened my job."

"He blackmailed you into seeing him?"

Emma's breath hitched. *What will he think of me?* She couldn't tell him everything. Only enough to satisfy his curiosity. Emma hugged herself. "My mother was sick. My father lost his job when the market crashed. I moved back into their home to provide for them. My income was all we had, and it wasn't nearly enough to support all three of us."

Her throat thickened. She fought to control the tremble in her chin. "My father was humiliated to watch his daughter struggling to support him. Every single day he tried to find work, but there wasn't any. I couldn't go to the school board for a raise because, as I said, Jasper's family controlled it. They controlled everything. Everyone was afraid of them. I—I had no choice."

Luke moved closer to the water, standing with his back to her.

Her shoulders sagged. "He was always a gentleman ..." The words sounded weak in her own ears.

"But you had no feelings for him. He had to have known that."

Staring at his back, a sense of rejection made her feel hollow inside. She hugged herself tighter. "It didn't matter." Helpless to stop the flow of information spilling from deep within, she continued. "When my mother was hospitalized and I couldn't afford to pay the bill, he proposed."

Luke seemed to move in slow motion until he faced her again.

Emma shrank back at the disgust in his eyes.

He muttered something she was pretty certain she should be

thankful not to have heard. He stepped closer to her, towering above her. His hat blocked out the sun. "You said no, right?"

She swallowed against the pain in the back of her throat. "I knew it would only be a worse prison." That much wasn't a lie.

"How did you break loose from him?"

Emma tugged at the collar of her blouse. "My mother got better." She closed her eyes and forced out the words. "I didn't need him anymore to pay the medical bills."

How had this escalated so quickly? She had to get away before he asked any more questions—and before she volunteered anything she would regret. She took a step away from him, but her foot found a gopher hole. She stumbled, bracing herself for a humiliating fall. Luke caught her. Being so close to him, his arms around her waist, stirred a dangerous yearning in her.

She ducked her head and attempted to free herself. "I'm fine. Thank you. I need to get back. I'm sure Barbara could use help."

Luke gripped her shoulders. "He gave you no choice, Emma. He used his power to manipulate you."

"But I didn't have to allow it. I could have—"

"Could have what?" Luke bent so she had nowhere else to look. "Let your parents go hungry? Let your mother die? You did what you had to do, Emma. He took your choices away from you."

Her vision blurred as hot tears filled her eyes. "But I used him for his money. I led on a man I didn't love."

"He didn't love you, either."

Emma blinked, freeing tears which spilled down her cheeks. "But he said— He kept saying—"

Luke's strong hands gave her a gentle shake. "He didn't love you, Emma." His lips formed a thin line before he continued. Anger brewed in his eyes. "He didn't want to love you. He wanted to own you."

For the first time she saw, and recognized, the truth. Why had she never seen it? How could she have believed everything Jasper did was out of some uncontrollable love? She had convinced herself he wasn't as bad as he was. That he was motivated by love, albeit a selfish and controlling love.

She'd only seen the depths of deception within herself. Her shoulders slumped. If Luke only knew... "I'm so ashamed."

"Don't be. The only person who should be ashamed is him. No real man treats a woman that way." Luke brushed a wayward curl off her cheek. His touch chased away the hollowness inside and awakened feelings that frightened her. "What about your parents? Where are they now?"

"When they found out I wasn't in love with Jasper, they told me to get as far away from the man as I could. They made plans to move to Colorado and live with my aunt." Again, that much was true.

"Wait a minute." Luke scratched his temple. "If you rejected his proposal, how did you end up living in that shack?"

Emma's mouth went dry. "He—he insisted I only needed time to think about things. That I would be back when I realized how difficult life is without money. I mean, that's what he said to you, right?"

Luke lifted a shoulder. "In so many words."

"I wanted to get away so badly, I accepted." She stared past Luke. "I didn't know what else to do. I know it's wrong..."

What must he think of her? She risked looking at him again. The fusion of emotions his dark eyes could project left her breathless. Anger, disgust, understanding, and compassion all mingled together and spoke with one glance things the man himself couldn't, or wouldn't, communicate in words.

Luke touched her cheek, tracing her jawline with his thumb. Words clogged in her throat. How easy it would be to simply lose herself in those eyes, in his arms.

The echo of voices in the distance grew closer, breaking the moment of intimacy.

Luke stared over the top of her head in the direction of the picnic. "I better go."

Emma wanted to grab his hand and beg him to stay. To stay with *her*.

"Thank you for your help—and not judging me." *Though you have every right to.*

He lowered his gaze to hers once more. "I know too much about how it feels to be judged to do it to someone else." He adjusted his hat, another nervous tic she'd picked up on. "I'll see you soon."

Her pulse quickened at what, from anyone else, would simply be a common salutation. Emma watched him as he disappeared over a small hill. She laid her hand over the letter in her pocket. She should have told him.

ELEVEN

Emma dropped chunks of ice into the pitcher of lemonade while Luke repaired a broken shutter outside. She snuck a peek at him through the kitchen window. What motivated Luke Morgan? For a man who clearly enjoyed his solitude, he had taken an interest in helping her, even in spite of everything she'd told him. Could it be... No. She couldn't afford to think that way. She had no right.

She reached for the sugar and worried her lower lip. Why was Jasper allowing Luke to do so many repairs? What if she told Luke the truth? But she couldn't. She didn't want to lose him. Her hand hovered over the sugar. *She didn't want to lose him*? He wasn't hers to lose.

Emma stirred the sugar into the lemonade. She stared into the pitcher as a tiny whirlpool formed in the center of the swirling liquid. How in heaven's name would she untangle herself from this complicated dance she'd begun? She didn't know. She only knew what she'd felt standing on the creek bank with Luke.

After giving a final stir, Emma held the spoon to her lips and tasted. Luke preferred his lemonade tart. Perfect. She picked up a glass and the pitcher and started to pour.

"I need to go back to the hardware store."

Emma yelped at his voice and dropped the glass, spilling

its contents on the floor. The lemonade in the pitcher sloshed, threatening to spill. She set the container firmly on the counter. The man was going to cost her a fortune in broken glass!

He tipped his hat back and grinned. "Maybe lemonade isn't your gift."

"Maybe knocking isn't your gift." She snatched a dishcloth from the sink and started to clean up. "Why do you have to go back to the hardware store?"

"Ran out of nails. You want some help?"

Surprised by the offer, she tossed the cloth at him. "Sure."

He caught it before it hit him in the face. His stunned expression prompted a bubble of laughter to erupt from her chest. "You think I'm not capable of cleaning?"

She cocked her hip. "I don't know. I've never seen you do any."

He took three steps forward and stopped inches from her at the sink. Her breath caught in her lungs at the glint in his dark eyes. He smelled of sawdust and sweat. He leaned in closer.

Good night, was he going to kiss her?

"You'll need to step aside." His voice was low and smooth, his breath sending a trail of gooseflesh down her arms.

Emma's mind stuttered, searching for a response. She stepped aside as he mopped up the spilled lemonade and put the broken glass shards in the waste basket. He rinsed out the wash cloth, then folded it and laid it across the faucet. He got another glass, filled it to the rim without spilling a drop, and held it out to her.

She took the glass, ignoring his teasing wink, and plopped into a seat at the table. He certainly did find pleasure in toying with her. What disturbed her was how much she enjoyed it.

Luke sat at the table across from her, with a glass of his own.

Eager to drown out the sound of her heart beating in her ears, Emma pushed her lemonade aside. "Can I ask you a private question?"

He studied her with a suspicious eye. "Depends."

"I've been wondering about this for a while now."

He took a long swig of the lemonade. "Wondering about what?"

"What is the project you're working on, out in the barn? The one I saw at your house." She could almost see the war going on in his mind, whether to answer or not. Whether to let her into his private world. Those intense eyes drew her in and held her at bay at the same time. In the quiet that followed, she traced the condensation on her glass with her finger. "I'm sorry. I don't mean to pry."

He shifted in his seat. "It's a— I don't really know what to call it yet. A cage? To help kids. Crippled kids. Blind kids."

Emma frowned, picturing the odd metal contraption surrounding a saddle. Understanding dawned, igniting wonder. "So they can ride a horse?"

"Yeah." He dipped his head, looking for all the world like a little boy who feared being laughed at.

She cupped her palms around her glass. "So it's a type of cage to help them stay in the saddle?"

"Yeah. So they don't have to balance on their own. Or worry about falling off."

Emma imagined crippled children, ordinarily bound to a wheelchair, riding atop a horse and enjoying the kind of freedom of movement they could never experience otherwise. And blind children, feeling the large animal move beneath them, the wind in their hair, carefree and unafraid of bumping into anything they couldn't see.

"I don't know if it would even work. It's an idea I came up a while back."

She reached out and covered his hand with hers. "It's a wonderful idea, Luke. It's—it's brilliant."

His fingers twitched beneath hers. She blinked at the realization of what she'd done and started to withdraw, but Luke turned his hand over and captured her. His dark eyes pulled her in and, like the tide drawn by the moon, she was helpless to fight the magnetic pull.

"Wha—" Her voice cracked. She cleared her throat. "What gave you such an idea?"

The vulnerability in his eyes shifted to a "No Trespassing" sign. He let go of her hand. "I don't know." He abruptly stood, sending the chair skidding across the wood floor. "I better get to the hardware store before Finn closes it up." The screen door slammed behind him.

Left sitting alone, her hand still warm from his touch, Emma wondered once again at the man's ability to tangle up her thoughts and emotions like an unkempt ball of yarn.

TWELVE

Luke slapped dust off his pant legs and swiped sweat from his brow with his sleeve as he made his way from the corrals back to the house. Keeping the horses safe in this heat was quite a challenge. Like him, they couldn't seem to get enough water, and their energy lagged. He wasn't one to shy away from hard work and, in fact, got to feeling restless when he was still for too long. Today, though, he would gladly sit in the shade with a cool drink and let someone else worry about the ranch.

Percy Slocum's black Cadillac pulled into the driveway. Percy exited the vehicle and waved at Luke. "How are you, Morgan?"

"Real good." Luke opened Mrs. Slocum's door for her.

She offered an elegant, poised smile. "Thank you, Luke. Children, come say hello to Mr. Morgan."

The couple's children, Matthew and Margaret, climbed out of the car and obediently greeted Luke. They all wore riding clothes and boots.

Percy pumped Luke's hand. "How are the horses doing?"

"They're in good shape. Follow me." Luke led the family to the corral holding their four horses. "I saddled them for you, and they've been fed and watered. They're ready to go." He opened the corral gate and let them inside.

Percy surveyed the horses. "They look in excellent shape." He patted his horse's neck. "By the way, Logan Prentiss asked me to let you know he and his wife will be here to ride next week."

"I'll be ready for them. Thanks."

"Good, good. How's the boarding business these days?"

"Holding its own, thanks to you spreading the word."

Percy shrugged. "It was nothing. I simply recommended you. You're the one who did the impressing. And believe me, I know how finicky some of those people I sent your way can be."

"Business is business. You won't hear me complain."

Percy chuckled. "That's the attitude to have these days. By the way, I received your letter about the business opportunity before we left. Are you free after dinner this evening?"

"Yes, I am. That would be fine." Luke helped twelve-year-old Margaret onto her horse. Once she was settled, he smiled up at her and winked. He wasn't oblivious to her crush on him. It was cute how she blushed whenever he showed her attention.

He double-checked the bit on Percy's horse. "You and your family have a good ride."

Percy guided his horse to exit the corral. "I'm sure we will. We'll be back in a couple of hours."

Luke contemplated the four horses again. "Be sure to stay near the creek. They may need more water in this heat."

"Good idea."

The family rode out of the corral, and Luke closed the gate. The busy season of boarding horses had begun. Every week for the rest of summer, owners would come and go. But this particular owner was especially important. If he could get Percy in on the idea of helping crippled children ride, he could expand the business to what he really wanted.

Hours later the setting sun splashed a watercolor scene of pink, orange, and lavender across the sky and clouds. Cool evening breezes off the coast brought relief from the suffocating heat of the day. Ruckus found a burst of energy and chased a brown lizard into a rosemary bush. The dog shoved his snout into the shrub, intent on sniffing out the reptile. Luke enjoyed being out here on the porch listening to the sounds of birds, wind stirring the tree branches, the neighing of horses, and the gentle tinkling of the copper wind chime Ruth had brought with her from Montana. A breeze carried the charred scents of a cookout.

What would Percy think of his idea? The man was a serious businessman, and Luke certainly didn't want to waste his time. He considered praying for a good outcome, but guilt quickly quashed the impulse. Who was he to ask God for anything? He'd stopped praying a long time ago. Asking God for help now would make him every bit a hypocrite as the people who had turned on him.

At last, Percy's Cadillac came into view. The man got out of his car and approached Luke with a smile.

"As congested as San Francisco gets," Mr. Slocum said, climbing the steps of the porch, "I forget what it's like to head up here to the country and enjoy the fresh air. This is a beautiful place."

Luke nodded his agreement. "I know what you mean. I lived in San Francisco for a while."

"Oh, that's right. You worked on the Golden Gate Bridge." Percy slipped his hands in his pockets. "I see you out here in the country, with all these horses, and forget you were a city boy for a bit."

"For a bit. I came from the country, though, and always planned to return."

"I don't blame you." Percy rocked back on his heels. "I'd be happy to buy you a drink in town while we discuss this business venture of yours."

"I appreciate that. But I think it will make more sense to you if I can show you what it is I'm working on."

"All right then. Lead the way."

Luke led Percy toward the barn near the back of his property.

"Yes, it's quite peaceful out here." Percy drew in a deep breath. "We're thinking of building a vacation home here. When the Depression is over, of course."

"Sometimes it feels like the Depression will never be over."

Percy patted Luke's shoulder. "Oh, it will be. It will. Seems you've done well enough for yourself though, eh?"

"I'm better off than some. But not by much. I was lucky. Just stubborn enough to not put my savings in a bank or the market."

Percy inclined his head. "A fortuitous move. Although my father taught me nothing invested is nothing gained."

Luke responded with a wry smile. "I think the past few years would prove that nothing invested is nothing lost."

Percy pointed a finger at Luke. "True enough."

Luke stopped at the barn door. "Here we are."

Percy studied the barn, as if appraising its value. Luke pulled open the creaking doors. His stomach clenched a bit. Percy was tall, well-groomed and well-dressed, with graying temples—the epitome of wealth and distinction. Luke was a simple country boy with a big idea and a crude prototype. He squelched a nervous cough. Ruckus barked at Percy, demanding his attention. Luke hadn't even noticed the dog had followed them.

Percy reached down to pet him. "I'd like to have myself a dog." He scratched behind Ruckus's ears. "But the missus, well, she likes cats."

"Ruckus likes cats, too. For lunch."

Ruckus answered with a low growl. Percy chortled and gave the dog's side a hearty pat. "I share your sentiments, old boy, trust me."

Luke brought the two hanging light bulbs to life, and Percy looked around the barn until he came upon the contraption of hay bales, metal, and the saddle. His brow quirked.

"It doesn't look like much right now, mind you. But that's only because I don't have the materials I need to build it properly."

"And, what is it, exactly?" Percy circled the project.

Here was Luke's moment. His chance to make this a reality. "It's a way to allow crippled and blind children to ride a horse."

Percy's eyes darted back to Luke. "Crippled and blind children? On a horse?" He studied the hay bales again. His furrowed brow began to relax. He pointed to the saddle and opened his mouth as if to speak but said nothing. He bent down and inspected the various joints and connections. He blew out a low whistle. "Well, I'll be." He stroked his chin. "How do you propose to lift the children up onto the saddle?"

Luke spoke with his hands in motion. "The kids would be brought up on a ramp to a platform that's a bit taller than the horse. We'd lower the kids onto the saddle and be sure they're safely strapped in."

Two hours later, Luke emerged from the barn with Percy Slocum. The night sky had swallowed the dusk. Luke flicked on the flashlight he'd grabbed from inside the barn.

"I think you've got quite an idea here, Luke. I've never seen or heard of anything like it before. But even if you were to build this with the proper materials, what would the use be? Patent it? Sell it in catalogs?"

"Actually, I had in mind inviting the kids to come here. To my ranch. A kind of vacation. A chance to spend time with other kids like them."

Percy stopped. "My niece had polio when she was six years old. It left her crippled."

Luke pushed away painful memories of his own. "I'm sorry to hear that."

"Do you know a crippled child? Is that what inspired this?"

Luke took a step back. "Not exactly."

"Hmm." Percy crossed his arms over his chest and raised a thumb and forefinger to his chin. "How much money do you suppose you'd need for the right materials? To build the cage and deck and such?"

Luke drew in a deep breath. This was the moment. "I figure about five hundred dollars, sir."

Percy's eyebrows raised. He released another low whistle. An unseen choir of crickets filled the night. "And your horses? You think you can train them for this?"

"I'm positive I can."

"How long do you think it will take?"

"I figure I should have the working product by spring. Once I have that, I can start training horses."

Percy rocked back on his heels. "Luke, I think if anyone can build this thing, train the horses, and make this a reality for children like my niece, it's you." He held out his hand. "I'll give you a first installment of two hundred. When I see it taking shape and agree it's going to work, I'll give you the rest. And success or failure, I'll expect my investment returned."

Shaking Percy's hand, Luke felt the muscles in his shoulders and neck relax. "Of course."

"I'll draw up a contract by next Wednesday and, providing you agree with the terms, I'll have the money wired as soon as I receive your signature."

After seeing Percy off, Luke returned to the barn and rested on a bale of hay, staring at the "cage." All the years of wondering why it had happened and what he could do to make it right had come to this. He spoke into the empty barn. "I did it, Sadie."

His throat constricted. He couldn't remember the last time he'd said her name out loud. Movement in the corner of his eye caught his attention. What was it? And why hadn't Ruckus barked?

"I'm sorry, I don't mean to intrude." Emma's voice carried to him.

"How long have you been here?"

She stepped carefully into the barn. "I came about an hour ago. I haven't seen Ruth in over a week. I heard she hasn't been feeling well so I wanted to check on her. She went to bed a few minutes ago."

"Yeah, she's been sleeping a lot lately."

"Is everything okay?"

Luke shrugged. "Her stomach bothers her off and on. Dr. Brighton thinks it's the heat. He said to be sure she doesn't spend too much time outside, make sure she rests when she needs to, and drinks plenty of water."

"Makes sense. Some people have a difficult time with this kind of weather. May I sit?"

"Sure." He leaned forward, resting his elbows on his knees.

The bales of hay and the metal cage held court in the middle of the room, as if it were its own person with a story to tell.

She pointed to it. "Not working on it tonight?"

"No." His left leg bounced up and down seemingly of its own accord. Should he tell her? She knew all about the idea anyway. "I talked to one of my boarders tonight about investing in it. He thinks my idea is good. He's going to give me two hundred dollars to start building with the right materials."

"Luke, that's wonderful!" She rested her hand on his forearm. "I'm so happy for you."

He stared at her hand, in awe at how such a simple touch could make him feel like he was...home. He'd never seen such clear blue eyes. So open and trusting. She made him want to share things he'd kept inside for fear of crumbling into nothingness if he said them out loud.

She lowered her hand. "Who is Sadie?"

His heartbeat thrashed in his ears.

"Did you do this for her? Is she a child you know?"

Luke closed his eyes, fending off the quiet compassion in her voice and the instinct to run. But she'd trusted him with her secrets about Jasper Loomis. She thanked him for not judging her. Maybe she wouldn't judge him either.

He interlocked his fingers to stop their trembling. "No. She's not a child." He'd kept it all locked inside for so long, he didn't know how to let it out.

"Luke?"

Tell her.

The thought, or voice, or whatever it was, incapacitated him. He couldn't move or speak. He pinched the bridge of his nose and allowed Sadie's memory to glide to the front of his mind, like an angel appearing to a lost soul. He clenched and unclenched his fists. "Sadie was my girlfriend when I was sixteen."

She sat quietly, which allowed him to tell the story at his pace.

"She was beautiful. Long, blonde, wavy hair. Hazel eyes that could see right through all my bluster. She was sweet and giving and—" The words caught in his throat. He blew out a breath, like an acrobat about to step out onto a tight rope. "We were in love. I knew I wanted to marry her the day I met her, and she felt the same. Our families went to church together, and they approved."

"Oh?"

He caught the surprise in her voice. "Yes, I used to go to church.

Every week. Believe it or not, I was good Christian boy. Made God the master of my life. Made my parents proud. Gave Sadie's parents every reason to consent to our relationship."

"What happened?"

His leg began its bouncing again. "She got pregnant."

Thirteen

Luke paused at Emma's gasp. He stared out the barn door into the night. "I'll never forget the look on her face when she told me. She was so ashamed. So scared." He worked his jaw muscles. "I did that to her. I made her feel that way. I made her feel dirty and ashamed and afraid."

Emma rested her hand on his arm. "What did you do?"

He rolled his head on his shoulders. "I asked her to marry me. It was the first time she smiled since she'd told me about the baby. She begged me to take her away. Live somewhere else so no one would know. She wanted to get married and have our baby and come back later if we chose to. I told her if that's what she wanted, that's what we would do. I would take care of her. I would protect her."

"And did you? Get married?"

Luke winced, staring at the dirt floor. "Her father was furious. He had a right to be. But instead of letting me take responsibility, instead of allowing me to take her away to avoid the shame, he forbade me from ever seeing her again. He said I needed to go to church and see the pastor. Get myself *right with God* again. As if I hadn't been begging God for forgiveness every minute of every day already."

Unable to sit any longer, Luke stood and paced. Nervous energy coursed through him. Ruckus rose from his blanket and paced with him, as if understanding his master's pain. "I went to the pastor. The man I had trusted for sixteen years to guide me in my relationship with God. The man who'd told me about God's love and mercy and *grace*. But this time he told me what a wretched sinner I was. As if I needed him to tell me that." Anger ballooned like swollen storm clouds and pressed against his ribs.

"He told me I needed to go to the altar and repent. I was so desperate to make things right, so desperate to be forgiven, I did what he said. I went to that altar and I repented. I cried like a baby." His voice grew in volume. "And the next week, he told me to do it again. And the next week he told me to do it again. Every sermon he preached for a full month was about sin and repentance."

Luke jabbed himself in the chest with his thumb. "And his eyes bored right into me every time he preached that over and over and over. He preached how God would destroy evil and that sinners would burn in the pit of hell. I realized it didn't matter how much I repented. It didn't matter how sorry I was or how badly I wanted to make things right. My new job was to be at that altar every waking moment, *repenting*. I asked him one Sunday, with all this repenting, when does the forgiveness come? You know what he told me?"

Emma's eyes shimmered with tears.

"He told me if I didn't *feel* forgiven, then I probably hadn't really repented. That there must still be sin in me. There must still be pride in me." He spread his arms. "How much *pride* could a terrified seventeen-year-old kid with a baby on the way have? I spent so much time at that altar, on that wood floor, my knees were bruised. And it was never enough. I was never, ever going to be good enough. I made a mistake, and God was angry, and that would never change no matter what I did."

He dropped his arms, recalling when the moment of understanding had dawned on him all those years ago. "And that's when I realized it was pointless. God wasn't going to help me. That preacher wasn't going to help me. I had to take matters into my own hands. I sent Sadie a note through a friend. Told her I would meet her at midnight. We'd leave and go where no one could find us. Get married and have our baby and live our lives."

The consequences of that decision hit him in the gut as if it were happening all over again. A roar filled the barn. He kicked a nearby bucket and sent it tumbling through the air until it crashed into the far wall.

Emma's hand flew to her chest.

Luke realized the roar he heard came from him. He collapsed next to her on a hay bale again. Pain and anger and frustration ripped at his chest in a physical ache. "I packed some things, took all the money I had, and at midnight, I rode my horse over to her daddy's farm. I didn't know if she would defy him to go with me.

"I waited and waited, and then I saw her sneaking out her bedroom window." He laughed the laugh of a lunatic. "I was excited. Excited that she chose me over her father. I was getting what I wanted. I was going to take care of her better than anyone else possibly could. Better than her father. Better than our preacher. Better than *God Himself*." He leaned forward, holding his head in his hands. Emma's hand caressed his back. He wanted to slap her hand away and at the same time he wanted to pull her to him and hang on for dear life.

She whispered, "What happened?"

He squeezed his eyes shut. The memories reappeared in still photos, each one holding more horror than the last. "I helped her onto the horse. And we rode away. I kept him at a slow pace because I didn't want to hurt her or the baby. We were about a mile away when I heard it. A rattle. There was a full moon that night and I didn't see the snake anywhere near us, but the sound was enough to spook the horse. He took off at a full gallop. Sadie wasn't prepared. She wasn't holding me tight enough."

Emma gasped. "Oh, no. No, Luke."

"She fell off." He felt hollow. A shell of a man with nothing of value in him. He could see it happening all over again. "I can still hear her scream my name. The sickening sound of her body hitting the ground."

He heard Emma's sniffle. He had no fight left in him. No pride. Nothing left to hide. His shoulders sagged. "I stopped the horse and jumped down. Ran back to where she was. I was so relieved to see her eyes were open. She was so strangely calm. She kept saying, 'The baby, the baby.' I checked her for injuries. I knew her arm was broken. I thought maybe that was all but then...then I saw the blood on her dress."

"Oh, Luke." Emma laid her cheek against his shoulder.

"She was losing the baby." He spoke through gritted teeth. "I tried to get her to the horse. I tried to pick her up, but she screamed out in pain. She kept saying 'The baby, Luke, the baby.' I couldn't get her on the horse. She couldn't sit up. I couldn't lay her over the horse, bleeding like she was and with the pain she was in. I didn't know how bad she was hurt. Doing that might have made it worse. I started to pray, but I couldn't. I was too far gone. I had committed a horrible sin. I had tried to repent. I begged for forgiveness and it never came. Why would God do anything for me? He was angry with me."

"What did you do?"

"I did the only thing I could. I brought the horse to her, handed her the reins, and told her to hang on tight to them so he wouldn't wander off. I laid my coat over her and gave her the canteen of water and my gun in case any animals came near. I kissed her and said I would be back. She told me to go, that I had to save our baby. Then I ran the mile to town, thinking about her lying out there in that field, bleeding. I was crying so hard I could barely breathe, but I ran as hard as I could and got the doctor. I nearly passed out when I got to him. He took me back to her in his carriage."

"Was she ... "

"She was alive. In and out of consciousness. We got her in the carriage and back to town."

"And her father?"

"He wanted to have me thrown in jail for kidnapping. But Sadie told the sheriff she went with me of her own accord."

"Did she recover?"

"Yes." He massaged his temples. "Without our baby. And without the use of her legs. I wasn't allowed to see her, of course. But she wrote letters to me. Friends delivered them. Can you believe she apologized to *me*? She asked *my* forgiveness? She was sorry to put me through that. Sorry she hadn't hung on to me tighter. Sorry that she lost our baby."

He shook his head, drained from the memories. "She said she would always love me, and if I still wanted her, she would marry me as soon as she was well enough. She said we would ride a horse together again. But for eight months she fought infection after infection. Then she got influenza." He drew in a breath that sent a sharp pang through his lungs. "She died. July 15th, 1917." Luke was spent. He'd laid himself bare. His limbs were jelly. There were no more words.

She didn't say a thing. She finally knew what he really was. She would never look at him with admiration—or desire—again.

FOURTEEN

Emma couldn't speak. Everything had gone still. It seemed fitting. What Luke had shared with her was sacred. She felt the need to spend a few moments paying respect to Sadie and their baby, the young family that never got to be. She ached for the pain, the guilt, the loss he carried all these years.

No wonder he was so protective of Ruth. No wonder he reacted so harshly to Grady. She saw his tough skin and gruff ways for what they were—protection. A wall of defense to keep people from getting too close. A barrier to protect the memory of Sadie and their baby.

Emma was honored he chose to let her be a part of that memory. She knew it had come at a great cost—his vulnerability. Something Luke Morgan did not offer up lightly.

She considered her words carefully. "What did you do after...after she passed?"

He didn't answer right away. "I joined the Army. Served in the final year of the war." He shrugged. "And then moved around a lot."

"You never went back home?"

He kneaded one hand with the other. "I couldn't go back to that place. I stayed in touch with my folks and with Kate. No one else."

"How did your parents react to it all?"

"The way they reacted to everything. With patience. Compassion. Mama tried to get me to come home. It killed me to hurt her. Daddy understood, though. So did Kate. I always let them know where I was. I told Kate if she needed me, I'd be there. But she never asked me to come back. Of course, now I know how much she hid from me, so I wouldn't feel obligated to return."

Luke straightened and pulled in a deep breath. He stood and crossed the dirt floor, to the cage. "Sadie wanted to ride again. She was sure I'd figure out a way to make it happen. For years I didn't even want to think about it. But when I bought this place and knew I'd be boarding horses, I...I don't know...I felt like she led me here."

"And that's when you got the idea?"

"Pretty much. I was watching Ruth ride one of the horses and, well, I can't really explain it. In my mind, I saw...this"—he motioned to the cage—"surrounding her. Keeping her on the horse."

Emma smiled at the thought that Ruth had inspired the idea.

Luke lowered himself to the hay bale again. His eyes softened. Emma had to remind herself to breathe. He traced her cheek with his thumb. "We're quite a pair aren't we, Miss Darby? Walking around with our deep dark secrets no one would ever suspect."

Oh, Luke. If you only knew ...

His eyes roamed her face and fixed on her lips. She allowed herself the sensation of drowning in the passion sparking in his dark gaze. He tilted her chin upward and leaned in to her. The touch of his lips on hers sent her mind reeling. She never imagined he possessed such tenderness. She kissed him back, lifting her hand to his cheek, his stubble scratchy beneath her fingers.

Ruckus barked, jolting Emma back to her senses. She held her hand to her thundering heart.

Luke lifted a brow. "Ruckus approves."

Ruth was still in her nightgown at three o'clock in the afternoon. Her stomach roiled. She and Olivia had made plans to go to a movie this afternoon, but at the moment the very thought of moving made her ill.

She hated to let Liv down. She had been talking about seeing *Showboat* for over a week. What an awful way to start their summer break from school. Ruth's spirits sank even further at the knock at the door. She lifted her head enough to call out, "Come in, Liv."

Olivia let herself in. "So, I was thinking maybe we should get there early so we can—Ruth? Why aren't you dressed?"

Ruth turned her head. Even that slight movement sent a wave of nausea through her. "I'm sorry, Liv."

Olivia pulled out the chair next to her. "You're so pale." She touched Ruth's shoulder. "What's wrong?"

"I don't know. I feel awful." Ruth laid her head on her crossed arms atop the table.

"I'll get you a glass of milk." Olivia rushed to the ice box.

"No," Ruth moaned. "No milk. Please don't even say the word again."

"Okay. How about some water?"

"No."

Olivia sat back in her chair and sighed.

"You can't be mad at me for being sick." Ruth held her sick stomach. "It's not like I planned it."

"I know, I know." Olivia crossed her arms. "It's just that we've planned to see this movie all week, but you and Grady—"

Ruth's heart thundered. What did Olivia know? "Me and Grady what?"

Olivia leaned forward. "Ruth, every time you make plans with me, you cancel them so you can sneak off with him. I don't understand the sneaking around anymore. Luke has been letting you spend time with Grady. Why all the secrecy?"

Ruth stared at Olivia. Her mind raced. "I—"

The kitchen door opened and Luke entered, saving her from having to come up with an excuse that would satisfy Olivia's curiosity.

Luke set a grocery sack on the counter. "I thought the two of you were going to the movies today."

Olivia answered. "We were supposed to go see *Showboat*, but Ruth is sick."

"Ruth, you're sick again? What's the matter?"

"I don't know. I'm sick to my stomach."

Luke pressed the back of his hand to her forehead. "Does your head hurt?"

"No. I want to go back to bed, though. Liv, I'm sorry I ruined our plans again."

"Don't worry about it. I probably shouldn't spend the ten cents anyway." Her stooped postured betrayed her seeming acceptance.

Ruth stood to go to her room. The room started to spin.

"I think she's going to faint!" Olivia's voice sounded so far away.

Ruth felt herself falling as the room faded. She braced for impact with the kitchen floor but it didn't happen. Was she floating? The dark swallowed her.

She woke up in her bed. Luke sat across the room in the floral chair she and her mother had recovered together. In two long strides he was at her bedside. He bent down on one knee. "How are you feeling?"

"Better. How long did I sleep?"

"About two hours."

She rubbed her eyes. "How did I get in bed?"

"I carried you."

"Before everything went black, I thought... Did you catch me?"

He nodded.

She'd never seen that look in his eyes. Was it worry? This must be the Luke her mother knew and talked about all the time.

"It's dinnertime. Do you think you can eat? Emma—I mean Miss Darby—is here. She made soup for you."

Ruth's head felt clearer and her stomach had calmed. "I am a little hungry. That sounds good." She started to pull her covers back to get out of bed.

Luke touched her shoulder, gently pressing her back. "No. You stay here. We'll bring it to you."

She moved a pillow and tried to sit up anyway. "That's not necessary."

"Ruth, you're not getting out of bed."

She knew better than to argue with that tone.

He brushed a strand of hair behind her ear.

"I'm okay, Luke. Really."

He stared at her for a long moment as if trying to remember every detail of her face, then he stood and left the room. When he returned, he carried a tray with food on it, and Miss Darby followed close behind with a glass of water. Luke positioned the tray on the bedside table.

Emma put the glass of water down. "Here, let me prop some pillows behind you so you can sit up." She stuffed pillows behind Ruth's back and helped her get situated, then picked up the tray and placed it on her lap.

Ruth's mouth watered at the bowl of chicken soup and two slices of bread. "It smells so good." She dipped one of the pieces of bread in the soup and took a bite. She leaned back, closed her eyes, and let her taste buds absorb the flavor. "Mmm. I think I can actually feel myself getting better." She opened her eyes. Miss Darby and Luke wore the same concern on their faces.

"I'm okay, really." She scrunched her shoulders. "I must have eaten something that didn't sit right with my stomach."

Luke finally spoke. "Well, your color is back anyway."

She tapped her cheeks. "See? Nice and pink. I'm fine."

Luke rubbed his neck. "Okay then. I'll be in the barn if you need me." He dipped his head at Miss Darby and left.

"I don't know this Luke." Ruth whispered in case he could hear her.

Miss Darby pulled the floral chair closer to the bed and sat down. "I think he's always been there, hiding under all that thick skin."

Steam from the soup swirled up from the bowl as Ruth stirred it. "He really does seem to care, doesn't he?"

Miss Darby cocked her head and smiled. "Yes. He does."

Ruth thought for a minute. Luke and Miss Darby seemed to be getting pretty chummy these past two months. Maybe she could gather some information from Miss Darby about her big silent uncle. She kept stirring her soup. "Did he tell you what that thing is out there in the barn?"

"Yes, he did."

Ruth wriggled herself into a straighter position. "What is it?"

"You don't know?"

Ruth lifted a spoon full of soup to her lips and gently blew on it. "He didn't seem to want me out there, so I've always been afraid to ask."

"Honestly, I'm not sure it's my place to tell you. It's a very special project to him."

"But he told you." A smile tugged at Ruth's lips. "Does that mean you're very special to him, too?"

Miss Darby's cheeks blazed. She shifted in the chair and crossed her legs. "He told me because I asked him. That's all."

"Oh, really? And since when does Luke Morgan tell anyone anything, just because they ask?"

Her teacher lifted one shoulder. "I don't know. I think he wanted to tell someone. I happened to be the one to ask."

"Or it might be the fact that you look like Ginger Rogers."

Miss Darby leaned forward and gave Ruth's cheek a playful pinch. "That might be the sweetest thing anyone has ever said to me. Now, eat your soup."

"But I want to know what that thing is." Ruth pressed her palms together.

Miss Darby closed her eyes. "All right. You eat your soup, and I'll tell you."

Ruth scrunched her shoulders. "Deal." She ate as much as her stomach would allow, which wasn't much. Miss Darby moved the tray to the bedside table. "So?" Ruth wriggled her brows up and down. "What is it?"

A smile crept across Miss Darby's face. She scooted the chair closer to Ruth's bed. "It's for crippled and blind children, so they can ride a horse."

Ruth pictured the metal contraption, a saddle in the middle, stacked on bales of hay. "That's—" She stared at her teacher in wonder.

"I know. It's wonderful, isn't it? Can you imagine? There are so many children in the hospital in Santa Rosa and San Francisco stricken with polio, bound to a wheelchair, or having to wear leg braces. Can you imagine them being able to ride a horse? Or a blind child able to ride without fear?"

"Where on earth did he get such an idea?"

Miss Darby's smile wavered. Her brows pulled inward. "That part is his story to tell."

"His story?" Ruth's curiosity was further stirred.

Emma straightened and smoothed Ruth's quilt. "Do you need anything else?"

Ruth chewed her lip. "Okay. I won't ask any more questions. Wait a minute, I didn't even think about why you're here. Did Luke call for you?"

"He sent Olivia to get me. Dr. Brighton couldn't be reached."

"Thank you for coming." Ruth couldn't suppress a yawn. How could she be so tired after all the sleeping she'd done?

Miss Darby removed the extra pillows from behind Ruth and helped her lie down. "You get some more rest." She picked up the tray from the bedside table. "I'll be back tomorrow to check on you."

"Miss Darby?"

Her teacher stopped in the doorway. "Yes?"

"I just want you to know...I miss my mom a little less when you're around."

Miss Darby's eyes glistened. "Now *that* is the sweetest thing I've ever heard."

FIFTEEN

September fifth. First day back in school. How had the summer gone so quickly?

Ruth sighed at the sight of another boy sitting in Grady's old desk in history class. Grady had graduated in June, and it wasn't the same being in school without him. Fortunately, this was her senior year. As soon as she graduated, they could get married and be together forever.

The new boy caught her eye. He winked at her. She lifted her chin and ignored him. If that boy thought he stood even a chance with her, he had another thing coming. She belonged to Grady Akins. Completely.

Miss Darby, having been reassigned as a history teacher this year, spoke about the record breaking temperatures across the country and their devastating effects on the Midwest.

"He's cute!" Olivia whispered. "I hear he's an Okie."

Ruth frowned at the term she hadn't heard before. "A what?"

Olivia rolled her big blue eyes. "That's what they're called. The people who come west from Oklahoma because of the drought." Olivia sighed. "I can't wait to hear his accent. I bet he sounds like Grady."

Ruth scrunched up her nose. She'd never heard anyone call Grady an Okie. "His mother could have at least washed his overalls for the first day of school."

Olivia slapped at Ruth's arm. "Ruth Morgan! What a rude thing to say."

Ruth winced at her own ugly, judgmental words. If it was true the boy's family had to flee Oklahoma and come to California in search of work, he deserved understanding and compassion. And he needed friends. Even if he was a shameless flirt.

She'd been so irritable and on edge lately. At least the awful nausea and tiredness seemed to be letting up. Which didn't make much sense if it was truly due to the heat. The sweltering temperatures hadn't changed one bit. A newly familiar uneasiness took up residence in the pit of her stomach.

Miss Darby directed a stick of white chalk in smooth *scratch-scratch* and *tap-tapping* against the blackboard as she wrote possible essay topics for the week. Ruth was thrilled to have two classes with her favorite teacher this year, English and History. "Class, your assignment for this week is to write a four-page essay on one of these current events. I encourage you to make use of newspapers, news reports on the radio, speak with people who may have firsthand information or may simply be well educated on a particular topic, and pay attention to the newsreels if you go to a movie."

Melissa Johnson raised her hand.

"Yes, Melissa?"

"What about listening to President Roosevelt's fireside chat?"

Ruth rolled her eyes at Olivia.

Olivia whispered, "Such a goody two shoes."

"The President's fireside chats are an excellent source of information, of course." Miss Darby held her hand out. "But unfortunately, I don't believe there is one scheduled before this assignment is due. Does anyone else have any questions?" She scanned the classroom. "All right then. Moving on, can anyone tell me how the Midwest became known as the Dust Bowl?"

The new boy slipped his hand up.

"Noah, you probably have a better understanding of the situation than any of us. Class, this is Noah Crossland. His family moved here from Oklahoma."

The class greeted Noah. Miss Darby prompted him to answer her question, and he stood beside his desk.

"My pa said some reporter called it the Dust Bowl sometime last year, an' the name jus' stuck."

Olivia nudged Ruth with her elbow at the sound of his southern accent.

"And why did this reporter refer to it as the Dust Bowl, specifically?"

"Well, ma'am, the soil started turnin' dry and loose. Farmers started takin' over the good grassland an' covered it with wheat. If that weren't enough, there weren't no rain at all. There's lots o' dust storms happenin' all the time." Noah seemed lost in thought for a moment. "They're somethin' awful, them dust storms. Last year in April there was a real bad one. Folks called it Black Sunday. Everyone saw the sun an' went outside to do chores and go to church and such. But come afternoon, a big cloud covered the sky. A black cloud full o' dust." Noah stared at his worn shoes. "Ruined some five million acres of wheat. Folks on the road tried to find shelter an' was in the dark for hours."

Ruth couldn't fathom the vastness of the devastation the boy described. She exchanged a wide-eyed look with Olivia.

Miss Darby clasped her hands at her waist. "Can you share with the class how this made life difficult for people like your family?"

Noah's shoulders sloped forward. "With the crops dyin' an' the soil so bad an' all, farmers couldn't produce enough food to live on, let alone sell. Folks weren't able to pay their bills. Where I lived, we had hard times gettin' food. Sometimes folks with no homes went to parks and ate there. Some of the parks have cookin' areas where you can build fires. Everyone shared whatever they had. Some would bring a kettle for water, and some brought food to boil. We might get to eat a potato, or sometimes a meat stew. I remember I had to put a plate over my cup of water so no dust would get in it."

Miss Darby's eyes misted. "Thank you for sharing with us, Noah, and helping us to better understand what is happening in the rest of the country. We're thankful you and your family were able to make it here to California."

"Yes, ma'am." Noah took his seat.

Ruth's respect for the boy had grown as she'd listened to him tell his story. How could she have had such an awful attitude toward him? She thought of Grady, thankful he'd lived in a city and not a farm in Oklahoma. She hated to think of him in such dire straits.

She shifted in her chair, trying to get comfortable. She'd been having sharp pains all morning long.

"Why are you so squirmy today?" Olivia whispered.

Ruth scowled at her friend. "I can't get comfortable is all."

Olivia cocked her head. "You're starting to look pale again. Are you feeling okay?"

"I'm fine."

"Girls." Miss Darby gave them a stern look.

Ruth and Olivia both sank a little lower in their seats. Miss Darby went on to discuss the World War, instructing the students there were would be a test on the subject on Friday.

By the end of the day, exhaustion had claimed Ruth all the way through. The simmering heat sapped whatever energy she had in reserves to the point that she didn't even want to get out of her seat.

The classroom emptied and Olivia gathered her books. "Ruth, should you see the doctor? Should I go get Luke?"

Ruth didn't answer. The sense of dread that had been creeping in over the past two months rendered her speechless. She couldn't say out loud what she was thinking. She heard Miss Darby's heels clicking on the classroom linoleum. The teacher sat at the desk in front of Ruth and positioned herself to face her. Ruth squirmed under Miss Darby's knowing eyes.

"I'm concerned about you, Ruth. I've been watching you these last couple of months, and you don't seem to be getting better."

"It's still really hot." Ruth shrugged. "Dr. Brighton says I'm over sensitive to the heat."

Olivia chimed in, "I heard the heat is breaking all kinds of records all around the country."

Miss Darby pulled in and slowly released a deep breath. "I need to ask you a very personal question."

Ruth fidgeted with a loose thread on her dress. "Okay."

"When was the last time you...had your cycle?"

Ruth's throat clenched. She whispered, unable to answer in full voice. "Two months."

Olivia gasped.

Ruth covered her face with trembling hands.

Miss Darby stroked Ruth's hair. "Sweetheart, I think we better go see Dr. Brighton."

Ruth's eyes flew open. Hot tears of panic spilled down her cheeks. Was this really happening? She couldn't control the quiver in her chin. "Does Luke have to know?"

Miss Darby gripped Ruth's hand. "We'll cross that bridge when we have to."

Sixteen

The small, sterile waiting area in Dr. Brighton's office sent a chill through Ruth's body. She stared at a painting of children playing on the shore. If only she could go back to her childhood when things were that simple. Innocent. If only she could go back to two months ago. Miss Darby picked up an issue of the *Saturday Evening Post* from the small table in front of them.

Ruth's stomach grumbled, and her palms were sweaty. Sharp shooting pains and the bloated feeling she'd had for over a month made finding a comfortable position difficult.

Oh, please, Lord, don't let anyone else come in while I'm here!

She wished Olivia or Miss Darby would say something. Olivia stared at the opposite wall. Miss Darby perused her magazine. The room was too quiet. The *tick-tick* of a grandfather clock in the corner of the room seemed unusually loud.

What if she was— She couldn't even form the thought. It simply couldn't happen. There had to be another explanation. At church on Sunday, Mrs. Eggert commented on Ruth's low energy and suggested a vitamin B shot. Maybe she was right. Maybe all Ruth needed was some vitamins.

"Ruth, Dr. Brighton will see you now."

Ruth jolted. She stared at the woman wearing a white uniform, white stockings, white shoes, and white hat. The color of purity.

"It's all right." Miss Darby gently nudged Ruth's elbow. "Go on."

The assurance in Miss Darby's eyes generated enough courage in Ruth to stand. She followed the nurse on trembling legs.

An examination table sat in the middle of the room, cold and ominous. On one wall a glass cupboard held dozens of bottles of mystery pills and liquids. On the opposite wall, a counter with a sink was lined with glass canisters filled with tongue depressors and cotton balls. Everything so sterile and unfamiliar. Ruth caught a glimpse of her reflection in the glass cabinet. She quickly diverted her gaze to the floor.

"Step on the scale, please." The nurse's leathery face held no expression.

Ruth stepped carefully onto the scale. Then she stood against the wall as directed so the nurse could measure her height.

The woman scrawled a pencil over a piece of paper attached to a clipboard. "How old are you?"

"Sixteen." She rushed to add, "I'll be seventeen in two months."

"And when was your last cycle?"

Ruth couldn't breathe. She didn't know this woman. She didn't want to have this discussion with a stranger. She didn't want to have this conversation with anyone.

The nurse looked up from her clipboard. Her mouth tipped downward and her dark eyes screamed of boredom. She tapped her pencil on the clipboard.

"Two months."

"You'll need to speak up. I can't hear you."

Ruth looked beyond the woman at the closed door. She wanted to run out of this room and keep running.

The nurse huffed and cocked one hip. "Young lady, Dr. Brighton needs this information so he can proceed with his examination. Now please tell me. When was your last cycle?"

Sheer intimidation pushed the words out of her mouth. "Two months."

Thin eyebrows raised.

Ruth hugged her arms around herself, fending off the sense of exposure beneath the nurse's scrutiny.

The nurse scribbled on the paper again and set the clipboard on the counter. She opened a drawer, retrieved a gown, and handed it to Ruth.

"Put this on and sit there on the exam table. Dr. Brighton will be in soon."

Ruth held the gown away from herself with quaking fingers. "You mean, take off my clothes?"

The woman's disapproving eyes scanned Ruth. "Yes." Nurse Horrible left and closed the door behind her.

Ruth stood in the frigid exam room alone, legs nearly giving way. She leaned against the table, remembering the nurse's condemning glare. Was that how everyone would look at her? Would the whole town see her as a loose girl? A floozy?

Please, God. Please help me.

She pressed her hand to her roiling stomach. At the thought of what may be growing in her belly at that very moment, she jerked her hand away as if she'd touched a hot stove.

A knock at the door sent her heart darting into her throat.

"Ruth? Are you all right?"

She nearly cried out at the sound of Miss Darby's voice. She flew to the door and swung it open. Miss Darby eyed the gown Ruth clutched. She closed the door behind her. "Honey, you need to put that on."

Ruth took a step back. "Why?"

Miss Darby drew her into a hug and held her for a long moment. "You need to put on that gown so Dr. Brighton can examine you." She cupped Ruth's chin in her hand. "Do you understand what that means?"

Embarrassed that she had no idea, Ruth shook her head.

"Oh." Miss Darby drew in a breath as if to steady herself. "All right."

Ruth stared at her scuffed shoes as Miss Darby describe what was about to happen to her. She clutched her hand to her stomach and fought the instinct to curl into a ball on the floor. How could she endure such humiliation? She didn't want a stranger to see her. To touch her. Her breathing quickened and the room seemed to close in on her.

"I—I can't do this." Ruth backed away from Miss Darby, shaking her head. "I don't want to do this." Unchecked tears cascaded down her cheeks. Saliva flooded her mouth as a tsunami of nausea rushed from her stomach toward her throat. Her veins buzzed with horror. "Please don't make me do this."

"I'm so sorry, honey, but you have to. And the sooner you get this done, the sooner we can move forward."

Even Miss Darby's gentle and understanding tone did not assuage Ruth's fear. She threw the gown on the exam table as if it had bitten her. "I can't. I just can't."

Miss Darby picked up the gown and placed it in Ruth's hands. "Enough of this, Ruth Morgan. You have to have this exam. This is not something you can ignore and hope it goes away. Now, you put that gown on."

Strangely, being yelled at was more calming than all the coddling. Ruth hung her head and unbuttoned her dress. Miss Darby helped her put on the thin gown and then pulled a little metal stool out from under the table.

"Here. This will give you a step up so you can get on the table."

Ruth scooted to the very edge of the table. "I don't have to lie down, do I?"

"Not right now." Miss Darby tenderly rubbed Ruth's upper arms. "You've got goosebumps. Are you cold? I can ask for a blanket."

Ruth crossed her ankles. "It won't make any difference."

Miss Darby tipped Ruth's chin upward. "It will be over soon. I promise."

"Will—will it...hurt?"

Miss Darby brushed Ruth's hair off her shoulder. "It shouldn't. I'm sure the doctor will be as gentle as possible." She pointed to the door. "Now, I will be right out there, in the waiting room with Olivia. We will be waiting for you, okay?" She kissed Ruth on the forehead and started for the door.

"Miss Darby." Ruth reached for her teacher's hand. "Can't you stay? Please?"

A knock sounded at the door. Ruth nearly jumped down from the table. Miss Darby motioned for her to stay where she was. She said, "Come in."

Dr. Brighton entered. A tall man with a bald head and strong brow, he could easily be an intimidating figure except for his friendly eyes and affable smile. Why did he have someone like Nurse Horrible working for him? "Hello, Ruth." He held his hand out. "How are you feeling?"

She accepted his hand, hoping he didn't notice how badly it trembled. "Nervous."

"A lot of people get nervous about seeing a doctor. But I promise, I don't bite, and I have a jar of lollipops at the front desk for all my patients after their visits. Even the old, cranky ones."

Ruth managed a smile. If she were here to see him for any other reason, she wouldn't be nervous at all.

Dr. Brighton acknowledged Miss Darby. "And you are..."

"Emma Darby. I'm one of Ruth's school teachers."

"Pleasure to meet you, Miss Darby."

He picked up the chart the nurse left on the counter. "I want to make sure you are comfortable with your teacher being here, Ruth."

Ruth answered with a mute nod. She watched the doctor and Miss Darby exchange a look that made her squirm.

Dr. Brighton took a pen from his pocket and redirected his attention to her chart. "Let's see what we're dealing with, shall we?"

His forehead wrinkled. He returned the chart to the counter and leaned back against the counter, ankles crossed, hands loosely clasped at his waist. His quiet demeanor began to have a calming effect on Ruth.

"I suppose we should begin with the most obvious question. Have you been intimate with a man in the past two months, Ruth?"

Shame hung on her like a heavy cloak. Her shoulders slumped forward beneath its weight. She ducked her head. "Yes, sir."

"And was this a decision you made on your own? Were you coerced or forced in any way?"

"No!" Ruth blurted, horrified at what he inferred. "Gra— He would never, ever force me."

Dr. Brighton gave a single nod. "All right then. I have to ask because of your age." He looked to Miss Darby. "I'll need to examine her now."

"Of course, but Ruth asked if I would stay with her. I understand if it's not possible, but she's so young and very nervous."

Dr. Brighton addressed Ruth again. "You'd like her to stay?"

"Yes, sir."

"If having Miss Darby stay for the exam is what makes you comfortable, then by all means. Miss Darby, you stand up by her head."

Ruth lay down on the table as the doctor instructed. She squeezed her eyes shut and held tight to Miss Darby's hand while Dr. Brighton conducted his examination. Tears slipped out from under her closed lids as she turned her head to one side and tried to block out what the doctor was doing. She was broken. Used. Dirty.

At last Dr. Brighton rolled his exam stool away and stood. "You can sit up now. I'll leave and you can get dressed. Nurse Corrick will bring you to my office in a few minutes." He gently patted her knee. "You did very well, Ruth." Somehow the small gesture and kind words helped.

Miss Darby helped her out of the gown, and she slipped back into her blue dress and saddle shoes. Nurse Corrick reappeared to usher her to the doctor's office.

Ruth grasped Miss Darby's hand again. "Stay with me?"

Miss Darby patted her hand. "Of course."

Dr. Brighton sat behind an oak desk in an even smaller room, its walls lined with books. It smelled of antiseptic and old wood. Two chairs were positioned across from his desk. He motioned for Miss Darby and Ruth to sit.

Images of the night she spent with Grady flashed through Ruth's mind. What had she been thinking? How could she have done it? The moments of pleasure she'd experienced that night were not worth what she faced now.

The doctor laced his fingers together and rested his hands on the desk. "Miss Morgan, I think you already know what I'm going to tell you. I'm pretty certain your teacher does as well, or she wouldn't have brought you to see me."

Ruth picked at a loose thread on her skirt. Her insides wobbled.

"Miss Morgan, you are going to have a baby."

Ruth hung her head. She squeezed her eyes closed and she saw her mother, the way she'd always looked, so happy and proud of her little girl. Mom had taught her how a young lady should behave and had warned her of the ways a girl could soil her reputation. Her mother was so beautiful and kind and...pure.

"Are you absolutely certain?" Miss Darby's voice sounded far off.

"Yes. I am certain." The doctor's voice held a gentle apology.

How disappointed would her mother have been? Would she have stopped speaking to her? How would Olivia react? What must Miss Darby think of her? And Luke? And Grady.

Oh, Grady, we've made an awful mistake.

SEVENTEEN

Emma carried Nella's silver tray into the living room and lowered it to the coffee table. She had never been in Nella's home and found the furnishings and artwork surprising. The woman always seemed like one more person trying to make their way through the Depression. Many things made sense now. One would have to have money to buy a new pair of shoes for a child in need, or a sack of groceries for a family expecting their fourth child, or any of the other philanthropic things she'd heard about and witnessed Nella doing around town.

Nella poured a cup of tea and handed it to Ruth. "Drink this, sweetheart. The ginger will help settle your stomach."

Ruth accepted the cup but stared blankly at it.

Emma studied Olivia, who sat next to Ruth but hadn't spoken a word past a gasp before they even made it to the doctor's office. She hoped this situation wouldn't have a negative impact on such a sweet friendship. Olivia struggled with her mother being away at her grandmother's house and depended a great deal on Ruth's friendship. Now Ruth's attention and energy would be needed elsewhere.

Emma knew before leaving the doctor's office she was in over her head and had no idea what to say to Ruth or how to help her, so she'd brought the girls to Nella's. Nella called Barbara Hudgins to come over. Emma was so grateful for the wisdom and life experience of these two older women.

Nella sipped her tea. "Isn't it true, Barbara, that there are no mistakes when it comes to babies?"

"Yes, it is absolutely true. The Bible says God knows us before we are born, before our conception even. He forms us in our mother's womb." Barbara rested her hand on Ruth's knee.

Ruth set her cup on the coffee table in front of her. "I'm sorry, but I don't think God planned this."

"Well, you're right in that God does make it clear we are not to be intimate until we're married. Bringing children into this world is one of the reasons why."

Ruth's eyes blazed. "But if God knows everything, then He knew Grady and I would—we would make a mistake—and He knew this would happen. If He knew we weren't ready for this, why didn't He stop it?"

Barbara took a sip of tea before answering. "Because that would be like stepping out in front of a moving automobile and expecting God to keep it from hitting you. There are consequences to our actions. Out of His love, He gives us free will. His Father's heart allows us to experience the consequences of our actions so we can learn from our mistakes and gain wisdom from them. But in His grace, He forgives and makes all things work together for the good of those who love Him."

Ruth turned with hopeful eyes. "You mean He'll make it all work out? He'll fix everything? How?"

Nella poured herself another cup of tea. "Well now, that depends on what you mean by 'fix everything,' chil'. He'll fix it all right, but it will be in *His* way. But His way is the best, you can count on that." She raised her cup for emphasis.

Ruth sighed. "What I want is for this to never have happened." Her tender brow lifted and her green eyes lit with fear. "How am I going to tell Grady? What if he doesn't want this? What if he doesn't want *me* now? And *Luke*? He'll hate me! Things have finally started getting better between us, and now this."

Emma lifted her hand to the ache in her heart. If she could take all of this off Ruth's shoulders and take it on herself, she would. "One thing at a time, Ruth. If you try to answer all these questions at once, you'll only make yourself sick."

"Yeah." Olivia spoke for the first time since they left the doctor's office. "You don't need to worry about all that right this minute."

Ruth swiped tears from her eyes. "Could you tell Luke for me, Miss Darby?"

Stunned, Emma stared back at Ruth, her mouth agape. She searched Barbara's and Nella's widened eyes for assistance but found none. She held tightly to the delicate china cup. "I—I don't know. I'm not sure that's my place."

"Oh, please. Please, Miss Darby." Ruth scooted to the edge of the sofa. "I can't face him."

Emma wanted to help. Ruth was under so much pressure. She had so much to adjust to, so many challenges and obstacles to overcome. Sixteen years old and her entire life had just been altered forever. But would bringing this news to Luke really help Ruth?

He would absolutely be angry. He would say things he shouldn't. Emma would rather any initial outbursts be directed at her, not Ruth. Luke's most predictable reaction helped make the decision for Emma.

She held her tea cup and saucer with both hands as she lowered them on the coffee table. "I'll speak to him."

Lord, Help me.

Emma poured lemonade into a mason jar. She set down the heavy pitcher, added ice to the jar, and screwed the lid on.

The ladies had all decided the sooner she told Luke of Ruth's condition, the quicker he could absorb it and hopefully help her through it. Emma placed the mason jar in her picnic basket next to the fried chicken, potato salad, and a piece of Nella's chocolate cake.

Nothing softens bad news like food, right?

She said a prayer for wisdom—and courage—and hooked the basket on her arm. She reached Luke's house and spotted him in the distance riding a chestnut-colored horse toward the house. Her breath caught in her lungs at the sight of him atop the beautiful animal. Her lips tingled at the memory of his kiss. Never in her wildest dreams did she think she would fall for such an unpredictable man. Then again, he really wasn't so unpredictable, was he? Difficult to read, yes. Frustratingly silent, yes. But at the same time, solid. Honest. Led by integrity.

Trepidation vibrated through her veins, though. She'd seen the pain and anger he still carried from the memory of what happened to Sadie and their baby. What would he do with this news? Emma lifted her hand to shield her eyes from the sun as the horse trotted closer. For the briefest of moments, his smile chased away her anxiety. His charming, crooked smile was rare. The fact that it showed itself for her made her wish she could forget the reason for this visit.

Luke jumped down from the horse and eyed the basket. "You read minds in your spare time?"

It wasn't fair for the man to be so handsome at a time like this. "Not really." She adjusted the food in the basket.

Luke's smile dissipated. "Something wrong?"

"Well, um, there's an...issue I need to talk to you about."

His hat cast a shadow over his eyes. "Okay. I need to put Lexi here in her stall." He motioned to the barn. "You want to sit out here? It's cooler than in the house this time of day."

Emma followed him and deposited the basket on a hay bale.

Hay bales. That seemed to be the seat where she and Luke held their most intimate discussions. She opened the basket and took out the food and lemonade while he put the horse in her stall.

"Looks good."

At the sound of his voice so close, she spun on her heel and discovered herself inches from him, staring at his chest. He smelled like trees and earth and fresh air. Her eyes moved from his chest up to his face., The spark of desire in his brown eyes held her hostage.

"Looks real good." He winked.

Oh, my.

Emma took a step back, dusted invisible dirt from her skirt, and busied herself taking out the single napkin, plate, and fork.

He reached for her hand. "Emma? Your hands are shaking. What's wrong?"

Pressure built in her temples. There was no sense in delaying it. The quicker she got it out, the quicker they could all begin to move on and help Ruth through this. Emma held the tips of her fingers to her forehead. "I took Ruth to see Dr. Brighton after school yesterday."

"You did? Why? I thought she was feeling better." He leaned sideways to look around her at the food in the basket. "Did she get sick again?"

"No, she's not sick. Not exactly."

"I don't understand. I talked to her on the telephone yesterday afternoon. She said she was going to Olivia's and would probably spend the night. She didn't say a word about going to the doctor."

Emma's fingers felt cold. No doubt this was going to rip open the wounds left by the deaths of Sadie and his own baby. Emma didn't want to be the one to do this to him. She wanted to kiss him and hold him and tell him everything was fine.

"Emma." The tone of his voice conveyed patience running thin. "What's wrong with Ruth?"

"She—" The words emerged with a rasp her voice. "She's pregnant."

Luke stared at her, unblinking.

She waited. "Please say something."

He finally blinked and stalked several feet away.

She stared at his back, the sound of her own breathing echoing in her ears.

He set his hands on his waist, and his head hung low. "Where is Grady?"

The gravel in his tone rattled her. "I—I don't know." She took a step toward him. "Luke. Please. Getting angry isn't going to help the situation."

He faced her again. For the first time since she had met him, fear of what he might truly be capable of struck her. Luke stalked closer, his eyes narrowed. "It may not help the situation, but it will sure make me feel a whole lot better to beat that boy to an inch of his life. And maybe further!"

"I understand you're upset right now—"

"Oh, you understand that, do you?" Veins on the sides of his neck protruded. He thrust his forefinger in the direction of the open barn door. "Do you understand that I'm gonna find that boy and make him wish he never laid eyes on her? Do you understand that?"

"He's a good boy, Luke—"

"A *good boy*?"

Emma jumped a step back.

Luke punched his own chest with his fist. "*I was a good boy, too!* Let me tell you something, Miss Darby, being a 'good boy' isn't worth spit when a young, innocent girl ends up pregnant. And who were you to take her to the doctor? Did it even occur to you to call me? Why was the good doctor examining my niece without my permission?" He spread his arms wide. "Why am I finding out about all this a full day later?"

Emma's back stiffened. "I suppose you think she would have preferred you to be with her?" She waved a hand at him. "Look at you. Look at the way you're acting. She was frightened enough already without you there pounding your chest, bellowing at everyone, and threatening Grady."

Luke thrust his finger at her. "Everything was fine before you stuck your nose in around here! I had rules and she followed them. I didn't have to worry about some punk kid ruining her life forever."

Emma clamped her temper. Screaming at each other was not going to do any good. Someone had to keep their composure and obviously it wasn't going to be Luke. She lifted her chin. "Grady Akins is not a punk kid. He is a kind, respectful young man who is going to be scared out of his wits."

"A kind, respectful young man, huh?" His dark eyes bore into her. "Your judgment in men certainly hasn't improved, has it? No wonder Jasper Loomis zeroed in on you."

She didn't know whether to slap him or kick him. Stunned at his hateful, biting words, she waiting for him to realize the cruelty of them and apologize.

He didn't.

Her hands balled into fists, her nails cutting into her palms. "You're right. My judgment in men seems to be permanently flawed."

Luke didn't flinch at her insinuation.

EIGHTEEN

Olivia squeezed Ruth's hand. "Do you want me to stay with you?"

Ruth considered her friend's offer. The thought of giving Grady this news alone terrified her. But Olivia had said very little all afternoon. Actually, she'd said very little in the last twenty-four hours. Ruth suspected her best friend was dealing with her own issues regarding the— She still couldn't even finish the thought.

"No." Ruth's eyes followed the long driveway toward Grady's house. "I have to do this alone."

"Okay." Olivia dropped Ruth's hand.

Ruth swallowed the sense of rejection. The sense that she was losing something very important. "Thank you for coming with me, Liv."

Olivia offered a half smile and walked back down the road the way they had come. Ruth tried to ignore how quickly Olivia agreed to leave. She stared at the house where Grady lived. So pretty and quiet and welcoming. Grady's family had money and, though they didn't flaunt it, their refinement let everyone know they were different from most of the farmers around here.

Elaine Akins, Grady's mother, stepped out onto the porch with a watering can and tipped it over a potted plant. She spotted Ruth and waved her over.

Ruth didn't move. She felt as rooted to the ground as the stately oak trees in the Akins' front yard. Once she took that first step, it would all become too real. Maybe she could turn around and catch up with Olivia. At Mrs. Akins furrowed brow though, Ruth forced her body forward.

Mrs. Akins descended the white porch steps and knelt beside of a patch of peonies growing in front of the porch. Her laughter sounded like crystals dancing in a breeze. "Mr. Akins warned me the heat would be no help for my flowers out here, but I'm too stubborn to give up on them." She stood and brushed a brunette curl away from her face.

I wonder if my daughter will look anything like her. Gasping at the unbidden thought earned Ruth a concerned glance from Mrs. Akins.

"Are you not feeling well, Ruth? Grady told us how this heat has made you ill. Can I get you a cold beverage?" She went back up the steps and fluffed a pillow on the porch swing. "Maybe you should sit and rest."

Ruth's stomach tumbled. "No. No, thank you." How could she be standing here wondering what this child would look like when she couldn't even believe it existed? And why would she assume it would be a girl? Ruth breathed a silent prayer she would not get sick in front of Mrs. Akins. She also prayed the woman would not be able to detect Ruth's condition. Did married women, especially if they'd had children of their own, have a kind of sixth sense about these things?

"All right then." Mrs. Akins winked at her. "I assume you're here to see Grady?"

Ruth mutely nodded.

Mrs. Akins opened the screen door and called out to her son. "Grady, Ruth is here to visit you." She motioned Ruth to the porch swing again. "Please. I would feel much better if you would rest."

Ruth nodded and slid onto the porch swing's seat.

"I'm so sorry your uncle wasn't able to come to dinner with you last week."

"Oh, yeah. He's been real busy with the horses. Folks come in the summer to ride and he has to have everything ready to go."

"He's a hard worker."

"Yes, ma'am."

"Ruth, are you sure you're feeling well? You look a little pale."

Had her heart leapt into her throat and lodged there? She stared at Mrs. Akins's questioning eyes, trying to swallow, unable to speak. Surely the woman would be able to tell if she stared at her long enough.

The screen door opened, then slammed shut, pulling Mrs. Akins's attention away from Ruth. "Grady Theodore Akins. How many times do I have to tell you about slamming the door?"

Grady smiled and planted a kiss on his mother's cheek. "Sorry, Mom. You wanna come in and have some iced tea, Ruth?"

"Uh, no." She stood. "Actually, I was wondering if we could go for a walk."

"Oh. Okay. Sure we can." Grady walked down the porch steps with Ruth. "See ya later, Mom."

"Be back in time for dinner."

Grady spun around and walked backward, rubbing his stomach. "Always!"

His mother laughed. Ruth heard the screen door open and close behind them. They strolled halfway down the driveway and met Mr. Akins, driving home in his Cadillac. Ruth took a step back. Grady's father always seemed to have a suspicious eye with Ruth. Grady had told her his father didn't want girls flocking around because of his family's money, but he'd assured his father she wasn't one of those girls. His father would surely think differently by the end of the day.

"You going out so soon to dinnertime, son?" Mr. Akins spoke to Grady as he eyed Ruth. She chose to focus on two squirrels scampering up an oak tree.

"Just goin' for a short walk. Mom knows all about it."

Ruth glanced back at Grady's father. He offered a cold smile that didn't reach his dark eyes. She managed a smile with trembling lips, wishing he would leave them.

"All right then. As long as your mother knows. Be sure you're back in time for dinner."

"Yes, sir. See ya later, Dad."

Grady took Ruth's hand and tugged her with him as he started jogging the rest of the way down the driveway. Ruth's stomach rolled over. She pulled her hand away and stood still, eyes closed, willing the nausea to pass.

"What's wrong? Did you twist your ankle or something?"

She shook her head. Tears burned. If she opened her eyes, they would spill all over her face. She felt Grady's hands on her shoulders.

"What's wrong"? His tender voice reached her ears.

She managed to choke out, "Not here."

"Okay." He leaned in and whispered in her ear. "We'll go to our place then."

"No!" Ruth jerked away from him. She opened her eyes. Sure enough, tears coursed down her face. "I don't want to go back to that place. Not ever again!"

Grady backed away. He rubbed his cheek as if she'd slapped him. "Okay. We don't have to. We can go wherever you want. But tell me what's wrong. You're makin' me nervous."

Ruth hurried ahead of him to get some distance. She clutched the fabric of her dress in her fists as her step quickened. How would she get the words out? How would he respond? She was about to ruin his life. Dash all his dreams. Ruth slumped against the trunk of an immovable oak.

Grady caught up to her and reached for her hand. She quickly hid her hands behind her back. His Adam's apple bobbed. "Ruth, you gotta tell me what's eatin' you. You're scarin' me."

"I don't know how to start." She kneaded her fingers. "I don't know how to say it."

"How to say what? What happened?"

She willed her stomach to stop its incessant tossing and turning. She drew in a trembling breath. "Miss Darby took me to the doctor after school yesterday."

"Okay. Did he say you needed vitamin B, like Mrs. Eggert thought?"

Ruth stared at her shoes. The words swelled in her throat,

threatening to pop like a balloon if she didn't release the pressure. She couldn't hold them in anymore. She had to get them out. Wanted to get them out and be done with it. "I'm pregnant."

The words that altered the course of their lives forever hung in the air between them for an eternity.

He dipped his chin, eyes not wavering from hers. "What?"

Ruth's lips trembled. "Please don't make me say it again."

Grady staggered a few steps away. He turned his back to her. He shoved his hands through his hair and paced. When he faced her again, his focus seemed lost in the craggy gray-brown bark of the tree that supported her.

Back home she knew a girl who got pregnant, and the boy she thought loved her left town without a word. Merely disappeared. Would Grady do that? She already sensed his father's disapproval. He would tell Grady she was no good and to get away from her as quickly as possible. She would be stuck here alone.

How could she ever raise a baby all by herself? Where would they live? Surely Luke wouldn't let her stay at his house. How would she make money to feed both of them? Who was going to hire a— For the first time it struck her. She couldn't go back to school. She would be a high school dropout.

"I sent my application to Stanford this morning." Grady spoke in a distant voice, with a blank stare at the tree.

What? That's all he had to say? She told him she was having his baby and all he could think about was his college application? Of course, that's what he would think of. This baby didn't really change anything for him, did it? It only changed everything for her. Her life was completely and utterly destroyed.

She wasn't even aware she'd made the decision to run. Her legs seemed to take off on their own accord. She heard Grady's rushed footsteps crunch on the dirt drive behind her. His voice called after her. But she didn't stop. She couldn't stop. All she wanted was to do the one thing she'd longed to since this nightmare began.

Run.

NINETEEN

L uke roamed into the front barn after a long night of tossing and turning. He'd finally gotten up at two a.m. and worked on the cage until dawn. The food Emma brought the day before remained where he'd left it.

How had the mice and raccoons missed such an easy feast? He worked his jaw muscle and sat down, rubbing away the tension in his legs. He had fought every fiber of his body that told him to chase after Emma yesterday. His mind was reeling. How had this happened? He did everything he could to prevent history from repeating itself. Why did he let Emma talk him into letting Ruth run with Grady when his instincts told him not to? And now Ruth was—

How many people knew about Ruth? The doctor did, obviously. And Emma and Olivia. He pressed his fists to his eyes. Emma's words still reverberated in his ears.

I suppose you think you're the one she would have preferred to be with her? Look at the way you're acting ... My judgment in men seems to be permanently flawed.

He groaned at the last expression he saw on her face. Hurt. Betrayal. How low had he sunk, to throw her relationship with Jasper Loomis in her face? What kind of man had he become?

Sadie's face eased into his mind. The devastation and fear in her voice when she told him she was going to have his baby. In spite of his own fears, his every instinct had been to protect her and their baby. An unwanted thought that Grady might feel the same for Ruth struck him like ice water in his face. He forced the idea out, refusing to accept any similarity between him and the boy who did this to his niece.

If ever there was a time he wished he could pray for wisdom and believe God would give it to him, this was it. Ruckus sauntered over and lay down at his feet, looking up at Luke with soulful, trusting eyes. Luke stared into the abyss of unconditional love and acceptance in the dog's eyes.

"Leave it to a dog to teach a cowboy his rightful place with his Master." J.D. leaned against the open barn door.

How did the man always seem to know right when to show up?

J.D. ambled into the barn, thumbs hooked on his suspenders. He pulled a handkerchief from his pocket and mopped his brow, pushed a hay bale closer to Luke, and straddled it. "Barbara said you might need some company this morning."

Add Barbara to the list of people who knew. Luke bounced the tips of his fingers off each other. "Emma came over yesterday."

"Mmm-hmm. Barb told me Emma would be the one taking the hit. How did that go?"

Luke couldn't look at the man. Taking the hit? So, everyone assumed he would handle it badly. And they were right. In J.D.'s presence, he was even more ashamed of his behavior, the things he'd said to Emma. He couldn't bring himself to answer the man's question.

J.D. sighed heavily. "I figured as much."

"I don't know which way is up, J.D." Luke removed his hat and shoved his hand through his hair. "I want to go after Grady and beat the living tar out of him. I want to go to Ruth, but I have no idea what to say when I do." A bluebird pecked at the ground beyond the open barn door. "And I hurt Emma."

"How so?"

Luke finally met J.D.'s crystal-blue-eyed scrutiny. They appeared more a stormy gray today. "She trusted me with personal information a few weeks back, when I helped her at the church social. Something no one else around here knows. And yesterday I—I used it against her."

J.D. grimaced and leaned forward to rest his elbows on his knees. "Boy, do you know what it took for that sweet woman to come here and tell you this news? Did she tell you it wasn't her idea? Did you know Ruth asked her to do it? She took Ruth's place, to protect her and try to make this whole thing a little bit easier on you both."

He'd suspected Ruth was hiding from him. Luke put his hat back on and tugged it lower over his eyes.

I suppose you think you're the one she would have preferred to be there? Look at you. Look at the way you're acting ...

"No. She didn't tell me that." His heartbeat echoed in his hollow chest. "I didn't give her much of a chance."

J.D. let the admission hang in the air for a long moment. "Did you have a chance to look at the book of Ruth like I suggested?"

What? With everything that was going on, J.D. wanted to talk about some Old Testament book in the Bible? But with J.D., even the most bizarre turns took you right to where he wanted you to go. "Yeah. A couple of nights ago actually. *Hmpf.* First time I opened the Bible in nineteen years and look what happens."

"Oh, come on now," J.D. growled. "If you're gonna play 'poor me,' I may as well go home. I came here to help you, boy, not listen to you whine. Now pull that blasted hat back so I can see your eyes while I talk to you."

Luke's lower lids twitched with irritation. But J.D. Hudgins had the same kind of power or authority...or whatever it was...that his dad had. Luke lifted his chin and slowly eased his hat back on his head. He raised a rebellious brow at J.D.

J.D.'s steely eyes did not waver. "What did you see when you read it?"

"Look, J.D., I'm not really in the mood for a Bible story right now."

J.D. leaned forward, one elbow on his knee, his other arm raised, forefinger pointed at Luke's nose. "I don't much care what you're in the mood for, son. I didn't come here to check your mood. I knew what your mood would be. Answer my question. What did you see when you read it?"

The thought of anyone, including J.D., talking down to him chafed against the respect he had for the man. "Ruth's husband died. She left her people to stay with her mother-in-law and follow God. She met Boaz and married him. A love story." Luke spread his hands in a *are you happy now?* gesture. "Like Kate always said. It's a love story."

And I'm not real interested in love stories right now.

"It's a start, I guess." J.D. motioned to the mason jar next to Luke. "Mind if I have a drink?"

Luke handed him the jar and the man drank half of the now warm, watery lemonade Emma had made.

"The real message in the book of Ruth is the kinsman redeemer."

He was going to get a Bible lesson whether he wanted one or not. Luke searched his memory of the text. He scratched his temple. "Yeah, I remember that. Boaz was Naomi's relative. He could marry Ruth and give her children. Only, there was another guy who was closer or something."

J.D.'s eyes lit. "Yes. The kinsman redeemer was the closest male relative of a widow's husband. If the husband had a brother, then he would marry her. If he didn't have a brother, the next closest male would marry the widow, take her as his wife, and have children with her to honor the dead husband and, most importantly, prolong the family name by providing an heir." J.D. grinned. "And you're right, there was another man closer to Ruth. But you see, Boaz wanted Ruth. He was pretty sneaky about the way he approached the other man."

"How so?"

"If you remember, Boaz told the closest kinsman redeemer about the land and got him all worked up about getting richer. The man saw nothing but dollar signs and said, 'Sign me up!' But then, and only then, did Boaz casually mention the fact that Ruth came with it. That cooled the man's heels right quick." J.D. laughed and swiped the handkerchief across his forehead again.

Despite his mood, Luke couldn't help but be impressed with the craftiness Boaz employed to get the woman he wanted. "I didn't catch that. Gotta admire a man who goes after what he wants."

"The most beautiful part of the story isn't even the romance, though." J.D. scooted forward on the hay bale. "It's actually the story of Jesus, and of us. You see, Boaz is an Old Testament representation of Jesus. And Ruth represents you and me." He placed the mason jar on the ground. "Just as Boaz took Ruth to himself, took responsibility for her, 'redeemed' her, Christ did the same for us. To 'redeem' something means to pay for it. And Boaz didn't do it because he had to. He didn't get stuck with Ruth. He did it because he wanted to. He loved her. Same as Christ loved us and wanted to pay the ultimate price to redeem you and me. He wanted to pay the price for our sins, take them on Himself, actually become our sin on the cross. He made us heirs with Himself. He prolonged the name of His father. He made us family. God is all about family. Especially *His* family."

Luke rubbed the back of his neck.

J.D. picked up the jar again and drank the rest of the lemonade. "Firstly, you need your Redeemer more than ever right now. You've been running long enough, son. You've reached the end of yourself and you know it. You can't help Ruth, who's your family, in your own strength and wisdom, and—let's face it—we both know you're running a quart low on wisdom right now."

Luke couldn't argue. His behavior with Emma was evidence of that fact.

"You have a choice to make." J.D. leaned forward. "Your situation is different from the Bible story, but you can still be like Boaz and represent Christ to your Ruth, or you can be the guy who hands her off to someone else because all of this is more than you bargained for."

Luke lowered his head. That's what he'd been doing, wasn't it? He'd been a little annoyed his life had to change, his plans interrupted, because of Ruth. He handed her over to other people to take responsibility for her. Her friend Olivia kept her occupied and entertained. The church kept her on the straight and narrow. Her teacher had become her confidant, her safe place. Emma'd even taken responsibility for Ruth's emotional and physical health.

The spiteful words he'd thrown at Emma regurgitated like bile in his throat. *"And who in the world were you to take her to the doctor?"* In actuality, Emma was the perfect one to take Ruth to the doctor.

And hadn't he done the same thing with Kate? Walked away, leaving her in the care of others? What kind of man had he become? He always thought of himself as a good person. Did he have a past filled with pain and regrets? Of course. But he'd never considered himself a person who abandoned those in need. Especially after quitting his job to take in his teenage niece. Didn't that count for something?

Luke pulled his hat down low over his eyes. He couldn't face this godly man's scrutiny. "J.D., this is a lot to take in right now."

"I know it is, son. But it's time you started taking it in. Because that young girl, *your* Ruth, needs you to point the way to her Redeemer. But you can't do it until you get reacquainted with Him yourself." J.D. stood and shoved his handkerchief into his pocket. Luke followed him out of the barn to the pastor's car, which he'd parked in front of the house.

J.D. opened his car door. "Barbara and I are here for you and Ruth. You know better than anyone, it's going to be a tough road for her."

They didn't need to speak further to share an understanding of the events of Luke's past. Luke scuffed his boot along the dirt. "Yeah, I know. I just wish I knew what to do first."

The older man rested his hand on Luke's shoulder. "God will show you the steps, and He'll put them in the right order for you. Pay attention. Walk through the doors He opens." He pointed his finger at Luke. "And for cryin' out loud, don't let that temper of yours get in the way again."

❧

Ruth helped Olivia fold laundry for her family. "Your mom sure has been gone a long time."

Olivia didn't look at her. "Yeah. She has."

Luke sent word an hour ago he would be picking Ruth up to go back home. She sat on Olivia's bed, waiting. He had given her permission to stay here two nights ago, but that was before he found out she was going to have a baby. Even though she dreaded going home to Luke, Ruth was a little relieved to be leaving. Things were strained between Olivia and her.

Ruth twisted the hem of her skirt. "Do you have any idea when she's coming home?"

"No."

Ruth suspected something was terribly wrong in Olivia's family, but she didn't want to add to the tension between the two of them by bringing it up. "I suppose Luke will be here soon."

Olivia shook out a white shirt and folded it in jerky movements before slapping it down onto the pile of folded clothes. "Yes, I suppose so." She folded three more shirts.

Ruth shifted her position. She bit her lip. "Liv, are you okay?"

"Sure." She tossed a pair of socks into a pile. "Why?"

"I don't know. Things don't feel right. I feel like—like maybe you're mad at me."

Olivia paused. She sighed and crossed her arms in front of her. "To be honest, Ruth, I kind of am."

Her friend's eyes held a scrutiny Ruth couldn't bear. She studied her folded hands in her lap. "Oh."

"I covered for you and Grady. All that sneaking off together—I helped you do that. And you promised me nothing improper was happening between the two of you."

"But nothing was!"

Olivia's high-pitched laugh jarred Ruth. "How can you say that? You're pregnant, Ruth! I trusted you. Here I am, stuck in this house, taking care of my brothers while my mother is off at my rich grandmother's house completely ignoring her responsibilities. I feel used by everyone around me and now I find out that you used me, too."

She grabbed a shirt from the basket. "If I had known what you were really doing, I would not have helped you. I feel like a fool. What did you think? That I was too gullible to have suspected what was really going on?" She folded the shirt with angry, quick movements. "I guess you were right."

"No, Liv, no." Ruth hopped down from the bed and rushed to her friend. "I promise you, nothing was happening. Not until—" Ruth's cheeks blazed. "It was only that last time. I would never lie to you, Liv. Never. Please, you have to believe me. I don't have anyone else." Hot tears rolled down Ruth's cheeks. She searched Olivia's eyes for a hint of understanding. Of compassion. Of ... friendship.

Olivia didn't answer for a long moment. "I don't know, Ruth." Her eyes shimmered. "Everything has changed. Us. School. The future. I don't know where we stand anymore."

Blood pounded in Ruth's ears. Her heart thundered. Her vision shifted, as if she were looking through a fish-eye lens. She was truly alone. Stranded. No one to help her. She had to get away. She grabbed the suitcase she'd packed for her overnight stays and darted for the door.

"Ruth! Where are you going?"

Ruth ignored Olivia's calls after her and bounded down the Hawkins' old porch steps.

Ruth studied the various bus routes and fares posted on the bus station's wall. She could go as far as Santa Cruz, but she didn't know anyone there or how much money she might have to use until she found work and a place to live.

She checked the money in her pocketbook. Enough to go to San Rafael. Only twenty-one miles away, but at least it was *away*. The fare would take her spare change, but she would still have the two dollars of babysitting money she'd saved.

Decision made, she requested a bus ticket.

The old man at the ticket booth raised bushy gray eyebrows. Gaps from a few missing teeth showed when he smiled. "Going south to visit family, young lady?"

What if he knew Luke? What if he ran and told her uncle where she'd gone? Part of her hoped that's what would happen. "Um, no. Just a friend."

He handed her the bus ticket. "Best hurry. It's getting ready to leave right now."

She set her suitcase next to the bus with the bags of other travelers, then climbed the bus steps and handed the driver her ticket. It wasn't until she took her seat and looked around at all the unfamiliar faces that she had second thoughts. She stood to tell the driver she'd made a mistake, but the bus rumbled to life and leapt forward.

"You better sit down, kid." A man spoke around the cigarette hanging out of his mouth. "You're likely to get knocked on your pretty little behind, acting a fool like that."

Embarrassed, she quickly took her seat. The scenery of Petaluma that had become so familiar—that had become home—was a blur beyond the bus window.

Tears slipped from her eyes.

TWENTY

Luke drove up to the Hawkins' house. The once green yard was now mostly dirt with patches of weeds. He got out of his truck and walked up the porch steps, which were sorely in need of repair. Maybe he could help Jack out with some of this stuff.

He knocked on the door and flicked one of the peeling chunks of white paint off the doorframe, revealing softened, black wood. A sure sign of rot. A single termite wiggled out of a hole in the window frame to his left. The old clapboard house was really in disrepair. But Jack didn't have much time to work on the place, taking care of four kids and working as much as he possibly could

The door opened and Olivia stared up at him, eyes wide, mouth gaping.

"Hi, Olivia."

"Um, hi, Luke."

Luke perused what he could see of the interior of the house beyond her. "I'm here to pick up Ruth."

"Yeah." Olivia seemed to search for something, or someone behind her. "I think she went home."

"She went home? You think? When?"

"About an hour ago."

"Why? She knew I was coming to get her."

Olivia seemed to have a difficult time knowing where to look. Too much so for Luke's comfort.

"Olivia? What's going on? Did you two have an argument?"

"Not exactly."

"Then why—"

"Hi'ya, Luke." Jack Hawkins stepped past Olivia out onto the porch. He shook Luke's hand. "You here to get Ruth?"

Luke assumed by the lack of awkwardness in his greeting, Jack had no idea about Ruth's pregnancy. "Yeah. I am. But Olivia said she left."

"Left?" Jack peered at Olivia. "When?"

"About an hour ago, Daddy."

Luke adjusted his hat. "The thing is, Ruth knew I was coming. I can't see her taking off an hour early and not getting word to me." He inclined his head toward Olivia. "I thought maybe they had an argument or something."

Mr. Hawkins looked at Olivia. "Did you?"

Olivia bit her lower lip. "Kind of."

Mr. Hawkins chuckled. "Well, there ya go. You know how girls are. They have their tiffs. I'm sure Olivia's right. Ruth is probably at home blowing off steam. I'm sure they'll be right as rain again by tomorrow."

"Yeah." Luke narrowed his gaze, eyeing Olivia. "Okay."

She ducked her head. She definitely wasn't telling the whole story. As if he didn't have enough to sort through with Ruth. Now he'd have to figure out what happened between the two girls that would cause her to leave her best friend's house the way she did.

Back at the house, Luke walked in the kitchen and tossed his keys on the counter, fed Ruckus lunch, and searched the living room for Ruth. Maybe she wasn't feeling well and had to lie down. He strode down the hallway. Her bedroom door was open, but no Ruth. The bathroom door stood open, the room empty. Unease began to percolate in his gut. He went outside and scanned the open areas, checked in all the barns, and even checked down at the creek. No sight of her. Luke went back to the house, grabbed his keys and got in the truck. Where would she go? Who would she seek out for help?

Emma.

Luke started the truck and pressed the accelerator to the floorboard. The old truck groaned and clanked as Luke pushed it past its abilities. Luke turned onto Emma's drive and spotted her sitting under the willow tree across from her yard. He slammed on the brake, pushed open the door, and got out.

Emma stood, holding a book.

He ran to her. "Is Ruth here?"

"No, she isn't. Was she supposed to be?"

Luke rubbed at his neck. "No. Maybe." He paced back and forth, took his hat off and scraped his fingers through his hair, then put the hat back on. "I don't know."

"Luke, what is going on?"

He broke stride. "She stayed at Olivia's last night. We still haven't talked about—" He pinched the bridge of his nose. "She knew I was coming to pick her up. But when I got there, she was gone. Olivia said she went home."

"Well, that's probably where she—"

He shook his head. "She's not there. I checked. But that's not all. Olivia was acting real strange. There's something she's not telling me."

Emma held her book to her chest. "What about Grady? Or Nella?"

Luke snapped his thumb and forefinger in the air. "Nella. That's it. If anyone knows about what's going on anywhere in this town, it's Nella." He ran toward the truck.

"May I come with you?" Emma called after him.

Luke didn't slow or look back. "Only if you're in the truck when I start it."

Emma caught up to the truck as Luke started the engine. She climbed into the cab and shut the door as he hit the gas pedal.

Luke massaged a growing pang in his left temple, urging the truck down the road as fast as he could force it. Where had Ruth gone? Why would she take off without saying anything? What a stupid question. He knew exactly why.

The last time he'd experienced this kind of fear-based adrenaline, he was climbing the first tower of the bridge, looking down at the freezing white-capped water over two hundred feet below.

"Did you check Grady's house?"

He'd forgotten Emma was even in the truck. He threw a glance her direction, then focused on the road ahead again. "No."

The dips and bumps in the road proved particularly rough at this speed. He could see Emma's white knuckled grip on door handle and heard her intermittent gasps. "I think maybe you should check Grady's house first." Emma bounced in her seat. "It's on the way to downtown."

Luke chewed on his inner cheek. He was not ready to see that kid yet. And what if Ruth was there? If she left Olivia's knowing he was coming to get her and ran to Grady's house, causing all this panic, he'd be hard-pressed not to padlock her in her room for the next five years.

They drew nearer and nearer to the Akins' driveway. Luke nearly drove past it, not wanting to interact with the boy who'd ruined Ruth's life, but at the last moment he jerked the steering wheel to the left. Emma nearly toppled into his lap. Luke sped up the long driveway to the fancy white house with its perfect flower boxes green lawn and manicured shrubbery.

Grady sat alone on the porch steps.

The truck brakes squeaked and the vehicle barely lurched to a stop, even as Luke threw it into Park, swung open the door, and got out. He stalked toward Grady.

"Luke!" Emma's hurried footsteps scuffed the dirt behind him.

Grady stood, fear in his eyes.

"Where is she? And God help you if you lie to me."

Grady stared, wide eyed, mouth gaping. "Who?"

Emma caught up to Luke and grabbed his arm just as he was about to lunge at Grady.

"You know who. Where is she?"

Grady backed up, stumbled on a step, and landed on his behind on the porch. He shook his head. "I—I don't know. She came to tell me and—and—I don't know what happened..."

Luke shook loose of Emma's grip. "What do you mean, you don't know what happened? What did you say to her?"

Grady hung his head. "Not what I should have. I couldn't think. I didn't know what to say. I'd just sent my application to Stanford and...I was shocked and...I was thinking out loud and she— She ran off."

"And you let her?"

"No! I ran after her. I kept begging her to stop, but she wouldn't. I thought maybe I should give her some time."

Luke recognized the fear in Grady's eyes and it irritated him. He didn't want to sympathize with the kid.

Grady stood. "Luke, we gotta find her."

Luke ran back to the truck.

Grady chased after him. "Where are you gonna look? You got any ideas?"

Luke spit on the ground, barely missing Grady's shoe, then grumbled, "Nella's"

Grady stumbled, sidestepping the spittle. "Can I come with you?"

Luke didn't answer, but it didn't stop Grady. He leaped over the tailgate into the bed of the truck. Emma hopped up into the cab, and Luke drove in the direction of downtown. He checked the gas gauge. This search was going to cost him a pretty penny in fuel.

His brain rolled over and over with haunting memories and nauseating possibilities of what could be happening to Ruth as he desperately tried to urge the '29 Ford to perform like a '37 Mercedes Streamliner. Out of habit, he checked the rearview mirror. Grady balanced himself on the left wheel well, jostled back and forth, gripping the truck panel on either side of him. His head hung low.

Luke was loath to admit he understood what the kid was feeling.

"She's probably sitting in a booth at Nella's being treated to a piece of lemon cream pie."

Luke's attention jerked to Emma.

"Or maybe at the five-and-dime, having a soda with Olivia. Or

Burke's. They have a nice selection of baby clothes..." Her voice trailed off, along with the confidence in her tone.

The drive to Nella's had never taken so long. "Olivia has no idea where she is."

"Oh, that's right. You said you think she's withholding information?"

Luke adjusted his hat on his head. "Yes. She was acting, I don't know, guilty."

"Guilty?"

"Yeah. Any ideas?"

"Well, Olivia has been very quiet, distant even, ever since we took Ruth to the—" She stared out her window.

Luke wished he could go back to their last encounter. Wished he could change how he'd spoken to her. "Listen. I know I could have handled things better the other day." Chancing a sideways look at her, he caught a skeptical raised brow.

"Is that supposed to be an apology?"

What else did she think it was? He drew in a breath, held it for a beat, and slowly released it. "Guess I could be handling it better now, too."

"I'm sorry." Emma waved a hand. "I'm on edge about Ruth. The truth is, I've gone over and over all the ways I could have handled things better as well. I can't believe I thought fried chicken would help."

"Yeah, well, don't be too hasty to abandon that tactic in the future."

Her hesitant smile alleviated the hovering anxiety.

"I really wish I'd put it in the icebox." He kept his eyes on the road. "Would have made a good breakfast."

"You mean you left all the food out? I'm sure the raccoons enjoyed it."

"Actually, it was all still there in the morning." He cocked his head. "Maybe they know something I don't?"

She reached across the cab and slapped his arm.

He couldn't suppress a grin. Grady's reflection in the rearview mirror caught his attention again. He heaved a weighty sigh. "Where could she be, Emma?"

The warmth of her hand on his shoulder made him feel less alone. "We'll find her. Don't worry."

જ

Ruth raised her hand to her growling stomach. Had she really run away from home? Obviously. Here she stood, holding a suitcase on a street corner in another city, on the doorstep of a diner she'd never heard of. What did she think she was going to do—get a job? Who would hire a pregnant sixteen-year-old high school dropout? What about a home? Who would rent her a room with no job and a baby on the way? What had she been thinking?

"You coming inside, doll?"

She'd been so lost in her panicked thoughts, she hadn't noticed the pretty young woman holding the door open for her.

"'Cause I'm in a hurry. The last thing I need is Buck the Bear to get sore at me two days in a row."

"Buck the bear?"

"Yeah." The woman's brown ponytail swung behind her as she motioned up at the sign above the building. "Buck owns the diner, thus the name, Buck's Diner. I call him Buck the Bear because he can be real grouchy. Not the greatest guy to work for, but hey, it's a paycheck, right?"

Ruth struggled to keep up with the sheer volume of words spilling from the woman's red-painted lips.

"So, you comin' in, or what?" The woman cocked one hip.

Ruth decided the best thing to do right now was to actually go inside and sit for a while. Figure out what in the world she was doing here. She stepped through the opened door, ahead of the woman.

"I'm Jessica, by the way." The woman—Jessica—snatched a menu and handed it to Ruth. "Follow me."

Ruth obeyed, though her stomach felt as bloated as a water balloon and she had trouble keeping up with Jessica, who walked every bit as fast as she talked.

"I won't be at this place forever." Jessica tossed the comment over her shoulder. "I'm taking night classes at the high school. Gonna be a secretary." She stopped at a booth. "No more greasy fingers pinching this behind, you know what I mean?" She paused long enough to smile. "Have a seat."

"Oh." Ruth began to form a mental picture of what a day at work must be like for the chatty Jessica. It sounded awful. A mean boss. Men putting their greasy paws on her. Waitressing was definitely out as an option. She'd taken typing in school. She was pretty good at it. She took good notes in school, too. And how hard could it be to answer a telephone and file papers? Secretary. A much better possibility. She wrestled the suitcase into the booth first, then scooted in.

"Take a look at the menu." Jessica handed her a letter sized piece of paper with the diner's options printed on it. "I'll be right back."

Ruth watched the fascinating young woman retreat behind the lunch counter. She couldn't be more than three or four years older than Ruth, but she seemed so much more... worldly. Did she go home to a mother and father? Siblings? Surely she didn't live by herself at such a young age. There was something about Jessica that told Ruth the two of them had lived very different lives. Ruth stared at the menu. How could she have no appetite and yet everything on the menu made her mouth water?

"So, what can I get you?"

Ruth's attention snapped to her right. Jessica was back, wearing a white apron tied behind her back and holding a pad and pencil.

A booming voice from behind startled Ruth. "Yer five minutes late, Jess!" A large, bald man with heavy eyebrows and a big belly scowled at the waitress.

"Aww, calm down Buck." Jessica waved him off. "I'll stay five minutes later." She touched Ruth's shoulder. "I'll be back again, Doll. Just gotta calm the bum down."

Gripping the edge of the red vinyl booth, Ruth's head began to spin. Everything was moving so fast. This wasn't what she'd expected. But what had she expected? Nothing. How could she expect anything when she hadn't even thought about what she was doing?

What was Grady doing right now? Did he know she was gone? And Luke. Oh, dear Lord, Luke would lose his mind. Miss Darby? Miss Darby...she would be so disappointed. How did all this even start?

Ruth stared out the window next to her table at the passing cars. Olivia. Her best friend. The one person in the whole wide world she thought would be there for her had abandoned her. How could Liv be mad at her right now? Liv wasn't the one going to have a baby. It wasn't her life that was ruined. Liv could keep going to school. She could giggle with friends and go to school dances and baseball games and—Ruth ground her teeth—graduate. All the things Liv would get to keep enjoying, all the things she would get to experience, Ruth never would.

"Every time you make plans with me, you cancel them so you can sneak off with him."

Ruth squirmed at the sound of Olivia's voice in her mind.

"I trusted you. I covered for you and Grady. All that sneaking off together—I helped you do that. And you promised me nothing improper was happening between the two of you...If I had known what you were really doing, I would not have helped you. I feel like a fool. What did you think? That I was too gullible to have suspected what was really going on?"

Ruth rearranged the salt and pepper shakers, trying to keep her hands busy. But Olivia's voice wouldn't stop.

"Here I am, stuck in this house taking care of my brothers, while my mother is off at my rich grandmother's house completely ignoring her responsibilities. I feel used by everyone around me, and now I find out you used me, too."

Liv was right. Ruth had lied to her. Used her. When was the last time she'd asked Liv anything about her life? Did she ever ask if Liv needed her help, or how she felt about her mother being gone so long? Losing her mom was the worst thing Ruth had ever been through, and yet she'd treated the absence of Olivia's mother as if it were nothing. She thought of all the work Liv had to do at home. All the things her mother should be there doing.

"Oh, Liv. I'm sorry. I've been so selfish."

"What's that, doll?"

Ruth nearly jumped out of her seat. How did Jessica keep sneaking up on her like that? "Um, nothing."

"Suit yourself." Jessica took a pad of paper and pencil out of the apron pocket. "What'll you have?"

Ruth stared at the menu.

Jessica tapped her pencil on the pad and leaned in. "Look, doll, I may not have been around long, but I've done and seen a lot for someone my age, and obviously something is going on with you. I'd like to help. Really, I would. But you can't sit here if you don't order. All you have to do is get some fries or a milkshake or something, and when I come back, maybe I can help you out."

"Oh." She wasn't wanted here either.

"Never mind." Jessica scribbled on her pad. "I'll bring you a burger."

Before Ruth could protest, Jessica moved on to the next table of customers. The thought of a hamburger turned her stomach. This was wrong. It was all wrong. But Jessica had offered to help her.

Ruth pressed her palms into her sandpaper eyelids. What was she thinking? The woman was a stranger. Ruth's own childish and irresponsible behavior struck an even deeper place inside as her stomach tossed and tumbled. She lowered her hands and laid them on her belly. And for the first time since learning of the baby, she held her belly.

The baby.

She'd known about it for two days, but only this moment had it become real. Only in light of this awful mistake did she realize she was going to be a *mother*. This baby, this little boy or girl, depended on her to keep him or her safe. Running away from all the people who kept her safe was not the way to do it. She had to go home. Facing Luke would be painful and terrifying, but it was the right thing to do. The responsible thing. Her life as a carefree teenage girl was over and she had to accept that.

Before Jessica could return, Ruth took twenty-five cents out of her pocketbook and left it on the table. She didn't want Jessica to get in trouble or have to pay for the food herself. She snatched a paper napkin from the holder on the table and a pen from her purse and wrote an apology to the girl.

Several hours and another bus ride later, Ruth found herself sitting on a bench at the Petaluma bus station again. It was much different at night than it had been earlier in the day. She clutched her pocketbook, doing her best to not let it be easily spotted. Nella had told her about a grifter in Petaluma a few months ago. Ruth assumed it was a rare occurrence. But the kinds of men she saw loitering at the depot now made her think otherwise. They drank out of brown paper bags. They were loud and clumsy and foul.

A woman with long, stringy brown hair pulled into a haphazard bun huddled with three children—two boys and a girl. They all appeared to be under the age of five. They were dirty and very, very thin.

Ruth touched her stomach, praying she and her baby would never find themselves in such dire straits. She whispered into the night. "Oh, Mom, how am I going to do this?"

Her mother's voice wove its way into her mind. *"Blessed be the Lord, which hath not left thee this day without a kinsman, that his name may be famous in Israel."*

Ruth caressed her belly and smiled at the memory of her mother's favorite Bible verse. Mom had explained to her that Jesus was their very own kinsman redeemer. That He would always be there to take care of her if she would let Him.

The familiar rumble of a truck drew Ruth's attention. Not knowing what she was about to encounter with Luke made her muscles go tense. Whatever it was though, she deserved it.

The truck rolled to a stop. A street light illuminated Luke's face in the cab. His eyes scanned the unsavory company she'd been keeping for the past hour and a half. She trudged to the truck as he got out and opened the passenger door. She saw no anger in his eyes or the set of his jaw.

"I'm glad you're safe." He took her suitcase from her and put it in the back of the truck.

Ruth got in the truck, her stomach rolling. She watched Luke walk around the front of the vehicle, hoping to decipher what he was thinking. But Luke was hard to read even in the best of times. The way his lips curled down at the corners and his avoidance of eye contact did not help her relax. He opened the squeaky door and climbed into the driver's seat. He put the key in the ignition and brought the engine to life. Ruth waited for him to yell at her, lecture her, shame her—something. Instead, he drove in silence. City lights sped past her window against the night sky. The motion caused her stomach to churn even more, so she leaned her head back against the seat and closed her eyes.

Ruth opened her eyes again. They were on Old Adobe Road, on their way home. She hadn't realized she'd fallen asleep. They neared Grady's house. The porch light illuminated a figure sitting on the steps. Grady.

Without thinking, she reached for Luke's arm. "Please stop, Luke."

"He's fine."

"No, he's not! I can tell."

Luke drove past the house. "There will be plenty of time to talk to him about your little trip tomorrow."

Ruth twisted to look out the back window. "Please stop!" With a heavy sigh, Luke stopped the truck. His dark eyes drilled into hers but she stood her ground. She could not pass by and leave Grady the way he was.

Luke jerked the gear shift into reverse and backed the truck up. He pulled onto the Akins' driveway and parked in front of the house but didn't turn off the engine. "Make it quick."

Ruth climbed down from the cab and ran to Grady. "I saw you from the truck and begged Luke to stop. I'm so sorry I ran away, Grady. I'm so sorry I scared you and worried you and everyone else."

He stood and folded his arms around her. "Scared isn't the word for it." He squeezed her tighter. "Where did you go?"

"It's a long story. Can I please tell you tomorrow? I'm so tired, I just want to go home and go to bed. Would that be okay?"

"It's fine, now that I know you're safe." He kissed her cheek. "I'm so relieved. And I'm so sorry I hurt you and made you run away."

"You didn't make me run away. I made the decision on my own. And it was stupid." She studied him. "What's wrong? Why are you out here? I hope it's not because of me."

"No. I mean, I was scared for you, but my dad kicked me out. I told him about the baby and—and he told me to find somewhere else to live."

"What? Right now?" Ruth peered up at the house. "But where are you supposed to go?"

"I don't know." Grady raked his hand through his hair. "But he said I have to leave tonight. He said I've humiliated him and my mother and that I'm being irresponsible with my future by not letting him give you money to make you go away so I can go on to college and move on."

Ruth held her hand to her chest. "He wants to pay me to go away?" She thought back to the woman and her children at the bus depot. No one paid attention to them. They were invisible. Worthless to those around them. An obstacle to get past on one's way to someplace better. Was that how Mr. Akins saw her? Invisible? Worthless? An obstacle to his son's future?

"It doesn't matter what he wants." He cupped her chin and searched her eyes. "I won't leave you or our baby, Ruth. No matter what he says or does."

Ruth began to cry. "This is awful. Everything is awful, and it's all my fault."

"Let's get going, Ruth." Luke's voice called from behind her.

Grady touched her cheek. "You better go. I'll be okay. I'll talk to you tomorrow and we'll figure things out."

She peered back at Luke. He looked away. She took Grady's hand, tugging him to walk with her. "Come with me."

"What? No!" Grady resisted her grip. "He'd as soon kill me as talk to me."

"What other choice do you have?"

"I can sleep in the pasture behind our house until I figure it out."

"No, you can't. Not with wild animals out at night looking for food. I've heard there have been mountain lion sightings around here." She pulled him toward Luke's truck. "Come with me."

"I'd be safer out there with the coyotes and the mountain lions than going anywhere near him right now."

But Ruth refused to let loose. They reached the truck, and Ruth drew in a deep breath. "Luke, Grady needs our help."

Luke's dark eyes narrowed, shadowed by his black hat. Surrounded by the night and illuminated by the yellow porch light, he was particularly menacing. "What that boy needs, I'd be more than happy to give him—but it's not help."

Ruth pressed her case. "Luke, please. His father kicked him out."

Luke studied Grady. "Didn't you say your father is a deacon at your church?"

Grady's Adam's bobbed twice. "Yes, sir. He is."

Luke stared through the windshield in front of him and muttered something Ruth couldn't understand. He motioned to the back of the truck with his thumb. "Get your stuff and get in."

Grady exchanged a bewildered look with Ruth. "Actually, it's just me." He shrugged. "My dad won't let me in to get any clothes."

Ruth touched his shoulder. "He locked you out of the house? Without your things?"

Luke muttered again and got out of the truck. He slammed the door and pushed past both of them, his boots clomp-clomping against the brick-paved walkway leading to the Akins' front door. He landed three solid knocks on the door and waited. Ruth and Grady watched warily from a few feet back.

The door opened and Grady's father appeared. The well-dressed man scrutinized Luke. "I don't have anything to say to you, Mr. Morgan."

"That's fine. I don't have anything to say to you either." Luke pointed behind him with his thumb. "Your boy needs some clothes."

Mr. Akins crossed his arms. "I told Grady he doesn't live here anymore."

Luke stepped toward the man. His hands formed fists at his sides. Ruth held her breath and squeezed Grady's hand.

"All the more reason for him to get his clothes." Luke's tone sent chills down Ruth's back.

"Look, Morgan, this is none of your concern. Why don't you go on and take that girl home and try to gain some control over her?"

Luke grabbed the man by his collar. He slammed him against the doorframe. Mr. Akins' eyes bulged. From inside the house, Mrs. Akins shrieked. Ruth's hands flew to her mouth, stifling a scream. Grady started forward, but she clutched his shirt, holding him back.

"Her name is Ruth." Luke's voice dropped an octave that nearly made the ground quake. "And that boy of yours is the father of her child, which definitely makes this my concern."

Luke released one hand and jabbed at Mr. Akins' chest, still clutching the man's shirt collar with the other. "I have had a very long day, I'm tired, and I am plumb out of patience. So I am asking you one more time, politely, to let your boy get his things. And trust me, Mr. Akins, you don't want to see my impolite side."

Grady squeezed Ruth's hand. He whispered, "He won't really hurt him, will he?"

Ruth swallowed hard. She didn't know the answer to that.

Grady's father shoved Luke away from him. "Fine. Get on with it, and get off my property."

Luke stared at Mr. Akins and he motioned for Grady to come forward, then followed Grady into the house. Mr. Akins tossed her a withering look and disappeared inside as well. Ruth hugged her arms around herself. Her knees trembled. She wouldn't breathe easily until both Grady and Luke came back out of the house with no one getting hurt.

Ruth paced the walkway. A curtain moved behind one of the windows. Ruth froze at the sight of Grady's mother watching her. Elaine Akins' gaze traveled from Ruth's face to her stomach. It paused there for a moment before traveling back up to meet Ruth's eyes. Elaine brushed her fingers across her cheeks and then disappeared. The curtain fell back into place.

Why was Mrs. Akins crying? Because she wouldn't know her grandchild, or because she also believed Ruth had destroyed Grady? Ruth began to pace again. Luke was helping Grady. This was a good thing, right? But worry niggled at the back of her brain. What was Luke going to do with Grady once they came out of the house? Where would he take him? Everything was out of control, everyone was fighting, she was losing her friends, her whole life was ruined. All because of one mistake.

As her thoughts tumbled, the trees around her began to spin. Her stomach roiled. She ran to a nearby bush, holding her arms out to steady herself. She bent over as the nausea overwhelmed her.

Ruth coughed and drew in a deep breath, praying the sickness had passed. A warm, firm hand settled on her shoulder. She looked up at Luke.

His brows knitted together and tilted upward. "Do you need a few minutes before we go?"

Fighting back tears, Ruth shook her head. "No. I want to go home."

She let him guide her back to the truck. Grady sat in the truck bed with a suitcase by his side. He stared at her, wide-eyed. Luke helped her into the truck and closed her door. They rode in silence. Ruth didn't dare speak.

A couple of miles down the road, Ruth could not stand the quiet anymore. "Where are you going to take Grady?"

"Home."

"Whose home?"

"Ours."

TWENTY-ONE

Luke checked the rearview mirror. Once again, Grady sat on the wheel well, head hung down and shoulders slumped. The kid looked lost. And scared. He bristled at the thought of Grady's father and his arrogance. Memories of the hypocritical church members in his past flashed by. He could have called out any number of sins he'd seen committed by those people back then. But the guilt and shame of what he'd done rendered him mute, not to mention terrified.

At least his own parents had stood by him. Telling them about Sadie and the baby had been the worst experience of his life to that point. He remembered how his knees shook and his voice cracked. But they showed him love and forgiveness and support. That should have been enough to get him through it. But the people in church, that bunch of self-righteous, judgmental—

"What did you say?" Ruth stared at him.

"What?"

"You were mumbling."

Luke returned his attention to the road ahead and adjusted his hat on his head. "I was thinking about Grady's father. Being a deacon and all."

"I know." Ruth sighed. "It's all my fault."

"No. No, it isn't. That man is a hypocrite. It has nothing to do with you."

"But if I hadn't gotten pregnant—"

"Cornell Akins would still be a hypocrite."

Ruth shrank back. In the rearview mirror, he could see he'd gotten Grady's attention as well. He didn't care. Everything was spinning out of control around him.

Luke steered his old truck off Old Adobe Road and started down the driveway. The truck's headlights illuminated the giant oak tree in the front yard, casting haunting shadows on the house. Ruckus bounded down the porch steps to greet them. Luke got out of the truck and went around to help Ruth down. Grady beat him to it. He watched Grady support Ruth's elbow while assisting her. Ruth started to lead Grady toward the house.

Luke cleared his throat.

The two paused and slowly turned back to look at him.

He wagged his thumb in the direction of the barn. "It's warm enough outside. He can sleep in there."

Ruth stepped forward. "Luke, it's a barn."

Luke held up his hand. "And it's a far bit more than what he had fifteen minutes ago." He begrudgingly acknowledged Grady. "If it gets cold, there are horse blankets. And if you need to use the bathroom—find a bush."

Ruth stomped her foot. "That's awful!"

Luke raised a brow at her.

She stepped back and rubbed Grady's arm. "Can he at least come in for breakfast in the morning?"

Luke focused his attention on the barn. Could the kid eat what the horses ate? He stalked past them and growled, "Fine." At the kitchen door he looked back and saw Ruth in Grady's arms. "Ruth!"

The girl nearly jumped out of her skin. Grady scurried two paces away from her, dust kicking up around his feet.

Luke ignored Grady, speaking only to Ruth. "If I have to come over there and get you, I will lose what little hospitality I'm feeling at the moment."

Ruth whispered in Grady's ear. Luke bit back another threat. He went inside, letting the screen door bounce loudly against the doorframe. He dropped his keys on the table. The loud clank echoed through the room.

The screen door creaked open. Ruth couldn't seem to settle her gaze on anything. Sixteen years old. Not even out of high school. Pregnant. What was she going to do now? What was he going to do? Deep down, he wanted to draw her into his arms and hold her and ease her fears. Protect her from the onslaught of pain and humiliation that was headed her way. But would she let him? Or would she push him away and withdraw to the point that he couldn't help her at all? At least she was home. The past eight hours had been a living nightmare. When he'd gotten the phone call from her at the bus station, he'd nearly fallen to his knees.

He opened the ice box. "You want some milk?"

"Sure."

What on earth was he supposed to say to her? He'd give anything if Emma was here right now to help them both through this. Luke retrieved the pitcher of milk from the ice box and picked up two glasses on the counter. He sat at the table and poured them each a glass.

Ruth pulled out a chair and sank onto the seat. He took a long sip from his glass. Ruth didn't seem interested in hers.

"So, uh..." He rubbed at the back of his neck. "I guess we've got some pretty important things to talk about."

"I suppose so." She stared at her hands in her lap.

"We can talk about the running away later. I think you understand what a mistake that was. And I trust you'll never do it again."

"I won't." Ruth slumped in her chair and picked at a hangnail. "I have nowhere to go."

Luke had no idea where to go from here. Ruth had never been a shrinking violet. She'd never had trouble speaking her mind, even arguing with him. But now she seemed so small and fragile, so frightened, looking for all the world like Kate when she was ten years old and got caught hiding a feral kitten in her bedroom.

"I guess you're ashamed, too, huh?" Ruth spoke quietly. "Like Grady's dad."

The muscles in his neck tensed. "I am nothing like Grady's dad." He rubbed his tired, burning eyes. "Ashamed isn't the right word. I'm disappointed."

Her brow pinched. Her lower lip began to quiver.

Luke leaned forward, linking his fingers together on the table. "I'm disappointed because of how this will change your life. How it will limit what you can do."

Ruth didn't speak again for a long moment. Tears slipped down her cheeks. "Would Mom be ashamed?"

Luke did something at that moment he hadn't done once since Ruth had come to him. He took her hand in his and held it tightly.

He stared into her green eyes. His heart jolted at the resemblance she held to his sister. "Your mother was proud of you. I can tell you without a doubt in my mind that there is nothing you could ever do to make her ashamed of you."

He didn't expect the way she came to him, practically crawling onto his lap, and cried against his shoulder. Her frame shook with her sobs. For a moment he sat, stunned, unsure what to do. But he recognized the protective urge that overcame him. He put his arms around her. Memories of Sadie flooded.

He whispered to Ruth the same words he'd whispered to Sadie. "It will be all right. I'll take care of you. We'll get through this together." He reached for the dishtowel on the table and handed it to her to wipe her eyes.

Ruth pulled back, sniffling, hiccuping, and wiping her eyes. "I'm so worried about Grady. Couldn't he sleep in here? Please? He could sleep on the couch or—"

"No." Luke guided her off his lap, stood, and took the milk glasses to the sink. "Just because I gave him a place to sleep tonight doesn't mean I'm ready to be in the same room with him."

"Why did you bring him here then? Why did you help him?"

"Because no one deserves to be treated the way his father treated him." He pointed his finger at her. "That doesn't mean I'm okay with that boy or what he did to you."

Ruth's eyes dropped to the floor. Her cheeks blazed pink. Luke grimaced, regretting his words. How was he going to make it through the next several months, not doing or saying the wrong thing every time he turned around?

Ruth sighed. "I think I'll go to bed now."

Luke leaned back against the counter, watching her retreat into the hallway and disappear. He spoke to the empty room. "Good night, Ruth."

Sleep was elusive for Luke, so as sunrise finally cast its customary golden warmth over the ranch and streamed through the kitchen window, he kept an eye on the sizzling bacon and eggs. Everything seemed the same. But everything was different. Punctuating that thought, the kitchen door opened. He glanced back at Ruth and Grady. Grady ducked his head as if anticipating a beating.

Luke chose to focus on the bacon.

Ruth stepped forward. "Grady milked Verna."

Luke flipped over a strip of the sizzling meat in the pan.

"And he chased a coyote away from the chickens last night."

Luke flipped the bacon over again. "I thought I heard a commotion out there." He glared at Grady. "Guess it wasn't what I'd hoped."

Ruth joined him at the stove. "Breakfast smells really good. Doesn't it smell good, Grady?"

Grady mumbled his agreement.

Luke pulled the bacon from the pan and put it in a dish. "Get the plates, Ruth."

"Sure. And I'm sure Grady won't mind pouring the coffee."

Grady bumped into a chair. It skidded against the wood floor, making an awful racket.

Luke stared at him. The boy's gaze flitted from Luke to the chair. Good. Luke didn't want the kid feeling too comfortable here.

Luke watched the two work together. Mostly he watched the way Grady treated Ruth. Listened to the gentle way he spoke to her.

Could it be possible Grady loved Ruth? Or was this all an act so he had somewhere to sleep and food to eat while he figured out how to get out of town? Just how much pressure would it take for him to fold and go back to his parents? Go to Stanford and forget about Ruth and their child?

The three of them sat down to eat. Ruth and Grady picked at their food. Luke had a hard time choking down his breakfast with Grady at the table. A knock came at the door. Thankful for an interruption, Luke got up to answer.

Two men wearing suits and slicked back hair smiled at him. The tall, thin one spoke first. "Mr. Morgan, my name is Olson Tate, and my friend here is Carl Mullen."

Luke acknowledged the shorter, pudgy man with a nod.

"We are on the deacon board at the Christian church downtown. May we have a word with you?"

Hesitant but curious, Luke moved aside, allowing the two men entry. "I'm sure you know Grady Akins, his father is also a deacon at your church. And this is my niece, Ruth."

The men's eyes widened in tandem. Luke may not want Grady in his house, but seeing how his presence startled these men made his morning a little brighter.

The tall one coughed once. "Yes, yes, we know them both."

Carl stepped forward. "We're wondering, Mr. Morgan, if we might have a word with you?" He tossed a look in the direction of the kids. "Alone."

Their slippery demeanor, their association with Cornell Akins, and the way they showed up at his door unannounced three days after Ruth found out she was pregnant made Luke feel less than hospitable. But he wasn't about to let these two escape before finding out exactly what business they thought they had here.

"Well, as you can see, we're sitting down for breakfast. If you'd like to wait in the living room for us to finish, I'll be in to talk with you when we're done."

The two men glanced at each other. Olson gave a quick nod. "Yes, yes, of course. We should have given more thought as to the time of day. We'll wait for you. I assume it's around that corner?"

"Yes." Luke held out his hand, motioning the correct direction.

The men left the room, and Luke took his seat at the table again.

Ruth stared at him. "You just sent two deacons to wait for you while you eat breakfast?"

He took a swig of coffee. "I sent two men who showed up at my house unannounced, expecting me to drop everything for them, into the living room to wait for me, yes."

Grady pushed his plate away. A pallor washed over his face. Ruth set her fork down.

Luke's appetite, however, had returned. He finished his eggs and bacon, drank the rest of his coffee, and stood. "You two clean up the dishes while I go see what these guys want." He ambled into the living room, suppressing a grin at the annoyed arch of Olson's brow and the firm line drawn on Carl's mouth. He sat in his chair across from where they were on the sofa.

Luke crossed an ankle over his knee. "What can I do for you?"

Olson scooted forward on the sofa. "I assume, Mr. Morgan, that you know, uh, know of your niece's...condition."

Luke's stomach clenched. He kept an eye on Carl, who fidgeted with his tie. "You assume correctly."

Olson pulled a handkerchief from his pocket and mopped his substantial forehead. "Mr. Morgan, we would like to do our part in helping Ruth overcome this unfortunate situation, reconcile her with her church family, and aid in guiding her back into a right relationship with God."

Luke's jaw twitched. He bit back the first response that came to him. He wanted them to spell it out. Give them enough rope to properly hang themselves. "I appreciate your concern. What did you have in mind?"

"We would like to hold a special service." Carl spoke now. Luke assumed his tone was meant to reflect the weight of this important discussion. "One that would provide Ruth with the opportunity to be reconciled, as Olson said, with the church and with God."

A slow boil of anger bubbled in Luke's veins. He bit the inside of his cheek. "And what exactly would take place at this service?"

"God's Word speaks to us of confessing our sins to one another. We will give her the chance, in the safe and loving environment of the church, to confess her sins."

Luke leaned forward, setting his elbows on his knees. "I guess that makes sense." The pair smiled and sat up straighter, adjusting their ties. It sickened him how pleased they were with themselves. "So, I assume this would include Grady?"

The two seemed surprised by the suggestion. But of course, they would be. The last thing they'd want to do was humiliate their fellow deacon, Grady's father.

"Oh, well." Olson shrugged. "I suppose it could."

"I mean, it only makes sense." Luke held out his hand. "The girl didn't exactly get pregnant by herself, right? If Ruth needs to confess, then surely Grady does, too. So, tell me, who else is on the list? Just so I know where in line Ruth will be."

The men offered blank stares. Olson leaned in. "I'm sorry, I don't understand. List?"

Luke spread his hands. "I assume you're visiting a whole lot of people about this today. I mean, if you're having some kind of special service for folks to confess their sins to the brothers, there must be a list." He fell back in his seat and laughed. "I mean, it's not like you'd single out one terrified young girl whose entire future has been upended for such a special event, right?"

The men's shoulders slumped a bit.

Luke stood. This little meeting was over. "Before you leave—and you are leaving—let me ask you, does J.D. know about this little visit?"

"We didn't see the need to bother Pastor Hudgins with this. Not until we had the details worked out."

"I see. Well, don't worry yourselves about that. I'll be sure and give him the details myself."

At their surprised looks, Luke added, "Oh, yes, I know J.D. We're real close, actually. I'm sure he will find this all very interesting." Luke went to the front door and opened it. The men took his not-so-subtle hint and left. Luke stood at the door, watching them leave.

"Luke?"

Ruth and Grady entered the living room. Unshed tears glossed Ruth's eyes. Grady looked downright green. Luke wondered if the kid might get sick all over his floor.

"Thank you." Ruth's green eyes were big as shooter marbles. "Thank you so much for not making me do what those men wanted." She shook her head, her auburn hair billowed around her face. "I can't imagine standing in front of all those people and—"

Grady held her. "It's okay, Ruthie. Luke would never let them do that to you. And neither would I."

So the boy really did consider himself responsible for her. Though it made a slight impression, Luke wasn't ready to trust that Grady wouldn't run off when things really heated up. And the kid had no idea how much heat was headed his way.

TWENTY-TWO

The three letters on Emma's desk drew her attention once again. She closed her eyes and took a long cool sip of water. The small cabin closed in on her. This couldn't be happening.

She'd managed to put the first letter out of her mind when it arrived three months ago. The second was delivered one month later. And now this one today. She worried her lower lip. Jasper was stepping up his threats. Thinking she could ignore him and still live in a house he owned had been foolish. Unable to stand the glare of Jasper's handwriting, Emma snatched up her pocketbook and left.

Beads of sweat trickled down her back as she walked. Only the orange California Poppies on the dusty road's edge seemed to thrive under the flaming noon sun. A lizard peeked its head out from an oleander bush, only to dart back under the protective shade. Even reptiles hid from the heat on days like this.

Coming to California had seemed like the perfect solution earlier in the year. A way to escape Jasper's constant scrutiny while she tried to figure out what to do. How ridiculous it seemed now that she'd been confused in the first place. How had he so easily manipulated her? Luke would never treat a woman that way.

She pumped her legs faster, as if she could outrun memories of Luke. His cutting words. His infuriating smugness. His kiss. His apology. Emma shook the memories loose until she found herself on Nella's doorstep. She rang the doorbell and waited. Momentarily Nella's bright smile appeared as always. The one constant Emma could rely on. Tears blurred her vision.

"Emma! What a delightful surprise." Nella pushed the screen door open and stepped aside. "Come in, come— Good heavens, cherí, what's wrong?"

Emma held her arms out to her sides and let them drop. "I wish I knew!"

"Well, let's sit down and see if we can't figure it out together. Have you had dinner?"

"Oh! I didn't even think of the time. I'm so sorry."

"Don't be." The woman's dark brows drew together. "I've never seen a beautiful young woman cryin' who didn't have reason to. Have a seat."

Emma slumped on the sofa.

"Now." Nella patted Emma's knee. "Are you hungry, honey?"

Emma shook her head. "I can't even think of eating right now. Thank you, though."

Nella eyed her as she perched on a chair. "All right then. Tell me what's botherin' you."

Could it be that simple? Simply blurt it out? No. She couldn't. Emma took the letters from her pocket and held them out.

"What's this?" Nella took the envelopes.

"Possibly the end of the most peaceful life I've ever had."

Emma waited for Nella to read the letters. She tried to decipher the woman's expression, but it never changed. Emma bit a fingernail.

Nella folded the last letter and slipped it into its envelope. She handed them back to Emma. "Well, he sounds like a very determined man."

Emma's shoulders sagged. "What am I going to do?"

"I can tell you one thing. If he's serious about talkin' to Luke, I suggest you beat him to it."

Emma stood and paced. "How do I do that? How do I work this mess into a conversation?"

Nella *tsk-tsked*. A grin tugged at her lips.

Emma propped her hands on her hips. "What on earth is there to smile about?"

"Two men vyin' for your affections. I'm sorry, but who would have guessed our sweet, demure Emma Darby could be a woman of such scandal?"

"I'm glad you find it so amusing." Emma sat on the couch again. "I don't think Luke is vying for anything from me." She picked at a loose thread on her skirt. "Not anymore, anyway. He hasn't spoken to me since the day Ruth ran away. That was nearly three weeks ago."

"You seem quite bothered by that particular thought."

The teasing in Nella's voice could not be mistaken. Emma's ears burned. Heat rose up the back of her neck into her cheeks.

"Oh, now, sweetheart." Nella rose. "You need to take your life back into your own hands." She reached and grasped invisible air in her fist.

"How do I do that?"

Nella poked her index finger in Emma's direction. "For starters, you move out of that shack Jasper's got you livin' in."

Emma lifted her chin. "*He* doesn't have me living there."

"Oh, doesn't he?"

Emma had no answer.

"You will move in here. With me." Nella gave a decisive nod. "Until you can find another place that suits you better."

Emma stared at her. "I— I—"

"I have an extra room." Nella continued as if not hearing Emma's attempt at speech. "If you ain't livin' in that place, and you get your bearings straight with both of those men, then Jasper will have no power over you anymore."

Ruth got out of the truck and closed the door. She checked her pocketbook to be sure she had the money Luke had given her earlier.

"I'll be over at the feed store." Luke rubbed his neck. "Are you sure you'll be okay?"

"Luke, I've been doing the grocery shopping ever since I came to live with you."

Luke stared down the street. "I know, but—"

Ruth held out her arms. "But nothing. I'm actually feeling pretty good today, and I've been cooped up in the house for so long, I'm going stir crazy. I'll meet you back here at the truck in twenty-five minutes."

"Fine. But if you need anything—"

"You're at the feed store. I know, I know. I'll see you later." She waved vaguely in his direction and headed toward the grocery store entrance.

Honestly, he treated her like an invalid lately. Sure, she'd been awful sick for a while, but it hadn't changed any— She caught herself mid-thought. It had changed things. This wasn't a bad cold or influenza. What caused her illness had, in fact, changed everything. She hadn't been able to go back to school, and shame prevented her from attending church. Especially after those men had come to the house three weeks ago. She'd talked to Olivia last week and apologized for her behavior. Liv had forgiven her, but still, things were different between them. Would she ever have her best friend back?

Pushing such thoughts aside, a skill she was becoming quite adept at, Ruth fixed her attention on the store's large window decorated with weekly sales ads. Once inside, familiar sounds met her. Metal shopping cart wheels squeaked against the worn linoleum floor. The *ching-ching* of registers and good-natured chatter of neighbors. She picked a cart and steered it toward the first aisle.

Paying close attention to prices, Ruth picked up only necessary items. Luke had given her two dollars and trusted her not to waste it. After putting most of the items in the cart, she noticed canned coconut on sale for ten cents. A coconut cake sounded divine. Surely Luke wouldn't mind one little treat. Especially if it meant coconut cake for dessert. She picked up a can and dropped it into the cart.

"Soap flakes," she mumbled to herself. "Don't forget the soap flakes."

A baby's cry startled her as she entered the aisle that housed the soap. Ruth stopped short. A young woman held a baby in one arm while grabbing at the sleeve of a squirming toddler with her other hand. Ruth stared at the scene. The noises of a busy grocery store faded away. Only crackling music struggling through old speakers echoed in her ears.

"Oh, hello." The woman blew a strand of hair away from her eyes. "I'm sorry, are we in your way?" She pulled the toddler to the side of the aisle.

Ruth gripped the shopping cart tighter. "No, not at all."

The exasperated mother tilted her head to one side. "Are you okay?"

Ruth mentally shook herself. The woman must think she was whacky. "Um, how old is your baby?"

The woman smiled down at the baby in her arm. "She's two months old today."

Ruth stood still, mesmerized by the tiny little person with a perfect little button nose, pink heart-shaped mouth, dainty ears, and bald head. The toddler at the woman's side started to whine and stomp his feet. The more his mother tried to control him, the more uncontrollable he became.

The sound of giggling reached Ruth's ears from behind. She spun around. Four girls from school huddled together, peeking at her not so subtly.

"Maybe she should offer to babysit. You know, for practice." Mary Dennison clearly did not understand the concept of whispering, as her words carried to Ruth.

A flush raced over Ruth's body. Did everyone in the store know her secret? Was everyone staring at her? She couldn't move.

Melinda Sharnell sauntered over. "Hi, Ruth." Melinda patted her bleached hair in its stylish finger wave cut. Melinda fancied herself a Jean Harlow lookalike, even if no one else agreed. Her squeaky clean oxfords and fitted gray dress grated on Ruth's nerves. Melinda always had to look perfect. Her family was rich, and she took every opportunity to let struggling families know it. Melinda's face drooped into a phony pout. "How are you feeling these days?"

Ruth refused to let the hateful girl see her tears. "I'm fine."

Melinda smiled. She leaned down and seemed to search Ruth's frame. Ruth bent to see what she was looking at. Was the pocket on her skirt torn? Did she have a stain? She did not need one more thing to be humiliated about.

"Oh, I'm sorry!" The girl crossed her arms and cocked her hip. "I thought for sure you'd have a wedding ring by now. Is Grady having second thoughts?"

Numb with fear and shame, Ruth opened her mouth but found no words.

"You know"—Melinda leaned in closer—"my sister has a friend who got herself in trouble, like you. And she just had it taken care of."

Ruth stared at Melinda, confused.

The awful girl's painted pink lips spread into a sarcastic sneer. "See you around, Ruth." Melinda rejoined her friends. Their giggles resumed as they sashayed away.

Panic buzzed like electricity through Ruth's body. Everything around her blurred except those evil girls and their laughter. She stumbled blindly for the front doors.

"Don't you want your groceries, hon?" the young mother called after Ruth.

Ruth didn't slow down. A store clerk yelled that she couldn't leave a cart full of groceries sitting in the middle of the store. Ruth pushed the large glass door open and ran outside to Luke's truck. He wasn't back yet. She looked down the street to the feed store. She didn't see him. Ruth climbed inside the cab and pulled the door shut. She sank down in the seat so no one could see her.

Why had she left the house? No wonder Luke worried about her. He probably knew that people were saying nasty things about her and laughing behind her back. She pulled in deep breaths to ease the pressure in her chest. It was no use. Violent sobs shook her shoulders.

At long last the vehicle rocked from Luke loading his purchases in the bed of the truck. Luke opened his door and got in behind the wheel. "Ruth, where are the grocer— Ruth?" The warmth of his hand on hers shattered her aching loneliness.

She buried her head in his chest and cried.

Luke wrapped his arm around her. "What happened? Are you hurt?" He pulled up his shirt tail and dabbed at her eyes.

Ruth shook her head and burrowed again. He let her cry a minute longer. She suspected because he didn't know what else to do with her.

"You're gonna have to tell me what's going on here."

Ruth sat up straight again, Then the hiccups started. She felt like a five-year-old. But she was a teenager. A teenager about to have a baby. She spoke as clearly as she could through involuntary gasps. "I had the groceries—*hic*. I even got—*hic*—a can of coconut on sale so I could make a—*hic*—a coconut cake. And I saw this woman with—*hic*—her baby. And she had a little boy, too. And the baby was so cute—*hic*—but the boy was throwing a tantrum and—and— all I could do was stare at them. I could only—*hic*—think, that's going to be me soon. And then some girls from school were—*hic*— whispering and laughing—*hic*—at me. And that horrid, hateful Melinda! She said such ugly things. I—I couldn't— All I could do was run. And you weren't here. And—and it was awful!"

Luke stared out the window of the truck, toward the grocery store, his dark eyes squinting. The muscles in his jaw flexed. Ruth started to regret telling him everything. He wouldn't go in there and yell at those girls, would he? That would make it all worse.

He sighed a heavy sigh and gave her a sideways look. Ruth held her breath. His eyes sparked. "I sure would have loved some coconut cake."

For a moment, Ruth thought he had missed every word she'd spoken. Maybe he'd gone temporarily deaf. But then his eyes softened and a grin tugged at his lips. She didn't know whether to scream, hit him, laugh, or cry. The sadness in his eyes though... He was trying to help the only way he knew how.

Ruth crumpled against him again. "You're really bad at this."

He chuckled softly. "I know. I'm sorry."

"It's okay."

Luke started the truck. "I'll take you home. We'll send Grady back for the groceries."

Ruth's heart weighed so heavy in her chest, her ribs didn't feel strong enough to hold it up. She rested her hand on her stomach and caressed it. It was so strange to her, how often she would catch herself doing this. How did that come so naturally? How did she go from not being able to look at herself in the mirror to embracing her growing belly?

Thankfully, Luke didn't try to make conversation. Sometimes his silence could be maddening, other times comforting. Like now. She knew he felt bad for her. But he couldn't change anything. All he could do was be there. And she knew he was. Did he know how much that meant to her?

She stared out the passenger side window. The beauty of wild grape vines and blackberry bushes was lost on her today. She'd felt so good earlier, so happy to get out of the house and feel useful.

Ruth reached for Luke's arm on the steering wheel. "I'll get out here. I'd like to go see Miss Darby."

A frown shadowed his eyes. "Uninvited?"

"Please, Luke. She doesn't care about an invitation. I need to see her. I need to talk to her. I haven't seen her since..."

Luke didn't take his eyes off the road. He reached for his hat and shifted it on his head.

Ruth touched his hand. "I really need to see her."

"All right." He pulled to the side of the road. "Be home in two hours."

Ruth's heart buoyed with the hope of seeing her teacher. "I will. I promise."

Luke steered the truck to the edge of Emma's short driveway. He drove away before she even had a chance to reach the porch. She considered his unease at letting her visit Miss Darby. Ruth hadn't asked him about the day her teacher told him she was going to have a baby. She knew they had searched for her together the day she ran away, but clearly, they weren't getting along. And it was her fault.

She trudged up the porch steps. Something was different. The potted flowers that normally brightened the porch were gone and the floor was littered with pine needles. Miss Darby swept this porch every day. Ruth knocked on the door and gazed across the quiet front yard while waiting for an answer. When none came, she moved to a window. The pretty, hand-sewn yellow curtains were gone. She cupped her hands around her eyes and peered inside.

The cabin was empty. She scanned the yard and field beyond. No, no, no. this couldn't be happening. She ran down the porch steps and around the back of the home, calling for Miss Darby.

"She moved, Ruthie!" Ben, the next to youngest of Olivia's brothers, batted a large rock with a stick as he shuffled along the road.

She caught up to him. "What do you mean she moved? Where to?"

"She lives over at Nella's now." His chest puffed up. "I helped her move her stuff. And Nella gave me cookies and lemonade and a whole quarter for helpin'."

Ruth blew out a relieved breath, falling into step with the boy. "What did you spend your quarter on?"

"Haven't spent it yet. I hid it so no one would find it till I figure what I want."

Ruth rustled his hair. "Sounds like a good plan."

"You goin' over to Miss Nella's to see Miss Emma?"

Luke's truck was out of sight, so she couldn't flag him back down and ask permission. Nella's house was quite a walk from here. But Nella had a telephone. Ruth could call Luke when she got there and explain.

"Yes. I think I will go see her."

"Can I go with you? I think Miss Nella might need to get rid of some more cookies."

Laughing, Ruth draped her arm around the boy's thin shoulders. "I would love the company. But does Olivia know you're out and about?"

"Yeah. She just said be home for dinner." Frowning, he squinted up at Ruth. "She's awful grumpy lately."

"Oh?"

"She gets real bossy. She don't take us to the river no more to swim. She complains about doin' the laundry and the cleanin' and cookin' and whatnot."

Ruth thought on Ben's description of Olivia's behavior.

"She was a lot happier when you came around all the time. Why'd you stop comin' over?"

Blinking at the pointed question, Ruth scrambled for an answer. "Oh, you know, I've been real busy."

"Livvy says you're gonna have a baby."

Ruth sucked in a breath and stopped walking. "She told you that?"

"Nah. She doesn't tell me nothin'. I heard her tell my dad."

Would Mr. Hawkins allow Olivia to spend time with Ruth now, even if she wanted to?

Ben dropped his rock on the ground and gave it a good whack with his stick. The rock sailed through the air then landed and wobbled to a resting place. He scratched his head. "Don't'cha gotta have a husband to get a baby?"

"Oh— I— It's not, um—"

"Hey! Look!" Ben pointed ahead of them. "A deer!" He beamed up at Ruth. "My dad shot himself a deer last week, and we've been eatin' on it ever since."

Ruth saw her chance to change the subject and took advantage of it, asking what Olivia had made with the deer meat. After that, Ben seemed to forget his question.

TWENTY-THREE

Emma swept a broom across Nella's porch for the third time. She couldn't focus on anyone or anything today. At least sweeping didn't result in an extra half cup of sugar in the lemonade or a burnt batch of cookies. She crinkled her nose at the charred smell still drifting from inside the kitchen.

The screen door opened with a lazy creak. Nella stepped out, fanning herself with a magazine. "Child, what are you doin' out here in this dreadful heat?"

"I can't sit still." Emma leaned the broom against the house. "I'm so worried. About Luke. About Ruth. About Jasper's reaction to my letter. He hasn't answered, and that's not a good sign. I don't know what to do with myself."

"There's nothin' that man can do to you. As for Luke, I've told you what you need to do. And there's nothin' stoppin' you from goin' to visit Ruth."

"I don't know." Emma dabbed at her forehead with the back of her hand.

"Miss Darby?'

The sight of Ruth chased away all momentary worries. Emma rushed down the porch steps and pulled the girl into a hug. "Oh, it's so good to see you."

"It's good to see you too. I've missed you." Ruth's brow pinched. "I went to your house but it was empty. I thought you had left town."

"Oh, I am so sorry. I should have sent word to you." She touched Ruth's shoulder. "I would never leave without telling you. I decided living in the cabin didn't feel right anymore. I'm going to stay with Nella until I can find my own place."

"I don't understand. I thought Luke got it all fixed up for you."

Longing simmered in Emma's chest. She wanted to ask how he was. But if he was interested in talking with her, he wouldn't have avoided her these last three weeks. Instead she mustered a smile, draped her arm around the girl, and guided her to the porch. "Why don't you join Nella and me for some iced tea?" She tousled Ben's hair. "As for you, Mr. Hawkins, I bet Miss Nella has some extra cookies."

The boy's head bobbed up and down, dirty blond hair falling in his eyes. "Okay!"

Ruth and Ben followed Emma inside to the kitchen, where Emma placed some cookies in a sack. "You go home and share these with your brothers, all right?"

"I will." Ben snatched the sack. "Thanks!" He ran outside, the screen door slapping shut behind him.

The ceiling fan in Nella's living room did little to alleviate the stifling heat, but the movement of air was better than nothing at all. Nella carried a tray holding a pitcher of sweet tea, glasses, and a plate of icebox cookies into the living room. Her brown skin glowed from perspiration. She put the tray on the coffee table and planted a kiss on the top of Ruth's head. "It's wonderful to see your sweet face. You two have a nice visit."

Emma sat forward in her chair. "Aren't you staying to visit with Ruth?"

"I have some things to do in the kitchen. I have a feeling you girls need a nice little chat." She pointed to Ruth. "But don't you forget to give me a hug before you leave."

Ruth made the motion of an X over her heart. "I won't."

Emma wrung her hands, her mind racing. She hadn't spoken to the girl since the day Ruth asked her to tell Luke about the baby.

And of course, it wasn't possible for Ruth to return to school. Sadly, word had gotten out already. Emma blamed the nurse at the doctor's office. She knew of at least one person who had heard the news from her. Emma hoped the hateful things being said about Ruth had not reached her.

She poured iced tea into the glasses. "How are you feeling?"

Ruth took a bite of a cookie and seemed to ponder the question. "I'm not as sick as I was before. I guess that's normal."

"Yes. I think it is."

Only the lopsided whirring of the ceiling fan disrupted the silence between them. Emma sipped more tea to moisten her dry throat. "How is Grady?"

"About as well as I am, I suppose." Ruth set her cookie back on her napkin. "He's staying at our place."

Emma nearly spewed tea all over herself. She patted her mouth with a napkin. "He's living with you? You and Luke?"

"Kind of. Grady's father kicked him out of the house. He wouldn't even let Grady in to get his clothes. Luke almost got into a fight with him. He made Mr. Akins let Grady get his things. Then, when Luke realized Grady had nowhere to go, he brought him home with us." Ruth frowned. "But he makes him sleep in the barn."

An unladylike spurt of laughter rushed past Emma's lips. "I'm sorry. I shouldn't laugh. It's terrible Grady's father would do such a thing."

Ruth grinned and bit her lip. As quickly as the grin showed itself, her countenance clouded. "Some men came to the house."

The tremor in Ruth's voice alarmed Emma. "What men?"

"They were from the church. They wanted me to—to get up in front of the church and...confess."

Emma stared at Ruth in stunned silence.

"Luke won't let it happen." Ruth sipped her tea. "In fact, he asked them for a list of all the other people who would be doing the same."

This time Emma managed to stifle her amusement. She could imagine the scene. "He is always going to protect you, Ruth. No matter what."

Darlene Wells

"I know that now. I'm worried about Grady though. I'm not sure what Luke has planned for him. I have a feeling it won't be much more pleasant than if Grady had stayed at home with his father. Luke pushes Grady so hard." Ruth fidgeted with her skirt, picking at invisible lint. She seemed to be avoiding eye contact.

"Ruth? Is there something else?"

Ruth peeked at her through her lashes. "I saw some girls from school today at the grocery store."

Emma caressed her back. "Tell me what happened."

"I was actually feeling pretty good for once. But then— Melinda Sharnell was there with her friends."

Emma fought the motherly instinct to track down the spoiled Miss Melinda Sharnell. She knew the girl all too well to think she had been anything but cruel.

Ruth touched her ring finger. "She made fun of me because Grady hasn't asked me to marry him."

To be honest, Emma had wondered more than once about the subject. "I'm sure he's simply trying to get his bearings."

"But what if he isn't? I mean, it's been weeks since I told him about the baby. What if he doesn't want to marry me? I don't want to force him because of the baby and have him hate me for the rest of his life."

"Grady is not going to hate you. He loves you."

Ruth's focus fixed on her shoes. "Melinda said something else. Something I didn't understand."

"What was that?"

"She said she knew someone—a girl like me." Ruth's brow creased. "She said the girl had it 'taken care of.'"

Emma suppressed her shock at such a vulgar comment.

"What did she mean?"

Emma frantically tried to think of the most delicate way to answer. Perhaps she wasn't the one who should answer. Maybe Luke— No. That was a bad idea. Emma drew a breath. "What she meant was, this girl lost her baby—on purpose."

Ruth cocked her head with a blank stare.

Emma thought for a moment. "She paid someone who...caused her to lose the baby."

A horrified gasp escaped Ruth's mouth. She leaped to her feet. "She thought I should— I would never! That's awful!"

Emma reached for Ruth's hand and gently tugged her down on the couch cushion. "I'm so sorry. It was a ghastly thing to say to you, and she should be ashamed of herself."

"I've never been so horrified in all my life."

Emma gathered Ruth in her arms again.

"Why did she do that? And why did all her friends go along with it? Why were they so cruel? It's just an innocent little baby. And it's not like I did this on purpose. It could happen to any of them."

"There's no simple answer, sweetheart. They aren't the kinds of girls to stop and think about how difficult this is for you."

"They think they're better than me because they didn't get pregnant in high school. And they're right."

"No, they are not." Emma gripped Ruth's shoulders. "Don't you ever, ever say that. What has happened can't be undone, but it doesn't mean you aren't every bit as good or worthy as any other girl out there. Those girls were plain mean and rude. If anything, you should pity them. They don't have the compassion to understand the pain of others." She held Ruth's gaze. "Ruth Morgan, you are a beautiful, sweet, kind, generous young woman. And you are going to be a wonderful mother to your child. Don't you let anyone make you feel like anything less."

Ruth seemed unconvinced. Emma knew it would take a long time for the young girl to overcome the guilt and shame of what she was going through. She picked up Ruth's glass and handed it to her. "Tell me how Luke and Grady getting along."

Ruth winced. "Luke told Grady they were going to do more chores today. And I know that tone in Luke's voice. He's going to be horrible to Grady." She rose and began pacing. "What if he chases Grady away? What if he is so awful to him that Grady leaves me?" She hesitated, lips pressed against each other. "I would never forgive Luke."

Emma knew how harsh Luke could be. But she also knew he would never willfully hurt Ruth. "Luke is probably testing Grady. To see if he will stay, regardless of how hard things get. And things are going to get very hard."

"But Grady says he won't leave me. Luke doesn't have to be this way."

"Then why are you so afraid?"

Ruth bit her lower lip. "I don't know. I'm afraid of...everything. All the time."

Emma met Ruth where she stood. "I know you want to protect Grady. But he is going to have to prove himself to Luke. And he will have to do that on his own. You need to step back and let Grady fight this battle. Respect the fact that your uncle only wants to protect you, and trust that Grady loves you enough to go through whatever Luke throws at him."

Ruth ducked her head. "I'm so worried all the time. I can't help it. My mind is so jumbled up."

"I know, sweet girl. But you aren't alone. You have so many people who love you and want to help you."

"I was stupid. So, so stupid."

"You made a mistake. We all make mistakes. And when this little one is born, the love you have for him or her will make all of this a distant memory."

Ruth sighed into Emma's shoulder and pulled back. "Everyone has changed. Olivia is different. Luke is different. And you—I haven't seen you since the day I asked you to tell Luke."

Emma hated that this was coming between the two girls. "I'm sure Olivia is trying to adjust to all of this."

Ruth crossed the room and stood at the window. "No, that's not it. She's angry with me. She thinks I lied to her all those times."

Curiosity piqued, Emma pressed, "All what times? What are you talking about?"

"I asked Olivia to help me sneak away with Grady. A lot. So she thinks we— But we didn't. Only once the last time." Her cheeks blazed pink.

Understanding dawned for Emma. "Oh. I see."

Ruth returned to the sofa. "I've hurt so many people. I know you and Luke were becoming close. But he hasn't talked about you at all, and you haven't come to see us. What happened? What did he say? And please don't tell me it's not important. I want to know. Please?"

Emma sat beside her again and released a long breath. Ruth needed honesty. Trying to hide anything from her would only add to her anxiety. "Well, as you can imagine, he was upset."

"You mean angry."

Emma tipped her head. "Yes. He was angry. But it was so much for him to take in all at once. And it sounds like he is beginning to deal with it. He's helping you and Grady, right?"

Ruth eyed Emma. "He was mean to you, wasn't he? He had to have been. He had to have said awful things to make you stay away like this."

Emma cleared her throat, smoothed her skirt. "He did say some hurtful things. But then when we were trying to find you, we made amends. Kind of. I guess." Emma rubbed her forehead. "I've wanted to give the two of you time to adjust."

"I'm so sorry I asked you to do that. I shouldn't have."

"It was the right thing to do. He was able to let his real feelings show without fear of hurting you. By the time he saw you, he was able to be a little more rational."

Ruth raised a brow. "You aren't going to tell me what he said, are you?"

Emma pressed her forehead to Ruth's. "No. I'm not. It doesn't matter. All that matters now is making sure you are safe and that baby is born happy and healthy."

TWENTY-FOUR

"Clean out all the horse stalls. There's fresh straw up there." Luke pointed to the loft above

Grady's gaze followed where Luke indicated. He reached for the shovel.

Luke couldn't believe what he was seeing. "What are you doing?"

Grady held up the shovel. "I'm going to clean the stalls."

"With a shovel?" Luke shook his head. "Good luck." He turned to leave.

"What should I use then?"

Luke answered over his shoulder. "Figure it out." He reached the corral gate where he kept Leah, the pregnant mare he'd agreed to board while her owners traveled. He blew out a whistle and clucked his tongue. The black mare ambled toward him with all her girth. Luke ran his hand down her neck and patted her back. "How you feeling today, ol' girl?"

Leah whinnied and nudged him with her head.

"I know, I know. You gotta be miserable. Let's move you to a corral with a little more shade." Luke slipped a halter on the animal, then a lead rope, and guided her across the field to another area. With the corral currently occupied by Raffle and Abbey, though, he had to tie Leah to the nearby tree and relocate them. Abbey didn't like Leah, and Leah didn't like Raffle.

Horses were more like people than folks knew.

After moving the two horses and getting Leah comfortable in her new environment, Luke went to check on Verna, their milking cow. Her water trough was empty. He kicked the ground and hollered, "Grady!"

The boy came running from the stalls, carrying the shovel. He stopped short at the sight of Luke standing by the trough.

Luke pointed to the empty metal container. "I told you to give her water."

"I know, but then you told me to clean the stalls."

Luke held his arms out to his sides. "So you up and walk away from this? Tell me, boy, do you like milk?"

Grady pursed his lips. "Yes."

"Then you better give the cow some blasted water. And for cryin' out loud, get rid of that shovel. Use a pitchfork." Luke stalked away. The kid was useless. How in the world did he think he was going to provide for a child? He didn't even know how to muck a stall.

Luke sought out the water barrel and brought the ladle to his lips. The water was still cool despite sitting in the sun. It ran down his throat, chasing away the burning grit of dust. He wiped his mouth with the back of his hand. What was he supposed to do with this kid? Why on earth did he bring him home?

Deep down, Luke knew the answer. But he wasn't about to go soft on the boy. Grady had no idea what he was facing, and Ruth deserved more than some seventeen-year-old kid who didn't have enough sense to give water to a milk cow.

Where was Ruth, anyway? He peered down the driveway for a sign of her. He'd been stuck here alone with Grady for the past two days while she went off and visited with Emma. Emma... An image filled his mind. Blond curls and blue eyes. The way she blushed when he winked at her. The way she felt in his arms. The way her lips felt against his ...

Luke threw the ladle into the water. It landed with a splash and bobbed a couple of times before settling. He didn't need all this aggravation. He was glad Ruth had someone to talk to, but did it have to mean him being alone with Grady so much? Most of the time he wanted to strangle the kid, and some of the time—he huffed a breath—he understood him. Even if he didn't want to.

Grady passed by Luke on his way back to the stalls. Luke watched him for a minute. He didn't want to feel the emotions that came to the surface when he saw the boy. He didn't want memories reemerging after all the years and the effort it took to tamp them down. Luke pinched the bridge of his nose and squeezed his eyes shut, trying to block it all out. He went to the vegetable garden and jerked up weeds. At least he could get rid of *something*.

The sun had begun its descent when someone's shadow cast itself over the garden. Luke pulled the last visible weed and looked to see who it was. Great.

"Wow. You cleaned up the whole garden."

"That's the point of weeding." Luke started to gather all the weeds he'd pulled and toss them in a pile. To his surprise—and irritation—Grady joined him.

"What do you do with the weeds?"

"Give 'em to Samuel down the road, for his goats."

"You want me to drive them over there for you?"

Standing up straight, Luke pushed his hat back on his head and eyed the kid. "Sure." Luke turned to walk back to the house.

"Hey, Luke? Can I talk to you for a minute? I need to ask you something."

Luke stopped in his tracks. He waited a beat then turned slowly, hoping it wasn't the question he'd been expecting.

Grady rushed to catch up. He reached Luke and cleared his throat. "Well, uh, I—I've been thinking, and"—he took a deep breath and stood to his full height—"I want to marry Ruth."

Luke knew it had only been a matter of time. He squinted at the kid. "Sounds more like a statement than a question."

"Right." Grady's eyes grew large. "Sorry. I would like your permission to marry Ruth."

Gazing out over the ranch property, Luke answered. "I still don't hear a question, boy."

Grady didn't respond, which drew Luke's attention to him again.

The young man's eyes hardened. Luke watched his hands form into fists at his side. Good for him. It was about time the kid started to grow a backbone. "May I marry Ruth?"

Luke considered him for a moment longer. "No."

❧

Things were definitely off with Grady and Luke. Ruth took another bite of peas, eyeing the two. Luke seemed perfectly content, but Grady... She had never seen him so upset. He seemed downright angry. What had happened between them today?

"Nella showed me how to make her dinner rolls today." She playfully flicked Grady on the arm. "I know how you love her dinner rolls."

No response.

"And Emma offered to help me sew some new clothes tomorrow. Mine are getting too tight. Nella has a whole trunk full of old dresses we're going to take apart so we can use the fabric."

Nothing.

Dabbing her mouth with a napkin, she tried to draw them in again. "So, how did the chores go today?"

Luke kept eating.

"Grady?"

Grady glared at Luke. "Fine."

"Just 'fine'?"

"Yes." Grady's eye snapped at her. "Just fine." He got up from the table so quickly, his chair nearly fell over.

Ruth stood with him. "Where are you going?"

Grady glared at Luke again, who still paid no mind to what was happening around him. "I'm going to the barn. With the horses. Where I belong." With the slam of the screen door, he disappeared.

Ruth whirled around to Luke. "What did you do to him?"

Finally, her uncle raised his head, as if he hadn't noticed anything at all. "Nothing."

"Then what did you say to him?"

"I said a lot of things to him. I had to work with him all day long. And trust me, it made for a long day."

"Luke! He is upset. You had to have done or said something to make him act this way."

Pushing back his chair, Luke wiped his mouth with his napkin and tossed it on the plate. "Why don't you go on out there and wipe his tears away then? I'm worn out from trying to teach that kid how to work for his keep."

Luke left the kitchen. The radio crackled, and then a news program came from the living room. She stared at all the half-eaten food—except for Luke's plate, of course—on the table. Should she go after Grady and find out what was wrong? But if Luke was awful to Grady, did she really want to know? Couldn't she simply ignore it all and pretend everything was fine?

She rested her elbows on the table. Her head was aching. Having Grady stay here wasn't working. Luke was making it as difficult as possible, she knew. But she couldn't let Grady leave. He might never come back.

TWENTY-FOUR

Luke lifted the ladle from the bucket of water outside the barn and drank. Seemed he spent more time at this bucket the last few days then he did working. Ruth was off at Nella's again, sewing clothes with Emma. He didn't want to think about where he'd be without Nella and Emma right now. Barbara Hudgins had also been a huge help, picking Ruth up a few times, and taking her out when she needed to talk. But why did it always come at the expense of leaving him with Grady?

Grady had been looking for a job for the past month and a half, but like a lot of people these days, he wasn't having much luck. That left him here all day, and Luke certainly wasn't going to let him sit around and do nothing.

Not that Grady loafed around doing nothing. Even Luke had to admit, the kid was a hard worker. But Luke wanted to see more from him. He wanted the kid to learn to be a man. Stand up for himself. How was he going to protect Ruth and their child if he just kowtowed to everyone?

Luke dipped the ladle in the water again, took his hat off, and poured the water on his head. He envisioned steam rising from his hair. What he wouldn't give for a crisp breeze to blow through and cool everything down. Even the animals moved in slow motion, barely able to garner the energy to eat. From inside the barn, the scrape of a pitchfork against the dry ground meant Grady was cleaning out the stalls. He'd had the kid working since sunup. And not once had Grady complained. Mucking stalls to loading straw in the barn loft, brushing down horses or pulling weeds in the vegetable garden, no matter what Luke threw at him, he did it. Luke knew he should be impressed, but instead irritation hammered at his nerves.

The scrape of the pitchfork stopped. Footsteps alerted him to Grady's approach. The kid stopped short. He stared at the ladle dripping with water and licked his lips. Luke handed it to him.

Grady drank his fill and slumped against the barn wall. He rubbed his arm against his forehead. "I want to thank you. For letting me stay here all this time. I appreciate the support."

"I'm not doing it for you." Luke adjusted his hat and stalked toward the corrals, swallowing a nasty remark when Grady followed him.

"I know that, but still. I appreciate you letting me stay here and be with Ruth."

Luke spun around so fast Grady stumbled. Luke stepped closer. "I am not letting you stay here so you can be with Ruth." For the first time since he'd met Grady, the kid didn't flinch.

The boy gave a huff and scowled. "Then why are you doing it?"

The last ounce of self-control Luke possessed began to evaporate. "I don't have to tell you why I do anything."

Grady stood taller and squared his shoulders. "With all due respect, I think I deserve to know why I've been busting my hindquarters these past three months for you, then."

The muscles in Luke's jaw tightened to a painful burn. "You think you've been doing all this for me? You ain't doing a thing for me, boy."

Grady closed the gap between the two of them, the veins in his neck protruding. "Then tell me who I am doing it for!"

Luke spoke in a low grumble. "I oughta knock you from here to next Sunday."

"Then do it. Just do it. Come on, punch me in the gut." He pounded his fists against his chest. "Do something besides glare at me and threaten me and make me feel like I'm worse than dirt around here." He pointed at Luke. "Let me tell you, Mr. Morgan, you can't possibly make me feel any worse than I already do. So why don't you go ahead and do what you really want to do to me and get it over with?"

"Because beating the tar outta you won't prepare you for what's waiting out there, boy." Luke's pulse throbbed in his ears. The muscle beneath his right eye twitched. "Do you have any idea what you are facing? Do you have any clue how you are going to provide for this baby? Have you ever had a real job in your life? Ever get those lily white hands dirty before you came here?"

Rage flashed in Grady's eyes. Before Luke had a chance to react, Grady's fist landed firmly on his jaw. Pain seared through his jaw into his skull. Luke bent at his knees, refusing to go down to the ground. His vision blurred. He sucked in air and fought the darkness closing in on him.

As his lungs refilled and his vision cleared, Luke gathered his senses and stood upright, fists clenched, retaliation overriding caution. He raised his fists, poised to beat the young upstart half silly.

Grady stood with his fists ready. As Luke drew back, prepared to throw his first punch, he suddenly saw all the overwhelming emotions bottled up in a kid only seventeen years old, facing a situation in life he didn't have the experience or the skills to handle. A kid who knew everyone had turned on him, including his own father. A kid who had always done the right thing and now found himself not knowing who he was or what he was capable of. The boy had had enough. He'd finally snapped and found someone to take it all out on. Grady's eyes were a crashing of emotions Luke had been trying to ignore. Fear. Pain. Confusion. And...grit

Luke's fists relaxed. He stared at Grady, wondering if he had lost it all those years ago and punched someone in the jaw, let them know how angry and scared he was, could things have been different for him and Sadie and their baby? He lowered his fists to his sides.

Grady glared at Luke, knuckles white against hardened fists. He spoke through clenched teeth. "I'm not sorry."

Luke worked his jaw, touching the painful spot. "I know you aren't."

Grady raised his fists higher. "Are you going to just stand there, or are you going to fight me?"

Luke spit the taste of blood out of his mouth. "I'm not going to fight you." He shoved past Grady, toward the garden. He'd taken several steps when, to his dismay, he heard Grady's shoes scuffing along behind him. Luke stopped at the garden and pointed to a pile of weeds that had been pulled.

"Clean those up. Put them in the wheelbarrow over there, and then dump it on the other side of the fence behind the corrals."

Grady didn't answer. All the huff and puff seemed to have gone out of him. But Luke could tell he walked a little taller. Grady retrieved the wheelbarrow and began to clean up the weed pile.

Luke touched his sore jaw again, wincing, and went about feeding the horses. He ruffled Leah's mane while she ate. "He's got more fight in him than I gave him credit for."

She bobbed her head up and down as if in agreement.

Even Luke never had the courage to do what Grady had done. Oh, he'd thought about it. A lot. But he kept it bottled up inside. Maybe Grady was better equipped to handle the storm headed his way than Luke had been. Maybe he was ready for the fight ahead.

The rumble of a car drew Luke's attention as he watered the last horse. He recognized Harold Graton's Cadillac pulling up to the house. What could he be doing all the way up here in Petaluma at this time of day? A twinge in Luke's gut told him it wasn't for anything good.

He tugged off a work glove and approached the man, holding out his hand. "Surprised to see you out this way. Can I help you with something?"

Graton shook Luke's hand. "Well, yes, you can. To be honest, this isn't exactly a social call."

"What then?"

"The truth is, Luke…" He let out a loud sigh and kicked at a rock. "I have to take the horses."

Luke stared at the man. "Why?"

"It's a bit of a sensitive matter."

Luke stepped forward. "I think I have a right to know why you're taking your business from me. Did someone else offer you a better deal? Because we can renegotiate the boarding terms."

Graton smoothed one hand over his slicked back hair. "I really don't want to get into your personal business. But...actually it's my wife. She heard about your niece."

Luke folded his arms across his chest. "What about her?"

Graton held his hands in the air. "Like you, I'm a businessman, and I have no interest in what goes on in other people's private lives. But the missus doesn't want our daughter coming here and seeing—" He clamped his lips shut.

"Seeing my pregnant niece."

The man offered a defeated nod.

Luke drew in a deep breath and held it. He blew it out slowly, removed his hat, and calmly brushed it off with his hand. He replaced the hat on his head. "May I ask exactly how your wife learned about my niece?"

"I guess she knows the Akins woman somehow." He shrugged. "I don't know, to be honest with you. I don't pay attention to all her women's leagues and clubs and whatnot."

"So your wife has no problem being around the mother of the boy who got Ruth in this fix, but she doesn't want your daughter at my ranch because Ruth is here?"

"Look, Morgan, like I said, I've got no interest in what goes on in your private life—"

"But your wife does, right?" Luke stepped forward. "Is that what you base your business decisions on? I have to say, if that's the case, I'm surprised you're as successful as you are, considering how fickle women can be."

Graton sputtered an unintelligible response.

Luke knew he should stop, but he didn't care. "Your wife does know it's not contagious, right?"

Graton stood to his full height. "Now, see here, I know this is a raw deal for you, but I won't stand here and listen to you besmirch my wife."

Towering over the man, Luke spoke through gritted teeth. "And I won't stand here and let you or your spoiled debutante wife belittle my niece, treating her like some kind of leper to be kept away from the pure, innocent children of the rich and privileged." He threw one arm in the air. "Take your blasted horses. I don't want your business."

Luke strode away from the man, his hands balling into fists.

TWENTY-SIX

Emma climbed the porch steps of Luke's home on feeble legs. This was a bad idea. In fact, now that she stood on his porch in front of his door, she was pretty certain it was the worst possible idea. But she had come all this way, carrying Nella's chocolate cake, and Ruth was expecting her. Was Luke? Had Ruth told him? Ruth hadn't really answered when Emma asked her.

Emma reached for the door and knocked. She stepped back, releasing a breath and praying Luke would not be the one who opened the door, remembering another time she'd breathed the same prayer. This time, her prayer was answered affirmatively.

Ruth stood behind the screen door, wearing a yellow and white checked, ruffled apron over the new maternity blouse they'd made. "Miss Darby, I'm so glad you came." Ruth threw open the squeaky screen door and hugged Emma.

Fears of Luke's reaction to her presence were, at least temporarily, averted.

Ruth inhaled dramatically. "Is that Nella's chocolate cake I smell?"

"Yes, it is." Emma handed the cake to her.

"Oh. How rude of me." Ruth's face fell. Concern worked into her eyes. "I should have invited her, too."

"I'm sure she didn't mind. When I left she was sitting in the living room in her favorite rocker, happily reading her favorite Faith Baldwin book."

Ruth giggled and straightened her back, lifting her chin. "You know, Mrs. Akins thinks reading romance novels is trashy. Not at all a ladylike pursuit."

Emma laughed. It was good to see Ruth in such high spirits. "I'd like to see Mrs. Akins say that to Nella." She followed Ruth into the kitchen, surprised at how the young girl seemed to have everything under control. "It smells wonderful."

"Thanks." Ruth placed Nella's cake on the kitchen counter. "I picked some rosemary that's growing out by the creek and added it to the chicken."

"I can't wait to taste it. Can I help with anything?"

"Sure." Ruth handed Emma a bowl of green beans. "These are fresh out of the garden."

"Okay." Emma reached into the bowl and picked up a bean, snapped the ends off, and tossed the bean into one bowl, the scraps in another. "I take it Grady and Luke are outside working?"

"Yes." Ruth opened the ice box and took out a jar of milk.

"You did ask him about inviting me, didn't you?"

Closing the ice box door, Ruth winced. "Actually, I never got the chance."

"Ruth!" Emma's gaze darted to the door. "Luke could walk in any moment. I thought you were going to be sure before I came."

"I was going to, I swear. But you know how stubborn he is. I really think this is best. Luke is trying to deal with everything, but it's hard for him. He needs someone he can talk to, and you know he doesn't trust people easily. Especially Grady. He—" Ruth gasped as the screen door creaked open behind Emma. Ruth's eyes widened.

Emma followed Ruth's gaze. Luke stood in the doorway covered in dust. The dust wasn't surprising. But the red and purple lump on his jaw was. He stopped short the moment he saw Emma. His dark questioning eyes and tilt of his head told her that indeed, he had not expected her.

"Luke!" Ruth ran to him and reached up to touch his jaw. He

flinched and backed away. "What happened?"

The screen door opened again and Grady stepped into the kitchen. Eyes still locked on Emma, Luke motioned behind him with his thumb. "Ask your boyfriend."

Ruth shoved past Luke. "Grady? Did you do that? Did you hit Luke?"

Grady shrugged his shoulders. "I didn't plan to."

Ruth slugged Grady on the arm.

"Ouch!" He grabbed his arm and took a step away from her.

"That's what you deserve! What possible reason could you have for hitting him?" Ruth turned to her uncle. "Luke? Please don't kick him out because of this. I don't know what happened, but please, he has nowhere to go. If you kick him out—"

"Enough!" Luke held up his hand. "No one is going anywhere. This is between Grady and me. And it's over. I've got bigger things to worry about."

"Like what?"

Luke rubbed his eyes. "Never mind." He stared at Emma, confusion etched into his forehead.

Emma swallowed hard. "I, uh..." His eyes still had the power to turn her into a bumbling idiot. "Ruth invited me. But I assumed she had told you. I should have made sure about that before I came. This clearly is not a good time, so I'm going to go." She picked up her purse from one of the kitchen chairs.

"Don't." Luke's hand on her arm sent gooseflesh dancing up to her shoulder. "I think I at least owe you dinner."

Emma's throat constricted. She somehow formed the word, "Oh."

Luke lowered his hand. Emma reached for the counter for stability. Warmth from his touch continued to tiptoe up her arm. He stared at her for a breathless moment. "I'm gonna go get cleaned up." He left the room and Emma released the breath she didn't realize she'd been holding.

Ruth's voice drew Emma's attention. "Grady, why on earth would you hit Luke? Why would you risk everything to do something so— so stupid!"

Grady scooted around her and washed his hands at the sink. He lathered his forearms with soap, scrubbed, then rinsed.

"Grady!" Ruth stomped her foot.

Emma handed him a towel. "Thanks, Miss Darby." He patted his arms dry with the towel. "I told you, Ruth, I didn't plan to hit him. It just happened."

"That bruise on his face doesn't look like an accident. I want to know what happened."

"Well, you're not going to know what happened. It's between me and Luke."

"Why?"

Grady stared at the ceiling. "Because even if I tried to explain it to you, you wouldn't understand."

"Why? Why wouldn't I understand?"

Grady muttered under his breath.

"What?" Ruth planted her hands on her hips. "What did you say? Why won't you tell me?"

Emma stepped in. "Whatever happened between Luke and Grady, Luke seems okay with it. He hasn't kicked Grady out. He hasn't threatened him."

"Yeah, I saw that." Ruth frowned. "It was weird."

"I can't argue with you about that. But you told me yourself, Luke seems to really be trying to handle all of this in the right way. I think you'd be wise to leave this alone. Trust them to work out their relationship on their own terms."

Ruth pouted, arms crossed, her brow furrowed petulantly.

Emma took Ruth's chin in her hand and lifted her face to look in her eyes. "Somehow, someway, Grady and Luke have reached some sort of understanding. I think that's a good thing."

The frown on Ruth's forehead softened. "You're right, I guess. It doesn't look like he hit you back." She touched Grady's chin, searching his face. "Did he?"

"No. He didn't." Grady wrapped his arm around Ruth's shoulders and kissed the top of her head.

Luke reemerged in clean dungarees and a fresh shirt, his dark curls still wet. Emma distracted herself placing the green beans on the stove top to cook. Grady took his leave. Emma's fingers trembled. She could feel Luke's eyes on her. She nearly dropped the knife as she sliced a freshly picked tomato for the salad.

"You need help with that pot?" Luke joined Ruth at the stove.

"Yeah. Thanks. You can drain it in the colander there in the sink." Ruth pointed to the colander.

Luke followed her directions. "Did you take my payment to your doctor appointment today?"

"Yes. He said thank you. I guess a lot of people aren't able to pay him right now."

Emma smiled. He really did love his niece and was committed to taking care of her. Who knew Luke Morgan's hardened shell contained such tenderness?

Ruth announced dinner was ready and Emma noted that Luke, Ruth, and Grady had clearly developed a rapport. She sensed genuine companionship between the three of them.

Ruth spooned mashed potatoes on Grady's plate for him. "Do either of you want to tell us now what happened between the two of you?"

Grady and Luke answered in unison. "Nope."

Emma smiled at Ruth's exasperation.

"Did you close the north corral?" Luke spoke between bites of chicken.

"Yep." Grady grinned at Ruth. "This is really good chicken, honey."

Ruth beamed. "Thanks, sweetheart."

Luke held his hand above his brow, shielding his field of vision. "I'm trying to eat here, if you don't mind."

Emma held a napkin to her lips, stifling a giggle.

"Do you want some more milk?" Ruth asked Emma.

"No, I'm fine."

Emma loved the way Ruth's eyes sparkled when she looked at Grady. The same sparkle reflected in the way he looked at her. Ruth was fortunate that Grady truly loved her and would not leave her to raise a baby on her own. She noticed though, that Luke kept an eagle eye on both of them. What a balancing act he had to perform.

"You look absolutely adorable in that blouse." Emma smiled at the way Ruth's skin glowed.

"Thanks. I'm so glad you know how to sew. I'd be in a heap of trouble. None of my clothes fit me anymore."

Luke shifted in his seat. Emma sensed his discomfort with discussing the pregnancy, so she changed the subject to less sensitive topics. After dinner, Emma started to clear the dishes from the table.

Ruth touched her hand. "Let's cut the cake and go in the living room to listen to the radio. I can do this later. Grady will help before he goes to bed."

Recalling Ruth's affinity for the evening radio programs, Emma agreed and sliced the cake while Ruth retrieved a pitcher of milk from the ice box and filled four glasses.

"I'm so glad Grady does the milking now." Ruth returned the pitcher to the icebox. "I hated fighting that old cow. And so early in the morning, too. It's bad enough that I feel like a cow myself."

Emma laughed at Ruth's wrinkled nose and squinted eyes. They carried a tray with the cake and milk into the living room where Luke reclined in his usual chair, feet propped up on a footstool. Grady made himself comfortable on a love seat where there was only room for one other person. Ruth joined him there, and Emma sat on the couch alone.

Fred Astaire's voice singing "A Fine Romance" filled the room like a warm embrace. The perfect song for the two young people on the love seat holding hands even under Luke's ever-watchful eye. After two more romantic songs, Luke seemed to have his fill.

He got up and walked to the radio. "I saw a headline today about Roosevelt visiting the Midwest." He moved the dial around, fighting through static and squealing sounds, and zeroed in on the station carrying the President's Fireside Chat. Luke relaxed in his chair again.

"I shall never forget the fields of wheat so blasted by heat that they cannot be harvested. I shall never forget field after field of corn stunted, earless and stripped of leaves, for what the sun left the grasshoppers took. I

saw brown pastures which would not keep a cow on fifty acres.

"Yet I would not have you think for a single minute that there is permanent disaster in these drought regions, or that the picture I saw meant depopulating these areas. No cracked earth, no blistering sun, no burning wind, no grasshoppers are a permanent match for the indomitable American farmers and stockmen and their wives and children who have carried on through desperate days, and inspire us with their self-reliance, their tenacity and their courage. It was their fathers' task to make homes; it is their task to keep those homes; it is our task to help them with their fight."

Emma thought of her student whose family had to move to California to escape the desperate situation in Oklahoma.

Ruth worried her lower lip. "Will it get that bad here in Petaluma? I mean, I know it's bad all around, and folks here are struggling, too. Olivia's family is having an awful time. But ..."

"Petaluma is lucky," Luke rubbed his chin. "We have the egg and dairy industry. As bad as the heat has been, it's nowhere near as bad as the Plains. We're lucky so many depend on what we have. And there are those who can still pay for it. Still, though, folks around here have it pretty rough, too. I passed a long line out by the quarry today. Men looking for work." He shook his head.

After the President spoke to the nation, news stories followed. Disturbing stories of Adolf Hitler and Nazi Germany.

Ruth slowly shook her head. "What exactly is he trying to do?"

"Nothing good," Luke responded dryly.

Finally, some levity broke the serious mood in the room as Stoopnagle and Bud's program began. Ruth and Grady laughed out loud, and even Luke snickered at times. He caught Emma watching him and grinned. She averted her eyes, heat rising in her cheeks like a lovesick schoolgirl's.

After the radio program ended, Emma offered again to help with the dishes.

Luke stood. "Actually, Emma, I was wondering if we could talk."

"Oh, well, I really don't want to leave Ruth with all those dishes."

"Don't worry about it." Grady slipped his arm around Ruth's waist. "I'll help her."

Emma watched a warning flash across Luke's face.

Grady pulled his arm back to his side. He took half a step away from Ruth. "I'll go right back outside after the dishes are done."

"Yeah." Ruth touched Grady's arm. "We can watch the stars from the porch."

Luke regarded them a moment longer. "All right." He pointed a finger at Grady. "You do not stay in the house alone after the dishes are done."

"Yes, sir."

TWENTY-SEVEN

Luke opened the back door and led Emma outside with his hand on the small of her back. Emma tugged her sweater tighter around her. The fog coming in from the Pacific brought a welcome break from the heat but could sometimes be a bit on the chilly side. Luke glanced back at Ruth and Grady through the kitchen window.

"I'm sure he will be on his best behavior." Emma's sweet voice carried on the night breeze, bringing a sense of peace to Luke's weary mind.

She was so beautiful. Not in the made-up Hollywood way so many women these days tried to emulate, but the kind of beauty that came from inside a woman and lit up the outside. He rubbed the back of his neck, resisting the ache building inside to reach and pull her close and forget—for a little while—all that was going wrong around him.

Her blond curls invited him to run his fingers through their silky-looking waves. And her heart-shaped mouth—so kissable. How had he managed to stay away from her all these weeks? How did he get close to her again? He'd treated her so badly. Would she forgive him? The thought that she might not landed like a rock in his gut.

Luke stared into her eyes. When exactly she had stolen his heart and made it her own?

Emma shifted and pulled her sweater tight again. "Did you hear me?"

Blinking, Luke cleared his throat. "Uh, no, I guess my mind was somewhere else. What did you say?"

Emma tilted her head to one side and considered him. "I said, I think Grady will be on his best behavior, you know, while he's in the house with Ruth."

"Oh." Luke watched Grady and Ruth through the window again. They laughed and flung soap suds at each other. "Yeah. I guess you're right." He allowed himself one more moment to wade in her ocean blue eyes, then adjusted his hat. "I thought we could walk down to the creek for a bit."

Emma kept in step with him. What a mystery how a man could live his life in solitude and be perfectly happy, but then a woman comes along, and everything turns drab and lonely when she's not around. He hadn't even known he was lonely until he met Emma.

Luke stared up at the stars starting to bring the evening sky to life. He breathed in the sweet smells of the night. "I, uh, I like your perfume. It's nice."

Her giggle danced on the night air. "Thank you, but I'm not wearing perfume."

Then what was he—

Emma pointed to a tree on their left. "Gardenias." She breathed in. "They're actually my favorite flower."

Luke had forgotten about the large tree that bloomed in big white perfumed blooms every summer. He walked to the tree, plucked a bloom, and carried it to Emma. His hands shook a little as he brushed back her hair and tucked the flower behind her ear. Being so close to her under the stars, under the influence of gardenia trees and jasmine vines, Luke's willpower began to crumble.

Her eyes lowered to his lips, then quickly made contact with his eyes again. "Thank you."

As Luke leaned in to kiss her, Emma spoke.

"I guess we should keep going if we want to make it to the creek before it gets too late."

Disappointment landed like an ax. Resisting the urge to grab her arm, pull her close, and kiss her anyway, Luke blew out a tense breath. They continued on in silence toward the second barn where Luke worked on his project.

Emma motioned toward the barn. "Have you been working on it?"

Luke took his flashlight from his pocket and flicked it on to light their path. "I was."

"Was? What happened?"

He led them in the direction of the creek bank along the north end of his property. "Mr. Graton, one of my best boarders, came by today."

"I've heard of him. He owns a lot of property around here, right? Lives in San Francisco?"

"Yeah, that's him."

"Why would his visit keep you from working on it?"

"Well, he came to take his horses back."

Emma stopped. "What? Why would he do that?"

Luke kicked at a large rock, sending it skidding across the ground. "Because of his wife. Apparently she knows Grady's mother and has decided Ruth is a blight to her privileged society. She doesn't want her precious daughter to come here and accidentally lay eyes on a pregnant girl."

Anger flashed in her eyes as she crossed her arms and cocked a hip. "What did you say?"

Luke grinned. Mr. Graton might be lucky he hadn't encountered Miss Emma Darby. He recalled his less than diplomatic reaction. "I'm afraid I didn't make the situation any better. In fact, I may have made it much, much worse."

"How so?"

"Graton is the reason all my other boarders came here. He talked them into it. If I've made him angry, all he has to do is say the word and I could lose all my business. Along with the money Percy Slocum promised for the project."

"Oh, no." Emma's voice lingered in the evening breeze, mingling with the mixed scents of jasmine and eucalyptus and hay.

They continued on until Luke heard the creek gurgling along the confines of the bank. He led Emma to two large, flat rocks.

Emma dusted one with her hand and lowered herself to sit. "I love watching the moonlight dance across the water's surface."

"I come down here a lot." Feeling her eyes on him, he shone the flashlight in her face.

She winced and covered her eyes. "Hey! Are you trying to blind me?"

"Just wanted to catch you."

She gave him a playful shove. "Catch me doing what?"

The moon reflected off her blond hair like a halo floating around her face. Her red lips were incredibly inviting. He recalled their kiss in the barn, what it felt like to hold her and how she'd trembled in his arms.

Luke swallowed hard. "Looking at me. You don't look at me like other people do."

"Oh?" She lowered her long eyelashes. "How do I look at you?"

"I don't know. Like I'm worth your time." He stared into the darkness, thankful for its cover. If she still harbored any hard feelings toward him, he didn't want to see it in her eyes. He listened to the water lap its way downstream. "I'm sorry, Emma. Really. For the way I treated you. The things I said when you told me about Ruth."

She didn't answer right away. "I understand. It was a shock."

"That doesn't excuse my cruelty. I just— I couldn't believe what I was hearing. I couldn't comprehend it was happening all over again. That another young girl's life is ruined because of me."

"Wait a minute." The touch of her hand warmed his arm. "How is it your fault?"

"I'm responsible for her. I knew Grady was trouble and I let him in. They were sneaking off, and I wasn't paying enough attention to know it. I should have kept this from happening to her."

"Let me ask you a question."

He waited, unsure if he wanted to hear what she was about to say. "Okay."

"Could anyone have stopped you from being with Sadie? Was it her father's fault she got pregnant? If he had placed more restrictions on you, would he have prevented any of it?"

Luke thought back to his time with Sadie. She was so sweet and trusting. And she loved him. Every bit as much as he loved her. "No. There's nothing anyone could have done to stop us."

"Then you must be able to understand there is nothing you could have done to stop this. Grady and Ruth made their choices. The consequences are theirs and theirs alone."

Luke stretched his legs out in front of him. Emma removed her hand from his arm. He marveled at how removing her touch could leave him so cold. He picked up a rock and tossed it in the water. "What do you think will happen to them?"

"I don't know." Emma sighed. "Do they have plans to get married?"

Luke answered into the darkness. "Grady asked me for permission to marry her. I said no."

Emma gasped. "Why?"

"Because I don't think jumping into a marriage because of a baby is the right way to start out. They both need to spend some time getting to know each other better. They need to figure out how they're going to manage the rest of their lives."

"But it would take so much pressure off Ruth if she were married."

"It won't change the attitude of folks around here. They all know what happened." He thought of the challenges facing them. "I don't think they're mature enough to be married."

"They aren't mature enough to have a baby either. But it's going to happen."

Luke removed his hat and ran his hand over his hair. There were no easy answers to this mess. So he listened to the rippling water, the chirping crickets, and croaking frogs. Luke loved this place of quiet solitude and contemplation, and sharing it with Emma brought a new and hopeful longing. Did he dare believe that the thoughts he had of a future with her could actually become a reality?

Every few moments a breeze carried the scent of the gardenia in her hair to him. He imagined walking down to this spot with her every evening, holding her close, and ending each day with her sweet kiss.

"It's getting late." Emma's gentle voice stilled the sounds of the summer night. "I have to teach in the morning"

Disappointed his time with her had been so short, Luke stood. "I'll drive you home."

"Okay." The smile in her voice lit the desire building in his chest.

After helping Emma into the truck, Luke got the engine rumbling, Luke drove down his driveway and turned onto Adobe Road. A half mile down the road he started to turn down the gravel driveway that would take them to the cabin.

Emma corrected him. "I'm living with Nella now."

"What? Why? I mean, I can't say I'm disappointed, but what happened?"

"I needed to make a break. From Jasper."

Hearing the man's name only reminded Luke of how he'd used her relationship with the man to hurt her. "I hope it wasn't because of me. Because of what I said."

"It was." She quickly added, "But in a good way. I realized some things I'd been refusing to consider. I decided I needed to break away from him completely."

They arrived in front of Nella's. Luke got out, rounded the truck, and opened Emma's door. Emma accepted his hand, and he helped her to the ground. "Thank you."

Luke accompanied her up the porch steps, and they stood at Nella's door. Was it the night air or was her presence creating the goose bumps on his skin? The moon sent a streak of light over Nella's yard. Somewhere a bullfrog let them know he was nearby.

"I really enjoyed my time with you and the kids." Emma smiled. "They're very special to me."

Luke's heart thumped in his chest and he moved closer. His lips nearly touched hers. He swallowed hard. "And what about me, Emma? Am I special to you, too?"

Her lashes fluttered. She licked her lips and swallowed. He'd caught her off guard. Made her nervous. For all the right reasons, he hoped.

"Yes," she whispered. "You are."

He placed his hand on the back of her neck and drew her close. She didn't resist. He kissed those red lips that had beckoned him all night. He felt her warm, tender touch on the bruise that covered his jaw. He registered no pain as he kissed her deeper. His heart pounded in his ears as she so sweetly returned his kiss. He could hold her like this all night if she'd let him.

Luke summoned every ounce of willpower he possessed and broke away. He never, ever thought he would fall in love again. But here he was, tumbling right into dangerous territory for his already battered heart. Seeing desire in her eyes only fed his own.

Emma pulled free. She stared at her shoes and rubbed her arms as if trying to warm up despite the warm weather. "There's something I have to tell you."

The way she stepped away from him raised a blaring siren in his mind.

"I—I don't know how to begin."

Luke made a move toward her.

She backed away again. Tears glistened on her cheeks.

He would do anything to stop her tears. Anything. "Emma, it's okay. Just say it. Whatever it is, it's nothing we can't deal with it."

She let out a humorless laugh. "I wish that were true. I really do."

What could possibly be bothering her so much that it made her cry? "Come on, after everything we've been through in the short amount of time we've known each other, it can't be that bad. Look, just say it. Just—blurt it out."

She searched his face. Sucked in a breath and opened her mouth. "Jasper has been sending me letters."

"He's been harassing you?" Luke ground his teeth. If he had to track Loomis all the way to Arizona deliver a personal—and very physical—message, he would.

She shook her head, swiping at her tears.

He stared into the blackness of the tree line beyond her. If Loomis wasn't harassing her, what was— A scene flashed in his mind. The day at the church social, when she told him about the man's manipulation. A sickening thought occurred to him. "For how long?"

Her voice was barely audible. "Since I moved here."

Luke's brain paused to question whether he'd really heard what he thought he just heard. He waited for her to correct herself. But she didn't.

He turned his back on her, squeezing his eyes shut. He held his hand to his forehead. His mind scrambled to understand, his thoughts tumbling over one another. Moments they'd shared. All the things he'd told her. The way she got him to open up about things he never intended to discuss. With anyone.

She let him hold her, kiss her, feel for her. And the whole time she'd been communicating with Loomis? Luke bit the inside of his cheek. The muscles in his jaw trembled. "He must be some great pen pal."

"I didn't say I wrote back to him."

He faced her again with a derisive laugh. "Apparently you didn't have to. So what's with the sudden burst of conscience?"

Did she have any idea what she was doing to him? Did she know what a punch in the gut this was? That it made him nauseated to think of her having anything to do with another man, especially that man? He forced himself to look away from her tears.

"He's threatening to tell you that he sent me here with a ring." Her voice trembled.

Luke stepped backward. A ring? Who was this woman standing in front of him? "You mean all this time...you've been engaged to him?"

Emma gaze darted to Nella's home. "Shh. You'll wake Nella."

"I don't care if I wake the whole blasted county. All this time you've been engaged to another man? The times you've let me kiss you?" He threw his hat on the ground and raked his hands through his hair. "I let you in, Emma, and you used me. What I can't figure is what you got out of it."

"You know me better than that, Luke Morgan. And I am not engaged to him!"

"I don't know you at all. I thought I did. You made me think I did." Luke jabbed a finger in her direction. "And he sure as blazes thinks you're engaged. Of course, I gotta say, if you were walking around with my ring, I'd be under the same impression."

Tears spilled down her stricken face. Luke steeled himself against them. She'd been lying to him. He'd allowed himself to fall for a woman he thought he could trust. He thought she could really be his. That he could actually be happy for once. And this is what he got.

"I had to get away from him." Emma's quivering voice barely rose above the chorus of frogs and crickets. "He told me he could get me a job here. He had a place where I could live. His condition was that I accept the ring and think about his proposal while I was gone. I never agreed to marry him."

Luke spoke through clenched teeth. "You never agreed not to marry him either."

"I have now. Nella invited me to live her until I can find my own place, and I sent the ring back."

His eyelids flinched. "Well, it sure did take you a pretty minute to decide, didn't it? Why did you send it back now?"

Her brows knitted together. "Do you really have to ask me that? Do you really believe I'm the kind of woman who would play with your feelings?" She moved toward him for the first time. "Do you really think I could kiss you like that if I didn't have true feelings for you?"

"From where I'm standing, it sure seems like you are."

She hugged herself and held his gaze long enough for him to regret his words, then she disappeared inside the house and closed the door.

Luke stared at the door as the night air seemed to grow icy cold. He sank down onto the porch steps. How many true loves did a man get in life? What happened when he burned through all of them?

TWENTY-EIGHT

Luke arrived back at the house feeling like he'd gone ten rounds with Max Baer. He'd been pummeled twice today. Once in the jaw by a seventeen-year-old kid and once in the gut by a woman no more than a hundred and ten pounds soaking wet.

A lonely plate with a lonely piece of chocolate cake sat on the table. Ruth must have saved it for him. He got a fork, poured himself the last of the milk, and took a seat for lack of knowing what else to do with himself.

A knock sounded on the kitchen door. What now? Did someone run over his dog? He trudged to the door and opened it. Grady. Luke let him in without saying a word and returned to finish his cake.

Grady took a chair at the table, looking nervous as a field mouse staring down a gopher snake. He wouldn't look at Luke, choosing instead to fidget with a crumb left on the table.

Luke spoke around a bite of the cake. "What's wrong with you? Is Ruth okay?"

"She's fine. I want to talk to you."

Luke spoke around a mouthful of cake. "So talk."

"I want to marry Ruth."

Great timing. Just great.

"Grady, this is not a good a time to—"

"She told me about what happened at the grocery store." Grady's eyes went steely. "I don't want my Ruthie to be treated like that ever again." He thumped his finger against the table. "I don't want her to be ashamed to go to the grocery store, or to church, or—or to walk down the street!"

Luke pushed the cake aside. This was happening now whether he wanted it to or not.

Grady's fists clenched. Beads of sweat formed on the kid's forehead. "Mr. Wayfair came by the house while you were gone to let me know I got the job at the D Street Bridge. I start on Monday. Between workin' there and here with you, I'm goin' to save up enough money to buy her a ring. I don't know how long it's gonna take, but I'm gonna do it." His determined gaze did not waver. "I'm gonna marry her, Luke. And I'm not lookin' for your permission this time. I'm going to protect her from ever havin' to deal with anything like that again."

Luke took a long drink of milk, then leaned back in his chair, frowning. "How are you going to support her with those two little jobs you have? Where are you going to live? Have you thought about those things?"

"Yes, I have. And I think I have a solution."

Luke raised a brow. "I'd love to hear it. Because those are some pretty big obstacles."

"Well, with you losin' boarders—"

"My boarders have nothing to do with you."

Grady held up his hand. "Hear me out. Now, we both know you're in danger of losin' more. But I have no doubt we can bring in new ones. Maybe even sweet talk old man Graton back on our side."

Irritation bubbled up in Luke's chest, crashing into the already churning anger that had taken up residence the moment Emma laid her little secret on him. "Excuse me. Did you just way *we*?"

Grady rested arms on the table. "Ruth and I get married. We live here. There's plenty of room. I bring in some money with the job I have. I figure I'd better be as invested in gettin' more boarders as you are, because we're all in it together. So, yes. *We.*"

Luke leaned forward. He stared into Grady's eyes. The kid stared right back. "Let me get this straight. You want me to give you my niece, let you live in my house, and let you be a part of my boarding business?"

"All while I bring in some much-needed cash. Yes. Look, I hate the way people look at her. I hate the things I hear them say about her. That she's an unwed mother, like she doesn't have a man." He poked his chest with his thumb. "She's not alone. That baby has a father. A father who loves it, and who loves her."

Luke shook his head as he took in the sight of Grady standing up for himself and for Ruth. "Are you the same gangly kid who came asking permission to take my niece to a church social a few months ago?"

"No, sir, I'm not. A lot has changed since then. I've changed."

At some point the kid had developed quite the hardened stare.

"Luke, I'm goin' to be a father. I want to be Ruth's husband. If you don't give me permission, with all due respect, I'm gonna do it anyway. If I have to take her away from here, I will. I'm not goin' to have my baby born without its mother and father being married. And I'm not gonna let Ruth endure one more day of this shame."

Luke saw himself in Grady again. He understood the determination. The conviction. He realized he couldn't stop Grady. But no way was he going to watch even more history repeat. He had to do what Sadie's father wouldn't allow. It was the only way to keep Ruth safe.

Luke stood. "Stay here." He went to his bedroom, opened a dresser drawer, and reached into the back. His fingers found the black velvet box he hadn't opened for eighteen years. The gold band was as pristine as the day he bought it. Not a scratch. Luke held the ring up to the lamplight. The tiny diamond, barely bigger than a chip but the only diamond he could afford at the time, still sparkled. He closed his fist around the ring. Would the ache ever go away? Would the longing ever subside?

He returned to the kitchen, placed the box on the table in front of Grady, then went to the coffeepot on the stove. It was still warm. He poured a cup then leaned against the counter.

Grady stared at the contents of the open box. His eyes widened. "What's this?"

Luke took a drink, buying himself a moment. "I was engaged once."

Grady's mouth fell open. He held the ring between his thumb and forefinger. "You were? What happened?"

Ruckus barked outside. Crickets chirped. Luke would rather be out there enjoying the peace and sounds of nature than here right now. He clenched and unclenched his fists. Memories flooded, determined not to be put off again. That night played in his mind as clear as if it had happened yesterday. Sadie climbing out the window of her parent's home. Her running to him and wrapping her arms around his neck. The kiss they shared. The pure joy that flooded his entire body. And then the shriek of the horse.

"Luke?" Grady's voice snapped Luke back to the present. "Who were you engaged to? Where is she now?"

"It doesn't matter. Just give the ring to Ruth."

"But it looks expensive. It even has a diamond in it. Don't you want me to buy it from you?"

Luke stared at the ring in Grady's hand. "That ring has been paid for many times over. Give it to Ruth, and give me your word you will not sneak off with my niece."

Grady eyed the ring again. "I give you my word. Thank you."

Smothering summer heat finally began to give way to the cool breezes of autumn. Leaves gave up their valiant fight and reluctantly exchanged their slick green complexion for brilliant reds and golds and oranges. Ruth slipped into one of her maternity smocks, already weary of having to wear them. Although she was thankful Miss Darby had helped her sew some new dresses and blouses, they only accentuated her growing belly. Even if she had tricked herself into thinking people didn't know, they could tell now.

She avoided going into town at all costs, though she longed to be in church, hearing the lovely hymns and messages of God's love. But for now, she listened to a radio preacher in San Francisco on Sunday mornings. He even had a few people sing hymns with him, and she sang along.

Sighing, Ruth made her way to the chicken coop and picked up the bucket of feed. Chickens clucking at her feet and flapping their wings normally drew a giggle, but today Ruth couldn't appreciate the glorious colors of fall or silly chickens. As she sprinkled feed on the ground and tried not to trip over the greedy little birds, she made a plan to go visit Emma this afternoon. Nothing lifted her melancholy like unburdening her heart to Emma.

Perhaps Emma would know if Grady had plans to marry her. She'd begun to wonder if he would ever propose. She was five months pregnant after all. Fear of being abandoned prevented her from pursuing the subject with him, although she suspected he and Luke spoke of it.

Ruth sprinkled the last of the chicken feed on the ground and made her way through the squawking birds, backing herself up to the gate to let herself out. She shut the gate behind her and walked to the house. Expecting the house to be empty, she gasped at the sight of Grady sitting at the kitchen table.

"I'm sorry." He stood. "I didn't mean to scare you."

Ruth held her hand to her stomach and laughed. "I was a little too lost in my thoughts. What are you doing here? Did you forget the lunch I made for you?"

"No. I remembered it. But I wanted to— I was going to wait until tonight, but I couldn't."

The grin on his face ignited suspicion. "What are you up to, Grady Akins?"

Grady took her hand in his. "Let's go for a walk down by the creek."

"But don't you have to be back to work soon? I have to work in the garden and get dinner pre—"

Grady's kiss silenced her protest. He smiled and winked at her. "Everyone will understand. Trust me. Come on."

Laughing, Ruth allowed him to take her hand and lead her outside. Ruckus danced around their feet as Grady led her away from the house. They reached the creek bank and Grady stopped. He stood and watched the water flow by. Why was he acting so strange? She'd caught him staring at her several times, only to quickly look away when caught. His forehead glowed with perspiration, and it wasn't even hot out.

Finally, Grady faced her. Fear struck in her belly. Was he about to tell her that he couldn't handle her or a baby right now? What if he and Luke had gotten into a fight and Luke kicked him out? What if he was leaving?

Grady took her hands in his. "You know I love you, right?"

She searched his eyes for a hint of what was coming. "Yes, I know. Why are you acting so odd?"

He gave her hands a little squeeze. His palms were sweaty. "I guess I'm a little nervous."

Ruth's heart started to thump in her ears. "About what? You're making me nervous. You aren't taking the job at the Golden Gate Bridge, are you? You aren't leaving me, are you?"

Grady dug into his pants pocket. He pulled out a ring. The moment Ruth saw the sun glint off the gold band, her breath caught in her throat. Grady's chocolate brown eyes were wide, anxious, and hopeful. "Ruth Morgan, I love you with all my heart. And I want to marry you."

She released the breath caught in her throat and sucked in another. Her hand rose to her chest as she stared at the ring in disbelief. "Really?"

His Adam's apple bobbed up and down. "I love you, Ruth, and I want everyone around here to know. I want them to know this baby has a father, you have a husband, and that it's me."

Hot tears rolled down Ruth's cheeks. Was this really happening? After all these months of being so confused and afraid, lonely and ashamed, he wanted to marry her. She held her hands to her cheeks. "Really? I mean, really-really?"

He laughed. "Yes, really. So? Will you? Marry me?"

"Of course I will!" Ruth threw her arms around Grady's neck and squealed into his shoulder.

Grady picked her up off the ground and swirled with her, laughing. When he set her down again, he took her left hand and slipped the ring on her finger. She held her hand up to the sun, admiring the colors bouncing off the diamond. Not even in her dreams did she imagine having a ring with a real diamond on it. "Where did you get the ring? How could you afford it?"

A mysterious glint lit Grady's eye. "Luke gave it to me."

"He—he what?" Ruth examined the ring again.

"He had it already." Grady ran his hand through his hair. "He said he was engaged once before. Did you know that?"

"No." Who was it supposed to belong to first? Clearly it hadn't worked out for Luke and the girl he was engaged to. She would talk to him. See if he would tell her.

Grady drew her close and lowered his lips to hers.

She melted into the safety of his arms and the tenderness of his kiss. They hadn't been close like this since— She fought the pangs of shame and became all too aware of her swollen belly.

He whispered in her ear. "I wish we could spend the rest of the day together, maybe have a picnic. But I have to get back to work." He kissed her again. "I'll be home as soon as I can."

Ruth hugged him tight and buried her face in his chest. She was so happy—and relieved. He wanted her for the rest of his life. She only wished she didn't have to share the joy of this moment with fears and regrets.

She spoke against his chest, tears pressing at her eyes. "We're going to be okay, right?"

Grady pulled back and cupped her chin, tilting her face upward. "Not only will we be okay, we're going to be happy."

His smile, the assurance in his eyes and in his voice, chased away her fears. She was going to be Mrs. Grady Akins! She stood on her tiptoes and kissed him again before having to let him go back to work.

The rest of the day's chores flew by much quicker than the

morning chores had. The heaviness in her heart was gone. The questions and fears that had swirled in her mind every day were now silenced. Grady wasn't going to leave her. She wouldn't have to have this baby alone. Her heart skipped every time her eye caught the ring on her finger or the sun glinted off the tiny diamond.

As dinnertime drew closer, Ruth eased herself onto a kitchen chair at the table. Nella had given her a sack of walnuts that had fallen from the tree in her backyard, and Ruth had picked a few apples from a lone apple tree behind the house. She began to chop them for a Waldorf salad to serve with tonight's chicken dinner. This was a special dinner, deserving of a special treat. She'd come a long way in learning to cook, thanks to Nella, Emma, and Barbara.

A knock at the door interrupted her task. She got up, wiped her hands on the towel hanging from the pocket of her apron and opened the door.

Miss Darby stood on the other side of the door. "Nella said Luke stopped in. He told her he was going to Santa Rosa for the day."

"Yes, he'll be gone another couple hours." Ruth knew something had happened between Miss Darby and Luke, but she knew better than to ask Luke, and Miss Darby wouldn't answer her questions.

Miss Darby's shoulders relaxed. She held out a magazine. A beautiful, glowing bride adorned the cover.

Ruth squealed with delight and ushered Miss Darby into the kitchen. "You heard already?"

"Yes. I saw Grady today at the store and he told me. He's as proud as a peacock."

A thrill raced down Ruth's spine. He wasn't simply happy, he was proud. Proud to have her as his wife.

Miss Darby reached for Ruth's left hand. "Let me see the ring."

Ruth held her hand out, wiggling her fingers.

"Oh, it's lovely. I didn't realize Grady could have earned enough money so quickly to buy such a beautiful ring."

"Oh, well, Grady didn't buy it."

Mrs. Darby cocked her head to one side. "How do you mean? He gave you this, right?"

"Right, but Luke gave him the ring to give to me."

"Luke?"

Ruth giggled at Miss Darby's wide eyes and raised brows She pulled out a kitchen chair for her. "Apparently, Luke was engaged before. He wouldn't tell Grady anything about it." She tilted her head. "Do you know who she was? Do you know what happened?"

"Yes, I do. But it's not my story to tell."

Ruth bit her lower lip, as she fingered the ring. What was this story of Luke's? Would Luke tell her about the woman who was supposed to wear this ring?

Miss Darby tapped Emma's hand. "We have a wedding to plan."

Ruth took the *Household Magazine* Miss Darby had brought over. The bride on the cover was stunning in a long, flowing silk dress. The image of the dress resurrected thoughts and feelings Ruth had struggled with these past few hours.

"What is it, Ruth?"

She ran her finger over the cover of the magazine. "I—I can't wear a beautiful white dress like this. My wedding won't be what I always dreamed of. I don't think I can even be married in a church." Ruth appreciated Miss Darby's silence. There was no arguing these points, and she was glad her teacher didn't try.

"There is no reason you still can't have a perfectly lovely wedding day. With all the leaves on the trees turning and the beautiful fall sky and sunflowers starting to bloom, you could have a wonderful outdoor wedding."

Hope sparked afresh in Ruth's spirit. "You really think so?"

"I know so. And the dress you wore to the church social with Grady is so beautiful, who says it can't be a wedding dress? How much more romantic could it be than to wear the dress you wore on your first date?"

Ruth held her expanding belly. "I'm pretty sure it doesn't fit anymore."

Waving her hand in the air, Miss Darby dismissed Ruth's fear. "It's only fabric. We'll let it out a bit. And if you don't want to do that, we can make a brand new-dress. Maybe a lovely soft pink."

"You really think we could plan a nice wedding?"

"I know we can." She pulled Ruth into a hug that dispelled all Ruth's concerns. Like her mother would have if she'd been here.

They spent over an hour planning together. They would ask Nella to bake a special cake. Certainly Pastor Hudgins would perform the ceremony. Luke would give her away. There were beautiful autumn wildflowers blooming on the hills and the fields around Petaluma. They could make a bouquet from those. The only thing that remained was Ruth's maid of honor.

Would Olivia stand beside Ruth on the most important day of her life?

The bell jangled as Ruth pulled the soda shop door open. She scanned the shop, heart pounding, hoping not to see anyone from school. No one looked familiar. Ruth's shoulders relaxed. She hadn't realized how tense she was coming here.

She spotted Olivia sitting at the soda fountain. Olivia offered a tentative smile as Ruth joined her at the counter. She tried to hide the extra effort it took to climb up onto the red vinyl stool. "Hi, Liv. Thanks for meeting me." She eyed the soda menu. "Chocolate?"

Olivia nodded. "Sounds good. Thanks."

Ruth ordered two chocolate sodas and an order of fries for them to share. It was such a strange thing to feel awkward with her best friend. "Um...how's everything at your house? Is your mom back?"

A pensive frown marred Olivia's peaceful face. "No."

Stunned, Ruth wasn't sure what to say. It had been months since Mrs. Hawkins left to visit her mother in Washington.

"You can say it. She left us."

Ruth gasped. "Oh, no, Olivia. I'm sure that's not true. She loves you and your brothers. And your father, too."

The soda jerk brought their drinks and fries. Ruth smiled her thanks. Olivia shrugged and took a drink from her straw.

"Have you heard from her at all?"

"Dad does. But he lies about what the letters say."

"How do you know?"

"I read one. When he wasn't home." Olivia sighed. "She told him she can't handle coming back to the 'shack' we live in or the secondhand clothes and dinners of beans and cornbread."

"I'm so sorry, Liv. I can't imagine." Ruth pushed her soda away. How could a woman leave her family like that? Ruth rested her hand on her belly. How could she leave her children?

Olivia suddenly put on a bright smile. "I don't want to talk about her anymore." She warily eyed Ruth's stomach. "How are you feeling?"

As difficult as it was to drop the subject of Olivia's mother, Ruth didn't want to say the wrong thing to Olivia about the topic. "I'm feeling pretty good." Ruth held her left hand out for Olivia to see her ring.

Olivia's jaw dropped. She reached out and touched it. "It's divine. It really is." Olivia's eyes misted. "How is Grady?"

"He got a second part-time job in addition to working with Luke. One at Adam's Box Factory, where he assembles boxes for eggs to be shipped. And the second, at the D Street drawbridge, learning the mechanics and how to fix problems on the bridge. He used to talk a lot about working on the Golden Gate Bridge, but I've done my best to discourage that."

Ruth shifted on her stool. She hadn't spent as much time with Olivia since finding out about the baby. She'd missed her friend. But Olivia was busy with school, her other friends, and her part-time job washing eggs at Poehlman's Hatchery. They seemed to find less and less they had in common. Olivia had never seemed to get over how Ruth lied to her, and for that Ruth felt awful. But Grady insisted Ruth had to think of their family now.

"I really am happy things are working out for you." Olivia offered a genuine smile.

"Really?"

"Yes. I know I haven't been around for you, and I acted terrible when you first found out about—about the baby." Olivia's cheeks blushed. "But I've missed you. I've missed our talks. Going to the movies together. Talking and laughing late into the night. I've really been needing to talk lately."

Ruth embraced her friend. "I've missed you, too. I'm sorry I haven't been there for you either." She paused to gather her courage. "I actually have something to ask you."

"Okay."

"The wedding is going to be small and simple, in Luke's back yard, and I was wondering—would you please be my maid of honor? You are my best friend, Liv, and I can't imagine anyone else there with me."

"I would be honored, Ruth. Really. Thank you for asking, in spite of how things have been lately." Shrugging, she added, "It's how I always imagined things. That we would be a part of each other's weddings."

"Me too." Ruth grasped Olivia's hand. "With so many of my plans having to change because of the baby, I'm so thankful to have you by my side."

TWENTY-NINE

Emma strode down the middle of Luke's back yard, holding her arms out to her sides. "You could put folding chairs on either side here and create an aisle for you to walk down."

Ruth walked alongside her, biting her lower lip.

"What's wrong? You don't like the idea?" Emma lowered her arms. "We can set up another way. I don't mean to take over your ceremony."

"No, no, I like it. It's...walking down the aisle. I mean..." She caressed her belly. "Most brides don't feel a baby kicking inside them as they walk down the aisle."

"Are you saying you don't want to do this?" Emma stroked Ruth's arm. "Because no one will force you."

Ruth stared at the ground. Golden leaves swirled at her feet in a crisp breeze. "I don't know. I mean, yes. I want to. I don't know if it's... proper."

"Proper to whom?"

"You know." Ruth waved her arm in the direction of the invisible chairs. "The people who will be here."

"Let me explain something to you." Emma took Ruth's hand in hers and squeezed it. "Look in my eyes and listen carefully. The people who will be sitting in those chairs are people who love you and want the best for you. There will be no one here who will judge you or attempt to ruin your wedding day."

A smile twitched at Ruth's lips. She fingered the ring on her finger. "My wedding day."

Emma drew Ruth close and held her tight. "Yes. Your wedding day. And when this little one is born and gets old enough to ask questions, you will want to tell him or her about the day you married his or her daddy, the many people who shared the day with you, and how beautiful it was. You will want to show your son or daughter photos of your wedding day."

Ruth looked in Emma's eyes. "I'm so glad you're here, Miss Darby."

"I'm glad to be here. And you know what, you are nearly a married woman. I think we are far past the student-to-teacher relationship. We're friends. Call me Emma."

The smile on Ruth's face touched a place in Emma's heart. A place that needed a friend as much as Ruth did right now. "Thank you. Emma."

With a smile, Emma redirected their focus. "Now, Barbara Hudgins said she can get a whole wheelbarrow full of flowers from her own garden and from the gardens of friends of hers. And Nella has lovely ivy growing in her yard. We could make an arbor here at the front for you and Grady to stand beneath."

"I love the idea." Ruth stood next to Emma. "Grady and Luke could easily build a simple arch. I'll go talk to Grady right now, and you talk to Luke. He's down at the creek."

"No!" Emma grasped Ruth's arm before she was out of reach.

Drawn to a halt, Ruth's eyes widened. "Why not, for heaven's sake?"

Emma stalled, rubbing her left temple while deciding how to answer.

"Oh, please don't tell he's acting like a twit again."

"No. No, he's not." At Ruth's raised brow, Emma pressed her palm to her heart. "He has reason. It's not really his fault. I mean, it was a lot for him to take in, and I should have been honest from the beginning." Emma raised her hands in the air. "I don't know why I keep fouling things up with that man."

"Well, for goodness' sake, what happened?"

Emma stared at the sky. "I told him the truth."

"The truth about what?"

Emma sighed. "Jasper has been sending me letters."

Ruth stared blankly for a moment, then her jaw dropped. "Why on earth..."

Emma rubbed her upper arms. "Because he—he sort of...thought we were engaged."

Ruth's eyes narrowed. "Why would he think that?"

"He gave me an engagement ring."

Ruth held her hand to her chest. "He proposed?"

"Yes." Emma shook her head. "I didn't answer. I didn't say anything at all. I was so desperate to get away from him, I took the ring to avoid an argument or any further discussion, and I came here."

"Hoping he would, what, forget he proposed? That you had his ring?"

"I don't know." Emma held her fingertips to her temples. "I simply wanted him to go away. I thought—I hoped—he would get the hint."

Ruth held a hand to her stomach and sighed. "That is quite a mess. I imagine Luke got real angry."

Emma groaned and leaned against a redwood tree. "Yes, he did."

Someone standing across the yard caught Emma's attention. Her brow furrowed as she squinted. She sucked in a breath at the sight of the man gazing back at her.

"Emma? Who is that? Do you know him? Should I find Luke?"

"No, no." Emma glanced at Ruth and held up a hand, indicating for her to stay put. "I know him. Don't worry. I'll deal with it." She left Ruth standing in the middle of the yard and crossed the short distance to meet the man, her arms crossed. She stopped a safe distance from him. "What are you doing here?"

Jasper smiled the smile that made women swoon. His blond hair glistened in the autumn sun. "I've missed you, Emma. I wanted to come and check on you. You haven't responded to any of my letters since you moved here, and then I find out you moved out of the cottage. Now I received the ring. I thought we should speak in person."

His phony act made her stomach sick. "I'm fine. You can go now."

"I've come a long way, darling. I'm not quite ready to leave yet." He perused the yard and the house. "I'm told this place belongs to someone named Luke Morgan. From what I've gathered he's a horse boarder for some very successful businessmen." He eyed her. "And not married."

How could he know so much? "You're the man Nella told me about. The one who was asking all kinds of questions when I wasn't home the other day. How long have you been here? Have you been watching me?"

Jasper only smiled. He tipped his chin in Ruth's direction. "Who's the young woman?"

She moved to block his view. "None of your concern. What do you want?"

"She can't be more than sixteen. But she's clearly going to have a baby. Looks like you're setting up for a party or...a wedding? Quite the upstanding company you're keeping these days."

The sarcasm in his tone flipped a switch in her. Was this what a mother's instinct felt like? Because Emma was certain she could inflict serious injury. Her jaw tightened. She straightened her spine, standing taller. "You are on dangerous ground, Jasper."

His touch on her arm sent a shiver of disgust through her. She jerked away. Jasper frowned. "Have I offended you in some way, darling? Please tell me so I can make it right." He took her left hand in his.

She tried to yank it free, but he held tighter.

"Why did you send our ring back?" A simulated pained expression crossed his well-bred features. "Did you want a different one, love?"

Emma's vision blurred, and she pulled on her hand, willing him to let go. "No, I—I don't want any ring. Not from you."

He abruptly released her, and she staggered one step. "You know, the least you could do is look at me right now." His smooth voice adopted a sharp edge. "What is going on with you, Emma? I've given you time to adjust to our engagement, I've given you time to come here and be alone for a while, but I'm tired of waiting to get on with my life."

It always came down to what he wanted. Emma pulled in a deep breath, holding her hand to her stomach. "I'm not going to marry you, Jasper."

His steel blue eyes transformed from twisted amusement to threatening irritation. "It's a little late for that, don't you think? You already accepted the ring. I already had an announcement printed in the paper back home. My mother has begun planning our engagement party. Whatever this is, you need to shake it loose. It's time to come home."

"I don't care what plans you've made. You made them without me and without my consent. I'm not going back."

He grabbed her arm. Yanked her close. "I will not be made a fool of."

Emma struggled against his grip. "Let me go!"

"Not until you come to your senses and agree to pack your bags." His fingers dug into her arm, sending pain down her fingers. Real fear took hold of her. For the first time she wasn't sure he wouldn't physically hurt her if he didn't get his way.

Suddenly, somehow she broke free and stumbled backward. She grabbed a fence post to prevent her fall and screamed at the blur of Luke gripping Jasper by his neck, fist raised. "Luke! No! Stop!"

Luke didn't seem to hear her.

"Luke, don't!" Emma scurried toward them. "It's Jasper Loomis! Let him go!"

Luke's dark eyes bore into her. He released Jasper with a shove. Jasper bent over, hand to his throat, coughing. Luke's eyes never moved away from Emma.

Emma startled at the touch of a hand on her shoulder.

"It's okay, Emma." Ruth's voice whispered in her ear. "It's only me. I saw him grab you and I ran to get Luke. Is that..."

Emma managed a nod.

The muscles in Luke's jaw flexed. He finally spoke to her. "I suggest you take your conversation somewhere else."

Emma shook her head, silently pleading with him to make Jasper leave. She hated the cry in her voice when she spoke. "I'd rather not."

She couldn't read what she saw in his eyes. Would he throw her out? Forbid her from being a part of Ruth's wedding day?

He faced Jasper. "I guess you'll have to leave all alone."

Jasper stepped toward Luke. "I have business to finish with Emma."

Ruth whispered in Emma's ear, "Is he crazy?"

Emma hoped Jasper's arrogance didn't earn him a broken jaw. He had no idea what kind of man he was dealing with. Luke would not bend to Jasper's will the way others did.

The veins on Luke's neck seemed to strain against his skin. "It seems Emma has already concluded your business here. Now, you're standing on my land. If you refuse to leave, I can either call the sheriff, or I can remove you myself." He paused. "Most men would rather face the sheriff."

Emma couldn't see Jasper's face. Luke blocked her view. She had never known Jasper to get into a physical altercation. His fighting tactics were far more subtle. Turning away in this situation would be humiliating to him, which would only make him more dangerous in other ways.

"No need to regress to your basic Neanderthal instincts, Mr. Morgan." Emma grimaced at the sound of Jasper's steely voice. "I will contact Emma when she's through here."

He turned, but Luke caught his arm. "I suggest you don't. Never know how long I'll be able to contain my basic instincts."

Luke stalked away from Emma and Ruth. The last thing he needed right now was two females babbling at him. He struggled to control his breathing. Every muscle in his body tensed like a rubber band, stretched to its limit.

He headed in the direction of his barn. The sight of a man putting his hands on Emma and seeing her struggle to get away laid bare a depth of anger even he didn't realize he possessed. His hands ached, and he realized they still formed tight fists, ready to fight.

If Emma hadn't begged him not to hurt the ingrate, he wasn't sure if he could have stopped himself. Why was Emma so desperate to save the blasted fool anyway? What was this hold the man had over her?

"Luke!" Emma's quick footsteps crunched the dry ground behind him.

He didn't slow.

"Luke, please stop. We need to talk."

Unable to ignore the pleading in her voice, Luke stopped and hooked his thumbs on his belt loops. He stood with his back to her.

"Please look at me."

He couldn't help but give in to her. Emma stepped forward and touched his hand. He took a step out of her reach. If he let her touch him, he might fall right into her kiss again. Her pained countenance sent arrows of regret searing through his chest. Did she know how much he longed for her touch?

"Why was he here?" Luke swallowed against the harsh tone he hadn't intended.

Emma folded her arms tightly in front of her. "Why do you think?"

Luke bit back the first response that came to him. The guy wouldn't have come here if Emma hadn't kept his ring, hadn't left him thinking he still had a chance with her. "You told me you sent the ring back to him."

She met his eyes briefly. "I did. He's been in town a few days."

Fury rolled in Luke's gut. "What?" He stepped toward Emma. "How long? Why didn't you tell me?"

Her blue eyes widened. "I didn't know."

"You know he's been in town for a few days, but you didn't know he was? Emma, I'm not in the mood for games."

Her brows gathered above stormy eyes. "I am not playing games with you. Nella told me there was a new man in town who was asking questions. I didn't give it much thought until ten minutes ago when I saw Jasper standing in front of me."

"You mean he's been following you? Spying on you?" Luke made a move to walk past her.

She grasped his arm. "Where are you going?"

"I'm going to find him and make sure he understands he isn't welcome around here. He needs to pack up and go home."

"Please don't. Just leave it be."

"Why?" Luke held his hands out to his sides. "Why should I let this guy wander around, watching you, watching me, and showing up on my property uninvited? Allow him around Ruth and her baby? He's nothing but a scheming louse."

"That's exactly why I'm asking you to leave it alone. Please."

"What are you so afraid of? You think that little weasel can hurt me?"

"Not physically, no." Emma stepped in front of him again. "Jasper Loomis doesn't fight fair. If you provoke him, he won't come after you physically, but he will come after you. And whatever he decides to do, you won't see it coming."

THIRTY

Autumn winds stirred the scent of earth and straw. Luke pounded one last nail for stability into the arbor he and Grady had built for the ceremony, being careful not to dislodge any of the flowers Emma, Barbara, and Nella had already attached. He'd tried to tell them not to decorate it yet, but trying to control a flock of women holding flowers on a wedding day was a fool's challenge.

He'd tried to avoid Emma as much as possible lately, but with her helping Ruth plan the wedding, it was impossible not to cross paths. He hated the way she became quiet whenever he showed up. The way her eyes averted from his and she busied herself with anything she could find.

Luke tested the strength of the arbor to be sure it wouldn't lean if a strong wind kicked up. Emma continued to plague his thoughts. Though she avoided him, she didn't shrink from him. She seemed to stand taller. Seemed to move and speak with confidence. He couldn't shake the feeling she avoided him more for his sake than her own. Like she'd given up. On him.

He twisted his neck and perused the chairs and decorations all prepared for the wedding. This day wasn't about Emma or him. He shoved down the feelings of loss that threatened.

Ruth would become Grady's wife in a few hours. Unease niggled at the back of his mind. If only he could know for certain whether this was the right thing or not. But what choice did he have? If he refused his blessing, Grady and Ruth would take off and get married anyway.

Luke stepped back. The last thing he wanted was for them to run away like he had. It was best to have them close so he could keep an eye on them. Make sure Grady treated Ruth the way he should and that Ruth had what she needed. He blew out a breath. Still, having them live under his roof with him was going to take some getting used to.

"It's beautiful." Ruth's voice interrupted his thoughts.

Luke turned. She sat on one of the folding chairs, toying with the ring on her finger. Luke sat next to her.

"Do you think we'll be okay?" Her question hung in the air, desperate for an answer Luke did not have.

He should say something to prepare her. Something wise and comforting. He watched tree branches above them rustle in the breeze. Who was he kidding? He had nothing wise to say. His entire life was one unwise decision after another. "Sure."

Ruth's shoulders slumped. She twisted her ring. "That doesn't sound very reassuring."

Sighing, Luke rubbed the back of his neck. "I'm sorry. I don't know what I'm supposed to say—or do." He watched her twist the ring round and round. Sadie's ring. His gut clenched. That was it. That's why he couldn't think of anything to say. Luke hung his head for a minute. "I need to tell you something."

Green eyes met his, wide, waiting.

"It's about your ring."

"Grady told me you gave it to him. Who did you give it to first?"

Luke braced himself against the onslaught of emotion in his chest. "I gave it to a girl named Sadie. She, uh, I mean we—we were going to have a baby."

"You mean before..."

How many more times would he have to tell this story? And would it ever get easier? "Yes. Before we were married."

Ruth stood and slowly crossed to the arbor. She fingered one of the roses. Luke waited for her to respond. He could imagine what she was thinking. How angry she must be at his hypocrisy. His chest constricted in pain as he tried to pull in a breath.

But rather than the anger he expected, he saw compassion in her eyes. "What happened?"

Luke stared at his boots, summoning the courage to tell her everything. "Her father wouldn't let me see her. Wouldn't give his blessing for us to be married." He pushed out a puff of air to relieve the pressure in his chest. "So we hatched a plan to sneak off in the middle of the night." As the words came out, relief seeped in. "Before we could get out of town, she was thrown from my horse."

Ruth sucked in a breath.

"She lost the baby and was paralyzed. She died soon after."

Her mouth formed a silent *Oh*. She returned to the chairs and sat beside him. "I'm so sorry, Luke." She paused. A duck quacked on the creek in the distance. "It explains a lot. Why you've always been so... protective."

"Yeah. I guess so."

"Did my mom know?"

"Yes."

"Are you sure you want me to have her ring?"

Luke met her tentative emerald gaze. "Yes." He gently squeezed her hand. "I think Sadie would want you to have it, too."

Relief tinted her smile before her eyes filled with questioning again. "Did you feel...trapped?"

Sadie's face drifted into Luke's mind. She'd had the same questioning eyes, the same fearful quiver in her voice, when she'd asked him the same thing.

"Trapped isn't the right word." Luke sighed. "All kinds of things went through my mind when Sadie told me about the baby. My own plans for the future suddenly didn't count for anything. From one second to the next I went from being a pretty carefree kid to having a kid of my own. I was more scared than anything."

"So you didn't blame Sadie?"

"No. Especially when I saw how scared she was. I knew I had to take care of her, regardless of what it cost me. Is that what you're so nervous about? You think Grady feels trapped?"

Worry formed lines around her eyes. "What if he's only doing this because he doesn't think he has a choice?"

"He has a choice." Luke brushed an auburn lock from her cheek. "He has always had a choice. And every time he's been faced with it, he has chosen you."

Ruth's brow knitted together. "How do you know?"

"How do you not know?" He tapped her forehead. "When his father could have made things easier on him—made this all go away—Grady chose you. He chose to come home with me and sleep in my barn rather than stay with his dad. Not once has he backed down to me, no matter what I've thrown at him. Ruth, if Grady didn't want to marry you, if he didn't want to take care of you and this baby, he has had ample opportunity to take off."

"I guess you're right." A cautious smile bloomed on her face. "You sound like you're starting to like him."

"'Like' is a strong word." Luke stood and took her hand and led her toward the house.

Ruth leaned into him as they walked together.

Ruth stared at her reflection in the standing mirror that had belonged to her mother. The intricate carvings in the redwood had always captured her imagination when she was a child. Flowers, leaves, and a butterfly here and there. She remembered her mother standing in front of it, twisting and turning to be sure her dress flowed perfectly, looking so beautiful.

"Oh, Mom." Ruth crossed the room and climbed onto her bed, fighting tears. A blanket of loneliness settled over her shoulders, causing a shiver. "I wish I weren't doing this without you."

A tap-tap at the door startled her. She swiped away her tears, cleared her throat and gathered her composure. It was probably

Luke checking on her. She didn't want him to see her crying. Ruth opened the door. A relieved sigh escaped her tight chest. She nearly fell into Emma's arms.

"Oh, sweet girl," Emma whispered in her ear. "Did you think I wouldn't be here for you on your wedding day?"

Ruth straightened. "I didn't know what—or who—to expect today. I feel so lost. I don't know what to do."

Emma's comforting smile eased the tremble in Ruth's stomach. "Well, I'd say the first order of business is to get you out of your robe and into your wedding dress."

Ruth drew in a cleansing breath. She just wanted someone to tell her what to do so she wouldn't have to think.

Emma helped her into the dress, and Ruth pivoted toward the mirror. Emma grabbed her arm. "No. Wait until we're all done."

Giggling, Ruth pointed at Emma. "You're having way too much fun with this."

Emma shrugged and tossed a playful look to the sky. "I suppose I am. Now, come sit here and I'll fix your hair."

Ruth did as directed. She closed her eyes, melting into the sensation of Emma brushing her long hair the way her mom used to do. She'd hardly slept at all last night and now felt as if she could fall right into a peaceful, deep sleep.

"Your dress is absolutely beautiful. I'm glad it turned out well." Emma gently pulled the brush through Ruth's hair. "It was so kind of Nella to pay for such lovely pink fabric."

"And of you to sew it for me. I couldn't have imagined I would have such a pretty dress for today."

Ruth bit her lip, tamping down the disappointment and shame of not being able to wear a white dress. Or to have a proper church wedding. Would she ever be free of such feelings? Would she ever be able to walk with her head up, unafraid of staring eyes and whispers behind her back, and even worse, the unkind words spoken to her? Would people think poorly of her as she walked down the aisle, pregnant?

"Are you all right?"

Ruth forced a smile. "Sure."

The knitting of Emma's brow said she didn't really believe her. But there seemed to be a silent understanding between them. A knowing. Ruth didn't want to talk about it and Emma didn't push.

"There we go." Emma cupped Ruth's chin, tilting it up. "You look beautiful. Such a lovely bride." She kissed Ruth's cheek and led her to the mirror.

"Oh!" Ruth gaped at her reflection. She twisted and saw the white pearl buttons Emma had sewn down the back of the pink satin dress. She faced forward again and stared at the white lace across the bodice.

"I have more." Emma opened her pocketbook. She pulled out a small compact and opened it. Then she dabbed her fingers on the pale pink color and softly swept it across Ruth's cheeks. Next she took out a tube of lipstick and put a tiny bit on Ruth's lips. She added a little bit of pink shadow on her eyes and a swipe of mascara, and then Emma stood back and examined Ruth's face.

"So, so lovely." Emma smiled and motioned for Ruth to look at her reflection.

"I—I've never worn makeup before." Ruth touched her face, afraid of rubbing off the pretty colors. "I look so...grown up."

Laughing, Emma fussed with Ruth's hair a bit more. "You are grown up. You're getting married, and in no time you're going to have a beautiful little one. You'll be a family."

"Thank you, Emma." Ruth hugged her teacher-turned-friend. "I don't know what I would have done without you. And not just today."

"I wouldn't be anywhere else. Now. One more thing." Emma dug in her pocketbook again, and drew out a beautiful, shimmering pearl necklace. She twirled her finger in the air, instructing Ruth to turn around. Ruth obeyed.

Emma looped the strand around Ruth's neck. "This belonged to my grandmother. She and my grandfather were married fifty years before he finally saved enough to buy this for her." She fastened the necklace. "And today, it's your 'something borrowed' and your 'something old.'"

"I don't know what to say." Ruth admired her reflection again, fingering the pearls.

A knock at the door alerted them to more company. Emma's smile spread as she rushed to answer it. What was she up to? Emma opened the door and Barbara Hudgins and Nella came into the room.

"So beautiful!"

"Oh my stars, if you aren't the prettiest bride there ever was!"

Emotions threatened to spill out of Ruth as she listened to their oohing and aahing. Her heart danced. Butterflies fluttered in her chest, and the baby wriggled its little toes in her belly. She couldn't remember the last time she felt such joy, such love.

"I see Emma gave you the necklace to borrow." Barbara winked. She reached into her pocketbook. She withdrew a light blue handkerchief. "Here is your 'something blue.' You see here on this corner?" Barbara pointed to some stitching. "I stitched yours and Grady's initials on it."

"Thank you so much." Ruth knew she must be absolutely glowing with happiness. Seeing her initial stitched on her very own handkerchief next to Grady's made it so real. This was going to happen.

Next, Nella approached. She handed Ruth a small red box.

With trembling fingers, Ruth lifted the lid. "Oh, my!"

Nella's smile lit her sparkling chocolate eyes and revealed her white teeth set so beautifully against her brown skin. "The 'something new' is supposed to be for you, but I know you weren't able to buy Grady a wedding band. I hope I didn't overstep."

"No, you didn't!" Ruth threw her arms around Nella. "It's wonderful. Thank you, Nella. Thank you so much."

Ruth drew back and stared at the plain gold band she would soon place on Grady's finger. He would be so surprised. A thrill dashed through her chest. She couldn't wait to give it to him.

How very, very blessed she was to have these women in her life. Even though she still wished her mother could be there, Ruth was certain her mom was watching from heaven with a smile, knowing these ladies were with her.

THIRTY-ONE

"**A**re you ready?" Luke held his hand out.

Ruth's green eyes widened like a fawn cornered by a grizzly bear. She offered her hand and allowed him to slip it through his bent elbow. "As ready as I'll ever be, I suppose."

They walked out of the house together, toward the backyard. As they got closer to the small group of guests, Pastor Hudgins began playing "Here Comes the Bride" on his harmonica. Ruth's fingers tightened on Luke's arm. He patted her hand and escorted her through the smiling faces, to the arbor where Grady and the pastor waited.

As Luke and Ruth approached, Grady's gaze seemed locked on Ruth. Her grip on Luke's arm loosened. Luke realized that to these two kids, no one else even existed. He was no longer calling the shots in their relationship, was only a spectator on the outside looking in, hoping they would always be as focused on each other as they were right now. Had she still worried that Grady wouldn't really be there?

"Who gives this woman to be married?" J.D.'s rich voice carried on the crisp air.

Luke cleared his throat. "I do." He bent down and kissed Ruth on the cheek, whispering, "You're going to be fine."

Then, turning to Grady, he shook the young man's hand. Grady's smile stretched across his face, and he offered a quick nod. Once

Grady took Ruth's hand, Luke stepped back and claimed a wooden folding chair next to Emma. It wasn't until he sat that he realized he had a nervous stomach. His left leg bounced up and down of its own accord.

I did the best I could, Kate. I hope I did right by you.

The ceremony went by in a blur. Luke's mind wrestled with memories. Occasionally he heard a sniffle from Emma and, from the corner of his eye, saw her dab her cheek with a handkerchief. Grady and Ruth said their vows and slipped rings on each other's fingers. Luke stared at his boots when they shared their first kiss as husband and wife.

He felt Emma's hand on his arm, tugging on him to stand. Luke became aware of Ruth standing before him, beaming.

She reached up and wrapped her arms around his neck. "Thank you."

Luke hugged her close, not wanting to let her go. "I wish I could have done better."

She pulled back and smiled through happy tears. Grady held out his hand and Luke accepted it.

"Grady, you've proven yourself more than once. I know you'll do good by her." He leaned in and whispered. "Because you know what will happen if you don't."

The two exchanged a smile that communicated a shared journey of distrust, anger, resistance, and finally respect.

Barbara Hudgins hurried the two away, chatting about cutting the cake and opening gifts. The hours passed quickly. Luke enjoyed watching Ruth smile, laugh, and enjoy her guests. She really was happy. He hoped things stayed that way for her.

At the end of the afternoon, Grady and Ruth rushed arm in arm to Nella's car through a shower of rice laughingly tossed by guests. Grady let Ruth into the passenger seat before rushing to the driver's side. Ruth leaned out the window, smiling, waving, and blowing kisses as they drove away.

A little piece of Luke left with her.

J.D. helped Luke clean up the yard while the ladies cleaned dishes and put leftovers in the refrigerator. Many hands made for light work, and one by one the guests offered their final congratulations and said goodbye, until Luke found himself staring at the arbor, a reminder of the day's meaning.

After the last guest left, Emma approached. Wavy blond hair brushed the tops of her shoulders. A blue dress he'd never seen her wear before made her eyes even more blue.

His heart hammered in his chest. His voice emerged, thick with emotion. "You look beautiful."

Emma's cheeks blushed pink. He loved how easily she was embarrassed. The blush crept down her neck. "Thank you." A breeze tussled her hair. She brushed a strand from her face. "It was a lovely ceremony."

"Yeah. It turned out pretty nice." He rubbed his neck. "Thank you, by the way, for the gifts you and Barbara and Nella gave her. She showed them to me before we came out."

"It was our pleasure." Her head tilted. She opened her mouth to speak, but closed it again and fidgeted with her pocketbook. "I heard Nella arranged a honeymoon."

Luke directed his attention beyond her, to the barn and corrals. There were some things he still avoided thinking about. "Yeah." He coughed once. "She has a friend who owns an inn down in Sausalito. I guess they'll, uh, stay a few days."

"And then the real adjustment begins?"

His attention jerked back to her.

She raised a brow at him. "Are you going to be able to handle them living in the house with you?"

"Don't see as I have much choice." He scratched his temple. "Grady doesn't make enough yet to support a family."

Awkward silence hung between them. So many things Luke wanted to say swirled in his mind, but he didn't have the courage. But he also couldn't stand the thought of watching her walk away again.

"I suppose I should go." Emma slipped her pocketbook under her arm. "Have a nice evening."

As she turned to leave, the thought of being alone in his house didn't appeal to him like it had at one time. "Emma?"

"Yes?"

He rubbed his neck. "I, uh, was wondering...do you want to stay? For a little while. We could have some lemonade on the porch. Or... something."

Her lips parted slightly, then stretched into a charming smile. "Sure."

Emma rejoined him and they went to the kitchen. "Are you hungry?" He peered into the icebox. "Looks like we've got some cucumber sandwiches. And of course, cake."

Holding one hand to her stomach and the other in the air like a stop sign, Emma shook her head. "I couldn't possibly eat another bite. Nella outdid herself. Again."

"Yeah. She did. And so did you."

"It was easy to do. We all love Ruth so much. Her poor mind was such a jumble. We wanted to make sure it was a day she could look back on with pride."

Her eyes held him spellbound. He opened his mouth to speak, but no words came. He wished he could tell her how much he needed her. How he ached to hold her when he was lonely and longed to talk with her when he didn't know which way to turn.

Emma busied herself with the sandwiches and cake. "I'm sure you're hungry. I didn't see you eat much.

Luke coughed and adjusted his hat. "Yeah. I could eat." He retrieved the pitcher of lemonade from the icebox and two glasses from a cupboard.

"Looks like you've got a pretty good early evening snack." Emma smiled. "Would you like me to carry the lemonade?"

Luke raised a doubtful brow and held the pitcher out of her reach. "Uh, no. I've managed to stay dry all day. I'd like to keep it that way."

Laughing, Emma swatted his arm with a kitchen towel. "I've never actually spilled anything on you."

"I'm sure it's only a matter of time."

She squared her shoulders. "Watch yourself, Mr. Morgan, or it will happen. But it won't be an accident."

Luke led her to the front porch. He snatched a blanket off the swing and spread it on the wood steps. They sat on the porch steps together, and Luke poured lemonade for each of them.

Emma took a sip and then sighed. "This is absolutely my favorite time of year, when the heat of summer dissipates and cooler temperatures prevail. The colors start to change. Anticipation of the holidays begins."

Luke nodded.

"Are you all right? I mean, I know it's been a big day and all..."

He couldn't look at her. He didn't know how to tell her what had happened. She'd feel guilty, and he didn't want that.

She touched his shoulder. "I know we've been through a lot, and we've bumped heads a lot, but I hope you know you can still tell me anything."

What was it about her touch that made him want to spill it all? And her voice. She had some kind of hold on him. An intangible that went far beyond, and much deeper, than physical attraction.

He rubbed the back of his neck.

"See? I knew it. Something's going on."

His gaze darted to hers. "What are you talking about?"

She lifted one shoulder. "That's your tell."

Chuckling, he raised his brow. "My *tell*? Do you even know what a *tell* is?"

"Of course I do." Emma straightened, tipping her chin upward..

"What is it then?"

"Well, it's when you—you know—you're playing cards, and you... cheat."

Now laughing to the point that he had to set down his glass, Luke leaned back on his elbows.

"What? What are you laughing about?"

"It's not cheating."

"It's lying. And that's cheating."

"Tell me, Miss Darby, how many poker games have you played anyway?"

Emma gasped. "I do not play poker!"

"Awww, come on now." He poked her in the ribs, enjoying the shock in her eyes. "You know the lingo. Tell me, does a full house beat a flush, or is it the other way around?"

She tipped up her chin. "I'm sure I don't know any of those terms, and I don't care to, so stop goading me, Mr. Morgan. All I'm saying is that when you're uncomfortable, you rub the back of your neck. Like you did just now."

Luke raised his hands in surrender. "Okay, okay." From the corner of his eye, he spotted her grin.

"So what is it? What's bothering you?"

He lifted his hand to rub his neck and stopped himself. How long had she been onto him? He wasn't even aware he did that, and all this time she'd noticed? How many times had she been able to read his mind while he thought he kept her at bay? One thing was for sure, he'd be more careful next time he was in a poker game.

Luke met her blue-eyed gaze. "I didn't want to say anything, but you'll find out soon enough."

She waited.

"I've lost all my boarders in the last five days. Most of them wouldn't tell me why, but it doesn't take a genius."

"Oh, no."

"Apparently Loomis reached out to my boarders and suggested another boarder down in Sausalito. He's cheaper, and he's closer. All they have to do is ride the ferry right across the bay to see their horses. And soon enough, the Golden Gate Bridge will be complete and they can easily drive across. He also made some financial offers that couldn't be ignored—investing in one guy's company, a donation to another man's favorite charity, that kind of thing. He's also getting a kickback from the new boarder."

Emma stood and paced. She held her arms out to her sides. "But these people don't even know him! Why on earth would they even listen to him? Your boarders love you, they're always complimenting you on the job you do with their horses, and they also say how they love coming up here. They want to get away from San Francisco, not closer to it!"

"Emma, it's—"

"It's what I warned you about." She rushed back to the porch steps. "I told you he doesn't fight fair." Emma covered her face. Her shoulders started to tremble. "It's my fault. I brought him here."

Luke wrapped his arm around her. "It's not your fault. This is why I didn't want to tell you. I knew you would feel responsible. But none of this is because of you. This is all Jasper Loomis. He's a petty, manipulative man who works in the shadows because he's too much of a coward to stand up to another man."

Emma took a deep breath, but she didn't pull away. She rested her head on his shoulder. Luke closed his eyes and breathed in the scent of lavender in her hair. This felt so right, sitting on his front porch on a cool fall evening, holding her.

She broke into his thoughts. "If I had only been brave enough to never have given him a foothold in my life, so much hurt could have been avoided."

"He's done his worst now. I'm sure he already slithered back to Arizona."

She pulled back and looked at him. "But can't you talk to your boarders? Explain who Jasper is and why he did what he did? Isn't there any loyalty at all in any of them?"

Luke brushed a stray blond curl from her forehead. "I tried." He shrugged. "It's business. It's the Depression. Even people with money are looking for ways to tighten their belts."

"What will you do?"

He sighed. "I still have some money squirreled away that I made while I worked on the bridge. Eugene Guy won't risk moving the pregnant mare right now, so he'll keep paying to board her at least until she foals. I bought a pregnant cow from Gerald Walters a few months back. He couldn't afford to keep feeding her. The calf will come in a couple of months and I can sell it. If it's a male, I can get a pretty good price for it." He paused for a moment. "I've been pretty lucky so far. The Depression has taken so much from so many, but I've managed to squeak by." He grinned and lifted a shoulder. "Guess I'll just keep squeaking."

THIRTY-TWO

L uke rested his elbows on his knees. Sitting beside her with no tension between them brought calm to his soul.

Emma bowed her head. "I'm sorry you're going through this. I'm sorry I brought Jasper and his vindictiveness into your life."

"I told you, none of this is your fault."

Her gaze seemed locked on the pine trees shading the porch. Her brow knitted together.

"Okay." He took his last swig of lemonade. "What's going through that pretty little head of yours?"

The tilt of her head and the pink flooding her cheeks charmed him. "There is a thought I've had for a bit now."

"All right."

"I was wondering if...if you would come to church with me one Sunday."

Luke broke eye contact and swallowed a frustrated retort. Maybe asking her to stay had been a bad idea.

The touch of her hand on his made it difficult to focus on much else. "Please don't be angry with me for asking. I know how you feel about church. I know you've been terribly hurt. But would you at least consider it? I know you respect Pastor Hudgins, and you adore Barbara. In fact, it seems to me there are several people in the church you have relationships with and—"

Luke held up his free hand. "Where is this coming from?" He stared at her hand resting on his. He made no move to separate their connection. He had no desire to do so. Things had begun to change in him since the day Emma appeared in his life. She softened his rough edges. Soothed his anger, even if it meant taking the brunt of it.

He wasn't sure when it had begun, but Emma Darby had pierced through the armor he built eighteen years ago. He knew what was happening even if he was still too afraid—or stubborn—to admit it out loud.

Emma's gaze followed a squirrel's path across the yard and up the oak tree. "I've been doing a lot of thinking, a lot of soul searching. I grew up going to church, and I've always attended." Her eyes brightened as she reminisced, but just as quickly a gentle frown crept across her forehead as she lowered her head. "At some point, though, it became more of an obligation than anything."

Luke turned his hand palm side up and captured her hand in his grasp.

She glanced at their clasped hands. "I think I began to pull away from God when I met Jasper. I was flattered by the attention. And, as difficult as it is to admit, I was drawn in by his wealth. His power. He offered everything a girl like me could ever dream of." She slowly shook her head. "Before I knew it, I was in his manipulative grip. I knew it was wrong. I knew I had stopped depending on God and had begun depending on Jasper. Even after I came here. I think that's when church became an obligation. I was there because I didn't want to feel guilty for not going. I didn't want others to think poorly of me."

Luke gave her hand a gentle squeeze. "But being in church carries its own guilt sometimes."

"Yes. When you know there is something standing between you and God. I pulled away from Him and I didn't even realize it." She smiled a sad smile. "I spoke with Pastor Hudgins. He's such a wise man."

Luke picked up a small stick and fidgeted with it. "I can't argue that."

"He helped me see that God hadn't gone anywhere. I had." Her eyes held a new glow, a new something that made them more beautiful than ever. "I pulled away from God because of my shame. I didn't think I had a right to ask Him for anything. I didn't even have the right to pray."

Her words hit too close to home.

"I prayed again, really prayed, for the first time in years. I can't tell you how much better I feel. How free, how...light." She slipped her free hand under their clasped hands, drawing his attention back to her. "I want that same feeling for you." Tears glimmered in her eyes, like a pool of clear blue water. "You've suffered for so long. With all the challenges ahead of you, you need Him."

"I don't know." His throat constricted. He'd felt the same pull over the last few months that Emma described, but he'd fought it with everything in him. Now, for the first time in eighteen years, he experienced the desire to be close to God again. To be part of a church body.

"Aren't you tired?" She touched his cheek. "Aren't you tired of being angry and holding everyone at arm's length? I know I was. I was so tired of trying to be two different people."

Everything in him screamed out to say yes. To agree to anything she asked. But he couldn't. "I don't know if I can."

"Why?" Her voice held a slight cry. "What could possibly be holding you back? Haven't you punished God enough?"

His back stiffened. "I haven't been punishing God."

"Who are you punishing then? Yourself? The pastor who hurt you? The church that hurt you? Sadie?"

"No!" Luke bolted up from the porch. "I do not blame Sadie for any of it."

Although the fight lit her eyes, the kind that transformed them into blazing sapphires, she remained calm. "I didn't say 'blame.' I said 'punish.' I'm not accusing you. And I'm not going to keep pushing. I only wish you would slow down enough to think about it." The look in her eyes took his breath away. "I can't be with a man who doesn't love the Lord." She reached up and lightly touched her lips to his cheek. "Please. Give it some thought."

Luke stood frozen in place and watched her walk away until she disappeared around the bend of his driveway. Anxiety crawled through his veins. She'd just told him she wanted him. But there was a condition. And he didn't know if it was a condition he could meet.

THIRTY-THREE

Ruth squirmed in her seat, rolled down the window, and stuck her head out, breathing in the scents of home. She could barely contain her excitement as Grady drove their borrowed car down the driveway.

Grady took her hand in his and kissed it. "You're going to give me a complex, Ruthie. I'm starting to think you'd rather have been home this past week than with me."

"Oh, stop it." She giggled and scooted over and planted a kiss on his cheek. "You know I loved our honeymoon. But I did miss Luke and Emma and everyone." And she was returning a married woman. She didn't have to be ashamed of being pregnant.

Although now and then a discouraging thought had forced its way into her mind while they were away—a young woman shouldn't be pregnant on her honeymoon. But whenever that mood threatened their time together, Grady distracted her by making her laugh or taking her for a walk on the beach.

The moment Grady pulled the car to a stop, Ruth opened her door. "I see him out by the barn!"

"Ruth!" Grady called after her. "Be careful!"

She tossed him a wave and ran, as best she could while holding her belly. "Luke! Luke!"

Luke stood up from the fence he was mending and tilted his hat back on his head. A smile spread across his face. Ruth reached him and threw her arms around him.

"Whoa!" He laughed, embracing her. "No one should be this happy to leave their honeymoon."

Ruth kissed his cheek.

Luke's eyes scanned the distance. "Did you lose Grady?"

"No. He's probably carrying our suitcases into my room." Her smile faded. "Um, I guess we never really talked about that..."

Luke looked back at the house and rubbed his neck. "I assumed I'd have a fight on my hands if I tried to keep Grady out in the barn after the wedding." He put his arm around her and directed her to walk with him to the house.

She scrunched her shoulders. "We've been a little worried about that."

Luke laughed. "Actually, I switched the rooms around. You and Grady can have mine. It's the biggest. The baby can have the small room across the hall, and I'll take the room at the other end."

Ruth wrapped her arms around Luke's waist. "Thank you."

They reached the driveway, and Luke helped Grady carry in the rest of their luggage and set it on their bed.

Grady scratched his temple. "Thanks, Luke."

"You're welcome." He adjusted his hat. "I'll, uh, let you two get settled." He closed the door behind him.

Grady and Ruth unpacked their things and began putting them away. Ruth balanced a figurine of a dolphin Grady had bought her on the dresser. "What do you think of this?"

"It's fine." Grady continued to fold shirts.

"Oh, and Luke moved these yellow curtains from my old room. Do you like them?"

"Yeah, sure." He put the shirts in their drawer.

"I was thinking when the baby comes, he could sleep in a bassinet right here at the foot of the bed. There's plenty of room to walk around even with it there. It was so neat of Luke to give us the bigger room."

"Sure was."

Ruth stomped her foot. "Grady Akins!"

Grady gave a start and twisted. "What? Are you okay? Is the baby okay?"

Ruth planted her hands on her hips. "I'm fine, except for being ignored."

"I'm not ignoring you. I answered every question."

"But you hardly paid attention to anything I've tried to show you. Don't you care how the room looks?"

"Honestly? No."

"Grady!"

He grinned in his own way that inspired goose bumps down her arms and legs. He pulled her to him and held her close. "I don't care what the room looks like. I don't care if we have room to walk around or not. I don't care what color the curtains are. All I care about is that you are finally my wife." He kissed her, leaving her breathless. "And that I don't sleep in a barn anymore."

Ruth giggled and wrestled free. She set a framed photo of her and Grady on her nightstand. "Luke made a joke that he figured you would fight him if he tried to make you stay out there."

"I'm sure there's a part of him that wishes he could."

"I'm so glad the two of you have found a way to get along. I couldn't bear it if you still hated each other."

After getting their things put away, Ruth perused the new bedroom, thinking of a couple of things to add, but they could wait. "Listen, I'm dying to see Emma. I'm going to go visit her, okay?"

"Sure. But I'd rather you not walk there, Mrs. Akins. I'll drive you."

"My own chauffeur." Ruth scrunched her shoulders. "But of course, Mr. Akins!"

They entered the living room together, laughing. Luke sat in his favorite chair, reading a newspaper. He glanced up but quickly returned his attention to his paper. He shifted in his seat. Ruth and Grady exchanged a look. It would take a while for Luke to get used to this arrangement.

Grady spoke first. "I need to return Nella's car, and Ruth wants to visit Emma. Could you follow us in the truck and drive me back?"

"Sure." Luke set the paper aside and rose. "We've got some business to discuss when we get back here."

❧

Emma patted Ruth's knee as they chatted on Nella's sofa. "I'm so glad you and Grady had a wonderful time. I wish I could have seen it when that crab chased him."

Ruth giggled. "Later on Grady was mad he didn't turn around and catch it so we could have it for dinner."

"It certainly sounds like it was big enough!" Emma reached for the pitcher on the coffee table. "Would you like some more?"

"Thank you." Ruth held her glass out. "I've never been able to get enough of Nella's sweet tea."

Emma poured Ruth's tea, enjoying this time alone with her. "So tell me, how are you doing with all these changes in your life?"

Ruth gently rubbed her expanding belly for a moment before lifting her gaze to Emma. "Honestly? Sometimes I feel like everything is wonderful, and other times I feel like I'm waiting for something awful to happen. I mean, I'm so happy to be married to Grady and all, but ..."

"But it's not exactly how you thought life would be."

"Right." Ruth traced her finger tip over the rim of her glass. "The wedding was wonderful and everyone was so kind, and I really did want to marry Grady, but...in the back of my mind I wished all day we had just snuck into the courthouse and done it quietly."

Emma witnessed the war going on in Ruth's mind and heart. Even when she smiled there was a glimmer of sadness in her eyes. The crease between her brows remained intact. Ruth still carried a great deal of shame. Emma ventured carefully. "I think maybe you got so used to hiding these past months, you feel you still need to hide."

Ruth tilted her head. "I thought that feeling would go away once Grady and I were married. But it hasn't. People still know. I still know."

Emma took Ruth's hand in hers. "You need to forgive yourself.

Yes, you made a mistake, but it's done. No one can change the past. But don't let the past steal the joy of your future." She patted Ruth's stomach. "I've never had a child, but I would imagine once this little one arrives, it won't matter how or when he or she came to be."

"I am starting to get a little excited. I lay awake at night and wonder whether it will be a little boy who looks like Grady or a little girl who looks like me." Her brow pinched, and she rested her hand on her stomach. "And then I think about the pain, and whether I can do this, and I get scared."

"Sounds perfectly normal to me." Wanting to get Ruth's mind off the fear of actually giving birth to her baby, Emma changed the subject. "Have you and Grady thought of names?"

Ruth's eyes lit up. She hunched her shoulders. "Yes. But we want to keep it a secret."

Emma held her hand to her chest and tossed her head back. "Well. How rude!" Eliciting a giggle from Ruth did Emma's own heart good. "Is there anything you need right now? Anything I can help with?"

"Actually, there is. I would love it if you would teach me to knit. The baby will need blankets and socks and sweaters."

Thrilled at the prospect of helping Ruth learn to knit and prepare for her baby, Emma quickly agreed. "I have an extra pair of needles, and Nella has a whole basket of yarn I'm sure she'll let us use. Would you like to start today?"

Luke tugged his coat tighter as the wind kicked up. It seemed as quickly as the heat of summer took a break, the wind and chill of autumn wasted no time replacing it. He'd moved Molly, a mare nearly ready to foal, into the barn to get her out of the harsh wind and cold. He felt bad for the old girl. Her back so bowed she looked as if she would bust in half if he pushed on her too hard. She'd stay until her foal was born, and then...who knew? He hoped he'd be able to keep her and the foal as boarders.

Clouds hovered low and dark in the sky. The scent of the first rain of the season hung in the air. Tree branches rustled loud enough they sounded like the ocean. Luke wanted to get inside where it was warm. He tugged his coat tighter and ambled toward the house. The windows glowed with yellow light. Beyond the curtains, shadows moved about, and as he got closer, voices reached him over the din of the trees.

Sundays had become Luke's favorite day of the week. Grady and Ruth left early for church, and they brought Emma back with them. Occasionally Nella joined them, but with the weather getting colder, she tended to stay home in front of her own fire more often.

Opening the door to the kitchen was like opening a door to another world. Outside, nothing but gray, wind, and cold. Inside laughter, warmth, and the scents of a roasting chicken and vegetables.

Grady drained a pot of boiled potatoes. "How's she doing?"

Luke shrugged out of his coat. "It'll be soon. I'm not sure how much longer she can hold out."

Ruth swirled a spoon in a pot on the stove. "Every time I look at her my own back starts to ache something awful!"

Luke accepted a cup of coffee from Emma. "Be thankful you're not a horse. They're pregnant for eleven months."

Ruth's wide eyes and dropped jaw evoked laughter from Grady and Emma. Luke couldn't even hold back a chuckle. He sat at the kitchen table with his coffee and relaxed, watching all the commotion around him. Grady and Ruth had an unspoken understanding between the two of them already. They seemed to know what the other needed before a word was said. Ruth and Emma had a sisterly relationship, giggling and chattering nonstop.

How had this happened? How had his life changed so completely? One day he was a loner, perfectly happy to avoid other people while he worked on the Golden Gate Bridge. He knew he was playing a part in a piece of history, but his only goal was to make enough money to buy himself a ranch out in the country and be left alone.

Then one day—Ruth. One sixteen-year-old girl without a mother turned his plans, his life, and his future upside-down. Just like another sixteen-year-old girl had. There had to be a reason.

"Luke? Are you all right?"

Luke looked askance at Emma. And with Ruth came Emma ... He swallowed. "Yeah. I'm fine."

"Would you like some more coffee?" Emma reached for the coffeepot.

He considered her for a moment and then smiled. "No. I've got enough. Thanks."

Emma tilted her head and her forehead wrinkled. "Are you sure? You seem a little far away."

"He's always far away." Ruth offered Emma a bowl. "Would you mind mixing these mashed potatoes?"

"Of course." Emma cast one more worrisome glance at Luke before joining Ruth again at the counter.

"Grady!" Ruth rushed toward the oven. "I told you not to put the biscuits in the oven yet!" She guided him away from the oven. "Darling, I love you, and I love that you want to help, but please—go sit down with Luke and let Emma and me finish."

Grinning, Grady kissed the top of her head and joined Luke at the table. There was a suspicious glint in his eye. Luke lowered his voice. "What are you up to, kid?"

Grady leaned close to Luke and whispered. "She only thinks she wants my help. If I mess it up bad enough, I help her realize she doesn't."

Luke nearly spit out his coffee.

Ruth's eyes narrowed, her gaze flickering between Grady and Luke. "What are the two of you up to?"

"Nothin', honey." Grady rested back against his chair. "Just enjoyin' the view is all." He elbowed Luke. "Right, Luke?"

Ruth gasped and held her hand to her mouth. Emma's eyes bulged.

Laughter bubbled up in Luke's chest, but he managed to control it. Instead, he shrugged. "Can't argue with that."

Emma's cheeks blazed. Luke loved the shy sparkle in her eyes. Ruth bit her lower lip and went back to preparing the meal. Luke noticed Emma's fingers trembling as she rejoined Ruth.

Watching Emma work, Luke tried to remember what his life was like before she came along. Before any of them came along. How had he thought he was happy then? This trio of people made him feel things. Things he didn't want to name or acknowledge and had spent a long time ignoring. His home was filled with life now. Comfort. Laughter. He may not always indulge. In fact, most of the time he found a way to get away from it. But that didn't mean he didn't notice it.

Another thing he noticed was that Emma had kept her promise not to nag him about church. For over a month now she and Ruth and Grady had gone to church together. Came back here together. Fixed a meal together then sat around the table, eating and talking, like a family. They always included him. So why did he still feel like an outsider?

THIRTY-FOUR

L uke got out of his truck, pulled on his coat, and stood in the empty parking lot. His gaze locked on the church's white steeple. He balled and unballed his fists in an attempt to stop the tremor. His stomach clenched, and his jaw muscles twitched.

The past month had been a confusing mess of events, thoughts, and emotions that left Luke exhausted and struggling for understanding. More and more he felt as if he were being sucked down into a pool of quicksand. The more he struggled against its pull, the faster it pulled him under.

Having Grady and Ruth under the same roof with him had taken some getting used to, but they eventually established a routine that worked for all of them. All in all, it really wasn't much different than when Grady slept in the barn. The kid had turned out to be a hard worker, and he took good care of Ruth.

The day Luke told him about losing the boarders because of Jasper Loomis, Grady simply nodded and said, "We'll make it work." And make it work, they did. Grady himself brought in three new boarders. He showed some pretty sharp intuition, contacting folks even Luke hadn't thought of.

Emma had become an everyday part of his life, one he wasn't sure he'd know what to do without. Grady and Ruth had found their niche in church. They wanted to give their child a proper foundation

275

of faith, and Luke not only agreed but encouraged their decision, especially since J.D. had dealt with the two deacons who had gone rogue and visited his house a few months back. Grady's parents attended a different church now, which was perfectly acceptable to Luke. He didn't want Ruth anywhere near those people.

Which caused conflict within him. If it was so important to teach a child to have faith in God, to trust Him and live for Him, how much more important was it for an adult? In the back of his mind, Luke knew it was important. He'd spent so many years pushing God and God's people away that it had become his way of life.

The white doors of the church stood before him like a final challenge. Luke walked to the doors and stood in the doorway. The place was sure quiet. No chatter of people or piano music, no J.D. up there preaching up a storm. Not the way he always imagined it when he drove by.

Luke took his hat off and rolled it over in his hands. His legs moved seemingly of their own accord. His boots echoed on the wooden floor as he cautiously approached the kneeling bar. The altar, J.D. called it. Luke was familiar with altars. With kneeling and praying and begging. He'd swore a long, long time ago he'd never do it again. He'd been so angry. So resentful and bitter.

"You know..."

J.D.'s voice startled Luke. He turned around.

J.D. wagged a finger at him. "I'd started to doubt I'd ever see the day you finally walked up there of your own accord."

The wooden cross that hung on the wall behind the pulpit drew Luke's attention. "I'm not sure why I'm here now."

"Oh, I think you know." The little church sanctuary stood silent for a long while. Then a front pew creaked with J.D.'s weight. "The only person you've been punishing is yourself, you know that now, right?"

Luke stared at his hat in his hands.

"You set out to teach that preacher a lesson. To teach those church folks a lesson. To teach God Himself a lesson. But that preacher kept on preaching. Those church folks kept on going to church. And God, well, He just kept on being God."

Luke let out a defeated laugh. "Guess I didn't have as much power as I thought I did, huh?"

"None of us do."

"So what now?"

"So now—you give grace a chance. You can't make it right. You can't do anything to fix any of it. That's why it's called grace. Unmerited favor. Nothin' you can do to earn it, nothin' you can do to run from it." J.D. stood and moved close to Luke. He placed a fatherly hand on Luke's shoulder. "Don't you think it's time you stopped runnin' and talked to Him, son?"

J.D. patted Luke's shoulder and turned away. The older man's shoes echoed on the wood floors until finally the door at the back of the church opened then closed. And Luke was alone again.

He eased himself down onto the pew J.D. had vacated. Drawing in a deep breath, he worked up his courage.

"I hope You'll understand if I talk to You from here, God. I don't have a whole lot of faith in the whole 'altar' thing. I spent a lot of time at one, a long time ago. I'm sure You remember." Luke sighed. "J.D. says I've got to get to know my Redeemer again. The One who paid for me. And I get that. I know what it means. But I don't quite know how to trust You, even though I've got nowhere else to turn. My business is just barely hanging on. Ruth is pregnant and married at sixteen. Grady's just a kid himself. And Emma..."

He leaned forward, resting his elbows on his knees and trying to swallow the lump stuck in his throat. He blew out a tense breath and sat back in the pew. He held up both hands, his hat in one. "I know You've been watching all of this, and I know it doesn't worry You. But I don't have Your vantage point. And I'm completely lost, trying to figure this mess out. So if I could get some kind of sign or, I don't know, flash of lightening. Anything to let me know You knew I came here today. That...I'm trying to find my way back."

꙲

Ruth awoke to the bed shaking violently. In her groggy mind she noted the shadows on the walls, of trees blowing outside the bedroom window and rain pounding on the roof. But what was shaking?

"Grady! Wake up. I think it's an earthquake."

"It's not an earthquake." Luke's voice cut through the darkness. "I'm trying to wake Grady up."

Grady bolted upright. "What's going on? What's wrong?"

"It's Esther. She's calving."

"Now?" Grady got out of bed and jumped up and down as he tugged on his pants. "That cow's not supposed to deliver for another month."

Luke's boots clumped on the wood floor as he left their room. "Meet me out there."

Ruth flipped on a lamp. Grady fumbled for his boots and a shirt. "Here, it's cold out there." She handed him his jacket. "I'll be out in a few minutes."

"No, you stay here." Grady kissed her on the cheek. "I don't want you and the baby out in this weather." He ran out of the room before Ruth could argue further.

She paced at the foot of their bed, stopping every few minutes to look out their bedroom window. Light from lanterns in the barn filtered past the curtain of rain. Standing by, feeling useless, did nothing to settle her nerves. She should make some coffee. She pulled on her robe and slippers and went to the kitchen. The world outside lit with flashes of lightning. Moments later a roll of thunder rattled the glasses in the cupboard. Ruckus stayed close, sniffing the air. Ruth measured the water and coffee and rested the pot on the stove. She bent down and petted Ruckus while she waited.

When at last the coffee was done, she poured it into a metal thermos, grabbed two cups and her coat and umbrella from the porch. Pulling the back door shut proved to be a challenge with her hands full and the wind fighting her every effort. She crossed the yard and driveway to the main barn, her slippers soaking up water and mud. Why hadn't she put shoes on?

Luke's voice carried even over the storm. She battled the barn door and stepped inside, then started to set the thermos and coffee down. But the sight before her sucked the breath from her lungs. She dropped the items. She wanted to run to Luke and Grady, who knelt next to Esther, but the horror of what she saw paralyzed her.

"Why are you doing that? You're going to hurt her!"

Luke's boots pressed against the cow's rump as if bracing himself as he struggled to keep his grip on a chain wrapped around two small hooves emerging from Esther. Muscles and veins in his arms and neck bulged. Esther's huge belly heaved up and down, her eyes wild and nostrils flaring. Luke glowered at Grady. "Get her legs tied so she can't kick!"

Ruth watched in stunned horror as Grady moved in quick, fluid motions, wrapping a short length of rope around Esther's legs. The cow reared back and thrust a foot at Luke's face. Luke lost his grip on the chain and let out a curse word.

Ruth screamed.

"Get that leg!" Luke scrambled for the chain as the calf's hooves began to slip back inside the cow. "We're gonna lose 'em both if we don't get this calf out now!"

Grady swiftly wrapped the rope around Esther's back legs and jerked it into a knot. "I got it."

"Get back here and help me pull."

Warm tears coursed down Ruth's cheeks. "Stop! You have to stop! You're going to hurt them both!" Her legs trembled so violently, she dropped to her knees. Her stomach tumbled and nausea threatened. They didn't seem to even hear her pleas. They continued barking orders at each other, grunting and pulling on that awful chain. Ruth cried, praying for the calf and its mother.

She didn't know how long she was trapped in her living nightmare, but finally, the calf was pulled free. Ruth sucked in a breath as if it were her first, along with the calf's.

Grady grabbed a blanket and vigorously rubbed the calf. "Oh, no. No, no, no..."

"What's wrong?" Ruth pulled herself to her feet and stepped forward. "Is it okay?"

Luke moved to Esther's head. "Keep rubbing him. I'll check Esther." He ran his hand over her stomach. "Come on, girl, come on..." He held one of her eyes open. He held his cheek to her nose.

Ruth's gaze darted from Luke and Esther to Grady and the calf. A chill spilled down her spine. "Luke? Grady?"

Luke rushed back over to Grady and stuck his finger in the calf's mouth and moved it around. He held his cheek to the animal's nose while Grady continued rubbing the newborn. Finally, Luke fell back and shook his head. He and Grady exchanged a look. Grady stopped massaging the calf.

Ruth's heart screamed, but no sound came out of her mouth.

Luke hung his head, wiping sweat from his brow with the back of his hand.

Grady dropped to his backside.

Ruth found her voice. "You mean..."

They both turned at the same time. Grady stood and trudged toward her. "I'm sorry, Ruth. Things like this...they just happen sometimes."

Luke kicked a milk bucket across the barn. It clanged against a wall.

Ruth shivered in Grady's arms.

Luke sat on a hay bale, elbows on his knees. Footsteps drew his attention. He lifted his head and tilted his hat back. J.D. Hudgins stood in the barn doorway.

"I've been looking for you." J.D. pointed to the cage. "You've almost finished it. Looks good."

Luke harrumphed. "It's all I was able to do." He spit out a piece of hay. "Percy gave me the two hundred up front, but he took the rest of his money with him when he took his horses. And I still have to pay that money back."

J.D. joined Luke on another bale. "I hate to see you give up on it."

"Yeah, well, it's pretty tough to get anything done without money."

"You never know. Anything could happen and change everything. You may still finish it. Just not in the time frame you'd planned."

Luke stretched his legs out in front of him and crossed them at the ankles. "Not much of anything has happened in the time frame I planned."

"I heard about the calf. Ruth was pretty upset."

Luke's shoulders lifted and fell. "She shouldn't have seen that."

"Well, she did see it. It frightened her. She's afraid of what may happen when her baby comes."

Luke met J.D.'s bright eyes.

"It's okay." The pastor lifted a hand "Barbara is speaking with her right now. Emma is with them, too. But still, it was a traumatic thing for her to witness."

Nodding, Luke stood and moved to stand at the open barn door. Rain splashed down into puddles in the clay earth. "Not nearly as traumatic as losing all that money in a matter of one hour." He stared straight ahead. "That calf was a bull. Do you know how much money I could have gotten for a bull and a milk cow?"

J.D. joined him. They both watched the rain fall for several minutes. Finally, J.D. spoke. "How did your visit at the church go last week?"

"I did some talking."

The older man smiled. "You mean praying?"

Luke shrugged one shoulder. "Yeah. For the first time since I left home as a kid, I actually felt comfortable sitting in a church. Praying didn't come as natural as it used to, but yeah, I did some praying. Asked God for a sign that He still saw me. That He knows I'm trying."

"And what happened?"

Irritation flashed in Luke's chest. "My cow died giving birth to a dead bull worth a fortune."

"You don't think God did that."

Turning his attention back to the rain, Luke snorted. "Well, He didn't stop it, that's for sure."

"For the life of me, boy, I cannot figure out how a man as smart as you, who knows the Good Book the way you do, continues looking for excuses to stay mad at God."

"Why not?" Luke's shoulders tensed. "Things were starting to go pretty good, you know? Ruth and Grady got married and moved in with me and we're getting along. Grady is working hard and taking care of Ruth. And when Emma comes over I— It was a waste of time."

"Praying is never a waste of time."

"It is when He doesn't listen."

"Oh, please." J.D. snorted. "Let me ask you this, did you do any listening? Or did you do all the talking and expect Him to follow orders?"

Luke stared at the man.

J.D. shook his head. "I don't think you'd even hear Him if He did speak. You're too fixed on what you want. You don't care what He wants."

Anger crawled up Luke's spine. "That's not true! I went to that church and I prayed because I was—"

"Was what?" J.D. stepped closer. "Say it out loud, boy. What were you doing there? Why were you praying?" J.D. poked Luke in the chest with his finger. "After all these years, why did you go back to talk to Him?"

"Because I needed help. Everything was falling apart around me. My business is gone." Luke paced. "Ruth got pregnant and then had to drop out of school. She's married now, but that doesn't mean her problems are over, not by a long shot. I got Emma, who is the most beautiful woman I've ever known, in my life, but she's made it clear she can't be with a man who doesn't—" He stopped pacing and sat back down on the hay bale. "I knew it was a waste of time. I had no right to ask anything from Him."

"Ahh. Now we're getting somewhere." J.D. wagged his finger at Luke. "You can ask anything you like of Him. You're His child. He's here to help you when you need Him. But He wants a relationship with you. It's a great thing you went to the church. That you prayed." J.D. shook his fists in front of him. "By doing that, you acknowledged your need for Him. You came to the end of yourself. And that is always the best place for a man to be in the presence of his Creator."

"So why did everything go so bad so quick? Is He punishing me for staying gone too long?"

"Son, if He was in the business of punishing us for taking too long to come to Him, there's not a person in the world could stand beneath the weight of their own guilt." J.D. rested his hand on Luke's shoulder. "He's not punishing you. It only feels that way because you've been trying to get through this old world on your own without His grace to pave the way for you and without your Redeemer to pay for those sins that you are so bent on paying for yourself."

J.D. stood. "I best be getting back to see if Barbara's ready to leave. Give it some thought. Instead of asking God to make your life easier, try asking Him to give you what you need to get through it when things go wrong."

Luke stayed put while J.D. walked away into the rain. He rubbed his hands up and down on his face. Would he ever get this right? "Okay, God. I guess we need to have another talk. And this time, I promise to do some listening, too."

THIRTY-FIVE

Christmas Eve, Ruth paced the living room, biting the nail of her left thumb. This was exactly like the last time. Rain pounding, thunder rolling, lightning flashing. And Grady and Luke in a barn helping another animal give birth. Her heart thumped against her ribcage.

The knock at the door startled her, stealing her breath, even though she knew who it was. She rushed to answer, not wanting to leave Nella and Emma out on the porch in this horrid weather. She opened the door and put on a smile.

Nella's wide smile greeted her first. "If I didn't know better, I'd think God was planning another flood!"

"I was afraid we wouldn't even make it this far." Emma pulled Ruth into a hug. "There are a few trees out there that might not stand much longer in this wind."

"Come in, give me your coats and umbrellas and bags." Ruth collected their things. "I have cocoa on the stove, and I'll get you some. You can sit down and have some cookies and popcorn balls now, though."

"Oh, that snapping, crackling fire is just what these old bones need." Nella rested herself on the couch and reached for a cookie.

Ruth took the coats and umbrellas to the kitchen, then poured three cups of cocoa, arranged them on a tray, and brought them to the living room.

Emma's gazed roamed the living room. "Where are Luke and Grady?"

Tears sprang to Ruth's eyes. "They're, um, in the barn. With Molly."

"Oh!" Emma stood and took the tray from Ruth. "There aren't any complications, I hope?"

"I—I don't know. I can't bring myself to go out and check." She studied the kitchen door. "They've been out there for about two hours."

"I wouldn't worry about it, honey." Nella bit into a cookie. "When I was a little girl, we had a mare that took six hours to birth her foal. Honestly, we thought that baby would never arrive. But she did, happy, healthy, and wise."

Emma offered a compassionate smile. "See? Sometimes these things take time." She glanced around the room. "I see the tree. Where are the decorations?"

"Oh, they're in the attic." Ruth grimaced. "We were about to get them down when Molly started bellowing. It sounded awful. Grady and Luke told me to wait. Not to climb the stairs."

Emma rubbed her hands together. "Show me where it is. Between the three of us, I'm sure we can get them."

Thankful for the distraction, Ruth led Emma and Nella to the closet that held the stairs leading up to the attic. Emma went up while Ruth and Nella waited.

"The string to turn on the light is on your left, at the stop of the stairs." Ruth called up.

"I got it. Thanks."

A dim light fought through the darkness above them. Ruth took two steps up. "My mother's ornaments are in the red trunk to your right. And somewhere nearby is a small box of ornaments that belong to Luke."

A giggle reached them from the attic. "Somehow I have a hard time picturing Luke collecting Christmas ornaments."

"I know." Ruth laughed. "My mom sent him one every year. And I think my grandma sent him a few."

Nella leaned in. "I've given him a handful over the years, too, though he's never bothered to put up a tree."

"If it hadn't been for Grady and me," Ruth said, "he wouldn't have one this year either."

"Okay." Emma called out. "I'm coming down with the trunk. It's a bit heavier than it looks."

When Emma reached the bottom step, Nella and Ruth took the trunk and placed it on the floor. Ruth's heart began to flutter. Her favorite memory of Christmas past was opening the old trunk and pulling out the ornaments one by one while listening to her mother's stories about each of them.

Nella took hold of a small handle on one end of the trunk. "I can drag this into the living room. Ruth, you stay and be sure Emma is all right."

A few moments later, Emma emerged with Luke's box. She cradled it as if it were a treasure. Ruth smiled. It had become so clear over the past months that Luke and Emma were falling in love. When would they give in and admit it?

Ruth trailed Emma to the living room. Nella had turned on the old radio. Bing Crosby's smooth voice filled the room, crooning "Silent Night."

Emma halted. "Oh! Wait one second. I forgot something!" She rushed to the kitchen and then reemerged with her purse. "I hope you don't mind. I brought two of my favorite childhood ornaments." She unfolded the cloth wrapped around two small ornaments. "I wanted them to be enjoyed by more than just myself." She held up a crocheted angel, yellowed at the edges. "My grandmother showed me how to make these on a rainy Christmas Eve just like this one, when I was a little girl. This is the only one I have left. And this"— she unwrapped the other ornament—"was given to my grandparents on their first Christmas together."

Ruth gasped at the beautifully ornate ornament. The red, gold, and green crystals danced in the light of the fire.

"And we have another gift for you." Nella disappeared to the kitchen. When she came back she handed Ruth a large paper bag. "Emma and I have been working on this for weeks."

Ruth opened the bag and giggled. She withdrew long strands of popcorn and cranberries. "It's perfect! Mom and I always had popcorn and cranberries on our tree, but I haven't had time to do it."

In the midst of their giggling another knock came at the door. Ruth rushed to open it, hoping it would be Luke or Grady. She opened the door and released a happy screech.

Olivia smiled. "Am I still invited? I mean, I know I haven't been around and all—"

Ruth threw her arms around Olivia and hugged her. "Of course you are! I'm so glad you came."

Emma and Nella engulfed Olivia in their arms as well. Joy danced through Ruth's stomach right along with the kicks of her baby. Having Olivia here made everything nearly perfect. She couldn't wait to start decorating the tree, but she wanted Luke and Grady to be here, too. This Christmas was important for so many reasons. It was the first for her and Grady as a married couple, her first with Luke, and her first without her mother.

Gentle hands rested on the back of Ruth's shoulders and Emma whispered in her ear, "Staring at the door won't make them come in any faster."

Sighing, Ruth caressed her round belly. "I know. I just want everything to be okay. I don't want Molly to lose her foal."

Olivia approached. "Do you need help with anything?"

Ruth swiped a tear from her eye and smiled. "Yes. You can help me make some more cocoa."

In the kitchen, Olivia poured milk into a pan on the stove and Ruth retrieved the cocoa and sugar.

Olivia's eyes traveled to Ruth's large belly. "I guess you'll be having your baby pretty soon, huh?"

Ruth rubbed her stomach and sighed. "Depends on what you mean by 'soon.' Three months from now seems like 'too soon' and 'forever' at the same time."

"Are you scared?"

Ruth sprinkled cocoa into the milk while Olivia whisked. "Honestly? Yes. Everyone tells me not to be, but I can't help it. Especially after..."

Olivia's brow wrinkled. "I heard about Esther. I'm sorry. It sounded awful."

"It was." Ruth pushed the kitchen curtains aside to peek out at the barn. "I hope it doesn't happen again with Molly."

"Ruth?"

Drawn by her friend's tone, Ruth dropped the curtain.

"Well..." Olivia removed the cocoa from the heat. "It's, um, I'm going to be leaving."

Ruth stared at her friend. "What?"

"Leaving Petaluma," Olivia clarified.

"Oh." Ruth's heart pinched in her chest. "I didn't know your family was moving."

"My family isn't. Just me."

"Are you going to see your mother?"

Olivia poured the cocoa into mugs. She shook her head. "Hollywood."

"Hollywood!"

Olivia's eyes widened and darted in the direction of the living room. "Shh!"

Ruth leaned in and lowered her voice to a whisper. "What are you talking about? Who do you know in Hollywood? Why would you want to go to a place like that?"

Olivia took a defensive posture. "I've been thinking about it a long time. My mother isn't coming back. As long as I stay here, all I will ever be is a second mother to my brothers. I will never be able to chase my own dreams, make a name for myself. And besides, with me gone, Daddy will have one less mouth to feed."

"I'm sure he would rather feed you than have you run off to Hollywood. What on earth are you going to do? How will you live?"

"I'm going to be an actress."

Ruth stared at her friend. "Has someone contacted you? Did you send your picture to a magazine?"

"No." Olivia shrugged. "I'm just going to go, get a job, and start auditioning."

"Olivia! This is crazy. Where will you live?"

"I'll figure it out." Olivia took Ruth's hand. "It will be fine. I'll be fine. I promise. And I promise not to leave until after your baby is born."

"What are you two whispering about in here?" Emma's voice interrupted their hushed conversation. "Is everything all right, girls?"

"Yes, ma'am." Olivia smiled brightly. "C'mon, Ruth, help me carry the cocoa."

Luke returned to the house with Grady close behind. It had been a long delivery and they were both weary from the fight. He opened the door, shed his coat and hung it up. The smell of hot cocoa, cookies, and popcorn balls wafted to him. Nat King Cole sang "The Christmas Song" on the radio, a fire crackled in the fireplace, and happy chatter in the living room brought him back to life inside.

For the past month the ice block that had formed around his heart had been slowly melting. At first, he wasn't even aware of it. But now it was as if he could feel again. Emotions he'd denied himself for so long, he no longer fought. He felt...at peace.

"Luke! Grady!" Ruth heaved herself up from the sofa, pressed a hand to her lower back, and moved toward Grady as quickly as her swollen belly would allow.

Luke smiled. "She's okay."

"She had a boy," Grady added.

Squealing, Ruth threw her arms around Grady and planted a kiss on his lips.

Luke raised a brow and dropped his gaze, rubbing the back of his neck. He caught Emma covering a giggle with her hand over her mouth and quickly dropped his hand from his neck.

Ruth released Grady and stood on her tiptoes to kiss Luke's cheek.

"Can we go out and see him?"

"Not right now." Luke smiled, enjoying the show of affection from his niece. "Mama had a hard time and didn't want to have anything to do with him. We couldn't leave him alone with her until she warmed up to him."

"She wouldn't have hurt him, would she?"

"Actually, yes, she might have. Especially if he tried to nurse. But we finally got them settled in together. He's nursing, they're happy and warm. You can see them tomorrow."

Feigning a pout, Ruth agreed and tugged them into the living room.

Luke couldn't recall the last time he'd decorated a Christmas tree or the last time he'd been so at ease, happy even, in a room full of people. The scene was like a photo on a Christmas card, and as they talked and laughed, he listened to the others sing with the radio while hanging ornaments on the strongly scented pine tree. By the time they were done, it was a sparkling symbol of a family. He stared at the tree until someone elbowed him in the arm.

Ruth grinned up at him like the Cheshire cat. "Did you happen to notice where Emma is standing?"

He scanned the room and found Emma talking to Nella in the doorway of the kitchen. Luke frowned at Ruth.

She rolled her eyes. "Look up."

It was Luke's turn to roll his eyes at the clump of mistletoe, held together by a bright red ribbon, hanging above Emma. "That has to be your handiwork."

"I figured Grady and I shouldn't be the only ones to get Christmas kisses this year. So?" Ruth wriggled her brow. "Are you going to kiss her or not?"

Nella tapped her wristwatch. "I hate to be a spoil sport, but it is awful late for this old lady. If I'm to be back here in time to help with the turkey, I should be getting home and go to bed."

Luke rubbed his neck and stepped away from Ruth. "Let me help you to your car, Nella."

Ruth held out Nella's coat. "Grady and I can drive ahead of you in Luke's truck, in case there are any trees down in the road. We can also give Olivia a ride home, too, right?"

Grady nodded. "Sure."

"Okay, then." Ruth tugged on Grady's arm. "Olivia, are you ready? We can help Nella to the car and wait for Grady."

Ruth ushered everyone out of the house and cast a final wink in Luke's direction. Luke stood next to Emma, pinching the bridge of his nose. Could his niece be any more obvious?

Emma looked up at him. "What's the rush to send everyone home? What's going on?"

"Oh, it's not a rush to get *everyone* home. Ruth wants the two of us to stay here for a minute."

Her brow knitted together. "Why?"

Luke pointed to the mistletoe above them without breaking eye contact with her.

Heat raced through his chest at the way her cheeks filled with pink. She whispered a barely audible, "Oh."

In the middle of the word, Luke touched his lips to hers. The familiarity of her perfume, the scent of her hair, her hand on his cheek, the way her lips moved with his... He wanted this more and more every day. She leaned into him, fully trusting. He didn't want to only kiss her. He wanted a life with her. He wanted to take her to a church and put a ring on her pretty little finger. Go to sleep every night with her kiss on his lips and wake to her beautiful face every morning.

He had finally surrendered to his Redeemer. In return, his Redeemer restored to him a life of joy and love. And he was finally the man he wanted to be for Emma.

EPILOGUE

If Luke thought the craziness of Christmas and New Year's Eve were over and life would settle down, he was mistaken. He couldn't get comfortable in the waiting room chair. His left leg bounced up and down uncontrollably. Emma rested her hand on his knee. The diamond ring on her left hand sparkled. He was still in disbelief at how his life had changed since the day Ruth walked into his life and everything was turned upside down. He had asked Emma to marry him three months ago on New Year's Eve, and she'd said yes.

He took her hand in his and lifted it to his lips.

"I know it's hard to wait, sweetheart," she whispered.

"Why do you seem so calm, then?"

"I'm pretending, trust me. Inside, I'm a wreck."

Luke wrapped his arm around her shoulders. She leaned into him. Nella seemed perfectly at ease in a chair across from them, her knitting needles in motion, but she checked the clock on the wall every few minutes. J.D. and Barbara Hudgins huddled together, looking at outdated hunting and home magazines. Olivia sat on the other side of Emma, chewing on her forefinger nail. And poor Grady paced back and forth.

"I don't understand why I can't be in there with her." Grady shoved his hand through his hair. "Did you hear her crying in the car on the way here, Luke? She was in so much pain. And she was scared to death. She didn't want to go in there alone."

"I know." Luke's leg bounced up and down. "But that's the way it's done. They'll let us know soon enough."

Luke knew his words landed on deaf ears. He imagined himself in Grady's place one day, waiting on Emma to give birth to his child, being kept away from her, feeling helpless. He squeezed her hand tighter.

Silence hovered over the waiting room again. For the next hour and a half, few words were spoken. Finally, a nurse arrived. The expression on her face revealed nothing.

Grady rushed to her and the rest of the waiting party leapt to their feet.

"Congratulations, Mr. Akins. It's a girl."

"A—a—a girl?" The wonder in Grady's tone matched the feeling in Luke's chest. "I have a daughter?" He spun around to face the others. "Did you hear that? I have a daughter!"

Everyone took turns hugging, slapping each other on the back, laughing and wiping away tears. The nurse led Grady out of the waiting room.

The moment they departed, Barbara turned a beaming smile on everyone in the room. "Let's go to the viewing window. They'll be showing off the new baby there soon. Let's be there to welcome her into the world."

Luke trailed the others down the hallway to the nursery window.

"I don't see her." Emma craned her neck, peeking through the glass at empty bassinets.

Nella clasped her hands beneath her chin. "I can hardly stand this. I just can't wait to see that precious baby."

Barbara pointed. "Here they come! There's Grady coming through the door."

The sight of a little bundle wrapped in a pink blanket and cradled in Grady's arms stole Luke's breath. Grady moved to the opposite side of the window, sporting the widest grin a human could possibly manage. He locked eyes with Luke.

Luke dipped his chin in approval. Was it possible Grady's smile grew even brighter? Luke slipped his gaze to the pink face of Ruth's daughter. She looked like a porcelain doll with her rosy lips, petite nose, and perfectly formed little ears.

Emma rested her head against his shoulder, and he sucked in big a breath. Images flashed through his mind. Sadie. Their baby. The accident. The family he'd lost. Running away from home. J.D., Nella, Kate. Ruth, Grady, Emma...the family he had now. He flexed his jaw and bit his inner cheek. Tears burned the back of his eyes.

You knew all along, didn't you God? You knew that every decision, every mistake, every angry outburst and thought of self-hatred would be redeemed. That it would all culminate in this perfect moment.

Emma slipped her arm around his waist. "She's beautiful."

He nodded, swallowing.

"Are you ready to go home now, sweetheart?" Emma's blue eyes gleamed, further confirming that he was a man graced with blessing he'd never dreamed possible.

He leaned in and kissed her forehead. "Not just yet. I'd like to talk to Grady first, make sure Ruth is really okay."

He and Emma waited in the waiting room until Grady returned. He grinned as he crossed the floor to Luke.

"Ruth has begged and pleaded with the nurses to let you come in and hold the baby. I don't know how she did it, but she convinced them."

"I really don't need to." Luke held up his hands as if blocking a stampede of horses. "I mean, I'm happy for the two of you, and she's the cutest little bug I've ever seen, but really, I'm fine."

"Seeing her through the nursery window and holding her are two different experiences, trust me." Grady cocked his head and scratched his chin. "You're really going to let Ruth down if you don't go."

Luke sighed and rubbed the back of his neck. "That's blackmail."

Grady rocked back on his heels. "Yes, sir. It is."

"Fine." Luke rose with a sigh. "Lead the way." He followed Grady to Ruth's room then froze inside the threshold. Ruth lay in the bed with the baby cradled in the bend of her arm. The sight struck him in a way he didn't expect. His chest expanded with pride, but his heart clenched with sorrow.

Kate, you'd be so proud of her. And your granddaughter is beautiful. I wish you were here to see them.

Ruth beamed. "Come in. Sit down in the chair there. Grady, come get her and take her to her great-uncle."

"You sound like a mom already," Luke quipped, crossing to the chair and sinking down. "Bossing everyone around."

Ruth lifted her chin. "I rather think it runs in the family."

Grady approached with the baby. Luke tensed. What if he dropped her? He looked up at Grady, shaking his head. "We really don't have to do this."

Grady laughed. "It's okay. I thought she would break, too, but she's tougher than she looks. Here, hold her head like this." Grady demonstrated, then placed the baby in Luke's arms.

If anyone else in the room spoke, Luke was oblivious. All he could see was this baby girl. All he could hear was her breathing. She opened her eyes and stared at him as if she recognized him. As if she'd been waiting to finally meet him. And he felt the same. He'd waited a very long time to meet little—

He jerked his attention to Ruth. "Did you decide on a name?"

Ruth exchanged a look with Grady and smiled. "Yes. Last night. Her name is Kathryn Sadie."

Luke's breath caught. "Sadie? My Sadie?"

Ruth eyes glinted with tears. "Yes. And Mom."

Luke gazed down at Kathryn Sadie and smiled as she wrapped a tiny fist around his pinky finger. "Welcome to the family, Kathryn Sadie. I'm your great-uncle, Luke. And you know what? One day I'm going to tell you all about your grandma's favorite woman in the Bible, and about someone called a Redeemer."

THE END.

ACKNOWLEDGEMENTS

Thank you, *Lord*, for teaching me what it truly means to have a Redeemer. And that You never give a dream without a plan to fulfill it.

Rick, for choosing me to share your life with, spoiling me rotten, making me laugh every day, and teaching our sons how a man should treat a woman.

My sons, *Zach* and *Kyle*, for revealing my strengths and weaknesses in ways I never saw coming. I'm so proud of you both.

My mom, *Linda Dodds*, for teaching me how to overcome when life doesn't turn out exactly as you planned, and being my partner in "just doing the next thing."

My dad, *Gerald Dodds*, my spiritual superman. No words can express how grateful I am that you were my father. I learned from you how strong a quiet faith can be. The day you left us, Heaven became a little sweeter to me.

The Posse, *Kim Vogel Sawyer, Eileen Key, Marjorie Vawter, Connie Stevens, Kristian Libel,* and *Jalana Franklin,* for all the encouragement, honest critiques, prayers, and good times that shall not be spoken of outside The Posse. See y'all at the next retreat!

My first writing mentor, *Beverly Sticken* (aka Kimberly Rae Jordan), for bringing me into a critique group that would change my life and for hysterics in a Nashville elevator.

The Coffee Girls, *Linda Dodds, Cheryl Bigon, Joyce Wilson* and *Faye Jackson,* for honest talks, prayer, and straight up goofiness.

Jim Peterson, the first editor I ever met back in 2004. I had no idea what a great friend and encouragement you would be in my life. Your words from that first meeting, "I'm proud of you," have rung in my ears for 14 years. You understood the undertaking it was for me to get to conference all alone.

Pastor Bill Funk, for being the first person to push me out of my comfort zone, put me in a pulpit in charge of a ministry, and constantly tell me, "Keep writing." It all terrified me, but I'm so thankful for your vision now!

J.D. and Barbara Hudgins. for being wonderful pastors and mentors to my family for three generations. I look forward to the day we are all reunited with you both in Heaven.

Pastor Ross Reinman, Barbara, and *my family at Calvary Chapel The Rock,* for teaching me to trust again.

Patricia Dodds for being my Fwend in Da Lawd!

TO CONTACT THE AUTHOR

EMAIL
gracewriter43@yahoo.com

FACEBOOK
Darlene Dodds Wells Christian Fiction Author

WEBSITE
www.DarleneWells.com

MORE BY DARLENE WELLS

A Thread of Hope
a novella in the *Threads of Time* collection

Chosen
a novella in the *A Place of Refuge* collection

UPCOMING TITLES

Finding Olivia
Book 2 in the Days of Grace Trilogy

Loving Tilly
Book 3 in the Days of Grace Trilogy